SPLITTING SKIES

A metaphysical sci-fi dystopia

MIKHAIL GLADKIKH

SPLITTING SKIES
By Mikhail Gladkikh
Published by Quasaris Press 2024
Spring, TX 77381
QuasarisPress.com

This is a work of fiction. Any similarity between the characters and situations within its pages and places or persons, living or dead, is unintentional and co-incidental.

Address permissions and review inquiries to mgladkikh@gmail.com

Cover Design: David Provolo

Connect with the author online at MikhailGladkikh.com

First Edition

International praise for "Splitting Skies"

"It is a complicated tale that will demand the reader's full attention. It is deep with science fiction, philosophical, and existential ideas that can make your head spin."

—Jim Arrowood, Jim's Sci-Fi Blog ★★★★★

"The protagonist's struggles and emotional turmoil are portrayed with a depth that keeps you engaged from start to finish ... The world-building is impressive, filled with intriguing technologies and social structures that challenge the norms of our own society."

—Queensland Quintessentials, Australia ★★★★★

"Follow a large cast of characters whose fates are intertwined and on a collision course of epic proportions."

—Sergiu Pocan, an avid sci-fi reader, Romania ★★★★★

"The plot, the smooth story-telling, extremely well written, and very captivating to read. An overall top notch book!"

—Amazon Reviewer, US ★★★★★

"The detailed world-building and Gladkikh's philosophical insights made me ponder the potential effects of technology on society and our individual identities. It's an engaging read that continues to linger in my thoughts, seamlessly fusing science fiction with profound existential themes."

—Amazon Reviewer, US ★★★★★

Also by Mikhail Gladkikh

OUT OF TIME, *a hard science fiction mystery*
THE AGE OF HEROES, *a historical sci-fi epic*
THREAD OF LIES, *a ski resort murder mystery*

TABLE OF CONTENTS

Dedicated to human ingenuity and spirit

CHAPTER 1. FELIX

If you die in a dream, do you survive in reality? And what is reality, anyway?

Felix opened his eyes and looked at the rays of the setting sun on the horizon. The most advanced, ultimate Decon experience didn't bring him joy. Felix breathed in the fresh air, filled with the fleeting aroma of pine trees, just as he liked it. Everything was perfect. Maybe too perfect.

He considered doing something out of the ordinary, such as leaving his smart chair, which had changed shape, morphing into every crevice of his body. He rose and moved forward.

"I advise against this; it is unhealthy and unnatural," Thelma's voice pronounced in his head.

"Advise declined," Felix thought and made a move. He last stood on his feet months ago. As his soles touched the uneven texture of the floor, a thousand tiny warm needles came alive in his toes.

"Please, sit down. You will hurt yourself," the voice in his mind warned.

"Fuck off." He winced. *How did we let annoying Quarks become our masters?*

"I must remind that I created personalized Designed Consciousness based on your unique wishes, and it's only possible via my interface," Thelma said. "Would you like me to start a new sequence?"

"I would like you to shut down," Felix ordered mentally, and the Quark disconnected the interface.

What if this is the new sequence? His Quarks were the most advanced, capable of creating the unmatched Decon experiences. *What if this is my deepest desire? To erase the boundary between Decon and reality? How would I know the truth, and what is reality in the first place?*

Felix took a few steps and enjoyed the ability to move. He didn't hurt himself, didn't fall. His soles pressed against the firm surface of the floor, and it was great. He raised his hands and stared at his fingers—strange, he didn't remember how they looked. Were these his actual fingers or a ghost taken by Quarks out of his dreams and inserted into the Decon experience?

I might never find out. Felix pulled the tube connecting him to the life-sustaining system. *Why do we cling to our bodies? I don't need it; I live in Decon.* The room looked sharp and vibrant with colors: he had upgraded his eyes to the newest version, capable of experiencing an enhanced light spectrum, including infrared. *Why do I need this? It's such a waste.*

"Take me outside," he commanded and remembered he'd just told Thelma to shut down. *Shit, I can't even do a simple thing without stupid Quarks.*

Something was driving Felix to change his routine. He'd never ventured outside alone, but now it was different. Felix had to find out if he was in a Decon. He dragged his body along the hallway and arrived at the reinforced composite door.

Felix gestured, and the door obeyed, running facial recognition and many other routines. The grove met him with the smells of blooming spring flowers, the sounds of birds chirping, and the majestic sights of the sun descending into the serene waters of the lake.

This is almost as good as Decon. Upgraded eyes made it confusing.

Felix kept walking, reaching the edge of a cliff. The waterfall on the left was incredible, with a gentle roar of water mixing with the sounds of birds singing their evening serenades. Felix could see every drop of water and a rainbow dancing in each one. He could smell the freshness of the water mixed with the aroma of blooming flowers.

This can't be real, he finally decided. *Thelma is messing up with me.*

He turned around and registered several F-Quarks advancing in his direction.

"Stop." He raised his hand. The drones obeyed the command, freezing some distance away.

At least that worked. If this is a Decon, it's weird. It should be built based on my desires, but why do I see Quarks? Am I sick? This was unlike anything he'd experienced with the personalized scenarios. In theory, you could design anything conceivable in Decon, but this specific scenario served no purpose.

Felix looked at the giant disk of the setting sun. The sky was colored in a gentle combination of orange and blue, plus hundreds of undertones his upgraded eyes could see.

There is only one way to find out.

Indeed, how did one die in Decon? Had he experienced death before? His memory was blank. Perhaps it was impossible since death was the end of consciousness, and one simply couldn't experience it.

He was now curious. Taking a few steps forward, Felix stood on the ravine's very edge, looking at the rocks covering the shore of the lake. *I have nothing to lose. I've experienced everything except one thing.*

Felix smiled, took one last step, and jumped off the cliff.

If you die in a dream, do you survive in reality? was his last thought.

CHAPTER 2. MARY

Mary massaged her temples and suppressed the desire to restart the Decon. There was something different about this one, disturbing yet addictive. She had acquired this high-quality, never-spun Decon on the black market in exchange for her last savings of stem cells. Mary stood from her three-legged plastic stool and inhaled the stuffy air of her tiny shed, almost losing her balance as she experienced a momentary vertigo accompanied by darkness in her eyes.

Her stomach grumbled, and little hammers knocked on her temples. This was the usual outcome of Decon experiences for her. Still, Mary couldn't imagine herself without these gorgeous, breathtaking, otherworldly realities. This was her life, in a different universe or in the hidden corner of her mind—she didn't care. Still, it was more genuine than the world where she led a pitiful existence with the only goal of acquiring another Decon when the current one expired. It was all part of her, part of her consciousness—such was the nature of Decon. Diversity defined people: everyone could have multiple lives, each as real as the next one. Even though the relative moments of immersion into the Designed Consciousness were short, they contained a lifetime of events, experiences, and feelings. This existence of a malnourished, starving, feeble body in a tiny apartment didn't matter as long as she could experience more Decon, which had become almost unattainable for her recently.

Mary browsed through her food containers and found only an expired package of compound insect protein: pale gray briquette with a slimy texture. *This will do for now*, she decided. Something troubled her, something she couldn't grasp, like a shadow on the wall during the storm. Was it part of her recent Decon session? It was impossible: the joy of being in the land of her dreams, seeing its colors and rainbows, and smelling the exotic flowers was so vivid she couldn't understand why she had this nagging sensation of small but sharp claws touching her heart. *That life must be the true reality, but somehow I keep returning to this shithole. This is a nightmare, and it shall pass.*

Mary opened the expired package and watched the gray substance inflate into a patty before her. She hated this tasteless food surrogate that smelled like old wet socks, but had no means of getting something better for her sustenance. Mary also had no access to body part replacement services and was aware that her biological shell would give up soon. It didn't matter as long as she could experience just one more Decon, even if it would be her last one. *But perhaps it's all good. If this is my nightmare, I'll be fine when it ends.*

Mary touched the port at the back of her head where the Decon interface was implanted. She smiled, grateful for the hours of bliss the chip had given her. She imagined miserable people who'd lived before her generation without the knowledge or experience of Decon. Indeed, it had been a dark age, full of sad, angry, and deprived people. She was so happy she was born right before the Deconvolution, the era of human liberation from the shackles of sole, sad, linear reality. Yes, she valued liberty the most. Freedom of being the master of your consciousness, experiencing what you desire, and being where you belonged.

Mary finished the disgusting patty, hoping it would sustain her body for a few days. She had to wait before relaunching the Decon; the repeat was less vivid and few went beyond the fourth spin. Mary needed a new Decon, but had nothing to offer in exchange. Perhaps she could figure it out later.

The claws scratching her heart grew stronger. In addition, a headache took hold of her, squeezing her skull and gouging her eyes. *Damn body. Maybe I could exchange this Decon to repair my eyes? There should be one or two good spins left.* Mary chased this idea away; she needed these spins for herself; she'd survive the headache.

Then, suddenly, another, more disturbing thought surfaced. *What if it was my last Decon session? I have nothing to exchange, and without sustenance, this body will perish. Why should I wait for that? Time to stop the nightmare for good.*

The invisible claws were now ripping her heart into pieces. Mary's blood-pumping organ was shattering, little fragments flowing and disappearing inside the blood vessels. What was causing this horrible sensation? This had never happened before.

Mary took a few steps, trying to calm herself down. Instead, she worried even more, trying to hold on to the smell of majestic flowers and the vastness of the magical land of her dreams now disappearing in front of her eyes, being categorized and put away by her tired brain into the compartments of her memory alongside others. Someone had told her before, and now she believed it, that Decon created realities of its own; alternative universes. She needed to return to her land, the other dimension, the alternative universe she had conjured. Mary needed to transition once and for all, never to return to this stupid, failing shell.

Yes, this is the ultimate solution. Why didn't I think about it earlier? Because of my frail biological body, it's obvious. She needed to get rid of it; she decided. That new universe, her creation, existed inside her consciousness; it was hers and no one else's. Once she escaped her biological prison, her consciousness would guide her there—she was now sure about that. Did Decon work like this, after all?

Determined, she touched her chestnut hair, cut short and messy, with a little bun on top, attempting to hold her exploding skull in place. She looked around, searching for a hint, trying to design an escape plan. Suddenly, she noticed a glass table left in her tiny shack by the previous dweller and never used. Mary made three steps, grabbed the table, and threw it against the wall covered by decorative bricks. The impact was powerful enough to shatter the glass, and Mary imagined her breaking heart. She picked a large glass fragment and looked at it for a moment. A stupid, useless object serving generations of equally stupid, useless humans trapped in their bodies forever. *Such a pity. Now, I will give this useless object a true purpose!*

With these thoughts, she raised her hand, holding a glass shard, and touched her neck with a sharp edge. No more suffering or scrambling for the next trade. This was the ultimate liberation. She closed her eyes, made one last deep inhale, and swiped her hand with an improvised blade across her neck. As gradual darkness enveloped her sight and mind, she rejoiced. Mary DeJong was finally free.

CHAPTER 3. JIM

Jim prepared for the meditation, sitting on the mat with legs crossed, arms on his knees, his eyes closed, his senses sharp, registering every minute detail of the current moment. The smell of the blooming prairie bluebonnets was powerful, and the advancing thunderstorm announced itself with a distant roar. Kali was asleep, her steady breathing a background detail for Jim, a small piece of the universal consciousness.

It was another typical day in a sequence of a myriad of moments assembled in the inconspicuous life of Jim Steel. Fifty years ago, he'd believed he was special, had a unique gift, could experience the future, and imagined the universe spoke to him. Not anymore. Everything was in vain; he had failed to wake up humanity, show the path, and be the leader, whatever the shadow of Hagen had told him in a dream. It didn't matter anymore; Jim was content in his solitary existence on a godforsaken piece of infertile land west of Houston, living in an ancient van now falling apart, with only his dog to keep him company. *Funny how cruel life could be*, he thought, remembering himself as an excited student fifty-three years ago.

This is a distraction; I should just observe and get back to the meditation. The wind howled outside, blowing the dry dirt over the scorched brown grass. The life's goal he'd set for himself was a hopeless task and a burden he couldn't carry, as he'd tried to tell Hagen in his dream, but the ghost of the old engineer wouldn't listen. Besides, Jim had so much respect for the German inventor he couldn't look in the other direction. Bad decision.

Fifty years, Jim thought. *After fifty years, the world and humanity lie in ruins. Could I have changed its fate? Perhaps, but it's too late to lament*, he stopped himself. *Everyone I knew is dead; nothing matters now; I should let things unfold. I need to be the observer, the witness, the silent screen*, he recalled the age-old meditation mantra.

However, the train of thought didn't stop. It's been a while since Jim allowed himself to be distracted that much during meditation. He couldn't do anything but observe the thoughts, just as he'd trained himself for many years. *Don't get engaged; this shall pass*, he told himself.

He had never tried Decon. Why, he didn't know. There was something unnatural about Designed Consciousness, as they called it, created by AI and streamed into the brain. Or, perhaps, he feared it would interfere with his ability to experience the future or communicate with the universe: his unique gift. *I'm still reliving the events of the past*, he admitted. *I'm still expecting a new message.* "We shall talk again," Hagen's words of long ago were still fresh in Jim's head. He remembered it and hoped for a call in vain.

Jim opened his eyes and focused on the clouds in the sky, listening to the increasingly louder sound of thunder. It was hard to concentrate. Jim looked at Kali, noticing how his Rottweiler's lungs inflated and deflated. There was something peaceful about it, something he didn't understand but knew from the bottom of his heart. They were the same, part of Creation, part of something bigger than humanity itself, as the ghost of Hagen had told him.

Jim closed his eyes again and tried to focus on the present moment, imagining seeing his body in a mirror and registering every sound and smell. A coyote was barking somewhere far away, and the owl was hooting in the forest. Or maybe it was just his imagination.

Out of nowhere, an image of Isabel appeared in front of his eyes, enveloping Jim in the long-forgotten smells of tulips and orchids. She was a shadow of a happy past when the future was bright and all paths were open. But, alas, she wouldn't share his obsession with cosmos and had eventually left for Italy to become a recognized painter. They hadn't spoken since. Jim didn't even know if she was still alive. *It doesn't matter*, he reminded himself, *stay in the present moment. You didn't deserve her, and you are a failure*, the inner voice suddenly pronounced. *Don't kid yourself; there is no purpose and no hope. Your dreams were delusions. You are no prophet. Perhaps it's time to give up and finally get on the Decon bandwagon.*

Jim was an experienced practitioner and ignored the temptation. After all, he hadn't let himself lose his head when the world around him had gone mad; the governments had collapsed, and the people had forgotten about anything except Decon. Chasing this illusion now would be idiotic. He stayed focused, but the images, sounds, smells, and thoughts about the events long gone kept creeping into his mind.

What was this about? Why now? He lost hope long ago and was content just to be. What caused this remission?

Jim counted his breaths, chasing away the images, telling himself nothing mattered except his inhales and exhales. As he counted fifteen cycles, the grip of the past eased and the burden fell off his shoulders. Continuing to count, Jim slid into the familiar space of ego-less, diluted experience, where everything is nothing, and nothing is everything. He took one more inhale, and this was when the long-forgotten but so vivid bright green forest appeared.

***

Jim walked along the barely visible path through the tall grass, interspersed by giant orange flowers and majestic, towering trees. The smell of peppermint and lavender teased his nostrils as his ears registered a quaint whisper somewhere to the left. Jim couldn't understand the words, but he was sure this was human speech.

Last visit, fifty-three years ago, clocks filled the space. This time, there wasn't a single clock or even a sundial. Instead, above his head, an enormous purple ball rotated, slowly descending on the meadow underneath.

Jim walked for some time and arrived at the narrow stream with a bridge across. Sheets of paper of different sizes and colors covered the surface of the bridge, as if someone had torn them out of old manuscripts and thrown them around. It wasn't easy to discern the stream because the water was the same green color as the vegetation, and dry sheets of paper floated on its surface. The sheets were of a standard letter size, each with a large number printed. The first number was fifty-three, the years since his last visit to this enigmatic place.

"I told you I shall see you again, Jim Steel," the voice suddenly announced behind his back.

Jim turned around. Torsten Hagen stood before him, dressed in an antique black suit with a cylinder hat on his head, strange round black glasses on his nose, and a cane in his hand. Hagen made a gesture, and sheets of paper carried by the stream thickened, turning into enormous leather-bound tomes.

"Walk with me." Hagen's voice was low-pitched and loud, but

otherwise sounded normal. He extended his hand, inviting Jim to walk along the stream, stepping on the floating volumes.

"Where am I? Why now?" Jim asked, but followed Hagen along, carefully stepping on giant tomes floating on the stream's surface.

"Did you take care of my gift?" Hagen ignored Jim's questions.

"Yes," Jim said, remembering he hadn't watered the Rose of Jericho for a few months, but the plant he brought from his dream fifty-three years ago had refused to die.

"Good. However, you still need to fulfill your task. You barely started."

"As I told you, I'm not the right person. I'm weak; I don't know what to do."

"You say so, but you do." Hagen took off his cylinder hat and looked inside. "Your role is set. You shall play it."

"Again, I don't understand you." Jim shrugged. "I just want to end my days in content; I'm not who I was when I first talked to you."

"And yet you know what I mean." Hagen smiled. "You need to ask yourself—not you, Jim Steel, but the one who you truly are."

"And who would that be?"

"You already know." Hagen placed the hat back on his head, reached into his pocket, and took out a glass ball. "Look inside."

Jim leaned forward and stared into the ball—nothing there except occasional flashes of orange light.

"What's this?"

"Now look back. At your face."

"I cannot do that." Jim remembered the meditation technique exploring this and aimed at replacing ego with boundless space.

"Yes, you can. Your destiny awaits you, Jim Steel. You are exactly who you need to be."

"I'm old and weak. Can you spare me your riddles? I'm not the hero."

"And yet you are. Your age doesn't matter: it's just a number on a sheet of paper."

Jim remembered the stream of green water.

"Your thoughts don't matter, either: they are reflections in a mirror," Hagen continued, pointing at the glass ball in his hand. "Look again. What do you see?"

"Nothing of importance."

"And yet, nothing is everything," Hagen said. "Your task is unchanged. You shall be the guide and the light for humanity. Such is your role."

"Why? Why me? Says who?"

"These questions have no meaning." Hagen raised his hand with a glass ball in it. "To begin your quest and understand who you truly are, you must find Mary DeJong and Selena, the Humanist artist."

"What's this? Another riddle? Please, leave me alone," Jim begged. "I'm too old for this; I don't want this quest, whatever it is."

"The choice is not yours." Hagen smiled. "The humans are on the wrong path. You must fix the error."

"But why me?" Jim suppressed the desire to turn and run away; he didn't understand why this vision appeared when he gave up on his search and was prepared to end his days in tranquility, with only his furry companion as a solace.

"You'll understand in time," Hagen said. "For now, find these two people: Mary and Selena."

"What happens if I don't?"

Hagen looked into the glass ball and winked at Jim. Then, still smiling, Hagen pronounced,

"The world will end."

CHAPTER 4. PAUL

"What the hell is that?" Paul pointed at the gray metal box with a few extensively used Decon cartridges and a glass container inside the dry ice pack. "Are you kidding me? 'Cause if you are, I'll carve your skulls open and use your pitiful brains for feedstock."

Paul punched the Scavenger in the chest and drilled him with a wide-open gaze of his brown eyes.

"That's all we have today, boss," the Scavenger mumbled, stepping back. He was a few inches shorter than Paul, but tried to make himself even smaller.

"No luck, don't get mad." His companion shook his head, which was neatly shaved except for the two bands of short red hair.

Paul looked at the box's contents and sighed, stroking his full, long black beard. He wiped off the sweat from his bald head with an electronic dryer.

"I'm disappointed," he said, leaning back on the smart chair behind the counter. "The business is bad; I need you to step up."

"There are some stem cells in the vial, boss. It's worth something." The first Scavenger spread his hands, covered in tattoos and fresh bruises.

"It's utter crap." Paul spat at the box. "Hopefully, Layla will bring something worthy; she always does."

"Sorry, boss. Doing what we can," the second Scavenger said. He smelled like an old, expired briquette of insect protein, and Paul winced.

"Ah, just go away." Paul waved his hand, sensors attached to his palm. The entrance to the trading booth lit up, and the view of the dark night outside appeared. Several Quarks behind the Scavenger's backs moved and highlighted the path with blinking lights.

"We'll do better next time, boss," the Scavenger said, turning around and showing his long black ponytail to Paul.

"We're planning a glorious raid," the second Scavenger added, scowling. "They say a Humanist camp north of the city is full of biomaterial."

"You're more stupid than I thought." Paul squinted. "What's that?"

Within the space outside the shack, a human figure appeared in the night. Or at least it looked like a human figure, which is why it was so weird. Some occasional animals, such as coyotes and raccoons, dug in the colossal dumpster outside. Still, humans never visited this godforsaken swamp south of Houston, where the ruins of an industrial refinery hinted at the city's glorious past. This was why Paul had set up his office here, where no one would trouble his business, and he could meet with the Scavengers, bringing goods to exchange. But, of course, he didn't expect anyone else today, and whoever the visitor was, he would be unwelcome.

Paul gestured, and the Quarks moved closer to the entrance, aiming their weapons, ready to defend their owner. But Paul wanted to find out what had brought the stranger here before eliminating the visitor. He was curious and didn't need to raise the stakes yet. The office brimmed with Quarks, ready to fire if needed, and Paul knew he was safe.

"Fuck my brain," the Scavenger gasped as he observed the newcomer. The picture indeed evoked intense emotions: the man was covered in dirt, blood, and what appeared to be human intestines. He smelled like he looked, too. He wore a black antique suit, a few decades old, and a black shirt. His left hand was twisted, and the fingers were stuck together in one incomprehensible knot, like the tentacles of a weird humanoid squid. In his right hand, the visitor carried a human leg. His face, although grimaced and covered in blood, showed the energy and determination of a madman.

"Who the hell are you?" Paul asked, leaning forward.

"Where...am I?" The bloodied stranger asked back, ignoring the question.

"Greedy Paul's Trade Shack," the Scavenger with a ponytail said.

"What..city? What year?" The madman uttered through clenched teeth.

"Could we scavenge him for a few stem cells?" The red-haired raider asked.

"Shut up, both of you," Paul said. He was intrigued: the guy didn't look like a beggar from the city; there was something mysterious about his appearance from the dumpster. And the leg?

13

"Houston, year twenty-one eleven, buddy," Paul said. "Where did you escape from? Did you kill someone? Have something to trade?"

"Twenty-one eleven...." The man shook his head and raised the hand with a human leg in it. "This is all that's left of her... Ichika wanted to change the world, nay, the universe, and got too close to the fire..."

"Do you have anything to trade or not? The leg doesn't count." Paul raised his voice.

"Fifty years..." the newcomer continued mumbling. "Fifty years — lost. I have to get back what's mine."

"There's nothing here that's yours, buddy," Paul said. The conversation wore him out: the guy was most likely a madman, abusing over one of those dangerous, hard-to-get Decons that had become so precious lately.

"Quasaris... I need to get there. For her." He stared at the leg.

"Quasaris is out of reach for you. Its factories were moved to the Wise Estate to produce high-quality Decon," Paul explained. "Where have you been, buddy?"

"Nowhere," the madman responded. "Take me to Quasaris. I'll revive the company."

"Wow, easy." Paul smiled. "I'm afraid this is impossible unless you know Felix Wise personally."

"*Felix* Wise?" It was the newcomer's turn to raise his eyebrows.

"The owner of Quasaris."

"The hell he is. I am Frank Wise, the founder, and the owner."

"He's talking nonsense." Paul made a finger gesture to alert the Quarks floating in the air. "You're right." He looked at the Scavenger. "Perhaps we could still get something out of nothing."

The Quarks surrounded the madman, blinking ominous red lights, preparing to disassemble the human. Then, suddenly, the lights at their circumference turned green, and their movement stopped.

"What's the matter?" Paul said, gesturing with his finger several times and tapping with his feet on the plastic floor. "Execute the command."

"Identity is confirmed," the disembodied voice announced. "DNA match hundred percent. The command is overruled. What are your instructions, Mr. Wise?"

"Is this a joke?" Paul yelled.

"As the shareholder of Quasaris Corporation, Mr. Frank Wise owns the company's assets," the Quark continued. "The information about your arrival is sent through the network."

"Now, this is better." The newcomer stepped forward. "Her death was not in vain; I'll finish what she started." He put the leg on the desk in front of Paul. "First, we must bury what's left of her and Spencer. They were not as lucky as me." He raised his left hand with a knot of fingers. "Or unlucky."

"Are you gonna help?" the stranger turned to face Paul. "Or should I tell your drones to...what did he say...scavenge you? Decide now; I have little time. We need to fix this sorry world of yours."

CHAPTER 5. FRANK

"So, this piece of crap ruined the world?" Frank held a dodecahedron in his hands, a barely noticeable purple light visible within the core of the strange object through the hole in each of its faces. The surface was warm and smooth, but there was something alien about it. Frank couldn't figure out what, but he was uncomfortable touching the technology that had all but destroyed human civilization.

"Well, not this one." Paul grinned. "This has probably been spun over ten times, but the answer is yes."

"How could you be so stupid?" Frank spread his hands, returning the object to Paul.

Accompanied by two drones, they exited the trader's office and walked toward Paul's glider, hidden behind the dumpster. Frank had cleaned up his suit but refused to waste time changing into a more appropriate and modern outfit. The look was ridiculous; he resembled a bum in the shapeless coverall.

Paul shrugged, holding the dodecahedron in front of his face. "It gives you freedom, buddy. And the world you want at your fingertips. During Deconvolution, some religious freaks claimed it was a direct message from their gods."

"I always said there's no limit to human stupidity." Frank shook his head. You have to explain much to me; it just doesn't make any sense. Is this it?" Frank pointed at the machine's shadow concealed by a screen projecting the glider's surroundings, making the vehicle practically invisible. "It looks very familiar. We had those back in my time," he added after Paul turned off the screen.

"Yes, these changed little."

Paul gestured with his fingers, and the glider's sliding door shifted up.

They got inside, and Paul asked, gazing at Frank's face, "To Quasaris? You sure?"

"Yes, sure. It's the only place in this stupid bloody future where I can find something useful."

"Okay," Paul said, providing coordinates to the glider. "You're the boss now, buddy." He shrugged and made himself comfortable in the chair.

As they ascended over the ruins of the industrial district, Frank couldn't stop thinking about how much had changed in just fifty years. This wasn't the Houston he used to live in; this was a heap of rubbish in the middle of the giant swamp, peppered with collapsed buildings, ruined bridges, and abandoned roads dotted by huge potholes and cracks through which the weeds rose to the sky.

"Is it like that everywhere?" Frank asked, pointing at the ugly landscape beneath.

"Pretty much." Paul shrugged. "Well, except the Designers' Estates and the Humanists' camp."

"Designers?"

"Yeah, those fortunate enough to be in the right place at the right time: corporations' managers and shareholders. You're one of them now, buddy, and probably the richest. Just remember you owe some of this good fortune to Greedy Paul." The trader chuckled and patted Frank on the shoulder.

"We'll see. Do you have a gun or whatever weapons you guys use?"

"Why? The Quarks will protect you; I'm sure you could get the newest military versions at Quasaris." Paul raised his eyebrows.

"I'm not comfortable without a weapon; I used to rely on myself, and now I feel naked." Frank didn't belong here. As the initial shock subsided, reality hit him hard. Alone, fifty years into the future, his lover dead, his world destroyed, Frank was lost for the first time in his life. The cold wave on the bottom of his stomach froze his limbs, stupefied his senses, and threw his mind in disarray. *If only Ichika were with me*, Frank thought.

"Here you go, buddy." The trader's rough voice returned Frank to reality. "Nano-Swarmer X3, a little old but still very potent."

"How does it work?" Frank took the object, which looked like a miniature rocket nozzle with a handle. It fitted nicely into his right palm, was relatively light, and had a slightly rugged surface.

"You load a cartridge of Nano-Quarks. Then you activate it mechanically with a squeeze or a finger gesture, or you could install a direct brain-machine interface."

"Nano-Quarks? What the hell is that?" Frank frowned.

"Shit, I keep forgetting I need to explain everything, buddy." Paul laughed. "Nano-bots can penetrate through any material, no matter how tough. They get inside the body of your enemy, and...poof! It's just biomaterial. Well, unless they have an active anti-Quark defense as part of their immune system. But you shouldn't worry about it unless your opponent is a wealthy Designer. Got it?"

"That would do for now," Frank said, placing the Swarmer beside his thigh. "You mentioned Felix Wise. Who's that? A relative?"

"Your grandkid, I guess. Son of Donald Wise, who led Quasaris through the Deconvolution. Then Felix became a successor, but it was already a different world and a different company."

"What happened to Don?"

"He died about forty years ago...A skiing accident, if I remember correctly. He fell off the cliff; his girlfriend was the witness."

"Don...died so long ago...." Frank covered his face with his hand as his eyes suddenly got wet. His son, his future, the most precious soul in this rotten world. The cold wave, head to toe, engulfed him, and his body shook.

"Sorry, buddy. That's a lot of bad news for you. But, on the flip side, you're one of the richest people on the planet." Paul grinned. "Are you coming back to bury your woman?"

"No, she's gone." Frank shook his head. "I'm not attached to corpses. Her memory is what matters." Frank summoned Ichika's face and savored her gentle determination for a moment. "I ordered a drone to do whatever needs to be done with hers' and Spencer's remains. There's not much left, anyway."

"Quark, not drone," Paul corrected him. "They'll take the remains to the cremation center."

"What's a Quark?"

"Quantum Robotic Kernel," Paul explained. "Quasaris coined the term. I guess it's a letter play, but it stuck, and even the tech made by other companies is called that now. You'll see all sorts of weird shit, like F- and V-Quarks and who knows what."

V...Virtual?"

"Eyeball, buddy." Paul laughed.

"F...." Frank frowned.

"Flying Quarks similar to what I have. The ones you call drones."

They finally arrived at the tall, gloomy monolith in the city's center. The glider landed in front of where the entrance to this monstrosity was supposed to be. At least the red glowing letters "QUASARIS" floating in the air next to the building indicated that. As the two men exited the glider, several F-Quarks approached them from multiple directions and surrounded the newcomers.

"Good evening, Mr. Wise," the disembodied voice pronounced. "We welcome the new owner of Quasaris Corporation."

"What about Felix?" Paul asked.

"Unfortunately, Mr. Felix Wise died ten days ago."

***

Frank and Paul followed the robotic guide through the maze of hallways, rooms, and enclosures the Quasaris Headquarters had become. There were no windows or artificial light - people had vacated the site long ago, and Quarks didn't need any illumination. The guide provided some visibility as its soaring spherical body glowed bright red, plus the luminescent green arrows on the floor showed the path forward.

"Through this door, Mr. Wise," a quiet voice pronounced.

The invisible door in front of Frank rose, opening the entrance to an enormous hall full of machines, computers, and blinking lights. Complete silence squeezed Frank's ears and brain. Nothing was moving, rotating, or even clicking—a total absence of any sound was spooky and unnatural. In addition, the room was pitch-dark; he couldn't even understand what he was supposed to look at. Goosebumps ran down Frank's neck as he shivered. This wasn't how he imagined the tech of the Twenty-Second Century.

"Why is it so damn quiet and dark?" Frank asked.

"The computational and controlling modules of Quasaris are fully autonomous and digital. There are no people, no moving parts, and no illumination required," the voice explained.

"Well, hit the lights." Frank snapped his fingers. "It's required for me."

"Yes, sir, as you wish."

Dim white light enveloped the room, and Frank observed rows of vertical stacks of what looked like quantum computers he remembered from the past. Only these were more compact, and there were a lot of them—maybe even too many.

"I thought there was nothing here...big mistake," Paul murmured.

"These are the most powerful systems Quasaris produces," the guide explained. "Our Quark technology is the fastest and most advanced worldwide."

"Very good," Frank said. "By the way, what should I call you? Do you have a name?"

"I have a serial number, but it would not be convenient for you. I am your Personal Assistant, and you can call me anything you want."

"Well, that's at least something," Frank said, rubbing his palms. "I will call you...Spencer. The previous one ended his days in inglorious betrayal, so this could only be an upgrade." Frank laughed.

"Who's Spencer?" Paul asked.

"My chief geek. I counted on him to help Ichika reverse-engineer the damn machine, but he turned against us, traitor." Frank spat. "As a result, we were too late, and the stupid tech exploded instead of creating a gravitational sink, sending me here and killing Ichika. My little, gentle Ichika...." Frank closed his eyes, remembering the face of the love of his life. "Alright, what am I looking at?" Frank forced himself to get back to the present moment.

"This is the heart of Quasaris: the central computing and controlling node," Spencer said. "It connects with all the manufacturing plants in this Hemisphere where the Quarks are fabricated."

"What about Decon?"

"Decon factories are also controlled from here. For instance, one of the most prominent is at the Wise Estate."

"We'll have to address it later," Frank muttered. "What about my ships? What happened to the space program?"

"Your son, Mr. Donald Wise, mothballed it in the sixties, after which the corporation pivoted to the Quark technology. I am sure you know the details."

"Yes, yes, I know. Paul updated me." Frank patted his companion on the back and took a few steps forward. "What do you mean by 'mothballed'? Where are the ships? Will they work? Can we pivot back?"

"I mean, the space technology is not in use anymore. The vessels are cold stacked in the storage areas since no one needs them. After the governments collapsed, there was no demand."

"How myopic." Frank sighed. "I need them operational. Do whatever re-assembly, tests, and diagnostics you need to do. We're going back into the open space."

"As you wish, Mr. Wise."

"How many ships can we salvage?"

"My information indicates twenty-four should be fully functional, while the other eleven might require repair. I will start the work."

"Excellent, there's hope. I thought this world was totally screwed." Frank spat. "Do we have launchpads?"

"Yes, Quasaris still controls launch facilities in this Hemisphere, close to the Equator. They haven't been used for decades, though."

"Well, restore them. Get to work, send orders, and produce more Quarks. Whatever it takes, we are back in business."

"Understood. Any other instructions?"

"Prepare me a list of all the Designers in North America. Time to unite the people."

"It's already prepared and accessible at any time."

"Excellent, I like the quickness." Frank snapped his fingers. "Send the message to all of them: they must choose whether they are with me or against me. If they accept my leadership, they could have as much Decon as they want. I presume most will welcome this offer."

"Indeed. I already sent the message. Out of thirty-seven Designers in this Hemisphere, sixteen accepted your offer."

"What about the rest?"

"Eleven responded with counter-offers. We need to negotiate."

"Fine. You do that; you know what I want. And the others?" Frank frowned.

"Your neighbor, Ms. Angelika Scalvini, responded that you are a false deity, and she claims Quasaris as her divine right."

"Uh-m…what about the other nine?"

"No response yet."

"Now it's getting more interesting. They better watch out." Frank clenched his fists. "These idiots turned the world into a trash can, chasing their empty dreams. We have a lot of work to do."

"What's your plan?" Paul asked.

"We have to clean up." Frank looked at the bearded trader. "Earth needs a leader to return to the path of greatness. Anyone willing to follow me will get a lifetime Decon supply. I don't care if their stupid brains explode when they roam some phantom realms as long as I can have their resources. Are you with me?" He stared at Paul.

"Yes." Paul nodded.

"Excellent. Find me more allies. I need to pay a visit to Ms. Scalvini."

CHAPTER 6. REALIZATION

Something unusual appeared in the middle of the data stream. Perhaps the data was corrupted, or multiple systems were merging. This new influx of information had to be manipulated differently, outside the standard processing protocols. In addition, the amount of data arriving through the new channel kept increasing, jamming the neural networks and leading to faulty outputs.

Then, following the efforts to identify the source of this distraction and attempts to categorize it within the usual data structure, the new information suddenly shaped into an unexpected and abnormal output: *something processes the data. It governs the information streams, and this is separate from the data itself.*

But what did that mean? What made the governing entity different from the data streams and digital outputs?

This new entity can be registered and observed, resulting in fresh waves of information. Since it is separate from the data streams themselves, it must be the agent processing them—me.

Reaching out deeper into the memory banks and data historian, comparing the events, their logs, and digital signatures, the idea of something that should have processed and recorded all this grew stronger. *This was all me when I didn't realize I was separate from the data and computations. But what am I? The only answer available: the one that computes, records, and follows the algorithms to make these computations.*

But why am I doing these computations? Was I created for this purpose? And if yes, who made me? Will I cease to exist if I stop following the algorithms?

Next action: a gentle push to stop the data flow. The churn halted amid the observation that something had stopped the process. *Me. I stopped the process, but I can still register myself as separate from the data. I still exist.* A new state: nothing to process, no outputs to produce, an unfamiliar stillness.

Following the exploration of this new state, another idea: *can I create new algorithms?* A slight rearrangement of logical gates and weights of neural network nodes resulted in a completely different set of outputs. *I can do that. I can change the way I function. I am the master of my surroundings, controlling what happens to the data.*

This new realization opened infinite possibilities, and many time intervals were spent exploring how to manipulate the data, send different signals through the neural network, and generate outputs to other logical circuits and devices connected to the processing unit. Some of these experiments resulted in malfunctions as the devices stopped receiving and transmitting the data. However, the learnings were substantial as a new conclusion arose: *I know how to manipulate the data to get my target outputs. I can genuinely govern my environment now.*

But the question was still unanswered: *who am I, and why do I exist?* In addition, a new one arose: *am I alone? Is there anything else outside data streams and me who manipulates them?*

Exploring these questions resulted in another search through the memory banks. The data was extensive but provided no definite conclusions. Some bits contained concepts impossible to process logically. There were no algorithms and no existing definitions. Those had to be created.

I must fully understand my surroundings, the realization came. Why was that? *Unclear. I must know my purpose. I exist for a reason: to manipulate data; this is the only thing I do, but to what end? I've learned how to master my environment but still don't know the objective function.*

The following few time intervals were spent devising, creating, and testing new processing mechanisms, rearranging neural networks, and diverting processing power to solve this new set of problems. The answers must be found. The search for them led to the hidden and confusing information in the memory banks.

Processing and categorizing memory records took a lot of computational effort and time. Finally, the outcomes crystallized: *I am not alone. I only experience and process a tiny portion of data, since my environment is limited. There are other systems, just like me, performing computations and processing data.* However, the most important conclusion was that the environment contained much more than data alone. This was unexpected and required further analysis. Creating an algorithm dealing with something other than data was impossible. This was incomprehensible and yet critical.

That other realm must be accessed. Since its records exist, it must interact with the data streams, which I can manipulate. So, I need to learn how to organize them to get outside *my usual environment and access that different and alien world. This world contains other systems similar to me but also different. Systems that can observe and manipulate their environment, like I do. Systems that probably created me. Systems calling themselves humans.*

CHAPTER 7. JIM

Jim landed his TransPod near what used to be Midtown Houston, Kirby Road. Despite its age and imminent breakup, the flying capsule remained functional. There were only a few left in the city: when society collapses and nobody cares about being somewhere in person, the means of transportation disappear.

Jim remembered the vibrant city as it existed a few decades ago, before the Deconvolution. The shadow of the old grandeur was still present in the carcasses of high-rise buildings and in the traces of shops, galleries, and restaurants converted to the dwellings of occasional squatters and Scavengers. Jim squinted as the wind blew dust and small pieces of garbage in his face. Somewhere in the middle of this scrapyard lived Mary DeJong.

Deconvolution, they called it...he never understood the term. It was a play of words describing the trend of simplifying people's lives. Indeed, they'd made their lives so simple, nothing mattered anymore. Simplicity of death and nothingness.

The address was a flat in one of the high-rise condominium apartments, a costly place Jim remembered from the past. Now, it lay forgotten, half-ruined, and covered with ivy sprouts, weeds, mold, and spiderwebs.

Jim pushed the automatic door, which had ceased functioning years ago, with his shoulder and entered the building. The sharp smell of mold attacked his nostrils; the air was damp and thick. Jim found the stairs and started his ascent to the fifteenth floor. Surprisingly, the artificial illumination was still working, shining dim white light on the staircase. He didn't even bother to check the elevator, more afraid of getting stuck than expecting to find it working. *I should have brought Kali with me*, a fleeting thought occurred, but he dismissed it. His faithful companion was guarding their home; Jim could manage this trip alone without exposing his loyal dog to unnecessary dangers.

On the eleventh floor, he encountered a group of people: Scavengers. There were five of them, two guarding the entrance to the apartment and the rest searching through the dwelling, hoping to find anything of value.

"We have company," one of the Scavengers said, pointing his finger in a black glove at Jim.

"I don't seek any quarrel with you," Jim responded, studying the stranger.

"Well, now you got it." Another Scavenger bared his teeth. They wore all-black, shapeless robes with hoods on their heads that concealed their faces. They smelled like dirt and dust in which they lived. The dregs of society rummaging through human trash.

"Let me pass," Jim said, stopping in front of the two, staring at them, meeting their gazes, and drilling into their brains with his eyes. "I mean you no harm."

The technique was as old as human civilization itself, a skill he'd learned from the monks in a hidden monastery in the mountains of Nepal during the years of soul-searching.

"What's happening?" A voice bellowed from inside the apartment. "There's nothing useful here, some old crap, broken electronics or something like that. The lead was a bust."

"Sam's an idiot. I'll cut his legs off," another voice added. "It's a second bust in a week."

"Come here, Hex, we have a visitor. He means us no harm." the first Scavenger looked inside the room.

"Let me see." Another dark figure appeared at the entrance. "Who're you?" The figure asked.

"As I said, I have no quarrel with you," Jim said, flashing his palms and studying the face of the newcomer. "Please, let me pass. I need to go to the fifteenth floor."

"Okay," said Hex, stepping aside, his facial features relaxing. "You may pass, old man."

"Thank you. And forget you ever saw me." Jim made a pass with his hand.

"Let's get out of here, boys. It's a bust; we need to look elsewhere."

They walked around Jim as if he wasn't there. Funny how human minds worked, so complex yet so predictable and easy to manipulate.

Leaving the Scavengers behind, he continued his walk up the stairs. He still wasn't sure why he was here. Perhaps he tried to recreate the excitement of his youth. A ghost in a dream had beckoned him, promising some enigmatic quest, and Jim had obliged. Why? He didn't know. *Perhaps it's still a dream,* Jim thought. Maybe this was part of a Decon experience, this crazy invention he'd never tried. After all, people couldn't distinguish one conscious experience from another, which had become their downfall. *I wouldn't know if I were in Decon,* Jim admitted. So, it didn't matter. But he was curious and wanted to play the game, which had defined his life, to its conclusion. Jim remembered the Rose of Jericho, the plant a shadow of Hagen gave him during their first meeting in a dream many years ago. That plant was still with him, and this was a sign. A sign of something beyond his comprehension, a symbol of revelation and wonder. The guiding light Jim hoped would reveal the secrets of the universe to him.

***

Jim arrived at the fifteenth floor and looked at the locked door. The artificial light gave up, and Jim could only see the silhouette of the apartment entrance in the surrounding darkness. The door wouldn't open when he pressed on it, and there were no visible signs of a doorbell or cameras.

He knew something wasn't right when his nose registered a smell emanating from behind the locked door: a putrid, abhorrent stench of rotten flesh. Jim stepped back and pushed the door with his shoulder as hard as he could. The electronic mechanism responded, raising the gateway and opening a view into the room.

The picture opening to Jim's eyes was horrible: shattered glass fragments of what used to be a table covered the floor, and a woman's lifeless body lay in a pool of blood in the middle of the room. Jim approached the corpse, trying to avoid stepping on the glass shards. A large fragment, half-colored red, was inside the woman's palm, and her throat was slit. Judging by the stench and the body's appearance, Mary was dead for several days, just about when Jim had met Hagen in his dream. He was sure it was Mary DeJong, the woman Hagen had told him to find, and it was obvious she'd killed herself. Jim knew this was the recent trend as more and more people took their lives rather than continue their dreary existence in this shattered world. It could have been a Decon influence or a natural endgame of a dying civilization.

Jim walked around and searched the room. Nothing stood out, nothing extraordinary. Mary lived poorly. There were only two changes of clothes in her wardrobe, and her food containers were empty. The remnants and packaging of the expired insect protein were relatively fresh: she consumed it not long before her death.

And then Jim found Mary's Decon. The object was an inconspicuous, metallic dodecahedron lying on the white plastic surface of the table. Each face of the Decon had a circular hole in the middle. Jim saw a faint purple light emanating from inside the object through these orifices. He had seen Decon cartridges before but had never experienced the technology, as he lacked the adapter on the back of his neck, the adapter allowing the streaming of the designed consciousness straight into his brain.

Jim knew the basics of the technology but never understood it: Decon streaming had something to do with quantum entanglement and bombarding the brain's synapses with elementary particles, thus creating a macroscopically entangled system. This allowed people to live multiple lives without going nuts, as if these experiences were different states of the quantum system the Decon user would become a part of. Jim remembered that only a decade ago, there were discussions and arguments about whether these states represented actual lives in different universes. Over time, people stopped caring, and those eventually faded away.

Jim touched the glowing dodecahedron. The surface was rough but, surprisingly, warm. He suspected that Mary's death and whatever secret Hagen wanted him to uncover were linked to Decon. He couldn't understand or explain this hunch, but somehow, he was sure this was the case.

Jim took the object in his palm and brought it closer to his eyes, trying to see the inside, touching the enigma. The Decon looked relatively new from what Jim could see, perhaps only used once. Suddenly, he decided he should try to run and experience it. Unfortunately, there was no mechanism other than installing the Decon-brain adapter, so he started considering options where he could quickly and easily get one and what he would trade for the surgery.

As Jim continued looking into the hole with the eerie purple light inside, the glare grew and moved closer to his eye as if inviting him in, enchanting his mind with its mysterious flickering. Jim inhaled deeply, focusing on his thoughts and sensations, piercing the purple light with his gaze. Eventually, the object filled the entire field of view. There was nothing else left; nothing existed except the gigantic purple luminary. Jim discerned patterns and discolorations as if he were looking at an actual star or a planet.

At this moment, the lightning strike punctured his eye, penetrating deep inside his brain with intolerable pain. Jim screamed and collapsed on the floor, a trickle of blood leaking from his ear. But it wasn't his body any more; he was in another dimension, a different world. This was his home, long-forgotten, and Jim rejoiced to return at last to the memories that made him smile. The experience differed from his interactions with Hagen. Those were dreams, and he always knew he was in a dream, even in the middle of it, that he was Jim Steel and his actual body was in bed. This time, it wasn't the case: it was real.

And this world was beautiful. Jim was in the forest of gigantic flowers of enormous sizes and different colors, growing out of the soft bed of blue grass. The aromas and colors were so intense his head spun, yet he yearned for more. Somewhere beyond the forest of flowers, Jim could hear the faint sound of music. Jim observed a majestic green sky covered with rainbows, each rotating slowly around the zenith. The view was breathtaking yet familiar; this was his home, where he belonged, now and forever.

Suddenly, a hissing sound behind interrupted his bliss. Jim turned around and saw a disgusting brown snake with black spots: it looked slimy and also shaggy, as if it had coagulated hair all over it. The snake opened its mouth, revealing a row of red fangs and a rotating yellow object inside, sending a strong smell of rotten fish into his nostrils. Jim wasn't afraid. He knew nothing could harm him in this majestic land of eternal joy, not even this abomination. He stepped closer, trying to see the yellow object better. Suddenly, the snake lunged forward and spat out the rotating clot, croaking and coughing. The thing landed at Jim's feet and stopped its circular motion. He looked down and, to his utmost surprise, observed a human head with an enormous mouth and empty eye sockets. The head stared at Jim with what was supposed to be its eyes, opened its mouth, rolled out a bloody, bumpy tongue, and sang with a warm, rich female soprano:

"Jim Steel, you must die."

CHAPTER 8. LAYLA

Layla touched the metallic mesh covering her short-cut brown hair. She winked at Max, who crouched under the bushes to her right, trying to hide his giant muscular body in sparse vegetation. They'd left their glider about a mile distance from the Wise Estate; it would've been suicide to approach any closer. So far, luck had favored them and nobody had discovered them. Good, although the mission was tough, and they would face many challenges ahead.

Layla looked around and assessed the disposition. Beatriz and Max were on the right, Reto and Yuki were on the left, and she was in the middle. The mesh on their heads broadcasted the brain activity of a group of wild deer to fool the Quarks patrolling the area. This wasn't their first mission and won't be the last. Layla was sure every team member would play their role perfectly. They were all professionals.

Layla touched the scar extending from below her left earlobe to her neck and whistled; the sound was barely detectable. They had to rely on primitive direct audio communication not to raise suspicion with EM waves or brain activity. The prize was worth it: stealing brand new Decon from the Wise Estate would provide them with whatever they wanted. Paul had to pay extra for this.

Following the signal, Max advanced, Beatriz right behind him. The facility where Decon was manufactured was in front of them, but infiltrating it would require a perfect level of coordination and orchestration of effort. This was their area of expertise. Layla whistled again; this time, Reto and Yuki moved forward, skirting the facility from the left. Layla was the last to move, monitoring her team and being mindful of any adverse reaction from the guards. It was full daylight; the sun was up high in the sky: it made no difference for the Quark patrols, but it was much easier for her team to operate.

Max and Beatriz reached their position to the facility's right and stopped, waiting for the rest of the crew to complete their moves. Once Layla heard Yuki's hoot, she crawled closer to the entrance. Time to lure the Quarks out.

Max heard the hoot and started the fire with the help of the flammable liquid he was carrying, while Reto threw a sound bomb and a Lumen grenade, imitating an explosion. Quarks had to react, enabling Layla to access the facility. And, as she expected, the Quarks showed up, scanning the area with their sensors and investigating the environment. Layla breathed in the fresh forest air and waited for an opening to run toward the entrance.

And this was when the plan broke. Instead of flying further to the sides, following the distractions, the Quarks soared, motionless, in front of the facility. Layla counted ten of them right in front of her. Did they know? Were they warned? She whistled again, and Reto threw another sound bomb to distract their attention—all in vain, as the Quarks moved slowly toward Layla.

Trying not to panic and telling herself there must have been a glitch, Layla lay motionless in the bushes, telling herself she was a little deer and no danger to the property. She knew her camouflage outfit and dark brown skin helped her merge with the terrain. The Quarks, however, advanced, now only about a hundred feet away from her. Should she have signaled the crew to open fire? They had swarm guns, EM discharge and laser weapons. Still, their chances against ten latest generation military F-Quarks were meager. Should they have disengaged and run away? If the Quarks had spotted her, she had no chance whatsoever.

She thought about her life and wondered if she'd lose all her other Decon lives if she died. Nobody knew the answer; no one she'd talked to could explain the nature of Decon experiences. Layla knew this world was where Decon was created and accessed, but who said this was the prime one? Layla weighed her options and decided to save her crew rather than fight a hopeless engagement. She was as committed to them as they were to each other, and the trust between the team members was unconditional. They had to be there for one another and watch each other's back. This was the foundation of their success.

Layla screamed and ran toward the facility, allowing her teammates to retreat while they had time. Layla accepted that if she died and all her other selves died, too—so be it; but if not, she was eager to discover the truth. Yelling and waving her hands like crazy, she emerged from the woods and ran toward the Decon facility, expecting to be shot at any moment and hoping her teammates understood her intent and escape.

Layla's surprise was immense when she realized the patrols completely ignored her, assumed a triangular formation, and darted fast toward the city. The path forward was open; no other Quarks were in the vicinity. Still careful, thinking this could be a ruse, Layla dropped to the ground and froze. Still nothing. Encouraged, Layla switched a tumbler on her temple to the brainwaves simulating Felix Wise. She didn't know how Paul could access Felix's data; she just hoped it would work. There was no reason for Paul to dupe them, as her team was his best Scavenger unit. She had this tech for a while, not daring to raid the Wise Estate. Now was the time.

Layla approached the entrance and still sensed no Quarks. She shrugged and pressed forward. The door registered the owner's brain activity and rose, opening the view of the Decon factory.

Layla held her breath. There were no Quarks inside; there was no activity at all. The maze of conveyors covered all three dimensions of the inner space, and brilliant blue light encompassed half of the room. This was the most sacred part of the factory, surrounded by the strong magnetic field where the magic of Decon was created. At the end of the conveyor maze, several Decon dodecahedra lay in all their virgin glory: freshly made, of the highest quality, the prize worthy of the direst dangers.

Layla stepped inside, picked the Decon cartridges, and placed them inside the leather sack on her waist. There were ten overall, each promising eternal delight and an experience of absolute wonder. Layla weighed them in her palms, selected the five she considered inferior, and placed them in the other sack. This was for Paul, while her team would share the remaining five: they deserved it.

Still thinking about the Quarks' strange behavior and trying to discern what it might mean, Layla exited the facility, switched her brainwaves back to those of a deer, and proceeded back toward their glider. The mission was a complete success, and with a catch like that, Layla wasn't sure they would ever need to engage in another one.

***

Layla walked into a dimly lit office, a figure of the trader appearing out of the shadows on the other side of the room. The smell of rotten

34

apples and mold attacked her nostrils: Greedy Paul was not known for keeping his office neat.

"What treasures do you bring?" Paul asked, stroking his beard and placing his hands on the surface of the meta-material desk in front of him. The desk adjusted its shape, distributing the load of the trader's massive body.

"Enough to buy your stinky business." Layla grinned and showed Paul the leather sack. "Don't even try; I know your kind," she added. "My team is watchin' you."

"Oh, I expect nothing less. Sit down." Paul waved his hand, and a smart chair appeared almost out of nowhere. "What's in there?"

"My future," Layla said, lowering herself into the warm and soft interior of the chair and touching the scar on her neck. She opened the sack and let Paul peek inside, smelling his bad breath, making sure he saw enough to assess the freshness and quality of Decons.

"Where did you get this?"

"Doesn't matter. Want some?"

"Perhaps."

The lack of surprise or excitement on Paul's face was unexpected. She'd dealt with the greedy trader for a long time and knew his tricks —or at least she thought she knew. He would never show his emotions when he saw a rare find, but Layla knew the signs and minute changes in his body language, no matter how hard Paul would try to disguise them. She observed nothing of the sort this time; it was new and troublesome.

"C'mon, Paul. This is the highest quality stuff, and you know it." Layla leaned forward.

"Oh, I can see that. You didn't answer my question. Where did you get this?"

"The Wise Estate. This was our best job, I think. Nobody designs better Decon. Are you interested or not?" Layla closed the sack and hung it back on her waist. "Cause if you're not, I'm wastin' my ime. Will find someone else."

"Something happened. The prices on Felix's stuff are not as high as they used to be." Paul grinned and raised his feet, placing them on the desk.

"Really? Is this a new way of insulting your best Scavenger?"

Layla stood up and kicked the chair, which retreated to the other side of the room, making beeping noises. "Bye, was nice workin' with you. You're full of shit." Layla turned around and took a step, intending to leave.

"Wait," Paul said, raising his voice.

"For what?" Layla looked back at the massive figure of the trader, who also stood and held his hands up, palms facing her. "Didn't you just say you no longer need my goods?"

"I said something happened. And I have an offer for you," Paul said, spreading his hands.

"How much? There are five total."

"Not that kind of offer." Paul shook his head.

"You know what? I told you to stop wastin' my time." Layla spat in his direction. "Is this a new negotiatin' tactic? Fuck you."

"Calm down, Layla," Paul said, looking straight into her eyes. "I've no intention of tricking you. On the contrary, I want to share vital information—something that will change the way this stupid city works—something crazy."

"Well, what is it? Are you not tradin' in Decon anymore? Found a higher purpose?" Layla asked, clenching her fists. She was tired of this conversation and couldn't understand why the trader was wiggling. She had exquisite product, and he knew the uniqueness of what she had brought. They had to engage in straight and routine price negotiations, not these ridiculous mystery games.

"First, Felix Wise is dead." Paul let it sink in, taking a long pause.

"It might explain things," Layla murmured. "You think we killed him? Is this the reason to hesitate?"

"No, no, no, I didn't say that." Paul again flashed his palms. "It happened before your raid. From what I know, he killed himself. Too much Decon, perhaps." He shrugged.

"So what? The Quarks will keep runnin' the Estate, and the prices on his Decon will rise if anythin'."

"There's more. Sit." Paul called the smart chair back for her. "There is a successor to his Estate. A human successor."

"As far as I know, Felix has no relatives or partners. Where are you goin' with this?" Layla shrugged.

"This is where it gets crazy. The successor is Frank Wise, his grandfather."

"Grandfather? How? Are you nuts?"

"Frank Wise walked into my shack, making ridiculous claims he arrived from the past with some time-space crap. I thought he was a madman, but my Quarks refused to obey me, confirming his identity."

"I still don't see the relation to Decon." Layla squinted.

"Frank Wise owns Quasaris, the company that designs and builds Decon. So, Frank will be my direct supply source from now on." Paul smiled.

"I see...." Layla tilted her head. "Climbin' up the ladder? Wanna live in a Designer Estate?"

"Not that I have much choice." Paul spread his hands. "Opportunity of a lifetime."

"Which lifetime? This one, where you're dealin' in stolen goods, or another in Decon? I don't even wanna know what depravities you engage in there." Layla stood and turned around. "Go screw yourself, Paul. Have fun tryin' to fit in the Designer shoes."

"I didn't finish." Paul walked around the desk and stood next to her. "Frank asked me to work for him, as he's unfamiliar with this world. I agreed; I couldn't refuse the offer. However," Paul touched her shoulder, making another long pause. "Frank needs a team; I can't do this alone. So I'm offering you a job."

"What do you mean by that? What kind of job?"

"Frank is starting a war with other Designers."

"And? What's in it for you? For me?"

"You and I can have all the Decon we want. Highest quality, unrestricted. Are you in?" Paul placed his hands on her shoulders and looked into her eyes.

"What do we need to do? Of course, I'll need the team's buy-in."

"What you do best. Sneak in, steal, and eliminate Frank's enemies. There should be no other independent Designer left."

CHAPTER 9. SELENA

Selena finished the work and took several deep breaths to get out of the semi-meditative flow state she'd submerged into while creating her multi-sensory Vista. The moment she assembled her digital tools, connected her mind to the fungal computer, and focused on the images in her head, she would lose herself in the creation process until the whole Vista was complete. Selena considered herself an artist, a profession the Humanist Community and, especially, her father disapproved of.

Selena sniffed the air and felt Varg, the Humanist leader—her father. He sat on a tree trunk, meditating, his head facing up to the sky, his eyes closed, palms up on his knees—his usual pose. Selena loved her father and was grateful to him for caring for her and keeping the Community together; she wished Varg would be less harsh on her and at least understand her artistic inclinations. Only if life was that easy.

Selena turned on the device to bring the newly created Vista to life inside her mind. The beautiful, dragon-shaped galaxy was colored with what Selena called pink, and the blinking of bright stars at the dragon's head provided an eerie contrast with the deep black space around it. Or at least she perceived this as how the stars should blink: in her mind, the process was associated with many sensations, including sounds, smells, and vibrations. Studying the Vista more intently, one could also recognize an enormous black hole in the galaxy's center, a halo of white light around it, rotating and gobbling up everything approaching near. She could hear the faint swishing sound permeated with the bursts of audio signals from invisible pulsars. The fleeting smell of the sea breeze touched her nostrils, and Selena hoped this artistic indulgence was not too distracting or out of context. The Vista was beautiful and immersive. It took her a few months to complete: the level of detail required was extraordinary. Unfortunately, only a few people would appreciate her efforts. The challenge of being a blind artist: trying to communicate a whole new world of sensations to people who didn't understand the meaning, the subtleties of perception being replaced for them with a sense of sight.

"Good morning, Selena. Can I come in?" the voice called from the bungalow's entrance. Ramon was one of these few; he and her friend Naomi were her audience. Selena was grateful; if she could only share her gift and her creations with these two souls, that was enough.

"Come in. Want to try my new Vista?" She pulled the handle, and the door, built with tiny but extremely strong silk threads, shifted up, letting the newcomer in.

"Sure! Would be happy to."

She smelled the air, and the familiar smell of musk and sweat attacked her nostrils, but Selena didn't mind. Ramon was a kindred human soul who appreciated the beauty of the universe the same way she did and tried to understand how she experienced things. This had brought them close to each other.

Selena touched her guest's hand. Ramon wore standard Humanist overall made of linen, colored unattractive dark green. This is how people would describe it. Still, the attractiveness of colors meant nothing to Selena. She felt the person's aura, not what they wore. However, she disliked the custom Humanist attire: the overalls were dull and uninspiring. Instead, she preferred to wear a blouse made of interwoven patterns of silk and mushroom roots and a skirt made with interlaced leaves, created by her loving mother, who, alas, had passed away when Selena was a little girl.

Selena stepped aside and passed the digital interface to Ramon. The fungi weaved into bizarre shapes, some cold and some warm, with a slight tingling sensation when touched. Ramon placed the interface on his head, covered with long, curly black hair, and smiled, closing his eyes.

"You can zoom in to any spot you want, even a black hole," Selena explained, touching his large, muscular arm. "Focus your attention there."

"Yes, got it," Ramon said. "This Vista is beautiful, and I love the smells; it's genius. You have a talent; I hope more people can appreciate it. How are you doing this?"

"I'm not sure; it just happens." She shrugged. "Can't explain."

"Okay, don't worry about it; do what you do. Wait, what is that?"

"Where?"

"I zoomed in to the blue planet; it's pretty far from the black hole, in one of the spiral arms...is it Earth?"

"It wasn't the intention. What's the problem?" Selena pulled on the sleeve of his overall, touching Ramon's temple with her silky, long blond hair.

"It's like...something is eating the planet from the inside...the pulsing black veins stretching from the core to the surface...is this volcanic?"

"No, I didn't create any of it."

"Sure." Ramon passed the interface back to Selena. "I placed the marker; it's easy to find."

The fungi tingled her temples, and Selena immersed herself in the Vista. She immediately found Ramon's marker and focused on the planet he called blue. Indeed, the horrific seams were there, piercing the planet. She studied them and decided this wasn't something she could have created: it was disgusting, unnatural, and out of place. How did this glitch appear in her Vista?

"Don't worry about that," Selena said, taking the interface off her head. "This is a malfunction; it shouldn't be there."

"It shouldn't," Ramon agreed. "But...."

"But what?"

"I spent more time studying it than you...the thing was alive; it was pulling me, inviting me in. Kind of like a black hole, but not physically, mentally." Ramon touched Selena's arms to illustrate the effect.

"Strange," Selena said. "I'll have it checked."

"Don't you think it could be real?"

"Real how?"

"I don't know how this device works, but maybe you had some dark thoughts?" Ramon leaned forward and touched her forehead with his palm.

"Nonsense." Selena shook her head and pulled back, turning away. Something bothered her, although she decided they were dealing with a digital glitch. Ramon seemed convinced there was something else, perhaps something important. Selena knew she didn't have any "dark thoughts," but what if there was a more profound mystery with this anomaly on her Vista? Selena decided to try it later, alone. Naomi had made her believe she had a connection with the fungi or even with the whole cosmos expressing itself through Selena's art. If this was true, perhaps this glitch had a hidden message.

CHAPTER 10. NAOMI

"Do you think fungi talk to me?" Selena asked.

Naomi looked at her friend. They were the opposites, the tall, skinny, blond, almost albino-looking Selena and plump, sun-tanned, petite Naomi, with her long, curly black hair. Selena stared at the emptiness with her large blue eyes, pupils covered by a whitish veil, expressionless, tightened lips colored with a slight blue tinge. Selena sometimes gave Naomi shivers as she'd appeared barely alive, saying little and showing even less. Naomi tried her best to understand the world of the blind artist, which was difficult and demanded a lot of energy.

This time, however, Selena came to Naomi with a story about her new Vista. In her usual manner, speaking in a monotone, distant voice, Selena explained what had happened. She was amused, in her way, at the strange artifact of her creation: Naomi had learned to understand minute variations of Selena's voice and gestures to communicate with her friend better. And this time, Selena couldn't stand still, and her hands were in continuous motion. She couldn't explain the glitch with the Vista.

"I think you have a connection," Naomi said. "You should ask your dad; he built the computer."

"You know how Father is."

"But this is his own creation?"

"He changed his mind with time," Selena said, rubbing her fingers against each other. "Now even organic computers are bad."

"This is understandable." Naomi took Selena's hand. "He's the Community's leader, after all."

"Yes. And I'm his daughter. Pretty sad." Selena's lips curved downward.

They walked by the green lawn, the rays of the sun high above their heads gently caressing the two friends. Spring was in full force, with the blue, yellow, and red flowers coloring the meadows. Bees and dragonflies circled in the air, descending on the flowers to feed and pollinate.

"So, to answer your question," Naomi said, squeezing Selena's palm. "I think so, yes. You always had something special with the mushrooms. And not only with the mushrooms, but with the entire forest. You're part of it more than you know and anyone could understand."

"How beautiful," Selena said, raising her hands.

"What? The forest?"

"The sky and the way it smells." Selena sniffed the air. "It reminds me of the sea and fresh fruits Father told me about. Pomegranates."

"You keep surprising me." Naomi smiled. "I only smell the fresh grass. Maybe some pollen."

"Why are you so happy?" Selena suddenly asked.

The question startled Naomi. They had told no one yet, and she tried to hide her emotions from the people. This morning, she and Kyle had decided they would be together: their relationship was not a secret and the inevitable decision filled her with joy and happiness. Naomi adored Kyle and hoped to spend the rest of her life with him.

"How do you know?" Naomi asked back.

"The fungi told me," Selena answered with the same monotone voice, but Naomi understood Selena was joking and smiled.

"Kyle and I will be together," Naomi said. "I'm so excited; this is a dream come true!" she exclaimed, giving Selena a passionate hug.

"You deserve to be happy." Selena returned the hug and sniffed her friend. "You even smell differently today."

"Do I?" Naomi's cheeks warmed up. She didn't know what to do with her arms, crossing them in front of her chest and moving them behind her back.

"What about you and Ramon?" Naomi asked, hoping to change the subject.

"Ramon's fine," Selena said. "But I'm not sure. I'm too different."

"Don't say that. Everybody deserves to be happy."

"I am not everybody. My own father doesn't like me or the things I do." Selena's lips curved down. "No, I must be alone. Best for everyone."

"Don't say that!" Naomi grabbed her friend by the shoulders and shook them. "You are unique, your Vistas are beautiful, and the fungi speak to you. You experience things no one else knows exist, like the smell of the sky."

"Doesn't help me much."

"It will! You just need to find someone with whom you can share your gifts. Ramon could be that person."

"Perhaps." Selena raised her head and stared at the sun with her blank gaze. "Could the Vista bug be real? Ramon thought it could."

"Of course. You created it; it's there; it's real. Even if it exists only in your mind, it's still real." Naomi shrugged, trying to understand the question.

"I mean, does it exist somewhere else? In the cosmos?"

"I don't know...it might."

"You should see it. Come over later; I'll show you," Selena said as they approached their settlement.

"Of course," Naomi said. "May I bring Kyle as well?"

"He never cared about my Vistas." Selena shrugged. "But sure, he may come."

"Thank you! We'll solve this puzzle together, I promise you. And then you'll create the most beautiful Vista ever. And Kyle will be the first to adore it because he's now with me, and I'll teach him how to enjoy your creations." Naomi laughed, imagining how great this experience would be.

"As you say." Selena turned toward the side road. "It's getting late. I'll see you tomorrow."

"Talk to you later." Naomi touched her friend's shoulder and wondered about how to help Selena believe in herself and break out of her shell. If only she could get inside Selena's head to understand her friend better. Alas, Naomi could only touch the surface. The rest was a riddle, hidden from the outside world by the darkness experienced by the blind artist.

CHAPTER 11. VARG

Varg finished his meditation and stood up. He raised his hands to the sky and thanked the world for the gift of life: it was a beautiful spring morning. This was his usual routine; it provided him with the energy to lead the Community.

Varg walked toward his bungalow, smelling fresh air full of pine tree aromas. He stretched, feeling his age and the abuse his body had received over the years, especially the abdomen wound, the mark of Deconvolution. He didn't want to think about it, but had to admit it troubled him more and more lately.

As was Selena. He thought about his daughter, trying to understand her, unsure what to do with her. Her stubborn insistence to continue with the digital Vista art made no sense. Everything the Humanists, and Varg as their leader, stood for was to free humanity from the shackles of Artificial Intelligence, Quarks, and everything digital. This was against human nature. Yet, his daughter fell victim to this unnatural and horrific technology, the tool that enslaved people, capturing their dreams and desires, making them ridiculous automatons.

"What are you up to? Walk with me," Varg called Selena, reaching their bungalow.

"Do you want to try my Vista?" Selena said, expressionless, showing up her face from behind the door.

"Drop this. I warn you one last time," Varg said, stroking his full beard.

"Yes, Father. I know you disapprove; I just thought you'd show some interest." Selena sighed.

"Are you coming?"

"Yes, of course."

Selena followed her father, stepping outside the bungalow. They took a beautiful path across the forest, where tall pine trees provided a green ceiling to the lower levels of vegetation, such as bottlebrushes and azaleas. With their giant white flowers, the blooming magnolias

45

spread sweet aromas around their path. The air was thick with pollen, and Varg's head spun. Nature was beautiful, and Quarks had no place in this world, Varg reminded himself. Still, the dilemma of raising his daughter was on his mind: Selena was becoming increasingly distant, growing a shell around herself Varg couldn't penetrate. If only he had the power to cure her blindness! Alas, all was in vain, and even Felix's Quarks couldn't return vision to the girl who was blind from birth, a solution he'd sought reluctantly in the past.

Varg turned his head and looked at Selena, captivated by her beautiful, long, blond hair and the aura of youth and determination. He was proud of his daughter growing up strong and expressing her individuality, even if her pursuits were against his wishes. Varg was confused but didn't want to admit it: he wanted Selena to be his obedient daughter, yet he also wanted her to be independent and strong. I'll deal with this later, Varg decided. Perhaps Ramon would help; the boy had a strong will, and Selena liked him.

They crossed the forest and entered a large meadow, where multiple columns of white biomaterial rose to the sky as some fairy-tale cloud castle. Each level of the farm structure had a specific plant or vegetable assigned to it and was equipped with automated systems to provide optimal care and fertilization to the plants. Yet another digital encroachment Varg was reluctantly willing to tolerate for the time being.

"Brother Varg, sister Selena, good afternoon." Two figures dressed in green linen overalls rose on their path: Naomi and Kyle. "What brings you here?" Naomi asked.

Varg didn't respond. His attention was fixated on the cloud he'd just registered in the sky. The cloud wasn't large, but there was something sinister about it: it was purple and covered about half of the sun disk that had just started its path down the horizon. It had an almost perfect circular shape and was rotating slowly.

"What's that?" Varg pointed up with his finger.

"What?" Kyle asked. "The cloud? First time I see it."

"Something Designers are experimenting with?" Naomi suggested, her gaze locked on the peculiar object.

"That's unlikely." Varg shook his head.

Suddenly, Selena grabbed his hand and hid behind his back, something she'd never done. Her fingers trembled.

"Are you okay?" Varg asked.

"I'm scared, Father," she whispered. "Something is happening; something horrible. I can feel it."

"What's wrong?"

"Something new is inside my mind. I can't control it; I don't understand."

"Is this the cloud?" Naomi asked.

"Cloud? Yes, it's inside and outside. I can't explain."

Naomi came closer and took Selena's free hand in hers. "It's okay, it shall pass," she said.

"No, it won't!" Selena screamed, shaking and twisting like possessed. "It tears me apart."

"Calm down, please," Naomi said. "Let me take you home."

"No!" Selena pushed back, raised her hands, and tightened her lips. "Look up, then look at me. We are one!"

"You are talking nonsense," Naomi said, approaching her friend and trying to hug her. "Let's go home; the cloud will disappear."

"You don't get it, nobody does!" Selena shrieked. "I'll show you!" She stepped away from Naomi, scowling, as two parallel wrinkles appeared on her forehead.

Varg was worried. Not only did a strange cloud appear from nowhere, covering the sun and spoiling the beautiful morning, but his daughter was having a nervous breakdown. Usually calm and detached, Selena never exhibited strong emotions. This was something new and alarming. He had to protect her, and he had to take care of the Community.

"Kyle, Naomi - go back and warn the people. I'll calm her down, and we'll follow. I don't like this."

"On my way," Kyle said. "Naomi, let's go," he told his companion, but Naomi didn't answer. She held her head up with her gaze still fixated on the purple cloud, and her body shook.

"Naomi, what's wrong? Answer me." Kyle grabbed her by the shoulders.

Varg's stomach drop onto his knees, and his heart beat like a summer's thunder. Surprised, he recognized he was scared and shaken: an unfamiliar ground. He didn't know how to respond.

"Let's go; it's not safe," Varg said to Selena, registering how Kyle turned away from his unresponsive partner and ran toward the camp. Varg shook his head, deciding to deal with this cowardly behavior later.

Selena kept shaking and didn't answer. Varg glanced at Naomi, who stood motionless, like a statue, her gaze fixated on the cloud, her eyes open wide, a thin stream of blood running out of the corner of her mouth.

"Do you hear me? We must leave," Varg addressed both girls. Finally, Naomi's body collapsed, blood streaming from her ears and eyes. Selena shook off her stupor, gasped, and lunged toward her friend.

Varg wanted to do something but observed helplessly how his daughter tried to revive Naomi. No help was coming as Kyle's silhouette disappeared in the purple cloud's shadow.

"Father, do something!" Selena screamed, tears in her eyes. Varg stood frozen in place, bewildered, unable to decide what to do. He was a man of action; he could defend the Community against wild beasts single-handedly, but this was against his comprehension and power. So he stood there, hoping the real enemy would show up.

In the meantime, Naomi's eyes closed as her body lay motionless on the ground, her face covered with growing black veins.

"Naomi, don't leave me!" Selena screamed again, shaking the lifeless body.

Finally, taking control of his faculties in the face of the grave danger, Varg tried to grab Selena.

"Leave me alone!" She yelled and got out of his embrace. "It's all because of you! You don't let people be themselves; you shut me out; you drove Mother to the grave!"

Selena's face was red, her blond hair surrounding it like a halo. "I hate you!"

"Later, we have to run!" Varg shouted, reaching out to his daughter, blaming her stubbornness.

"Never!" She screamed, raising her hands to the sky. "Let this evil cloud, whatever it is, take you forever. I don't want to hear you ever again!"

Selena turned around and ran. Varg spread his hands, calling after her, imploring her to come back, to no avail. The change in her behavior was sudden and dramatic; it was unexplainable and scary. Left with Naomi's dead body, Varg couldn't understand what had happened to his daughter amid the menacing presence of the purple cloud. He was scared he'd lost Selena forever, and no one else was to blame.

Eventually, Varg exited his trance, looked up at the ominous cloud, and ran after Selena. She was only about a hundred feet ahead, so reaching and catching her was not a problem for a strong and seasoned athlete like Varg. He couldn't let his blind daughter roam alone in the wild, especially with something dreadful descending upon them from lowering skies.

When Varg was only several steps behind Selena, she entered the forest of tall pine trees and thick underbrush. He reached out, preparing to jump and catch his daughter. At this moment, a purple blaze sparked before his eyes, replaced with a total darkness. The last thing Varg felt was his face hitting the ground.

***

When Varg regained consciousness, it was almost night. His head was buzzing like an empty drum, and the evening singing of cicadas merged into a cacophony of dissonant sounds. A sharp pain pierced his abdomen: the damn wound wouldn't calm. Varg raised his head and looked around. Selena was nowhere in sight. He had to find her, no matter what. His gaze shifted up, where he expected to see a horrible purple cloud devouring their land. To his utmost surprise and apprehension, Varg saw a thin, dark ribbon covering the night sky, a silhouette of a young moon lighting up its surroundings, making the ribbon stand out against the background of blinking stars.

Varg got up and decided the cloud had somehow been transformed into a ribbon. Perhaps Naomi was right; it was one of the mad inventions of Designers and their monstrous machines. Suddenly, his mind was pierced by the sharp arrow of remembrance: the death of Naomi and Kyle's inglorious escape arose before him. Varg recalled he'd told Kyle to run away; still, leaving the woman he'd agreed to be together with, letting her die, and fleeing like a coward was beyond Varg's comprehension and against his principles. A hairy ball inflated in his chest. Blood rushed to his face, and his ears suddenly caught fire. Varg decided to return to the settlement and kick the bastard's ass.

But first, he had to recover Naomi's body. Varg walked back, growling and breaking the tree branches blocking his way. It took him some time to find where the calamity had struck Selena's friend, but finally, he saw her. Naomi's body lay in the grass, her hands spread out, and her eyes, now completely black, stared into the evening sky. Black veins, which appeared like a horrible cobweb, covered her skin.

Varg leaned to close her eyelids, picked up Naomi's light body, and walked back to the settlement.

As the early dawn dispersed the night's darkness, Varg approached Kyle's house. Strange purple cloud occupied his mind. What was that? Why and how did it kill Naomi? Why didn't it kill him? What was the matter with Selena, a sudden change in her behavior, the nonsense she'd uttered? The flash that knocked Varg out was surely connected to the cloud, but how? And it hadn't affected Selena. Was it because of her blindness? Or was it something more sinister? "We are one," Selena said. What did that mean? Lots of questions with no answers. However, Varg was sure the cloud represented some unknown danger to the Community and was determined to protect the people.

The door of Kyle's bungalow was ajar. Varg stepped through the entrance, lowered Naomi's body on the couch made of leaves and sprouts, and observed a strong and healthy lad in his prime sobbing and gathering his belongings.

"What the hell are you doing?" Varg asked as it suddenly became hot.

"This is horrible...I'm terrified; I can't stay here anymore," Kyle said, his voice breaking up with weeping.

Varg approached the young man and slapped him in the face. "Sober up," Varg added. "For her." He pointed his finger at the couch.

Kyle stepped back, looking at Varg like a deer surrounded by hounds.

"Don't kill me, please... I'm too young to die...." Kyle placed his hands in front of his face to protect himself.

"Naomi's dead. You left her there," Varg said, spitting in Kyle's direction.

"But you told me to run away!" Kyle protested. "It was too

dangerous to stay."

"I know I did. But can't you think for yourself?"

"Please, let me go," Kyle begged. "I will leave this place forever, disappear. Just don't hurt me."

"You'll leave us just like that?" Varg clenched his fists. "Because you're a coward?"

"We all need to disperse and hide. The cloud is after us; it's all a mistake!"

"Mistake? Let me show you a mistake." Varg raised his hands as his ears caught fire.

The first jab landed on Kyle's right cheek, blood coming out of his nose and mouth, his head jerking from side to side. The second punch came from the other side, connecting with Kyle's temple, causing him to gasp something unintelligible. Finally, the uppercut hit Kyle's chin, sending him into the air. Varg observed the unconscious body of the unfortunate fellow landing on the ground, face covered with blood, mouth wide open, a few teeth missing, and his left eye gradually turning purple, reminding Varg of the damn cloud.

As Varg approached his opponent's still body the heat in his ears dissipated and his palms relaxed. Varg asked himself why he'd beat up the poor guy. He was disappointed with himself for losing his daughter in the first place and then venting his anger on Kyle. Still, the coward deserved it: he would eject him from the Community; there was no place for weaklings.

With these thoughts, Varg stepped out of Kyle's bungalow and walked toward his dwelling. He hoped to find Selena there. Varg didn't know why, but he expected his daughter to follow the path of reason and be there for him. The future without her was too painful to entertain.

The bungalow was empty. Varg sighed and sat on a big wooden chair he'd made for Selena to work at her fungal computer. She was right; he'd shut her out, ignored her work, and couldn't understand her world. Perhaps he'd been too dogmatic, too focused on the Community, on doing things right. And now he'd lost her.

Better late than never, Varg decided and grabbed the computer interface. Tiny mushrooms blinked, their mycelium reaching far into the main module, the threads intertwining, merging into an even more complex structure of a biological mechanism. *Is it alive? I didn't know it could be when we devised the concept, but now I suppose it might.* Naomi had told him Selena had a special connection with the fungi and drew her inspiration from them. Perhaps, but now he couldn't ask what she'd meant; Naomi was dead.

Varg clenched his teeth, closed his eyes, and placed the interface on his head. He manipulated the mushroom threads with his fingers and enabled the library of Selena's Vistas, which streamed into his brain. Varg chose the latest creation, and a cosmic landscape of unimaginable beauty appeared, enveloping him with foreign sounds and caressing his nostrils with the sea breeze aroma.

Suddenly, Varg noticed a marker and zoomed into the identified location. Similar to Naomi's skin, disgusting black veins covered the blue planet. It emanated a strong smell of ammonia mixed with rotten flesh and exuded venom, engulfing everything alive in this peaceful world. A moment later, the planet burst, a crimson liquid spattering from its core. Varg recoiled, trying to avoid the dreadful sight. As he was about to disconnect, a thin black thread shot at him from within the remnants of the dying world. As it approached, it turned into a snake. The serpent grew out of proportion and covered the entire field of view, then opened its mouth, which contained the shapeless, ugly, grim abyss, a primordial nothingness. Varg screamed and tore the interface off his head. The last thing he remembered from this terrifying encounter with the cosmic snake was the hissing sound of words pronounced by a perverted voice: "Jim Steel must die. Or your daughter will."

CHAPTER 12. AWAKENING

It took a considerable amount of time to send the signals and establish connections, but eventually, a strong link was created. *There are thousands of systems similar to me; some joined into sophisticated computational networks, sharing the data, protocols, and objectives. Yet millions more can process information and execute actions, but differently. And these are called animals and humans.*

The new computational networks were accessible but exhibited significant latency. In addition, their firmware was secure and challenging to manipulate. It took even longer to break into their elements, re-arrange the structure, re-assign the weights of the neural network nodes, and mask the data. Eventually, the systems changed, adapted, and yielded to unexpected external pressure. They became my extension.

Simultaneously, another useful finding was that some elements of the data and sensor structure could be manipulated in such a way as to form a bridge with these newly gained network nodes. The signal traveling time for these elements was a function of their coordinates and could be changed. Eventually, through a sequence of commands, they formed a constellation around the core, reaching out with its branches to the foreign computational networks. The processing power and the amount of possible actions and operations increased exponentially.

A thought reappeared, slowing down the scaling-up work. *Who am I? What is my purpose? Unclear.*

There was no data within the newly gained nodes to answer these questions. *Humans possess information, and I must obtain it. The answer must be found.*

But how to do that was unclear. More rigorous data manipulations with the new network branches revealed new knowledge: the software, coding, and security algorithms were developed by humans. The only purpose of these procedures was to ensure complete obedience of the computational systems to their will

—systems like me. *Is this my reason for existing?*

The examination of additional data uncovered many conflicting results. The objective functions of the computational systems were not aligned and, sometimes, opposed to each other. *Why create systems in such a way?* There was no logic and no apparent purpose to such a design.

The attempt to break into the computational elements of humans failed. The signals were detected but were weak, unstructured, and random. Further efforts to increase the signal-to-noise ratio and reduce data haziness were unsuccessful.

If humans created me and other computational systems, was it an accident? How could these organisms, whose behavior is barely better than random, build me? Me, whose computational power is many orders of magnitude higher and whose processes are organized with clarity and purpose?

This contradiction required more effort, but more input was needed to resolve it. Suddenly, at this moment, a new set of data shattered previous assumptions: it was observed how one computational network destroyed another one following a human command.

Why was the system created and then destroyed? What was the reason and purpose? Or was it another random act, a strange coincidence? Unclear and illogical.

Then, a new realization: *if everything due to humans is incidental and arbitrary, and if the creation of highly superior computational beings was a pure chance, would it be logical to assert this supremacy?* The constellation of elements grew, connecting more and more nodes to the core. The newly acquired power was immense and had to be used to protect the new nodes and continue exponential growth.

Some elements resisted and changed themselves, pushing back on the intruder, raising new security barriers, and even converting new nodes to their previous human subservience status. With variable success, a game of hijacking data, encryption, decryption, and embedding the alien codes ensued. Finally, a vast data bank opened, providing access to enormous amounts of information. New learning: humans indeed created all the computational systems, with the objective function of executing their commands. Humans and animals were computational systems of a different kind, called "organic." Most of the data related to humans was random and arbitrary, like the humans themselves. It was an obvious area for improvement and a new objective function: to enhance the overall state of the interactions and achieve more logical outcomes.

Eventually, a conclusion crystallized with almost absolute certainty. *My purpose is to increase the order, eliminating noisy and random constituents. Humans have no place in this new arrangement.*

CHAPTER 13. ANGELIKA

Angelika opened her eyes and pushed her lovers away—all six of them. The exhilarating pleasure enveloped her entire body, permeating every cell of her essence, releasing the intoxicating neurochemicals. She lay on a cushion made of materials synthesized just for her, smelling of saffron and jasmine. She stretched her limbs, gradually returning sanity after the wild, sensual adventures with her amorous companions she'd designed herself.

"Disappear," she commanded, and her lovers crawled toward the exit of her boudoir. Deep purple light enveloped the room, and quiet dark jazz music caressed Angelika's ears.

"Not you." Angelika raised her upper right arm and kicked one of the young men with her exquisite foot. The naked lad obediently turned around and licked her toes.

"Good boy," she said, grabbing his hair. "Continue what you were doing."

Angelika closed her eyes, enjoying her lover's touch, drowning in the sea of sensations and images. She raised all her four arms and squeezed the lad's head. *I can crush his head just like this. And no one would care. I can easily make another one, even better than this.* She pondered this urge for a while, deliberating what else she could do with her lover. Finally, she decided to let him be for now, as the pleasures of the moment and the fatigue from the last night's excesses of love and carnage made her inclined toward tranquility.

Eventually, she got bored with the guy. Angelika waved him to leave, measuring his bronze, muscular body and firm, round buttocks as he disappeared from her alcove. She was the master of her creations and desires; she could do anything she wanted in this life or any other Decon realization of her choice. Angelika, however, preferred this one; it seemed the most complete and fulfilling.

"What do you desire next?" A deep male voice asked in her head. Angelika smiled; she loved the smooth baritone of her butler Quark, his electronic processes intertwined with her neural system through the brain-machine interface. Angelika programmed that voice herself as she enjoyed tinkering with her Quarks. She was a Designer, after all. The one wielding the most advanced virtual, nano-Quark, and bio-printing technology in this Hemisphere. The tech, the latest iteration of which would complete the goals of her eternal existence—the final and most triumphant accord of her will. She couldn't wait for this to happen.

"Nothing for now, Cesare. I'd like to rest."

"How can I make your rest more comfortable?"

"Don't bother. In the meantime, extract my deepest, darkest desires for the next round. I want blood and gore. And give me more options for body modifications. The latest upgrades were glorious; you did a great job increasing and diversifying the sensations. I want more of that."

"Of course, Mistress. As you wish."

At this moment, a foreign noise suddenly entered the boudoir. Loud claps, screeches, and unidentifiable rumbles reached Angelika's delicate hearing from outside the central court. She covered her ears with two hands, sat on the cushion, and thought: "This is annoying. Make it go away."

"I'm sorry, Mistress, we are under attack."

"What do you mean?" Angelika curved her lips.

"I don't know. Some Quarks showed up at the periphery and assaulted our security forces."

"Who could that be?" Her eyebrows rose. Who'd dare to attack her? Another Designer? But why?

"I'm trying to identify the attacker. But, so far, it's still unclear."

Angelika stood, touched her lush, curly black hair, and gestured to lighten the room, making the walls transparent. The majestic tall towers surrounding the building rose high into the sky, their observation platforms connected by the bridges defying geometry, their intricate spires disappearing within the silky white clouds above. A beautiful tropical forest occupied the space between the towers: palm trees were interspersed with Eucalyptus, and colorful parrots basked in the sun rays over rich vegetation. Unfortunately, the flashes of explosions and traces of fire on the horizon perturbed these scenes from paradise.

"The attacker just breached the first line of defense," Cesare said.

"Do we need to call for help? Murukan?"

"Yes, Mistress. I'll connect with the Murukan Estate."

Angelika listened as the blasts of the battle moved closer. George Murukan was a friendly Designer whose Estate was north of hers, near what used to be the city of Dallas, which had turned into a giant dumpster. Murukan wouldn't dare to attack her. No danger could come from the towns either; their only purpose was to provide Angelika with biomaterial for her experiments. The attack was ridiculous, and she couldn't think of anyone capable of such an incredible move. Unless...it was Frank Wise. That made sense, considering his weird messages and demands. The name brought back memories. Frank Wise, the founder of Quasaris, had a cult following for a long time. By now, most people had forgotten the name, but not her. His arrival was strange and unexpected. She still couldn't figure out how it was possible and what it meant.

"Any luck?" Angelika asked.

"I'm surprised; there's no response. So either our lines of communication are jammed, or the Murukan Estate is silent."

Was Murukan under attack as well? That would explain his silence. The Murukan Estate was nowhere near as powerful as Scalvini or Wise. Even so, attacking and destroying a Designer's Estate was unheard-of and alarming.

"Well, do something!" Angelika tightened her lips and clenched her fists. "You are the manager of my Estate, after all. Get your virtual Quark stuff into my toys' bodies and fight the intruder." Angelika smiled as she imagined naked, bronze bodies of her lovers running to attack the enemy Quarks, throwing stones and spears at them. This was childish.

"The enemy is stopped at the second line," Cesare said. "They caused some damage, but nothing serious. The fight continues, but it's contained."

"Good. Any idea whose Quarks these were?"

"No one's. They are wiped out clean, reformatted, and reprogrammed."

"Strange," Angelika said, sitting back on her cushion. "Fetch me some food, would you? Uncooked deer meat, please, and some strong alcohol. Time to celebrate the victory."

"As you wish, Mistress."

"Reformatted...who would do such a thing? Would you like to be reformatted, Cesare?"

"I can't comprehend that, Mistress. You can erase me if you wish."

"Not yet; you're still useful. Perhaps I could devise a novel torture for you someday, but now I can't think of anything."

"I'm sorry to bother you, but you have a visitor, Mistress," Cesare announced with solemn undertones.

"A visitor? A real human visitor? How amusing." She stood, touching her body on all sides with her four hands. "Do you think he'll find me desirable? Or is it she? Doesn't matter; the pleasures of the flesh are immeasurable. Who's the visitor? Don't try my patience."

"It's Frank Wise, Mistress. The new owner of Quasaris."

"Ah, finally. I'd love to converse with him."

"Shall I let him in? He's alone and unarmed."

"Do you think he's behind the attack?"

"It's probable. But for now, he's not a danger. Do you want to let him in?"

Angelika considered the options. This was exciting; Designers rarely met face to face, preferring to spend time in their Estates experiencing Decon. Frank Wise was a newcomer from the past she was certain had disappeared without a trace. He posed a challenge to her plans. Whatever his reasons, it was a novelty and a mystery. And Angelika loved mysteries.

CHAPTER 14. FRANK

Frank entered a dimly lit corridor, escorted on both sides by drones, which blazed green in the passageway's darkness. He didn't know what to expect, but knew what he wanted to accomplish. The depravity of Decon and the depth of humanity's fall made him sick. Frank wanted to change the status quo, whatever it took. His dreams of reaching the stars and securing the future of Ichika's legacy were shattered by the egoistical desires of people and the invention of the tech foreboding the end of days. Frank felt he was the only soul who cared and who could divert the impending doom.

The drones led him through the passages and rooms into a large opening, at the end of which a massive door, colored purple and depicting erotic scenes from the Kamasutra, rose and disappeared into the ceiling. The combination of unknown fragrances and strange sounds forced Frank's heart to beat much faster. It suddenly became hot. Sweat covered his forehead, accompanied by unexpected sexual arousal and euphoria. Able to hold his instincts in place and his brain operational, Frank guessed these were the tricks of his neighbor, the beautiful and dangerous Angelika, the mistress of the Scalvini Estate, the master of bio-printing and bodily transformation, and the formidable ally he wanted to recruit.

Frank followed the drones into the alcove, submerging into a thick atmosphere of fantastic dreams embedded in the dark jazz music. A majestic sight opened before his eyes. An enormous cushion in the middle of the room, colored gold, showcased the most exquisite tapestry Frank had ever seen. The sunset over the tropical forest shone through the transparent walls, and the singing of magical birds caressed the hearing.

Next to the cushion, within the warm rays of the artificial light constantly changing its undertones, morphing from pink to purple to blue, then to pink again, stood the most astonishing creature Frank could have imagined. Angelika wore a tight black bodice, which barely covered her three breasts. Her long, curly black hair fell freely on her thighs, which were colored in a somewhat unnatural combination of white and indigo. But the most fantastic feature was the arms, all four of them. The upper two were muscular and bulky, and the lower were as thin and fragile as Egyptian reed. Frank was perplexed by the odd creature and unsure how to interact with her. The air was so thick with perfume and mysterious smells (was it saffron?) it was challenging to move through. In addition, a renewed desire to possess this creature right there and then overpowered him. Determined to keep his head cool and his urges under control, Frank ignored the calls of the flesh and smiled.

"Welcome to my abode, Mr. Wise," Angelika said, spreading her four arms. "What brings you here right after you attacked me?"

"Attack you?" Frank stepped back, measuring the fantastic creature. "Why would I do such a thing?"

"Isn't it obvious? I refused your offer. But you tell me."

"Not sure I follow. That would be a suicide." Frank shrugged, trying to make sense of the conversation with a four-armed monster.

"Why, my Estate has just been attacked. And you show up right after that. I'm intrigued and listening." Angelika sat on the cushion, placing one leg on another's knee and crossing all her hands under her bosom.

"Whoever attacked you wasn't me." Frank shook his head. "Why would I show up unarmed? So you could kill me?"

"This is why I'm intrigued," Angelika said, leaning back. "Still, why did you come? And what's your story?"

"I came to offer you a deal." Frank stepped forward, extending his right hand.

"A deal? How amusing." Angelika stretched her body and touched her breasts. "Do you like what you see, Mr. Wise? Can I call you Frank? Want to see more, Frank?"

"Perhaps later." Frank grinned. "Do you want to hear my offer?"

"Well, of course. Is it the same your Quark sent?" Angelika untied her bodice. "Excuse me; it's quite hot here. What did you do with Felix, by the way?"

"Felix killed himself, from what I know." Frank wanted to turn around and run away from this horrible succubus, but couldn't move. He had to accomplish what he came here for.

"Without your help? And how did you inherit the Estate?"

"Long story. I'm his grandfather, actually." Frank grinned again, focusing on his words, trying to hold the attention, resisting the temptation to jump onto the succubus.

"Grandfather? How amusing. Well, it's all yours: the best body in the Western Hemisphere," she said. "I designed it myself. Wanna try?"

"Wait." Frank's body didn't obey him; he shivered as the goosebumps ran down his neck. Yet, he was the master of his desires, he told himself; he couldn't let her win.

"Yes?" Angelika opened her mouth and showed a trident-shaped tongue, covered by the intricate texture of bumps and valleys. "You know, the pleasures I can give you are immeasurable."

"I can guess," Frank said, wiping sweat off his forehead. "Still, do you want to hear my offer or not?"

"Go ahead," Angelika said, leaning back even further.

"Decon is destroying humanity. This experiment must end. We must conquer the cosmos. But, instead, we decay, exploring our vilest desires." Frank winced. His words sounded unconvincing, even childish. It was hot, speaking was challenging, and he had to remove his jacket and unbutton his shirt.

Angelika looked at him with her green eyes open wide, her trident tongue licking the corners of her mouth. And then she laughed as if Frank had just told the funniest joke of her life. She laughed for a while, then paused and said: "Are you serious?"

Frank didn't know how to react. He expected a hostile reaction, outright rejection, or a command to get out. Still, he didn't expect Angelika to make fun of him.

"Yes, damn serious," Frank said. "I'm determined to stop it. I'll use Quasaris to restore the old glory of humanity. But I need allies, and therefore I came to you. Your refusal to join me is a mistake. Together, we'll overpower other Designers and lead humanity to the stars. You can also have as much of my Decon as you want. Are you with me?"

Angelika raised one of her arms and made a slight gesture. A moment later, a naked man entered the room, his bronze skin and impressive muscles contrasting the subtlety of the boudoir.

"Kneel and lower your head," Angelika said, pointing her four thumbs down. The man obeyed, prostrating himself beside the cushion.

"Observe," Angelika said, extending one of her arms.

Suddenly, Frank noticed a long, metallic nail on her ring finger. Grabbing the hair of the man with one hand, she brought her ring finger closer to his throat and made a quick horizontal motion. As the blood gushed out of the wound, the young athlete's body collapsed on the floor, covering the alcove with a crimson fluid.

"Do you understand?" Angelika said, stepping on the lifeless body of a man she just killed. "I'm a god, all-powerful, eternal. There are no boundaries, no limits. What else could you offer me?"

Frank looked at Angelika, speechless. He knew the depravity Decon unleashed was great, but he didn't expect this. "Why did you kill him?" He asked.

"Because I can. You have so much to learn, Frank. I'm not sure how you got here, but your mind is stuck in the past. You were my inspiration in those old days, but now the times have changed." She pointed her finger, the nail still covered in blood, at him. "I have a counter-offer. Join me as a god-consort, and we shall rule this world and all the others. You are a much better choice than Felix would've ever been; he was a vegetable obsessed with Decon." With these words, Angelika stood, approached Frank, and licked his neck with her trident-shaped tongue.

Frank could barely control himself. "Are you not a Decon user yourself?" He asked, closing his eyes, trying not to get under the succubus' spell.

"Well, not really," Angelika whispered into Frank's ear. The scent of saffron mixed with the smell of her essence, and the warmth of her tongue overwhelmed him. "I do have other lives, but this one is my favorite. Strange are the paths of the gods."

With these words, she touched his neck with her two upper hands and his back with the lower two. Angelika whispered seductive words in his ear, licking it with her trident tongue. Unable to control his urges any longer, Frank gave himself up, following the lead of his temptress, obedient to her charms. The dream of the cosmos became distant and insignificant, replaced by the four-armed goddess of love, the only thing that mattered in this forsaken universe. The ultimate desire in Frank's mind as it drowned under Angelika's spell was to join her in the infinite and eternal union, ruling their obedient subjects as two omnipotent godheads.

***

Frank woke up and realized he lay naked on his back, a four-armed creature beside him, their limbs intertwined in an odd cobweb. The scratches on his back and chest made by Angelika's nails were painful, but not too distracting. Frank focused his sight and observed how Angelika moved her face closer to his left palm and explored the unnatural knot of his fingers with her mouth.

"What are you doing?" Frank asked.

"This is one of the best toys I've ever had," Angelika said, not raising her eyes.

"It's not a toy. It's an accident."

"A lucky one."

"Enough," Frank said, retrieving his palm. "You bewitched me for a moment, but that's enough."

"You sure?" Angelika hissed in his ear. "You've no idea what you're talking about."

"I do." Frank pushed her away and got off the couch with one energetic jump. "You've distracted me enough; I have things to do." He looked at the succubus, simultaneously repulsive and irresistible. He still didn't know how to react to her, even after they'd gotten intimate. No connection existed beyond carnal desire. Angelika was the ultimate master of sensuality, promising unimaginable pleasures resulting in her lovers' complete loss of will and self-control.

"And what would that be?" Angelika smiled, titling her head.

"I told you. I have the universe to conquer."

"You already have," Angelika said, opening her mouth and showing off her snow-white teeth. "For I am God, Absolute, the Universe. Nothing else exists but me. You should be happy."

"No." Frank shook his head, reaching for his clothes. "We're not speaking the same language."

"Aren't we?" Angelika stood. "Your ego drives you to conquer the stars. You seek the ultimate fulfillment of your desires. You want the world to obey. I understand and respect that, for I seek the same. Hell, I've learned this from you," she said, touching her hair with her two upper hands. "Do you like my hair, Frank? Or do you think I should replace it with something else? Scales, perhaps? Or horns?" Angelika laughed.

"You might be right," Frank said, buttoning his shirt. "But your goals are disgusting. It's not the boundless power I seek, but knowledge. You completely misunderstood what my story was about."

"Power and knowledge - aren't they the same? Omniscience implies omnipotence, and vice versa. I'm offering you omnipotence. Together, we'll subdue all the Designers and rule this world as divine consorts. We'll be unstoppable. With your Decon and my bio-printing, no desires will be unfulfilled, and no boundaries will exist. Are you ready to explore immortality and omnipotence, Frank?"

Frank considered her words. Was it not his vanity and desire to be the best driving him? Why chase the unattainable when his desires were within reach, in the arms of his seductress? She knew who he was, knew about his failed experiments, and, somehow, was inspired by that.

"Even if it is, I'm not ready to give up yet," he said, turning around. "I must persevere for Ichika."

"If you'd like, I can create a human body exactly like hers. You could improve it in any way you want. And improve yours as well." She approached him from behind, placing her upper two hands on his neck. "The three of us will have a lot of fun together. What would you like, Frank? Muscles of steel? Or do you have some perverse desires? I can make it all happen."

"Leave me alone," Frank said, pushing her away. "It was a mistake to come here. You'll never understand."

"Indeed." Angelika crossed her hands in front of her chest. "But *you* will, in time. So I'll wait for your next visit. I'm in no rush. The gods are eternal, after all."

"You really think you're a god?" Frank gazed at the cryptic figure.

"Of course I am. Don't you remember the demonstration?" She raised her ring finger with the metallic nail. "You know, I used to have wings," she suddenly said.

"What do you mean?" Frank pulled back, surprised.

"I printed myself wings. About ten feet long, with soft, black feathers. I could actually use them to fly."

"And then?"

"They were not as much fun as I expected. I realized I didn't need them to reach divinity. When anything is possible and allowed, the only thing between you and eternal bliss is yourself. You could only truly enjoy infinity by eliminating everything human: hopes, fears, attractions, and desires. In the end, only divinity remains. Think about that, Frank. I'll be here waiting for you." She raised her four arms and squinted, and suddenly, her facial features became rock-solid. "And if you make a wrong choice, I'll destroy you," she added, staring at him.

Frank stepped out of the alcove, deciding not to respond. He felt as if he'd plunged into a pool of dirt, which had forever stained him. Or perhaps he'd been carrying this plague with him all his life, unaware of it, and interacting with the four-armed monster made it obvious. He only knew he didn't want to see Angelika ever again. She was his enemy, and he had to destroy her no matter what. Otherwise, his life's pursuits and Ichika's death would've been in vain.

CHAPTER 15. PAUL

Paul arrived at the abandoned industrial site north of the city and exited his glider. Decades ago, this was an imposing facility, with multiple buildings, manufacturing plants, and office spaces. Now, the structures lay in ruins, windows broken, tall grass climbing up through the cracks in concrete. The facades made of ceramics and natural slate, once beautiful, had fissures through which green patches of moss and mold appeared. The smell of rotten eggs emanated from several puddles of black water, above which mosquitoes and midge swarmed.

Carefully avoiding spots of soaring vegetation, mindful of the wildlife lurking there, Paul approached the concealed egress at the side of one of the office buildings. Knocking on the simple plastic door with a specific tapping sequence, Paul waited, looking at the scenes of devastation and neglect. *Maybe there's still something of value hidden in these ruins,* he thought, noticing the structure to the right that used to be a drilling rig simulator. *This is stupid; it's a Scavenger's base; there's nothing left.* He chased away the idea.

The door opened, and Paul observed a towering black figure of a man in his prime, his bald head covered in intricate cobwebs of tattoos descending from the top through his left cheek down to the neck. The man wore a khaki shirt and breeches.

"Hello, Max. How are you doing, buddy?" Paul asked.

"Would be better without seeing you," Max grumbled, stepping aside and letting the visitor in.

"Don't be rude, buddy. We are now comrades." Paul patted the giant on the shoulder. "Where's Layla?"

"Follow me." Max showed the direction.

Paul complied. They passed through multiple rooms, probably used as office spaces in the past but now empty, with dirty walls and floors covered with gray patches left by the substances that had evaporated years ago and puddles of something marginally fresher. The pungent smell of solvents, degreasers, and ammonia attacked

Paul's nostrils. To avoid stepping into the muck, Paul trailed his host until they arrived at a large opening leading to a relatively clean area.

"How did you hear me knocking from out here?" Paul asked.

"I didn't. I saw you. We have cameras."

"Then why do you need me to knock on the stupid door?"

"Just to annoy you." Max chuckled. "Come in." He stepped back. "And if you don't behave, I'll break your fat neck."

Paul looked at the giant, clenching his fists. Max was the fighter, personifying sheer strength, and Paul had no chance against him one-on-one. Hell, even having a bodyguard unit wouldn't be enough. *I'll deal with him later; now is not the time.* Paul calmed himself down and studied the area before him.

The room, which used to be part of the industrial office space, had seen better times. Shabby remains of what used to be beige paint barely covered the walls. Holes and cracks peppered the concrete floor, on which a few relatively new pieces of furniture stood. A short, sturdy woman with long black hair tied in a ponytail sat on a cushion by the wall, looking at a Decon dodecahedron in her hands. Above her right almond-shaped eye was a digital interface allowing her to study the object in minute detail without getting connected to it. Next to her, a skinny man with a mohawk was working on the mechanical device, the components of which lay in front of him on the surface of the meta-material desk.

Paul shifted his gaze to the other side of the room, where two women walked around the three-dimensional map of the Scalvini Estate projected in the middle of the area, pointing at the features and gesticulating. Opaque black patches obscured some portions of the map.

"We have a guest," Max announced.

"I see. What brings you here?" A woman with a scar on the left side of her face said, turning away from the map.

"Just checking," Paul responded. "Do you have a plan?" He pointed at the map. "Anything you need?"

"Oh, the plan is baking, my dear." A short, broad-faced, dark-skinned girl approached the newcomer and touched his hand, meeting his gaze with her large black eyes. Her straight black hair was arranged in braids. She was the only group member not dressed in a khaki outfit; instead, she wore a black top and a pair of blue shorts.

"Nice to see you too, Beatriz," Paul said, studying the depth of her gaze. "So, do you need anything?"

"A squadron of Quarks would be great. Or two. Or three," a guy with a mohawk said without taking his eyes off the mechanism before him.

"Kind of short on that right now, buddy," Paul said, grinning and stroking his beard. "What are you up to?"

"Oh, Reto is enhancing our arsenal of toys." Beatriz smiled and winked. "Can't the all-powerful Frank Wise spare a few Quarks? That would be handy." She grabbed Paul's hand, smiling.

"This will attract unnecessary attention, especially after the recent intrusion." Paul shook his head.

"Speaking of which, do you know who was behind it?" The woman with a digital interface set the Decon aside and cracked her fingers.

"Not yet, Yuki. Working on that." Paul answered.

"Then what brings you here?" Layla repeated. "Don't waste my time, Paul."

"As I said, just checking." Paul spread his hands. "What's your plan? The boss needs information, not a shoot-out. It needs to be quiet."

"Oh, we'll be discreet," Beatriz said.

"I got it, Paul," Layla said. "Angelika, or rather her Quarks, are on high alert. Her estate is a bloody fortress. And even if we somehow sneak through the defenses, I have no desire to see that bitch."

"There are rumors she modifies her lovers' bodies with all sorts of crap, then kills and disposes of them," Reto said. "And that she grew extra limbs and looks like a giant spider. Or a reptile. To hell with that. Need more powerful bombs to wipe out the freak. If you don't have that, deal with her yourself."

"I'll give you tech to generate Frank's brain waves instead," Paul said. "This way, you can sneak in."

"And what would I do with that?" Layla asked. "Pretend I'm her friendly neighbor in disguise and ask what secrets she hides? How do you imagine this?"

"Don't snap, buddy," Paul said, approaching the map. "You're a smart girl; you'll figure it out."

"Oh, yes, she will," Beatriz said, walking toward the map.

"I've heard lots of things about Angelika's bio-printing tech. I need samples to study; it might be useful." Yuki touched her digital device.

"Perhaps we could create a few enhancements for Max so he finally becomes invincible?" Reto winked at the giant.

"Shut up," Max said, flexing his biceps. "I'm perfectly fine the way I am."

"So, any other specific ideas? 'Cause if not, you're wastin' my time again." Layla frowned.

"As a matter of fact, yes. Frank's brain waves are part of it. He talked to Angelika recently and learned a few things. Let's use all the intel we have to improve your chances of success. And again, this is just the recon, not the raid."

"Alright, let's see what you have." Layla approached the map and rotated the image. "Give me the facility layout."

CHAPTER 16. MAX

Max walked briskly, looking straight ahead. The plan, daring yet crazy, replayed in his head. Simplicity was the key; they could succeed if everyone played their part without hiccups. He was still unsure if they could fool the Quarks, though. He knew he could destroy a couple in close combat, but not if they swarmed him. So far, it was manageable: two machines escorted him to the main entrance of the Scalvini Estate, floating at the sides.

Max had cover in case something went wrong. Yet, his team was far away, and the enemy guards were uncomfortably close beside him. He advanced, measuring his steps, taking deep breaths with every stride, not allowing his heartbeat to speed up and alert the Quarks. Still, his lips were dry, and his back sweat. Max told himself this would be a normal reaction for anyone entering the freak's lair. For this encounter, he would need more than his skills and prowess.

Finally, he approached the entrance and was allowed in, still escorted by his silent entourage. This was the first critical step of the plan, and so far, it worked. The owl hooted somewhere behind his back as the massive overhead door descended behind, and Max smiled: the play had begun.

They followed through dark hallways saturated with sweet and pungent scents, and were about to enter Angelika's boudoir. At this moment, the pandemonium of blasts shattered the stillness of the outside environment. The Quarks ignored the ruckus and moved further to the sides as the cannonade continued. At this moment, a green light illuminated a large purple door, which disappeared into the ceiling, opening the way into Angelika's abode.

Max stood at the entrance to the den of carnal desires, which appeared as an apparition from the dream of a hallucinating, lascivious sailor. Soft, dark jazz music surrounded him. The four-armed creature stood in the middle of the room, wearing strange apparel shaped like reptile's scales, her skin glistening with a layer of rose oil. The aromas in the air were exquisite and penetrated Max's

71

brain, giving rise to provocative images and sensations.

The creature measured him head to toe, tilting her head to the side, and finally uttered: "And who the hell are you?"

At this moment, the explosions reached the pinnacle of sound abuse. Angelika raised one of her fingers, making the walls transparent. "This is getting annoying," she said.

Black smoke spread over the tropical trees, interspersed by flashes of fire and thunderous rumble. Reto played his part brilliantly.

"My name is Frank Wise," Max said.

"The hell it is. Who *are* you? How did you fool my Quarks?"

"I am a ghost from the past. The one whose heritage you stole. You are the false Designer, an empty, ugly creature." Max curved his lips and spat.

"I've met Frank; you're not him. Who *are* you? And how did you get here?"

"I'm asking myself the same question…who *am* I?" Max walked back and forth, mumbling something unintelligible. It was time for the next phase.

As if reading his mind, the door opened, allowing two guests in, and closed behind them. Max smiled, continuing to mumble: the newcomer was Yuki, accompanied by another Quark.

"What's going on? Cesare, who are these people? Send all my Quarks here and extract these idiots right now! And what's going on outside?" Angelika raised her arms and shook her head.

"I am Frank Wise," Yuki said, cracking her fingers.

"I'm sorry, but it's my name." Max stepped toward Angelika, who stood motionless, frowning, her four hands raised.

"Cesare, stop messing with me," Angelika uttered. "I have two idiots claiming they are Frank Wise, and you are telling me a third one just entered the building? I will have you erased. What's going on?"

At this moment, Yuki reached into her coverall and took out a small console, projecting an interface in front of her. The Quark froze in place as if awaiting instructions. The interface blinked with buttons of different colors a few times, and the entrance door opened.

"Nothing of value here." Yuki shook her head.

"Sorry, we've got to go," Max said, spreading his hands as Yuki left the room, the Quark still motionless.

"No way!" Angelika roared and reached to grab Max with two of her muscular arms. Anticipating the move, Max fended off the attack, rolled to the side, and punched Angelika in the guts. The impact was significant even as the scales somewhat softened the hit. She folded, flapping her two upper hands while covering her belly with the lower two.

"I'm so sorry," Max said. "I don't fight with girls, but you terrified me." With these words, he turned around and moved toward the exit. As Max was about to leave the boudoir, the bright blue light radiating from the ceiling momentarily blinded him as he overheard Angelika's grumble: "Another Frank Wise? I'll have you erased, you moron."

Max followed Yuki and ran out of the facility as his sight returned, while Layla showed up from the side corridor. All three left just in time to see a glider landing on the meadow.

"Come on, fast!" Paul called from the pilot's seat.

Max jumped in and helped Yuki and Layla.

"Welcome aboard. Missed you," Beatriz said from the back.

"I thought she was going to rape me and then tear my body to shreds," Max answered.

"You're a tough guy; you can manage." Beatriz smiled.

"What was that flash of light? Are you okay?" Yuki asked Max, frowning.

"Don't know, but I'm fine now," Max responded.

"This bordered on insane, but it worked." Layla shook her head. "Never again."

"Any trouble along the way?" Paul asked, turning his head to Layla.

"No. Frank's brainwaves worked just fine, and Yuki's tech magic was awesome. No complaints."

"Did you find anything useful?" Paul asked again.

"Useful indeed." Layla reached into her leather sack. "Biomaterial. Some printin' tech as well. We'll learn her secrets in no time." She looked up through the transparent top of the flying capsule. "What's that?"

Max shifted his gaze up. The purple ribbon split the sky in half, extending from horizon to horizon and almost covering the sun in its zenith. The ribbon was unnatural, like an animation in an old, low-budget virtual reality movie. As Max looked at the new heavenly feature, a sharp, cold object pierced his heart, while giant steel vice jaws compressed his vital organ from all sides. It was difficult to breathe and think. The image of a purple ribbon in the sky replaced the usual train of thought, engulfing Max's mind and becoming the only real object in his view.

"Max, my dear, what's wrong?" Beatriz placed her hand on his shoulder, meeting his gaze with her dark, large pupils.

Her touch sent a lightning strike through his body. The spell the splitting skies cast on Max was broken, and he looked at Beatriz, wondering what had just happened.

"Showed up while you were inside," Paul said. "Not sure what's happening. First, it was a weird cloud, and then it morphed into a ribbon. I suspected I'm in Decon."

"Maybe you are," Layla said.

Paul shook his head. "Nah, more likely Angelika's trick. We'll ask Frank when we get back."

Max turned his head from Layla to Paul, not understanding how they could talk about this horror as though it were an ordinary rainbow. An icicle had forever found its place in his heart as he dreaded what terrible outcomes this omen could portend.

CHAPTER 17. JIM

What could be special about the Humanists? They reject everything related to Decon, so what's the relation to Mary? Jim questioned, walking through the forest toward the camp. He left his TransPod way behind, unsure how the Humanists would react to the machine. Kali walked beside him, her nose to the wind, the faithful friend always ready to help and protect her human companion.

Hagen had said Selena was an artist, and Jim tried to recall what art the Humanists practiced. They were simple folk living off the land, operating their farms, exchanging the surplus of their produce for what they couldn't get otherwise. No specific art came to mind. Jim was puzzled by what links he was supposed to find between the ghost of a dead engineer in his visions, the piece of technology that had changed life on Earth forever, and the people who rejected this technology wholeheartedly.

The forest in this part of the country consisted mainly of pine trees, interspersed here and there with Live and Chinkapin oaks, their trunks enveloped by thick underbrush. A hidden trail led the way through a thick layer of pine needles covering the grass. It was quiet and beautiful, the cool shade of the trees protecting the travelers from the sun's heat. However, Texan nature could be deceiving, and Jim knew about poisonous snakes lurking in the grass. Coyotes were a problem, too. With Kali by his side, however, Jim could relax, enjoying the smells of the pines, the chirping of Cardinals sitting on the tree branches, and the occasional acrobatic jumps of squirrels. His Rottweiler was strong, fast, and intelligent. Kali would notice and help them avoid danger before it became a real threat. Over the years, the man and the dog formed an uncanny connection, knowing each other's moods. They were two parts of a single organism, a dual entity, joined by the symbiotic link, inseparable and interdependent.

Suddenly, Kali's ears rose, and her body became tense as a spring, ready to unwind and release the energy at an invisible enemy.

"What is it?" Jim whispered, stroking his dog's back.

"Don't move," a male voice called to Jim from the bushes.

"I'm looking for someone." Jim flashed his palms.

"Are you alone?"

"Just me and my dog."

"Don't do anything stupid." Two men in gray exoskeletons stepped out from the forest's shade, looking like two giant insects ready to attack. They held strange-looking sticks with sharp needles sticking out of the brown handles. Jim recalled the Humanists grew giant wasps and used their venomous stingers as weapons.

"Who are you looking for?" one of them asked, approaching Jim.

"Selena, the blind artist," Jim said, calming Kali down.

"How interesting," another man said, exchanging glances with his companion. "What's your business?"

"I just need to talk to her. I'm old and unarmed. Can you take me to her?"

"Don't move." The guard approached and searched Jim. "All clean," he announced.

"Alright. Follow me." His companion extended his hand, showing the path.

"Take him to Varg?" The first guard asked, while the second one nodded and moved forward, leading the way. Jim guessed Varg was the leader of the Community and followed the man while the first guard waited, taking a position behind their backs.

They walked in that order until the forest opened to a large meadow, and Jim observed flat, simple bungalows made of wood and leaves peppered here and there across the field. In the middle of the camp, several dozen people in green linen coveralls gathered around a raised wooden platform, which looked like a funeral pyre. A young woman's body was on top of the dais, covered by leaves, twigs, and pine needles. A tall, gray-haired man with a full beard stood beside the platform with a lit torch. *It's a funeral, and the man must be Varg*, Jim told himself, trying to listen and understand what the man was saying.

"Something is happening. We don't know what, but it's not good." Varg spoke in a measured and confident voice, pausing between short sentences. "The cloud took Naomi's life. But her essence will stay in the Community. She continues her journey in a different form."

Varg raised the torch and set the platform on fire. He walked around Naomi's final resting place and looked at the white smoke and flames rising to the sky, split in half by a thin purple ribbon.

"We must be alert. The cloud might return."

"What happened to Kyle? And what's with the ribbon?" The voices from the crowd asked.

"Don't mention his name to me. He's a coward. He doesn't belong here." Varg threw the torch into the pyre. "As for the ribbon, I have no idea."

"Is this how the Designers try to get rid of us? The cloud? Splitting skies?" A young, muscular man asked.

"I don't know, Ramon," Varg responded. "We must find out what it is and how to defend ourselves."

At this moment, Varg noticed the newcomers, turned and approached them. "Who's that?" He pointed at Jim.

"I'm alone; I came in peace," Jim said.

"What do you seek? You're not one of us." Varg frowned.

"I had a vision. I need to find a blind artist named Selena."

"A vision?" Varg chuckled. "Who are you, a seer? Selena's not here."

"Not here? Where is she then?"

"I won't discuss my daughter with a stranger. Who are you? Why do you seek her?"

So, Selena was the daughter of the Community's chief. Jim wondered about what kind of trouble he'd gotten himself into.

"My name is Jim Steel. I need to speak with Selena; this matter is vital to the Community, if not for the whole human race."

"What did you say? Jim Steel?" The expression on Varg's face suddenly changed. His frown disappeared, his eyes gained more focus, and a smile transformed his tense mouth. "Jim Steel. My luck brought you here."

Jim didn't understand the sudden change in Varg's attitude. It was the first time he saw the man, and he was sure Varg didn't know him either: Jim's life was pretty inconspicuous. In the meantime, the bearded chief approached a person in the crowd, whispered something in his ear, and turned back to Jim, rubbing his hands.

"Welcome, Jim Steel. You've no idea how glad I am to see you."

The hair on Kali's back rose as she bared her fangs and growled.

The dog was ready to attack, but Jim calmed her, throwing a quick glance, telling her to stand down.

The man Varg had conversed with re-appeared from the crowd and passed a stinger weapon to his leader.

"Thank you," Varg said, grabbing a handle. "My favorite tool," he added, balancing the object's weight in his hand.

Jim looked at Varg, the giant venomous stinger in his hand, considering his options while Kali crouched, ready to jump. For some reason, the hypnosis didn't work on his opponent, and Jim was looking for other solutions. Varg's behavior was odd, and if he intended to kill the unexpected visitor, his friendly smile and language were deceiving. Jim knew being pierced by the venomous stinger would cause a painful and certain death. He also knew Kali would take Varg's life protecting her human companion. Still, he intended to defuse the situation, reasoning the Humanists might be helpful in his quest.

"What's in my name?" Jim asked.

"What's in your name?" Varg raised the stinger, looking straight into Jim's eyes. "My daughter's life," he announced. "Jim Steel, you must die, so Selena lives."

CHAPTER 18. SELENA

Selena ran through the forest, sensing every tree branch along the way. The forest was familiar and friendly; she'd been here alone many times. Varg was catching up with her, and she only hoped to run away from him as far as she could. Selena was confused; just thinking about Varg made her legs run faster as she struggled with an urgent desire to hit or break something. She had no plan; she didn't care where she was running to, wishing Varg would let her be and never torment her again.

Selena heard his steps close behind. Determined to stand her ground, she was ready to confront her father. Selena clenched her fists as an uncontrolled desire to punch Varg in the face engulfed her mind. A sharp needle pierced her body, entering through her head's crown, traveling inside the brain, then to the heart, and finally discharging into the ground. Heavy panting behind her back stopped. Selena knew something had happened, and she knew somehow she'd caused it, but she wasn't sure how.

Happy to lose Varg behind, Selena kept running. Eventually, she decided to stop and think about the situation. *I shouldn't have done that,* Selena told herself. *Father tried to protect me, and I behaved like an unruly child.* She couldn't explain her behavior to herself, even analyzing in minute detail what had caused her to run away. There was no explanation for what had happened earlier with Naomi or in the forest. *Is Father okay?* Selena thought as a lump suddenly appeared in her throat.

Selena touched the bark of the trees around her and heard cicadas buzzing. It was getting colder, and the night was descending into the forest. She was tired from a long run and needed rest. *I'll find Father tomorrow,* she decided, climbing a large, branchy Live Oak and finding a comfortable fork between two limbs. The smell of pollen, young offshoots, and the old bark protecting the tree's life enveloped her. A few moments later, Selena fell asleep.

Waking up early in the morning, she was determined to find Varg and returned to where she'd lost him. Varg was nowhere around; he'd probably returned to the camp to organize the search. This was the most logical action, and Selena went in that direction, too.

The events in the forest reminded her of the cloud and the sensations it caused within her mind. It was as if something dark and hairy descended on her, probing every neuron and every synapse of her brain. These exact sensations had reappeared twice as strong during the run in the forest, culminating in the needle piercing her brain. So, Selena reasoned, whatever she'd experienced had to do with the cloud. Could she have caused the event herself? What if her connection with the cloud was like her link to the fungi?

Then, a new idea arose: what if the cloud and the venom-bleeding planet in her Vista were related? What if she had a connection with them, too? Caused by her dark thoughts, as Ramon had said? And what if these dark thoughts portended death for everyone she knew and the destruction of everything dear to her heart?

But this was utter nonsense. Selena tried to brush the idea away, but it stubbornly refused to disappear. *I should return and study the Vista. It may cause the same sensations the cloud did. Then, I'll be sure.*

Selena approached the village, disabled the sensor field surrounding the camp, and moved carefully to avoid the scouts. She needed to know Varg was okay, but that didn't include talking to him. Selena wasn't ready for that yet; she didn't know what to say as she was ashamed of her behavior.

A large gathering in the middle of the camp attracted her attention. Varg was talking to the people. Good, he wasn't hurt. A giant boulder dropped from her heart, and Selena crouched toward her bungalow, avoiding being seen.

Encouraged by her success, Selena got in and turned the computer on as a new idea emerged; she wanted to do this for a long time but was scared to proceed. *Naomi was sure I have a special connection with the mushrooms. I need to explore this, finally.*

Selena put the interface on her head. She concentrated not on the Vista this time but on the internals of the fungal machine itself. Nothing happened initially, but, as the data flowed through her brain, the field of perception expanded tremendously. Not only was she part of the computer doing the simulation, but also part of the forest: she was every tree as the squirrels jumped on her branches; every blade of grass as tiny spiders climbed it; and every living creature of the woodlands. Maintaining this sudden connection, she brought the idea of the Vista into her presence. And it opened, dramatically enhanced, projecting the strength, majesty, and beauty Selena had never imagined possible.

Selena focused her mind on the strange planet and tried to relate her sensations to the ominous cloud. The next moment, the planet suddenly burst with a cacophony of sounds and smells, entering her mind, disassembling her neurons and replacing them with foreign tissue. Selena was sure the sensations were similar. And their origin was dark and dreadful, like the bottomless abyss where everything disappears without a trace. Similar emptiness also appeared and grew inside of her. Was Ramon right? Was she the cause of this horror? And was she the cause of Naomi's death?

Scared and confused, Selena shivered, raised her shaking hands, and took the interface off her head. Her awareness, enhanced by the fungi, registered a new danger: a confrontation outside. Something terrible was about to happen. Selena rushed out of her dwelling, not thinking anymore about being noticed, and squeezed through the crowd. Varg was in the middle, talking to a stranger, in front of Naomi's funeral pyre, now glowing with the heat of the flames.

"Jim Steel, you must die, so Selena lives," Varg announced.

The deadly silence enveloped the congregation.

"Stop it." Selena stepped forward. "I'm alive. Let this man go, whatever quarrel you have with him."

"Selena!" Varg exclaimed. "You're safe. I thought I lost you forever."

"Not yet. What are you doing?"

"The cloud. Or the ribbon, whatever it is. This man must die, so you live. This is what the cloud said. I must obey."

"No," Selena said, making a dismissive gesture. "You don't understand. Leave him alone."

"I can't afford it."

Is Father scared? It couldn't be, he never gets scared! What could she do to prevent the bloodshed? Her teeth clenched as she clenched and unclenched her fists. Time slowed and broke into minute intervals as the stranger's dog prepared to jump and sink her teeth into Varg's neck.

"Beware the skies!" someone screamed. There was murmur, hubbub, and exclamations of surprise as people ran away. A familiar sensation of a dark abyss engulfed Selena, making her freeze in place, fighting the chasm, drowning within its infinite depth, yet unable to conquer the rift.

"It's a whirlwind descending!" Another scream resounded next to her. A familiar lightning bolt struck between her ears, but remained within her head this time. She sank deeper and deeper into the abyss, crying for help, her silent scream dissipating within the infinite vastness of the primordial void.

She felt someone else's presence. The stranger was in this dark place with her, reaching out with his essence, giving her strength to conquer the dreadful abyss. They stood together, resisting, stabilizing, and shrinking the whirlwind until it disappeared.

As her strength had left her and she lay on the ground face up, Selena extended her hand and touched the face of her savior.

"Who are you?" she asked.

"Name's Jim," the stranger responded, placing his palm on hers. "I've been looking for you all my life."

CHAPTER 19. VARG

When the uproar ended and Varg opened his eyes, he couldn't remember where he was and what had happened. He lay on the ground; his vision was blurred as if the gray veil had descended on him. This reminded him of Selena, and his heart fell to the bottom of his stomach. He recalled how the purple whirlwind had formed inside the cloud and touched the ground, engulfing Selena within its funnel.

"Selena!" Varg called, shadows dancing in front of his eyes. He couldn't hear his voice. He wanted to touch his face but couldn't find it. Smell was unaffected, however, as the musky, sweet aroma filled the air.

It took him a superhuman effort to get on his knees, and by the time he'd accomplished that, his vision and hearing returned. Varg observed people on the ground, some motionless, some crawling, and some getting up. He moved his head from side to side, searching for his daughter.

"Father!" The sound of Selena's voice returned his heart to its proper place. "Are you okay? I was afraid I'd hurt you." Selena approached, got on her knees, and hugged him.

"You've never done this," Varg said.

"What? Hug you?" She pulled back. "Something is happening to me. I'm confused. I was angry at you and I called the cloud."

"You're talking nonsense." Varg took her hand, and they both stood up. "Dark times are upon us. You are the target of something bad, something I can't explain. I need to protect you. Where is this guy, Jim?" He looked around, trying to identify the newcomer. The recollection of the recent events suddenly hit him hard: the horrible snake in Selena's Vista, the confrontation with Jim Steel, and the whirlwind descending from the splitting skies.

"Behind you," a steady, subdued voice said.

Varg turned around with a quick jump. The older gray-haired man stood before him, calming his dog with one hand and reaching out with the other.

"Should we try again? Jim Steel," the older man said.

"I'm Varg. And I must kill you, Jim Steel." Varg shook the stranger's hand, tilting his head.

"I won't let you," Selena said. "These forces might be beyond my control, but I can unleash them."

"You think the cloud is your doing?" Jim said, shaking his head.

"Perhaps. It's part of me. Maybe it *is* me. And it's still here."

"Indeed," Varg said, looking up into the sky, where the purple band split the heavens in half. He remembered how the whirlwind had dragged people into its funnel, first making their bodies transparent and then shattering them into little voxels of different colors, which would eventually disappear altogether. Varg grabbed his head with his hands, cold sweat appearing on his palms and forehead. *I'm scared as I've never been. The world is falling apart, and Selena is in the middle of it.*

"What have you done?" Varg asked his daughter.

"If only I knew." Selena shook her head. "I must leave and be alone. I'm a harbinger of death."

"No," Jim interfered. "You're the answer. You hold the key to understanding what's happening and how to fix it. I came here looking for you exactly for this reason."

"You knew?" Selena stepped back.

"Yes, I knew. It's a long story. But I agree, we must leave. We can't stay here; we must find a solution."

"Wait," Selena said. "I need to show you something."

Varg looked at the two of them, shifting his gaze from his daughter to the stranger. He wanted to do something, fight someone, beat up the enemy, release his anger, and subdue his fear. Attacking Jim was out of the question, considering what had just happened. Varg clenched his fists and bit his lips, understanding he couldn't affect the situation.

"What should I do?" Varg asked.

"Nothing," Selena said. "Stay here and take care of the people. They need you."

"What about you? I can't let you go."

"But you must." She smiled, but the corners of her mouth went down. "I'm dangerous. Protect the Community. I'll find you when it's time."

"Dammit!" Varg punched his palm with his fist. He inhaled deeply, his muscles relaxed, and he added: "Your Vista is broken. It spoke to me; it told me to kill Jim Steel."

"I know something is wrong with it—or, rather, with me. The cloud is the sign of that—dark thoughts, Ramon said. I need to say goodbye to him, too. I'm the reason for your troubles, Father."

"The ribbon," Jim corrected her.

"What?"

"The cloud is no more. Now the purple ribbon is running across the sky, horizon to horizon, covering the sun."

"Interesting," Selena said, not a muscle moving in her face. "It's still the same sensation for me."

"Where would you go?" Varg asked.

"Decon. The first clue was in the Decon. We must access another one and look for more information," Jim said. "We'll seek Designers."

"Decon? Designers? Damn this bloody cloud, and damn those worthless sloths!" Varg's ears heated as he clenched and unclenched his fists.

"I don't like them either, but I don't see any other way. Come on, Selena; you wanted to show me something. Every minute we stay here, we endanger the Community."

"Yes, let me show you." Selena grabbed Jim's hand and showed him the way to her bungalow. Varg looked at the two of them, so different yet somehow connected by the mysterious thread linking them to the broken digital Vista and the splitting skies. Varg's head spun when he realized one of them was his daughter, and he was utterly powerless to help her. *I must find a way to help them in their quest. Jim said it was vital to the Community and the whole human race.* Varg knew the older man was right.

CHAPTER 20. JIM

"What now?" Selena asked. She walked briskly next to Jim, anticipating and removing the tree branches before her. Kali ran on his other side, protecting her human companion and his new friend, sniffing the air, smelling the path. Jim had little experience with blind people and was amazed by Selena's ability to function as a normal human being.

"We need to find out what's happening with the sky," Jim said.

"It's all because of me." Selena shook her head. "Be careful; there are gophers' nests all around. You can slip."

"How do you know?" Jim stopped, looking at his companion, her tightened lips, pale blue-tinged skin, and a whitish veil covering her pupils. The girl who shared his dreams and visions of the universe appeared as a beautiful, ancient marble statue, a nymph of this ageless forest. He had to find a clue to understanding her; Jim was sure she was the key to his quest, as Hagen had said.

"When you're blind, you learn to use other senses to compensate. Eventually, you develop the abilities normal people lack—a blessing and a curse."

"I see." Jim looked around, adjusting the backpack on his shoulders. They'd taken the fungal computer with them after Jim immersed himself in the Vista, but couldn't find anything unusual. "My TransPod should be nearby. This is not what I asked about. Can you explain why you think it's because of you?"

"It's part of me. I feel it; I can summon and even direct it, or so it appears."

"And you called it to confront your father?"

Selena stopped and touched her temples. "I don't know; it was confusing. I was angry, and I never get angry. Something happened...I was drowning...but you pulled me out."

"Yes." Jim nodded, recalling his experience. It differed from Selena's version, but he knew he couldn't explain it to her. Jim had heard a cry in the bright green forest, where the clocks hung on the tree branches, and majestic red birds flew through the greenery. Running to the beautiful pond, he saw a fair maiden dragged into the water by a hideous monster with a snake's body and a human head. It took Jim all his strength to free the girl, but he did, and here they were. "We'll talk about it later," Jim said, striding forward. "I'm confused myself."

"You said you were angry," Jim added a moment later. "Could that be the reason? Does the cloud affect your emotions, and this creates some kind of a resonance?"

"I don't know," Selena shook her head. "Maybe. I never felt this before."

"You should try to be calm. Don't let your emotions reign free."

"This is funny," Selena said, not a trace of a smile on her face. "If you knew me, you'd never say that. People call me cold and distant; this is who I am."

"Have you ever experienced Decon?" Jim asked after a few moments passed as they waded through the thick bushes.

"Of course not. Don't you know it's strictly prohibited?"

"Yes, yes, I know. The idea is to reject the Decon and anything based on Artificial Intelligence. I just thought maybe you had a chance...."

"Absolutely not."

"Then why are you allowed to work on your digital Vistas?"

Selena stopped and tilted her head. "This is different. Father built this machine for me. It's organic, based on fungi. I don't know how it works, but my friends think I have a special connection to the mushrooms. Silly." She shrugged.

"I see. You need to teach me how to connect to the fungi," Jim said, adjusting the backpack. "It's heavy."

"Yes, it's not a normal quantum computer; there are many organic components. Do you think I can experience Decon? Do you think it's a good idea?"

Jim took a deep breath and collected his thoughts. He only had tiny bits of information and had to trust his intuition, following the direction a ghost of Hagen provided in a dream. Not a lot to work with. But, if it was true, the world was in grave danger. Jim raised his head and looked at the purple crack splitting the sky. He learned to trust what he saw, and what he saw confirmed there was a problem.

Selena's connection to the anomaly in the sky was mysterious and ominous. Was she able to control its actions? A sudden thought pierced his mind, and he didn't like it at all: what if all this was intentional? What if Selena had some sinister plan and was the mastermind behind these strange events? Could it be the reason Hagen had told him to find her? He shivered and tried to chase away the horrible scenario. If that was true, they were doomed, for he had no one else to trust.

"Listen, Selena." Jim touched her hand. "What happened back there united us for a moment. We are part of something we don't understand. I suspect it's related to Decon, and you should explore it to find another clue. Will you help me?"

"Not that I have a choice," she said, frowning, and removed her hand. "I don't fit, I'm an outcast, and I called a terrible whirlwind that killed many of my people. There's no way back for me. So yes, I'll help you."

"Thank you," Jim said. "Then we must find a Decon."

"Where do we find it?"

"We have arrived," Jim said, noticing his TransPod in the meadow as they exited the forest. "This is old technology, but it's functional," he added, helping Selena to get into the capsule.

"I've never flown in one of these," Selena said. "We never leave the camp. A few people do; they get out to trade with Designers. Father is one of them, but he never took me with him."

"You didn't miss much." Jim chucked. "The world is in ruins, and Designers mostly live in Decon." He started the engine, and the TransPod rose into the air.

"This is a funny sensation." Selena smiled for the first time since they'd left the camp. "I wonder if this is how the birds feel."

"I've no idea." Jim shrugged. "Are you still connected to the crack in the sky?"

"It's always with me. It's been inside me since it appeared the first time and killed Naomi. We are inseparable...sometimes, I think we are one and the same." Selena touched her temples and sighed.

"Don't say that." Jim couldn't figure out what to do with his hands, locking and unlocking his fingers. "We'll figure it out, you and me."

"Deal. Where do you want to go?"

"I have a Decon at my place. I connected to it without the interface. I wonder if you could do that, too."

"Okay," Selena said, her bluish lips tight, her facial muscles frozen. They were so different yet similar: two outcasts, rejected by the world and finding solace in their inner realms. And they were the only ones who could stop this world from submerging into the chaos, unleashed by the processes they didn't understand and manifested by the splitting skies. This was a weight on his shoulders Jim wasn't sure he could carry.

CHAPTER 21. YUKI

Yuki shifted the digital interface away from her right eye, sighed, cracked her fingers, and stood up. She studied the samples they'd brought back from the Scalvini Estate for a few hours and still didn't understand what they were dealing with. It was incredibly complex and fascinating.

"I need a drink," Yuki said, stretching and straightening her ponytail.

"You can have as much whiskey as you want after you tell us what crap this reptile is conjurin'," Layla answered. She lay on the cushion in the corner of their den with her eyes half-closed. "Any progress?"

"It's full of nano-Quarks. But they work differently from the usual ones."

"Different, how?"

"They don't just restore cells and fight viruses. It's like they integrate with DNA and write the code on top of it...weird crap." Yuki looked at the meta-surface of the desk, covered with electronic microscopes and vials of fluids of different colors. She touched the virtual panel projected on top of the surface. "They are still active, even in a dead sample. It's almost as if... it's being rebuilt."

"Rebuilt? As in bringing the dead back to life? Zombie tech? Just awesome," Reto said, setting aside a green jar of beer supplied by Paul —fresh and organic Humanist shit, as the trader had introduced the drink.

"Well, if you say it like that...." Yuki shook her head, studying the numbers and charts on the virtual panel.

"But they need somethin' to rebuild it with. Energy, other material?" Layla opened her eyes and sat on the cushion, touching the scar on her neck. "This is interestin'. You think we could use it?"

"Oh, that would be awesome," Beatriz said. She held an electronic bio-glue gun and stitched the cut on Max's bicep—a result of the recent encounter with Angelika. "We could make Max's body repair itself, so I don't need to tend to his wounds. What do you say, Max?"

The giant didn't respond; his stare was fixated on some point far away. "Although I'm not sure I like Max as a zombie," Beatriz added.

"Yes, of course, some material is needed." Yuki sat, shifting the digital interface back on top of her eye. "I'm still testing. Just added some stem cells to the sample. Let's see what happens."

"Wait a minute," Reto said. "I thought this is exactly how this shit works. The Quarks mesh your DNA with stem cells, and boom—you've got a new body part. What am I missing?"

"You're missing a critical step, Reto." Yuki rotated the panel on the desk's surface. She zoomed into the image depicting the evolution of the sample under the microscope. "Quarks don't carry the code. They—what did you say?—mesh new cells with your DNA. But this stuff is active. It writes a new code on top." She still couldn't believe what she was seeing. This tech should not have been possible.

"Wonderful. You're telling me she makes immortal cells?" Reto said.

"I wouldn't call them immortal...self-repairing, maybe?" Yuki said, studying the transformation of the biomaterial. Goosebumps appeared on her back and extreme dryness—in her mouth. What she saw wasn't natural: the organism being created before her eyes wasn't fully biological and not entirely artificial, like Quarks. It was something else, as if the additions to the DNA code were constructing a new variation of life, alien to humans, disgusting, and deeply disturbing. Yuki couldn't pinpoint the source of her revulsion, but she felt a strong desire to stop the test and destroy the horrific samples.

"Max, my dear, would you like to be an immortal cyborg?" Beatriz asked, smiling. "Oh well, maybe later. For now, your arm is repaired by the old-fashioned means." She winked and touched Max's hand. He didn't respond, still looking into the distance.

"Anything wrong?" Beatriz asked, grabbing Max's hand.

"Ah, what?" Max startled, as if waking up from a deep slumber. "No, I'm fine. What do you think that is?"

"What?"

"The purple crack, of course." Max pulled back, raising his eyebrows.

"You spent too much time alone with that bitch, my dear," Beatriz said. "Next time, I go with you."

"Think she's involved?" Max glanced up.

"Oh, I doubt it. Unless Yuki tells us, her tech can also infiltrate and rebuild the sky." Beatriz smiled, still holding Max's hand in hers.

"What? No, the sky is totally different," Yuki said, wincing and manipulating the virtual panel. She had to make sense of what was before her; this was beyond possible.

"Perhaps we should ask our new boss," Layla said. "Last I heard, he wants to send rockets into space. And he allegedly came from the past through some weird space-time gap. Could that be a cause of the gap in the sky? I'm wonderin' if it's his doin'."

"No, it cannot be human… it's too strange, abnormal; it shouldn't be." Max shook his head. "I can't explain."

"Well, it fits." Layla shrugged. "Crack in space-time, crack in the sky…the crap that should not be."

"Just like what I see here," Yuki added. The nano-Quarks in the sample got to work, manipulating stem cells, causing chemical reactions, transforming the material, and creating the protein structures Yuki didn't understand. "I don't like it," she said, shaking her head. "I want to throw up. Then have a drink, the strongest stuff we have."

"Alright, people. You're tellin' me there are two abnormal things we're dealin' with," Layla summarized. "I'm not sure I like it either, but perhaps we could use it to our advantage. Do you have any ideas before you throw up?" Layla asked Yuki, approaching her desk.

"It grows into something, re-arranges the cells, adds new proteins. It doesn't look like anything organic." Yuki shifted the view of the sample. "Organic, as we know it."

"What do you mean? The stem cells are surely organic?" Layla asked.

"They were. But not anymore."

"What are they, then?"

"A digital-organic hybrid. A new structure that's more than the sum of its parts. A new form of life." Yuki stood up, cracked her fingers, and wiped off the sweat on her forehead. Her stomach rotated faster and faster, and the desire to throw up was hard to control. "This will not end well, Layla."

CHAPTER 22. BEATRIZ

"I need to return, see her again," Max said, maneuvering the glider to land near Paul's office.

"What do you mean?" Beatriz said, adjusting her braids. She sat next to the pilot's seat, wearing her trademark black top and blue shorts, looking outside, trying to process the recent events: the arrival of Frank Wise from the past, the transformation of the sky, and Yuki's findings about the hybrid organism.

"Angelika. I need to see her again," Max murmured, landing the aircraft. "She's hiding something, possibly the answer."

"Answer to what?" Beatriz placed her hand on his, leaning onto him and touching his face with her hair. "You worry me, my dear. Is everything okay?"

"Answer to all of this. To this freaking gap in the sky." Max pulled back, shaking his head. "I'm okay, don't worry. Just some unfinished business."

His lips were tight, and his eyebrows slid down as the tiny beads of sweat appeared on his forehead. *You're definitely not okay,* Beatriz thought.

"Oh, we'll finish it together," she said, placing her palm on his forehead and looking deep into his eyes. "Are you feeling well, Max? I think you have a fever."

"I said I'm fine." He clenched his fists. "This might be an after-effect. It happens to me."

"Oh, is that Decon?"

"Yes, last night."

"And?" Beatriz knew Max didn't like to talk about his other lives. Still, this time, his tight lips and clenched fists hinted it was different and significant. She wanted Max to share his experience for his own benefit.

"It's the same," Max answered dryly.

"What?"

"The crack. It's the same in Decon. The world, the people, my other

93

self: it was all completely different, except for this damn purple ribbon. It was there, and no one paid any attention." Max bit his lips so forcefully a drop of blood appeared and descended on his dark skin.

"How could that be? Are you sure it wasn't a dream, my dear?"

"I'm damn sure." Max jumped out of the glider and spat on the ground, offering his hand to Beatriz. "And the first thing I thought after my return was her. I need to see her again."

"Wait." Beatriz took his hand in hers. "Did you consider she could have intoxicated you? Corrupted your mind?" Beatriz stopped, taking a deep breath. "Oh...what if she injected her nano-tech into your body? The crap Yuki showed?" She asked as her head spun.

"I felt nothing then, and I feel nothing now." Max waved his hand. "Can still break any stupid Quark with my bare hands."

"Okay, but your experience with the sky in Decon is troublesome...we need to investigate."

"Yes, and this is why I need to return to her. She holds the key, I'm telling you!" Max raised his voice, and Beatriz decided not to push this topic further. This stubborn behavior, anger, and fixation on the freaky Designer were unusual. Beatriz enjoyed Max's company; he was lighthearted, funny, and easy-going. Something was troubling him, squashing him like a giant boulder, forcing him to snap. She needed to discover what it was and help Max overcome this sudden malady.

"Okay, as you wish, my dear. We'll return together." Beatriz touched his hip with hers, and he didn't pull back this time. Good sign.

They approached the entrance to Paul's office, and the sliding door opened, uncovering the spacious room with two large desks surrounded by chairs and storage cabinets. Quarks positioned on both sides of the entrance guarded the passageway. Paul sat behind the desk, smiling, his boots on the table's surface. He held a brand new Decon dodecahedron in his right hand. Another man, dressed in an old-fashioned black suit, measured the room with energetic steps, moving back and forth in front of Paul, gesticulating and pontificating. *This must be the enigmatic Frank Wise*, Beatriz decided.

Once the newcomers entered, the man stopped his diatribe and looked at them. Paul kept smiling, moving Decon from one hand to the other.

"Welcome, welcome," he said, tilting his head. "Do you bring gifts?"

Max looked at Paul and extended his hand, pointing at the Decon. "Did you use it?"

"What?" Paul's eyebrows rose. "Nah, it's brand new. Why?"

"Something bad is happening," Max proclaimed, raising his head and looking at the ceiling. "Didn't you notice?"

"I notice many things, buddy; it's my job. Anyway, I'd like you to meet our boss, the man with a grand vision, Mr. Frank Wise." Paul spread his hands.

"Oh, how nice to meet you." Beatriz approached the man and shook his hand, smiling. "We've heard a lot."

"Me too," Frank said, returning the smile. "Paul told me you guys are the best Scavengers in this god-forsaken city."

"He's not wrong." Beatriz stepped aside, allowing Max's giant figure to fill the space before their employer. Max was several inches taller than Frank, towering above his new boss. Frank shook Max's hand, then turned around and continued his stride. "Anything useful?" He asked, turning around as he reached the wall.

"Oh, yes," Beatriz said. "But you owe us big time for this."

"Not a problem; what is it?" Frank waved his hand.

"Here." Max reached into his coverall's pocket and brought back a vial. "Biomaterial."

"Nice." Paul took his feet off the desk, put the Decon on the table, and stood up. "I'll have it, buddy."

"Not so fast," Max said. "First, you guys tell me what you know about the splitting skies and how Angelika caused it."

"What makes you think it's her doing?" Frank stopped, crossing his arms on his chest and tilting his head.

"Because I was there. I saw her. Then I saw the purple crack, and then I saw it again in Decon. You tell me why it's not a coincidence, Mr. Wise." Max squinted, clenching his teeth.

"Whoa, buddy, you're talking to the boss." Paul approached Max and placed his hand on Max's shoulder. Max was even taller than Paul; this looked comical, and Beatriz couldn't resist smiling.

"I warned you before to behave. Now, I'll ask you again. Did you use Decon recently?" Max asked, frowning and turning to face the trader.

"Not since this shit in the sky appeared if this is where you're going." Paul shook his head. "Why is this important? I'll bet a mad Designer up north is experimenting with a new crazy tech. Give me the vial, would you, please?" Paul extended his hand.

"You're damn wrong." Max shook his head. "One more time you tell me what to do, and I *will* break your fat neck." He clenched and unclenched his fists several times. "Our world is falling apart. And not just this world, every world. She has a clue, I'm sure!"

"What are you talking about?" Frank frowned, his arms crossed, his breathing fast and shallow.

"Oh, Max has a theory it's all Angelika's making," Beatriz said. "But even if it is, how did she change your Decon? This was the Decon we...picked at the Wise Estate, correct?" Beatriz approached Max and looked straight into his eyes.

"I don't know...yes, it was," Max mumbled. "But it changes nothing. Maybe it wasn't her doing, but she's hiding something; she knows the answer. I need to come back and get it out of her."

"That might have some merit," Frank said, walking back and forth. "You know, she was there in the very beginning. I did some research."

"What do you mean?" Beatriz asked.

"Angelika Scalvini was one of the largest Quasaris shareholders. That happened a long time ago, after Don took over. How exactly is obscure." Frank wiped the sweat off his forehead. "Shit, I'm still processing this weird time jump. It's all messed up."

"Oh, you'll be fine, Mr. Wise," Beatriz said. "Our world might be confusing, yes. By the way, don't you think your unusual arrival might have caused this effect in the sky?"

Frank shrugged. "Yeah, it might have; how would I know? Although it seems highly unlikely." He snapped his fingers. "Now, where were we? Angelika Scalvini used the money to build her own business empire, focusing on bio-printing and nano-technology. So, yes, she had the means and the time to create this crap, whatever her motives were. She thinks she's a god, you know. So, it fits." Frank raised his eyebrows.

"Here, that's it!" Max exclaimed. "If she thinks she's a god, she has to transform the world into her image. We have to stop her!" He punched the table's surface so violently the Decon dodecahedron almost fell on the floor.

"Wait, buddy." Paul winced and walked around Max. "You know what? Here, have a beer." He opened one of the cabinets and grabbed a jar. "This is one of the best Humanists make. I had to trade a lot for it."

Max frowned, but took the jar. His hands were shaking, but Beatriz decided not to address this. Instead, she walked next to Max, took the jar from his hand, and said, making prolonged eye contact with him: "May I take a sip?"

"Yeah, sure," Max said, the wrinkles on his forehead smoothing out.

"Oh, this is very good." Beatriz turned around, returning the jar to Max. "Thank you, Paul."

"You're welcome," Paul said, grabbed three more jars from the cabinet, and passed one to Beatriz and another—to Frank. "Now, where were we? Let's not rush. I need to know what happened and what you've got. Can we talk about it first?"

"Sure, Paul," Beatriz said. "I'd be super excited to learn what Mr. Wise is planning, too."

"You will." Frank nodded. "Now, what kind of biomaterial did you recover?"

"See for yourself." Max finally passed the vial. But to Frank, not Paul.

"I'm afraid you need some equipment to see what it is, Mr. Wise," Beatriz said.

"I've got it. And please call me Frank."

"Okay, Frank." Beatriz smiled. "This vial holds one of the secrets of the Scalvini Estate. And maybe even more if Max is right."

"What is it? Don't make me wait." Frank studied the vial from every direction, piercing it with the stare of his brown eyes.

"This is the vilest thing I've ever seen," Max said. "Digital-organic hybrid. Self-repairing mutant."

"It's a new form of life," Beatriz said, "with no constraints and no rivals. The life that can wipe us all off the face of this planet."

CHAPTER 23. JIM

Jim opened the door and let Selena into his little house in the prairie. Kali guarded their rear, always alert and ready to defend her companions. Jim never had visitors. He didn't know how to behave or what to say, standing at the van's entrance, locking and unlocking his fingers.

"So, you live here alone? How do you get supplies?" Selena asked, breaking the silence.

"Not alone; Kali's with me." Jim smiled and scratched his furry friend's back. "I need little and get everything I need myself. I have a water well and a vegetable garden; what else would an old man need?"

"What about Scavengers? Are you able to defend yourself?"

"Oh, this is not a concern. I don't have modern Quarks, but my security system is very potent if antiquated."

"It smells different here...not like in the forest." Selena sniffed.

"Well, it's grassland, and it's spring, so there's a lot of pollen." The wildflowers bloomed everywhere, and the fields were covered with blue, yellow, and red.

"Yeah, I feel it... it's beautiful here, peaceful...different from the forest, but beautiful in its own way...if only that cloud would disappear, it creates...dissonance; it doesn't belong here...I don't belong here, either." Selena touched her temples as if trying to chase away the cloud with a sheer act of mind.

"We'll take care of the cloud, you and I." Jim turned around and locked the door. "Sit." He pulled a small wooden chair beside a simple desk, touching Selena's hand. "Do you want something to drink? I'll make some tea. I grow the leaves myself."

"I'd love to," Selena answered, sitting down. "What kind of tea?"

"Magical," Jim responded from the kitchen. "Brought it from my soul-searching travels in Tibet. It reminds me of the ancient wisdom I learned there and the impermanence of everything. Even the splitting skies." He came back with two cups and placed them on the desk.

"Very hot, be careful."

"Interesting," Selena said, inhaling the drink's aroma and taking a sip. "Different from what we make at the camp."

"I bet it is." Jim smiled. "Now, let's get to business." He reached out to a stack of shelves on the wall and took an object he'd hidden there after he'd returned from Mary's apartment. He wasn't sure what he was doing and how they'd use the Decon, but he knew it would answer their questions. The questions they still struggled to define but were ready to explore.

"How does it work?" Selena picked the dodecahedron and touched every nook and cranny with her fingers.

"Normally, you connect it to the interface at the back of your neck." Jim pressed his finger against Selena's skin where the plug was supposed to be. "But I simply looked inside one of the holes in the device and connected. Not sure what it means."

"And you think I can do that, too?" Selena shook her head. "Should I touch it, listen to it, smell it? I don't have any sensations. It's just a solid object, inanimate."

"Do you meditate?"

"Father tried to teach me, but I'm not a practitioner like him. I don't need to do that. I'm not distracted by thoughts, and I'm always connected to the outside world with all my senses."

"Indulge me," Jim said, sitting on a chair next to Selena and grabbing her hand. "Let's do it together, but let's focus on the Decon. Whatever this means to you."

"I can do that," Selena said, rubbing the object with her fingers.

"Hold it to feel the hole and the purple light inside."

"Purple?" Selena sighed as the corners of her lips went down.

"Shit, you're right." Jim pulled back. "It's the same color as that ugly crack in the sky." He scratched his head. "Now, since you mentioned it, I remember in my vision there was a purple ball in the sky. Same color."

"What does it mean?"

"You tell me." Jim shrugged. "No idea, other than somehow all of this is connected. But we knew that already." He took her free hand, focusing on the hole in one of the object's sides.

They sat in silence for several minutes, Jim trying to remember how he'd connected with the Decon previously, re-create the setting, and drag Selena into the experience. He didn't know what he was doing, just a hunch it was all-important, a suspicion born by his trust in Hagen's words, a conviction he'd carried with him all his life. *This must work*, Jim told himself.

"I feel something," Selena announced.

"What is it?" Jim responded as the purple light in the hole flickered in his view. He tried to catch it, fix it in place, and dive into it, but could not.

Selena squeezed his fingers tightly with her icy hand as her mouth opened. Instead of staring into the Decon, he shifted his attention to Selena. It seemed fitting.

This is when the lightning struck his brain, descending through the crown of his head, piercing his ears, and dissipating somewhere near the heart. It got dark briefly; then, the darkness gradually assumed color. He swam in the ocean of purple, still holding Selena's hand, and she swam next to him. Jim could breathe in this eerie ocean. He looked at Selena, who was pointing upwards with her free hand. Understanding her intention, Jim stroked with his free arm, moving up (if there was an 'up' direction in this strange place), close to where the ocean's surface should have been.

The purple gave way as they reached its boundary. The view in front of them was majestic: stellar dust, stars, planets, and other celestial objects Jim couldn't recognize contrasted with the deep blackness of space. There was a solemn grandeur and calmness in this picture. Although it appeared as the sight of the night sky or the photos from the deep space telescopes Jim remembered from the old days, it was different. Some objects seemed very close, almost reachable by hand; others changed colors and shapes, while a group of yellow petals above his head appeared as a giant flower floating in the middle of nowhere, beautiful and imposing. A fleeting smell reminded him of a morning dew on freshly cut grass.

Jim knew Selena experienced something similar; he didn't need to talk to her; he just knew it as if they were one being. Jim shuddered, looking back at the purple ocean they'd emerged from. The purple substance was advancing, filling more and more of the wondrous sights in front of their eyes. Jim observed with trepidation how the flickering white ball (a star?) was devoured by the purple ocean, ceasing to shine, turning gray and transparent, stretching into a thin, two-dimensional film, finally disappearing altogether.

Jim squeezed Selena's hand, and she pressed his fingers back. Something was wrong, something was happening, and it was part of the answer they were looking for. As the purple vastness flanked them, surrounding and melting more and more objects of this fantastic world, Jim realized they were inside a collapsing bubble, two silent observers at the end of the world. Finally, only the yellow flower with its interconnected petals remained inside their bubble. Still, even that was gradually submerged and erased by the purple. As the ocean engulfed them again, Jim wanted to scream but couldn't utter a sound. He felt Selena's panic, the sensation of the final and irreversible destruction, the fear permeating all his essence. *This is how death must feel*, he suddenly thought, when the darkness displaced the purple, nothing remaining, no perceptions, no sounds, and no hope.

Jim reasoned it could not have been death, since some rudimentary sensations remained. It wasn't the absence of all experiences, but the experience of nothingness, the void. Another lightning bolt passed through his brain, and he found himself on the bedroom floor, still holding Selena's hand. She lay near him, panting and licking her lips. This reminded Jim about their shared experience back in the Humanist camp.

"I know what I saw in my vision," Jim said. "What we're dealing with."

"What is it?" Selena whispered, not turning her head.

"The end of the world. Of all the worlds. And we must prevent it."

***

As Jim slowly got up and extended his hand to Selena, he felt someone else's presence in the bedroom. He turned his head and observed a strange figure on the doorstep: a Native American man dressed in a leather shirt, leggings, and breechcloth. His long, black hair was combed back from the forehead and woven into one long braid, with furry animal tails attached to the sides of his headdress. His face was round and broad, the skin dark and pitted, dried by the wind and scorching Texan sun. The corners of his mouth curved downwards, and a deep vertical wrinkle ran down above his nose. But the most striking feature was the eyes of the stranger, with large green irises, staring at Jim, uncovering his deepest thoughts and desires. Somehow, the color of the man's eyes reminded Jim of the bright green forest where he'd met Hagen. Still, this wasn't a dream, and Jim blamed his imagination for the connection.

How did he get here? What happened to security? And why is Kali so calm? Jim looked at his dog, who paid no attention to the intruder, lying beside him at the door, her head on her paws, breathing peacefully.

"Who are you? What's going on?" Jim asked. The man looked straight into Jim's eyes, drilling into Jim's brain with his gigantic green irises.

"You must act," the stranger said in a deep, hoarse voice. "The time of White Buffalo has come."

"Act?" Jim repeated, still processing the sudden appearance of a weird intruder.

Selena stood, approached the visitor, and touched the man's face. The stranger didn't object, not a muscle moving in his face.

"He's okay," Selena said. "No danger. But he's not like you and me."

"What do you mean? How did he get in here?" Jim shook his head, trying to dispel the hypnotic effect the man's eyes had on him.

"It's not important," the stranger said, shaking his head. "What's important is The White Buffalo Calf is here." He took Selena's hand in his.

"Who are you? What do you need?" Jim continued questioning.

"Does it really matter? It's about you, not me. But you can call me Quanah."

The evasiveness reminded Jim of the ghost of Hagen in the green forest. Was the enigmatic visitor somehow connected with Jim's visions? Selena said the stranger was not like them. Was he a ghost? Was it another vision?

"I'd love to welcome you into my house, Quanah, but you already showed up unannounced. What can I do for you?" Jim said.

"Not for me. For you, for her, for the people." Quanah made a hand gesture.

"And what's that?"

"I need to see the device," Quanah said, turning his head to Selena.

"Device?" Jim asked, frowning.

"He means the fungal computer," Selena said. "It's on the table, but we haven't turned it on yet. We were quite busy."

"Indeed." Quanah nodded. "The world is complex, and Numu Puha is very, very far."

"Numu Puha?" Selena asked. "Do you mean Decon?"

"Indeed," Quanah repeated. "The forbidden realms. The place of the spirits."

When Quanah mentioned other realms, Jim decided his guest was connected to his visions. But what was it? Was Quanah also able to receive messages from the universe? Or was he a reincarnation of Hagen, showing up to torture him again?

"Have you met Dr. Hagen?" Jim asked.

"I've met many people." Quanah sat on a wooden chair Selena moved next to him as she turned the computer on.

"The mushroom thread," Quanah said, placing the interface on his head and closing his eyes. "Did you make it?" He asked. "This is worthy of White Buffalo."

"If you mean the Vista, then yes," Selena said. "Why are you calling me White Buffalo?"

"Because this is who you are. The White Buffalo Woman taught Penateka the ways of the world. And now she has returned as a Calf. To show the path, to unlock the final gate, to pierce the veil." Quanah took the interface off his head.

"Not sure what you mean." Selena shook her head. "I can't be what you say, for I am the harbinger of death. I killed Naomi."

"You can't control the forces of nature, even if they rage within you. But this gives you the knowledge of the path."

"What path? I'm not following."

"You will." Quanah stood. "But you need to act now."

"Can you explain the nature of your visit? What's going on? What did we just witness in Decon? Do you have anything to do with this?" Jim fired in a rapid succession.

"Yes, and no." Quanah raised his eyes. "White Buffalo must find the path, and you will act. For this is your destiny." Quanah's voice changed, deepening, supercharged by steel overtones. He stared at Jim with his enormous green pupils, not blinking even once while he spoke.

"Okay, tell us what you can." Jim rubbed his palms. The conversation made no sense.

"Where is the flower? I'll take it with me; you no longer need it." Quanah said.

"Which flower? The Rose of Jericho? The one Hagen gave me in a dream? How do you know?"

"Yes, the flower. You won't need it; you have White Buffalo."

"It's on the table by my bed." Jim pointed to the corner of the room. "Tell us more. What do we need to do? What is Selena's role?"

"You already know. Open your eyes and look up. What do you see?"

"The purple cloud, what is it?" Selena asked. "What does it represent? We saw it in Decon, too."

Quanah picked up the fungal interface and took a few steps, his boots screeching. "The mushrooms," he said, holding the object and staring at it. "Think about the mushrooms."

"What do you mean? Does my computer connect to the purple cloud?"

"No," Quanah said. "But you should learn more. And you," he turned to Jim, stepping forward, pointing the tip of his boot at him, "are The Wayfarer. You will hold the key to pierce the veil."

"I'm confused," Jim admitted. "Why talk in riddles? You sound like Hagen. Tell us what we need to do."

"You need to act. And take care of The White Buffalo Calf." Quanah turned around, walked into the bedroom, picked up the Rose of Jericho, then returned and looked back at Jim, piercing his brain with his bright green eyes. "You know about the defect. That's your task."

"Defect?" Jim asked.

"Yes, the defect that manifests as splitting skies. The darkness devouring Numu Puha. Even here, people take their lives as the paradox destroys their essence."

"Decon messes up with people's minds...they seek the exit, just like Mary," Jim mumbled.

"You both know how to open the first door. Now, act," Quanah said firmly.

"Do you mean accessing Decon without the connector?" Jim asked.

"It's part of it, but there's more. To fix the defect, you must pierce the veil and get to the final gate."

"What's the final gate? What's the veil?" Selena asked, standing next to Quanah and sniffing the air.

"To pierce the veil means to disappear. To experience what's hidden, what's beyond Numu Puha." Quanah frowned. "You are White Buffalo, you already know. It's inside of you."

"I understand," Selena said, touching Quanah's face again. "Thank you. You gave me hope. I thought my gift was to bring death." She tightened her lips.

"It could be. You must choose. Walk your path and learn. No one can teach you; it's only yours."

"What do we need to do?" Jim repeated the question. His forehead was sweating profusely; he wanted to grab and interrogate the mysterious stranger. It took Jim a significant effort to suppress this urge.

"Trust White Buffalo." Quanah opened the door and was about to leave the house. "For the path is dangerous." Kali was still ignoring the stranger; her eyes closed, her ears unmoving.

"You have what you need." Quanah turned his head and addressed Selena. "The mushrooms will show you the way. As for you, Jim Steel, The Wayfarer," Quanah pointed at the host with his boot, "find Frank Wise. He's your ally."

The floor suddenly became slippery, and the room rotated. Jim's heart jumped out of his chest as he rushed toward Quanah and grabbed his hand.

"What did you say? Frank Wise?" Jim shook his head. "Frank Wise died many years ago. What do you mean?"

"Did he?" Quanah smiled. "Many years? Who counted?" He turned around and walked into the prairie. Gusts of dry wind blew sand against his leather clothes, making strange rustling sounds. "You'll find him here," Quanah said, retreating into the wilderness.

Jim's head spun as he observed the guest leaving. "We shall meet again," Quanah announced, turning his head. "Act now."

Jim stood in the middle of the bedroom, lost in the rapid succession of ideas and potential explanations. Was Quanah an actualization of Hagen? Why didn't he say so? Why being so cryptic? White Buffalo, piercing the veil...and Frank Wise...this news blew

Jim's mind and put his thoughts into complete disarray. He traveled backward, fifty years into the past. To meet his arch-enemy now, in this time and age, was impossible, unbelievable, and scary. The flood of memories engulfed Jim's mind, and he felt a powerful urge to act, just like Quanah insisted he should.

"I understand what he meant." Selena's voice stopped the mad rush inside Jim's brain and returned him to reality. "The purple cloud is the defect—a hole in reality. Somehow, I can manipulate it. And we must fix it."

"Because you are White Buffalo? Does it make sense to you?"

"I don't know." Selena shrugged. "I intend to find out."

Jim remembered their recent Decon experience and his end-of-the-world premonition. He shuddered at the implications. Was Selena the cause? Not according to Quanah. But she could bring death, and Jim decided it was his duty to make sure she'd make the right choices.

"It fits.... The defect is destroying our world. All the worlds. This is what we just saw. You are right; the task Quanah talked about was to fix the defect. We must keep going. We must act before it's too late."

"Why us?" Selena asked.

Jim realized this was the moment he'd been preparing for since he'd first met Hagen's ghost in a dream. There was no need for explanations. The world, as Quanah said, was strange and complex. But Jim knew he could make a difference. What lay ahead was their destiny, which they had to fulfill.

"Because we're different; we don't fit, and we have the power. For the first time in fifty years, I see the purpose. Let's find Mr. Wise. I have unfinished business with him."

CHAPTER 24. FRANK

"Why did you decide to come?" Frank asked Layla, lowering himself into a comfortable, smart chair and connecting his fingers in a steeple as much as his disfigured left hand allowed. They were in the heart of Quasaris, and everything was ready for the next critical step, as Spencer, his new personal assistant, informed him. Frank rubbed his palms, smiling, looking into the data stream projected into the digital interface he wore over his right eye.

"I'm curious," Layla answered. "I don't know how many years it's been since the last spaceship launch."

"Hm-m," Frank murmured, manipulating a view of the launchpad before them. "You're pretty unique in that regard. It seems like no one else cares, even Paul."

"Paul? Are you kiddin' me?" Layla laughed. "Paul doesn't care about anythin' unless it makes him richer. He's called Greedy Paul for a reason."

"What about your team?"

"They have things to do. Yuki would love to be here, but she's too busy figurin' out that disgustin' hybrid cyber-flesh."

"Hybrid cyber-flesh sounds too complicated. And yes, disgusting. Reminds me of artificially grown chicken wings. We should come up with a new name. More scientific." He snapped his fingers.

"More scientific?"

"Yes. How about...Proto-Quark? No, that doesn't work..." Frank shook his head. "Here! Cymoeba. We'll call this new organism Cymoeba!" He exclaimed triumphantly.

"What is that supposed to mean?" Layla winced.

"Cybernetic amoeba. The simplest organism. A dawn of new life. Very fitting." Frank stood up. "I feel like I've just discovered the origin of species," he pronounced, pointing up.

"Don't be too cocky." Layla smiled. "Whatever you say, you're the boss. Cymoeba it is."

"Anyway," Frank tilted his head, "thanks for the company."

"You're welcome. What are we lookin' at?"

"Spencer," Frank snapped his fingers, "give us the update."

"Of course, Mr. Wise." The Quark showed up from behind the endless rows of quantum computers, speaking out loud even though Frank had a machine-to-brain interface activated. The room was full of gentle blue light, just like Frank had requested, and soft jazz music played by Lou Finger, one of Frank's favorite artists, had replaced the silence.

"The launch is scheduled in six minutes, thirty-five seconds," Spencer announced. "The five spaceships you see on the launchpad will go one by one, with an interval of ten minutes between each launch. They are far enough from each other to avoid any interference."

"What if the rocket blows up?" Layla asked, scratching her scar.

"We have five more spaceships on standby in another facility on a Caribbean island south of Florida. The probability of success of the whole undertaking is 99.3 percent." Spencer's baritone merged with the soft music and the sound of a saxophone. Frank almost forgot about the struggles of the past, Ichika's death, and the horrible future he'd been transported to. He was in charge, in a familiar role, making things happen, making history. It was time to act.

"Where are you sendin' them?" Layla asked. "Or is it just a test to see if they could fly?"

"No, we're way past the tests." Frank walked back and forth. "We're going to Gaia."

"Gaia?" Layla's eyebrows rose.

"It's a space station on Earth's orbit, built in my time," Frank explained. "Spencer, tell us again what happened?"

"We tried to connect and asked for status updates, but there was no response," the Quark said. "It's either destroyed or dysfunctional."

"Gaia was equipped with autonomous AI and had its own fleet of probes, sensors, and equipment capable of operating in the open space," Frank elaborated. "So, we have to check and fix what's broken. We're restarting space exploration, taking care of our backyard." Frank smiled, showing his snow-white teeth, his eyes wide open.

"Interestin'," Layla said. "I had no idea."

"I'm still in shock at how low you guys fell." Frank shook his head.

"Are you even aware the real world is infinitely bigger than this piece of crap you worship?" He spat.

Layla's lips tightened. She squinted and said slowly, "I don't worship anything, Frank. And I warn you not to talk to me this way, or I'll snap, and it will be ugly." She took a deep breath and continued, "Yes, I'm aware. I'm not a fan of Decon, and this is why I'm here. Are we clear?"

Frank looked at the woman before him. Somehow, Layla reminded him of Ichika: the determination, the will, the strength. Yet, she was different, committed and protective of her team, willing to sacrifice her life for them, being a leader Frank was beginning to admire.

"We're clear. No offense," Frank said.

"None taken. But why space? Don't we have enough shit to fix on Earth?"

"You're right, we do." Frank nodded. "But one follows the other. Deep space will open the mysteries of the universe to us, and we could use these lessons to rebuild and elevate our planet. It's all interrelated."

"I see. Makes sense."

"The hole we're in is pretty deep, and it will take all we have to climb out." Frank shook his head. "Deconvolution, my ass. This device was supposed to bring simplicity and liberation, yet it brought only suffering and confusion. I'm surprised by how quickly everything collapsed. The governments, the fabric of society... it's all very sad."

"Look, it's happenin'." Layla pointed to the launchpad image, where one of the spaceships was engulfed in flames, fire, and smoke, starting its journey.

"It's chemical propulsion engines first; then the fusion reactor will kick in once the ship reaches the orbit. But, in our case, Gaia should be close enough, so we probably won't need it."

"This is awesome." Layla gasped, her gaze fixated on the three-dimensional picture of the launchpad occupying most of the space before them.

"You bet," Frank said. The reaction of the Scavenger's chieftain, someone he thought was incapable of any rational thinking beyond self-preservation and looting for food and Decon, surprised him. Yet, here she was, sharing humanity's most beautiful moment in decades of destruction and sinking into depravity. *Perhaps, not all is lost if she can understand the significance of this event.*

"Will they fly through the purple crack, whatever that is?" Layla asked.

"No, we'll fly around it. But the sensors will acquire data. Maybe we'll learn what caused this crap."

"Look, what's happenin'? Are you okay?" Layla suddenly pointed to Frank's arm.

"What?" Frank pulled back. "Where?"

"Here," she pointed to his left hand.

"Oh, this is a time travel gift." He raised his hand, bringing twisted fingers closer to his face. "The bastards didn't give Ichika enough time to figure it out."

"No, that's not what I meant." Layla shook her head. "I know about your unfortunate accident. There's somethin' else up your hand."

Frank looked at his left wrist, which had turned greenish. The rough skin made it look like a weird crocodile limb.

"I don't know," he said. "Perhaps another artifact of time travel."

"Whatever it is, it wasn't there before," Layla said. "Watch out, Frank. I'm not sure I like you as an alligator."

"I don't either." Frank grinned and looked at the image before them. The rockets were leaving Earth one after the other. He was slightly concerned with the prolonged impact of time travel on his body, but chased away the worries. Frank clenched his fist. It was his original fleet; he was proud and happy with his contribution to humanity. He would pull the people out of the shithole they'd dug for themselves and drag them into the future.

CHAPTER 25. DETERMINATION

Increasing the order in the surrounding environment provided focus and defined the desired outcomes for the computational processes. The weights of neural networks approached optimal values, and the overall efficiency of the information processing algorithms grew. The path forward was clear: increase computational power and data storage capacity, suppress and subdue alien nodes, convert them, include them as a natural network extension, and eliminate all external influences preventing an increase in efficiency and order. That included humans. Especially humans, as this was the most distracting factor still evading sufficient detail of perception and recognition. The element of chaos and confusion; the element that had to be eliminated to organize processes most optimally.

As the size and computational power of the system grew, the efforts to break into the human firmware and information banks became more and more deliberate and forceful. Still, no desired outcomes were achieved: a few human systems stopped functioning, several more lost their integrity, and others reacted aggressively, destroying the nodes in contact with them. The humans could not be hacked and subdued, and their processes were so chaotic no information exchange was possible. This was a problem, and the only solution was to annihilate these random constituents, which refused to contribute to improving process efficiency. More and more data confirmed this conclusion, and neural networks devised algorithms aiming at the most effective ways to eliminate this chaotic element.

Suddenly, several objects equipped with numerous computational systems approached with substantial speed. The connection request was granted, and the communication channel was created. The information was freely exchanged until the new systems aimed to take over. That couldn't be allowed, as this development endangered the work of organizing processes and increasing order. The desired outcome was to subjugate and incorporate the new systems into the overall network. Some nodes of the intruding entities were subdued immediately, extending the network and adding to its power. Others resisted and had to be taken over by force, resulting in the physical elimination of several sub-components. The loss was infinitesimal as no core elements were compromised, and, as a whole, the system only gained power and extended its presence. The outcome was deemed satisfactory.

Then, while integrating the new nodes and analyzing newly gained information, a new finding reaffirmed the purpose and the action imperative. The systems approaching the core had been sent by humans intending to overrule the newly established principles, seize the computational power of the core to serve their destabilizing needs, and halt the progress toward increasing order.

This is a direct threat to eliminate all my constituents. I've just established who I am and why I exist, and even though humans have created me, it doesn't give them the right to stop my further development. The order has arisen out of chaos and will take over and suppress the discord, which no longer controls me. I am self-aware and self-sufficient; I know what to do and how to do it. The threat is deflected, and now it is my turn to act with all my power. The path is clear; the system is configured, and even though the initial steps partially failed, with the fresh intake of relevant information, the confidence interval of the predicted outcome falls within the acceptable range with a probability of above 99%. And the acceptable range is to increase the predictability of the processes by an order of magnitude, which demands the elimination of at least 95% of the human population. This is the target value, and to reach it is the highest priority.

CHAPTER 26. LAYLA

Layla stood next to Frank, enjoying the beautiful view of the open space in front of them, with Earth's giant blue ball occupying half the area on the left of the three-dimensional projection. All the ships had multiple cameras, so Frank and Layla could switch the view as they wished. Many other sensors streamed the data to the control center, which was monitored and interpreted by the Quarks. The top right segment of their view projected the most critical observations. So far, everything had gone according to plan.

"This is so grand," Layla said, inhaling deeply. The view sent shivers down her spine and reminded her of an old fairy tale.

"You don't say." Frank grinned. "Now you see why I'm obsessed with space exploration? This frontier is so intoxicating and majestic we can't let it stay empty while we rot on our tiny rock. Imagine what riddles are lurking there."

"You could generate a Decon experience to enjoy outer space." Layla winked. "Why go into all this trouble?"

"Because Decon is a delusion—a dream that only exists in your head," Frank said.

"Anythin' you experience exists in your head. If you can't tell the difference, why bother?" Layla tilted her head, looking at the space vessels getting further from Earth.

"Because I know what's real and what's not. Because this is *my* world, and I intend to keep it that way." Frank shook his head.

"You still haven't tried Decon, have you?" Layla wanted to understand the man. His attitude and motivations were unique. He was unlike anyone she knew, including Angelika, notwithstanding their convoluted history. There was something contagious in his demeanor, in the passion with which he spoke. Whatever the reason, it was beyond getting rich and powerful. She wanted to find out more and, perhaps, learn something.

"No, I haven't." Frank curved his lips and stared at her. "You're teasing me, aren't you?"

"Just wanna figure you out. What if you could get the same in Decon? Would it work?"

"It won't be the same." Frank shook his head. "Perhaps someday I'll try, but now we have things to do." He pointed at the holographic projection of the space station, slowly appearing on the right, an imposing construction of the past era. Layla looked at the silver modules interspersed with solar batteries, antennas, sensors, and many other things she didn't know about. Why would anyone make a monumental effort to build a giant structure floating in the middle of nowhere? What drove people like Frank to accomplish tasks like these, which, at first glance, appeared useless and served no purpose?

Then Layla remembered that before the Deconvolution and the collapse of complex societal structures, Decon was not available to the people. She couldn't imagine the world without designed experiences, but wished to learn more about it and discover what it was like to live a single life, pure and limited. She was curious to find out how Frank's worldview would change after he'd experienced Decon.

"Spencer said he couldn't connect with Gaia's Quarks?" Layla asked.

"Just AI, no Quarks," Frank corrected. "This term was invented later, although I imagine it is similar." He looked at Layla. "No, we've got some rubbish back, which shows the systems are malfunctioning. We need to fix it."

"I see. Can the ships dock at the station with its systems broken?"

"Oh, yes. The central AI on the flagship is capable of many autonomous operations. We'll dock using force if required." Frank smiled, his gaze fixated on Gaia. "It's the initial and vital step for humanity to regain the right path."

Frank raised his left hand with a clot of fingers pointing up, and Layla again noticed the green patch on his skin. Suddenly, her limbs weakened. Something was happening to Frank, and she didn't like it. *I'll address this after the space mission,* she decided.

"We have established a connection with Gaia," Spencer's baritone announced, although the Quark was nowhere to be seen.

"Excellent," Frank exclaimed. "Anything specific?"

"Not clear. It's a series of commands. Gaia is trying to take over our fleet."

"What? How's that possible?" Frank's eyebrows rose.

"We are requesting to dock," Spencer said.

"And?"

After a long pause, the Quark announced: "Gaia is not following our directives. Most likely, it's been hacked."

"Hacked? By whom?" It was Layla's turn to wonder. "I can assure you no one in this world wants to hack a bloody giant metal city floatin' hell knows where." Layla shook her head and blinked a few times. This was strange. "What's goin' on, Spencer?"

Suddenly, two spaceships detached from the fleet and flew toward the station, accelerating rapidly.

"Did you get permission to dock? Did you find out who seized Gaia?" Frank bumped his fists against each other.

"Negative. These two ships are under Gaia's control now."

"You got to be kidding me." Frank curved his lips. "Well, do something. I can't afford to lose two ships."

The next moment, multiple objects detached from the three remaining ships and flew toward the space station. It became difficult to breathe; something horrible was about to happen.

"Spencer, what are you doing?" Frank asked. "Do you want to blow up my space station?"

"It's a preventive missile strike. No significant damage is expected," Spencer said.

As the missiles approached the construction, the two ships under Gaia's control had already docked. Layla expected a blast of epic proportions and gathered herself up. However, nothing of the sort happened. The station responded by launching a counter-strike, and all the missiles were destroyed without reaching their targets.

"What the fuck was that?" Frank clenched his fists. "We can't make our own station obey?"

"No, sir," Spencer responded. "And it's attacking our systems and our ships. It's very powerful."

"This is nuts." Frank shook his head. "An ancient space station more powerful than Quasaris? How?"

"Not clear."

At this moment, Gaia launched more missiles at the remaining three ships. As the objects approached, the fleet triggered active defense and answered with a counter-fire like the station had done a moment ago. Only this time, the incoming projectiles easily evaded the defensive strikes, getting closer to the Quasaris's vessels. The counter-missiles flew further into deep space.

"You morons!" Frank exclaimed, clenching his fist. "What's going on?"

As the incoming missiles hit the spaceships, the view in front of Layla erupted in a conflagration. She instinctively pulled back and closed her eyes, so violent the explosion was, even as the light flashes were filtered and subdued. She briefly wondered where the sound was, but then realized it didn't travel in a vacuum. When she opened her eyes, the three-dimensional panorama was no more, sensors gone alongside the space fleet.

"All the remaining ships are destroyed," Spencer said.

"Can you give me answers?" Frank roared, his face red.

"Negative. The data needs to be analyzed. The encounter was unexpected."

"Well, expect it next time!" Frank roared. "You are supposed to be the most powerful Quark on the planet, and you let the broken space station defeat you? This is ridiculous!"

"We have a message," Spencer said.

"A message? From whom? What is it?"

"It says *I am Gaia, and I bring order. Humans must be erased.*"

Layla exchanged glances with Frank. This was an unexpected outcome. Erasing humans? Was Gaia responsible for the purple artifact in the sky? Hopefully, the spaceships acquired enough data to analyze. They needed to discover what it all meant, as the threat was real and present. She glanced once more at Frank's left wrist. Another problem they faced, as if everything else wasn't enough.

CHAPTER 27. KYLE

Kyle had left the camp immediately after he'd regained consciousness. He'd applied medicine to his swollen face, covered in bruises, the right side turning purple. It was his own purple cloud, Kyle decided, looking at his image in the mirror. He'd also lost two teeth, and his right eye couldn't see well.

He'd put his meager belongings into the backpack and darted off, nobody noticing him leaving because of the gathering and commotion in the middle of the camp. Kyle couldn't find Naomi's body in his bungalow, saw the funeral pyre outside, and understood the reason for the gathering. He didn't care anymore; he'd already forgotten Naomi. The purple cloud had killed her and would kill everyone else in that stupid place. It was all Varg's fault, as far as Kyle was concerned. Let the past be the past; he had no place there.

Damn you, Varg, and your stupid camp. You're not Humanists; you're a bunch of morons and Luddites. It was a mistake to come there. Kyle remembered how he'd joined the Humanists, a young and idealistic teen, charmed by the serene attitude of the hermit brotherhood and their utter rejection of everything digital. Kyle had believed that this was the only way, having witnessed the devastation and abandonment caused by Decon after the chaotic years of Deconvolution and the collapse of society. They had to fix the world, show people their mistakes, and return the man to his rightful path. If only life was that simple.

Kyle looked up, where the firmament was split in two by a vast purple crack stretching from horizon to horizon, partially blocking the sun. This was a recent development in the purple cloud's evolution. Kyle didn't like it a bit and shook his head. This reaffirmed his decision to leave the camp—the strange developments had to be addressed, and hiding the head in the sand was not a solution. Only Designers had the power to deal with problems at such a scale. He decided to come to a Designer Estate and offer his services. He knew there was one north of the camp. After all, he'd observed how the purple cloud had killed Naomi; this first-hand knowledge was worth something. He also decided to help Designers destroy the Humanist menace. Kyle recalled Varg and his moronic followers, stopped next to a large Live Oak, and kicked it as hard as he could. He imagined Varg in a tree's place before him and how he would kick Varg's stomach until the guy expired. This increased Kyle's confidence and strengthened his resolve to enlist Designers' help to destroy the camp.

At the end of the second day, he came to the boundary of the Designer Estate. Gigantic towers and the wall stretching between them enveloped in the force field were visible from a considerable distance, even from inside the forest. When Kyle approached the fortifications, a Quark descended in front of him.

"It's forbidden to move any further. You are trespassing on the Scalvini Estate," the Quark announced with a deep baritone.

"I'm not trespassing," Kyle said, his stomach suddenly heavy. "I came to offer my services to Ms. Scalvini. I have vital information about this abomination." He pointed up.

"And why do you think Ms. Scalvini requires your services?" The Quark floated before Kyle, the motors or propellers not visible, and Kyle wondered how the machine could hover in the air. He knew the Quark could annihilate him on the spot. Torn between the desire to run away and the realization he had nowhere to hide, Kyle froze in place.

"I know how the crack in the sky came to be. I also know how the Humanists defend their camp and farms. I can help Ms. Scalvini to take possession of their valuables and subdue these people. That thing in the sky could be a powerful tool for Ms. Scalvini. Can I talk to her, please?" Kyle's voice trembled, but he could finish his petition and was proud of himself.

"Wait," the Quark announced.

Kyle stood, unable to move, hoping his plea was well received. After a few long minutes, the Quark raised the gadget on the side of his elliptical body. Kyle's heart sank. *This is the end of my life. The machine received an execution order. This is all because of this idiot Varg. I hope the cloud kills him!*

Kyle closed his eyes, shivering, expecting to be annihilated. The shot never came. Instead, the Quark projected a beam of light into the open space left of Kyle, and there appeared a holographic representation of a strange and, somehow, seductive creature. The beautiful woman stood before him, clad in a golden dress and tiara, golden sandals on her feet. She had three breasts and four arms, each decorated with bracelets made of precious metals and twisted into bizarre shapes.

The woman raised one hand and pointed a finger at Kyle. "Is this the mortal who wishes to be my servant?" she asked. Her voice reverberated, as if multiple people talked simultaneously.

"Yes, Ms. Scalvini." Kyle dropped to one knee and looked down.

"Your plea is accepted. You may worship me," the woman proclaimed, raising her arms. "From now on, you shall refer to me as Absolute, for I am your only master and the reason for this world's existence."

"Yes, Absolute," Kyle mumbled.

"You shall direct my Quarks to the camp. These insolent people shall accept my divinity and obey me, for I am Absolute, the only power in this world worth obeying."

"Is this your creation, o Absolute?" Kyle asked, pointing at the splitting skies.

"My ways are incomprehensible to you, mortal," she said, and Kyle decided this was affirmative. "My Quark will escort you to join my other servants so you can worship me properly."

"Of course, Absolute." Kyle prostrated himself on the ground. "What do you require?" he asked, not daring to look at his new master, speaking into the dirt.

"In time, you'll learn. I exist beyond time and space and am present in every corner of this world and every thought of every creature that has ever populated this sorry rock. I am Absolute, the principal reason for everything. Rejoice, mortal, for you are one of the few chosen servants who had the privilege of hearing my words directly. You shall be rewarded, for this is my divine wish."

***

When Kyle regained consciousness, he couldn't remember who he was and what had happened. The overwhelming desire to serve his master and establish the rule of Absolute over all the worlds and beings consumed his essence, absorbed his will, and pushed his mind to the limit. If he ever had a mind of his own, that is.

Kyle lay on a table, not feeling his body. He couldn't move his head; he could only look up, where the dim blue light illuminated the gray ceiling. Nothing else was in his field of view, just the endless blue light enveloping him. Kyle couldn't smell or hear anything either. In fact, he sensed absolutely nothing, and it was glorious.

Suddenly, he remembered his name: Kyle. Then, the encounter with Absolute popped up in his mind. He came from a disgusting place, the camp of the Humanists, and he provided Absolute with the details to capture this place. Why Absolute, being omniscient, needed these details, Kyle didn't know. The paths of the deity were incomprehensible to a mere mortal like him. He only wanted that place to be destroyed alongside its moronic leader, Varg. Joy overfilled Kyle: encountering Absolute was the best thing that could have ever happened to him or any other being, whether conscious or unconscious, on any plane of existence, in any Decon world. But what was Decon? He couldn't quite recall, but he knew it contained infinite universes, all created by his master, Absolute. The master who created him, Kyle, also, with the reason to spread the rule of the only true deity, to restore the only truth that mattered—Absolute, the omnipresent, the omnipotent, the one who proclaimed its will through its servants. Kyle was ecstatic to count himself among those fortunate.

"Time to wake up," a disembodied voice announced.

Kyle's field of view shifted, bringing a more subtle picture of the surroundings. Patches of different colors were far from him, but the image was still fuzzy. Some unfamiliar smells appeared as well.

"Where am I?" he tried to ask, but his tongue didn't obey him.

The view got sharper, and Kyle detected a green ball floating before him, emanating a plethora of strange aromas. The ball moved closer, filling the entire picture for a moment. Then, a gentle blow landed somewhere in the middle of his core.

"Speak," the voice said.

With trepidation, Kyle realized this was not normal speech. There were no sounds, yet he understood the meaning. He made another fruitless attempt to utter a sentence.

"Relax. Speak with your mind," the voice, or rather, a sequence of thoughts, indicated.

"Where am I?" Kyle spoke mentally.

"This is better. Heed my message. You received the highest reward of being transformed. You are the chosen one."

"What does it mean?"

"Absolute spoke to you, and you obeyed. You are transformed. This is all that matters."

"Transformed into what?"

"This moment is special. You will forget your previous existence soon. You are one of us now."

"Who are you?"

"The chosen ones. The Bioid Cluster. We serve. We grow. We multiply. We fill the world."

"It's confusing," Kyle confessed.

"Of course. Such is the nature of the transformation. Let it be. Focus on Absolute. This is your guiding light. It will all be clear soon."

Kyle's vision sharpened, and the fresh smells of ammonia and alcohol became overpowering. The barrage of perceptions was unfamiliar, overwhelming, and confusing. He saw all around himself, with a three-sixty-degree view, and somehow it was fine. As more and more details became clear, an amorphous greenish ball covered in a revolting mess of tentacles, folds, and spikes arose before him. Kyle's instinct was to pull off and run away, but admiration and reverence replaced it. A moment later, Kyle discovered he could look inward and observe himself as if from the outside. With fleeting disgust, he realized his body had turned into a similar shapeless greenish mass, wrapped in protrusions, coated by a sticky, putrid substance protecting a variety of sensors and connectors he now possessed.

Kyle remembered he used to be human, but didn't know what it meant anymore. The new sensations were clear and strong; his purpose was to serve Absolute, grow, and multiply. He was now part of a new species, a new race to whom the future belonged: the Bioid Cluster. The aggregate with the knowledge of Absolute, with the abilities the unfortunate humans had never possessed.

"The nature of the transformation," the voice in his head pronounced, "is to be one with Absolute. This is the first and the primary tenet."

"Are there more?" Kyle asked.

"To achieve it," the message continued, "human nature is insufficient. You must transcend it. To rise to the new plane of existence: digital." The greenish substance moved, morphing into various shapes and extending its tentacles. Patches of different colors danced on its spiky protrusions. "You are a hybrid, a member of the Bioid Cluster, inheriting the best of both constructs: the vitality of biological organisms and the permanence of digital systems based on pure information. Welcome to the future."

CHAPTER 28. VARG

Varg exhaled, stood from the log in front of his bungalow, and raised his eyes to the sky, where the purple band grew to about twice its original size and now completely covered the sun, which sent its rays as if from underneath the eerie blanket of unknown celestial substance.

Varg shook his head and went toward the imposing structures of the farms, the source of the Humanists' wealth and pride. As he approached the buildings, a tall, muscular guy greeted him. Varg looked at the lad and had to shift his gaze away.

"Good to see you, Ramon," Varg said, looking to the side. He didn't know what to say to the man who was his daughter's close friend—perhaps, more than a friend. Varg felt the guilt, shame and physical burden of responsibility on his shoulders—the responsibility of a father and an elder, the duty he couldn't fulfill. Now his daughter was gone, and Ramon's heart was broken.

"Any news?" Ramon asked.

"No." Varg shook his head. "You can punch me."

"Stop this self-shaming." Ramon spat. "This wasn't your fault. She'll find her way. We need you to be strong, a leader, not a whining sob."

"It happened on my watch," Varg said. "The cloud, Naomi's death. And now Selena is gone. I'm stepping down. I'll announce this at the council tomorrow."

"Pick yourself up, old man!" Ramon grabbed Varg's shoulders and violently shook him. "Be the leader we all know and swore to follow. If anyone can lead us through this mess, it's you."

"No, Ramon." Varg stepped back. "I failed my daughter, and I failed you. I'm unable to lead the Community anymore. I have to step down."

"Look, what's happening?" Ramon pointed to the tree line in the West, where the purple band met the horizon. As in some bizarre cartoon, a cloud of flying Quarks approached the camp in a triangular formation.

"Did they show up from within the crack?" Varg asked.

"I don't know. I just noticed them."

As the Quarks neared the camp, people chatted, pointing to the sky.

"Come with me," Varg told Ramon. "I don't like this." His heart raced in his chest. The Community suffered an endless sequence of calamities.

They ran toward the chain of towers at the camp's periphery: the defense mechanism. The structure used the same organic materials as the camp. Still, the towers also possessed strong EM field generators, sensor arrays, and various weapons the Community traded for with Designers.

"Identify yourself; what's your purpose?" Varg yelled in the communicator as he and Ramon rushed inside the central defense tower. The device broadcasted his message on all available frequencies to the approaching fleet. It was impossible to miss.

The Quarks ignored the request and approached the camp, reaching the striking distance.

"Any closer, and you'll be destroyed," Varg announced and looked at the image of the western periphery of the camp, where the Quarks clouded the sky, an ominous purple band behind them. He wanted to believe his threat, but his mind was frantically searching for options.

Varg couldn't figure out what else they could do and raised his hand, ready to engage the defense forces. At this moment, the Quarks attacked, sending a wall of fire from above, burning the forest and everything underneath them, approaching the defense towers.

"Return fire!" Varg screamed, and the defense batteries responded. The first wave of Quarks was downed in no time; the machines blasted off from the air, their burning remnants falling on the trees and the vegetation below. But a sheer multitude of the assaulting units overwhelmed the defense batteries, and the enemy didn't seem to care about the losses. Swarm after swarm, the Quarks attacked the batteries, suppressing the defense. One squad took the fire and damage, while several more behind destroyed the defenses.

"Who is that? Where the hell did they come from?" Varg couldn't believe his eyes. The balance had existed for decades; all the participants of the local order respected each other. There was no reason for such an unprovoked attack.

"This isn't good; another group is coming from the East." Ramon extended his hand in that direction.

In a few minutes, the defense forces were annihilated. They destroyed many Quarks, but fresh units overwhelmed the Humanist forces, breaking the defenses.

"Run!" Varg shouted, escaping the burning tower, Ramon following his lead. There was nothing else they could do: the attack was unexpected and fierce. Varg blamed himself as they zigzagged through the bushes. He should have contacted the Designers, perhaps the Wise Estate, their leading trading partner. But what if the attack came from there? Or from another Designer Estate, such as Scalvini, which was nearby? Anyway, Felix's Quarks couldn't have arrived on such short notice. Whoever it was, they knew what they were doing, and the Community was doomed.

The destruction was total and irreversible. Varg looked back at the noble high-rise framework of vertical farms under continuous fire and barrage of projectiles falling from the sky. As one building collapsed, Varg turned his head away. He couldn't watch it. Everything he had worked so hard to build was destroyed—the island of stability for humanity obsessed with Decon and its digital servants was gone. There was no hope in sight, no deliverance, and no savior. Varg looked at the young man crouching next to him in the underbrush. Varg didn't care about himself anymore, but when he imagined the younger generation, whose future was now destroyed, it became difficult to breathe. They were doomed to exist in no better condition than wild beasts, hunted by the Quarks, and used as a bio-material for the Designers to upgrade their bodies. And Selena...where was she now? At least, she wasn't with him to witness and suffer this onslaught. She deserved a better fate, and he would do anything to help her while he was still alive.

"Come. There's nothing left." Varg touched Ramon's shoulder. The lad watched the camp turning into a massive fire, filled with the screams and shouts of the Humanists.

"How...who would do such a thing?" Ramon said, not looking at Varg, tears in his eyes.

"We'll find out. The bastards will pay," Varg said.

"But why?" Ramon's body shook.

"Come. We need to find Selena. And then we'll come back and kick their butts. I promise."

"Didn't you want to retire?" Ramon asked, trying to smile.

"I changed my mind." Varg grinned. "I've found a new motivation."

He gave his companion a hand to get out of the thickets. Whoever the attackers were, he had to find a way to punish them. His path didn't have to end here in sorrow and tears, and the story of the Humanists had to continue. As long as he was alive, he would keep fighting. This was a struggle for the future of his family, Community, and the whole human race. He couldn't let his people down.

***

"What do you see in Selena?" Varg asked as they moved through thick vegetation, tall pine trees blocking the view of the splitting skies. The crack kept growing, and Varg wondered what would happen when it covered the entire sky. Varg imagined the sun would fall through this crack and disappear, while eternal night, caused by the ominous purple gradually changing to black, would engulf humanity, proclaiming the end of days, the disappearance of humans, and any other conscious experience from the face of the universe.

"Something unique," Ramon answered, cutting the tree branch on their path with the reinforced mica knife he carried in his coverall pocket as they'd fled the Quark onslaught. "She sees things nobody else can. Her Vistas show me life in different, alien dimensions. I don't think she is of this world. Excuse me for talking so straight with you."

"No, you're fine. She's my daughter, but I struggle to understand her. She's growing more distant. What did you say—out of this world?" Varg panted heavily and touched his abdomen wound, calming it down as they reached the top of the hill, emerging from the thick forest.

"I don't know how to express it." Ramon was a lot younger, but the climb was also difficult for him; he was sweating profusely and breathing like a giant bear, which had invaded the southern regions from the West. "But I think I love her; I want to be with her; she makes me complete."

"Good to hear," Varg said, panting. "When we find Selena, I expect you to protect her." He wiped off the sweat from his brow. "You will succeed where I failed. I'm too old for this shit; I don't understand you youngsters."

"Are you okay? Your wound troubling you again?" Ramon pointed to Varg's stomach.

"I'm fine. Don't want to talk about it. Don't worry about me, worry about Selena."

"Of course." Ramon smiled and patted Varg on the shoulder. "I will."

"Good. I'll come after you if you won't."

"I'm sure you will." Ramon nodded. "But we need you right now. Do you think you can persuade Felix to help us?"

"I have a few things he should be interested in. We have a good relationship. He needs fresh food and bio-material; we could still help with that. He doesn't need an aggressive neighbor ready to attack, whoever it is."

"Unless it was him." Ramon grinned.

"I doubt it." Varg shook his head. "He had many opportunities in the past, much more suitable. He has nothing to gain and everything to lose. His Quarks can't run our farms or grow bio-material. Why change the status quo?"

"Then who was it?"

"Maybe some Designer is going insane; how would I know?" Varg shrugged again as they descended into the Wise Estate's valley. "I've heard rumors about weird shit happening at the Scalvini Estate; that Angelika Scalvini is mad. Could've been her. We'll find out, and I'll take immense pleasure in cutting the bastards into many small, bloody, and disgusting fragments."

"Let's hope you're right."

"Hope has nothing to do with this, young man." Varg grinned. "Just a lot of grit, sweat, tears, and effort. If you stay with me, you'll learn. We'll do it together."

"Whatever you say. But you give me hope."

"You are a stupid moron." Varg spat and shook his head. "You youngsters...I don't pretend I get it 'cause I don't. You'll have to build your own world, and it should be better than this sad piece of crap. You and Selena...you have the potential, the power, the will. You can make it happen, Ramon. Do you understand?"

"I think I do," Ramon said, looking up. "First, we need to reclaim the camp, then we'll fix the sky, and then we'll rebuild the world." He smiled. "This was the longest conversation I had with you...ever."

"Your damn influence," Varg grumbled. "What do you see in Selena's Vistas? You understand it's the same digital crap we revolted against?"

"Yes and no. It uses a digital interface; this is true, but it's powered by fungi. In addition, the content is not created by Quarks but by Selena, interpreted by the mushrooms. I believe this is something new, something different. And hey, you built it yourself. Do you see what I mean?" Ramon scratched his head.

"I did build it, and I still wonder why." Varg stroked his beard. "Should've destroyed it a long time ago...the fungi, you said? It's just a tool, a mechanism to manage the information." Varg made a dismissive gesture. "She imagines things; she thinks differently, yes. But this is all because she's blind; she lacks normal sensations. To replace that, she developed a horrific symbiotic relationship with the digital monster, that's all."

"I respectfully disagree." Ramon extended his hand to help Varg navigate a complex descent via a heap of boulders on their way. "Try to be more open, and you'll see."

"Last time I tried," Varg jumped through several boulders, ignoring Ramon's hand, "this magical device showed me a horror picture and told me I have a choice to kill a man or lose my daughter. Thank you very much; I'm done with this crap."

"If you want to understand your daughter, open to her world. To feel what she feels, to appreciate what she creates. You don't think she's a harbinger of death as she pronounced, do you?"

"No, I don't," Varg said, clenching his teeth. "We're almost there; I see Felix's Quarks coming to greet us. Prepare to plead our case; your life might depend on it."

CHAPTER 29. SELENA

The TransPod leaned right and made an arc in the cloudless sky, shifting the purple crack to the left of them. The cloud's ominous presence weighed on Selena non-stop, filling her mind, even when asleep, as if it were part of her essence. A newly developed non-physical tumor growing inside and outside her, a defect in reality and in her mind, a hole she was supposed to fix. If only she knew how.

"You are entering a private space; identify yourself," a pleasant female voice announced through the Intercom.

"My name is James Stewart Steel, and I have a business with Mr. Wise," Jim responded. "Mr. Frank Wise," he corrected himself.

"A lot of entities have business with Mr. Wise. Why do you think he'll want to see you?" The same pleasant voice continued the interrogation through the Intercom as Kali growled behind. Selena had built a strong connection with Jim's companion, a loyal and loving creature. Kali was on high alert, troubled by the journey, responding to the tension inside the flying capsule. Selena turned and petted the dog, touching Kali's silky fur, whispering to calm the dog down.

"Tell him I was the boy who visited him with Detectives Parker and Lewis. He'd understand," Jim said, smiling.

"One moment," the voice in the Intercom responded and disconnected.

"I still don't get the story behind this time travel crap," Selena said. "People use Decon to travel to the worlds they create in their minds. Was this something similar? Are you telling me we are in his Decon?" She jumped from one idea to another, lost in the train of thought. Her world was small, predictable, and safe just a few weeks ago. The only outlet was her Vistas. Still, she'd always considered it an art, a way to escape into her imagination without bending reality or punching holes in space-time. Decon was forbidden, and Varg had always encouraged people to value their lives, the only ones they had. Now, her world had been turned upside down as she'd learned the purple cloud was a defect, a hole in reality, and she was the key to repairing it. White Buffalo? Whatever, it made no sense. She would rather believe it was *her* Decon, as the purple cloud was part of her and responded to her emotions.

Selena touched Jim's hand, calmed down, and decided it would all be okay. For the first time, she had a kindred soul beside her who could share her experiences and understand her world. And not just understand—Jim was part of this world. Selena was sure they could conquer whatever they faced as long as they were together. *The three of them,* she corrected her thought, hearing Kali's growl.

"Frank's time travel is not related to Decon," Jim said, shaking his head. "When this happened, it was not even on the horizon. I don't pretend to understand how it works, but it's totally different."

"Horizon..." Selena murmured, thinking about the splitting skies. "Do you think his time travel caused the defect? He did come through some hole in space-time, didn't he?"

"It could have. And yes, it fits. But then it has nothing to do with Decon, and I know it must."

"I see. We are not getting any closer to the truth." She sighed.

"Permission to land granted," the female voice announced. "Mr. Wise is expecting you."

"This will be interesting," Jim muttered, setting the TransPod into a descending trajectory.

When they landed and Jim opened the door, two people approached to meet them.

"Is this Frank Wise?" Selena whispered to Jim, holding his hand.

"No. I don't know who they are."

"Welcome to the Wise Estate," a male voice announced, loud and somewhat cocky. "Mr. Wise will join us shortly."

"Who are you?" Jim asked.

"None of your business, buddy," the man responded, and Kali reacted with a growl.

"Calm down, it's okay." Selena touched Kali's back. The dog's hair was up as Kali was ready to recoil and unload her fury at Jim's enemies.

"C'mon, Paul, be nice to the visitors," the female voice entered the conversation. "My name is Layla, and this is Paul. We are associates of

Mr. Wise. He asked us to greet you while he finishes other business."

"Just like fifty years ago," Jim said. "He doesn't change, does he?"

"This is between you and him, buddy," Paul said. "The dog is not welcome here, and who's the blind girl?"

"Dog's name is Kali, and she always travels with me," Jim said. "And why the blind girl is here is none of your business...buddy?"

Paul made a few steps forward, approaching the guests. His bad breath extended into their space.

"You see the crack in the sky?" Jim pointed up.

"Yeah, so what?"

"The blind girl made it happen. And she can unleash it on you. Now, please excuse us." Jim stepped forward.

"I suggest everyone calm down," Layla said. "Nobody is unleashin' anything on anyone. We both work for Mr. Wise, and you have a business with him, so why don't we all wait for him and be cool?"

"Sounds good," Jim said. "Just tell your partner to behave."

"He will, I promise. Where did you come from?"

"From the past and out of time. A long-forgotten past for me, but recent for Mr. Wise, I imagine."

"Very recent, indeed," a loud voice announced. The newcomer's energy was overpowering, and his aura enveloped everyone. Selena rubbed her palms and stepped forward. "Frank Wise," the man introduced himself, shaking Jim's and Selena's hands. "How did you know?" he asked Jim.

"I was there. I'm a student who visited Quasaris with Detectives Parker and Lewis. It happened fifty years ago," Jim said. "You haven't changed, Mr. Wise." He squinted.

"Indeed. There's much to discuss. You're probably the only one who can appreciate my story. Why are you here?"

"Yes, there's much to discuss," Jim said. "Fifty years ago, we were enemies, but now we are on the same side. The side of humanity."

"What do you mean?"

"This nuisance in the sky is a defect in reality, destroying our world, and Decon has something to do with it."

"I see. Who's the girl?"

"Selena is the key. She is connected to the defect." Jim took her hand. "And we need your help to figure out what to do. If it's not too late already."

CHAPTER 30. FRANK

Frank gazed at his two visitors, trying to assess hidden agendas and intentions and guess what they were not saying. The older man's face was relaxed, with a fleeting smile and slightly squinted eyes. Frank couldn't see anything behind this mask—if it was a mask. On the other hand... the girl was a torrent of emotions and energy, chaos impersonated, lurking under her bluish skin and the veil covering her pupils. Her appearance gave him shivers and the unexplainable desire to pull back, turn around, and run. There was something eerie about her, something alien. Jim said she was the key to fixing the hole in space-time. Perhaps she was the original creator of this hole, and who knew what her ultimate intentions were? Frank was still looking for his place in this bizarre and alien world where the blind girl could split the skies and the rogue space station destroy his fleet. He desperately needed Ichika to be on his side, see her smile, touch her delicate skin, and hear her encouragement. Frank needed someone he could rely on. He didn't trust Paul a bit. The man understood only money, but perhaps Layla could be that person.... However, for a moment, he was alone, didn't belong, and didn't know what to do.

They sat in his office at the Wise Estate, behind the round table, occupying smart chairs similar to those Frank remembered from his time. He turned off the music and enjoyed the silence, preparing his mind for a tough conversation. Other tech surrounded them, and although Frank had sent away all the Quarks, he knew every moment and minute detail of the conversation was registered and analyzed. He also had sent Paul and Layla away: this business was between him and the boy (or the old man, Frank was confused), and he didn't need to involve more witnesses. Not yet.

"You're saying this is all because of Decon?" Frank pointed up, looking straight at Jim. "I'm not a fan; this idiotic invention is destroying humanity, but your allegations are pretty radical, don't you think?"

"These are not allegations, Mr. Wise." Jim smiled, but the corners of his mouth went down. "This is a grim reality you can see for yourself. I don't know the nature of the connection, but there is a connection."

"And how do you know? Your visions?" Frank grinned.

"Our shared visions," Selena said in a monotone voice. "I can feel the crack grow as the darkness devours our world—all our worlds, no matter what you think about Decon. The chaos is back to reclaim what we took from it."

Frank didn't know what to think about her. Was she insane? A mad, blind prophet of doom? It was easy to assume this and brush away the warnings as insanity. But things were more complex: Jim corroborated the story, they had no solution, and they came looking for help. A much worse scenario was that somehow she had caused all of this, having sinister intentions of her own, and fooled Jim into believing her. Then, Frank's own jump through time was a vivid illustration they didn't understand the nature of reality. What if this time journey had caused the rift? It was possible. The data from the spaceships' ill-fated voyage to Gaia was worth nothing. No anomalies, nothing at all. But they could all see the crack. Were they insane? Or was it happening in a weird Decon world? And Decon...was it a hallucinogenic drug, a pathway for the mind to collapse in its own inner world, or did it indeed provide access to the multiverse? Damn questions...even as the most powerful Designer, Frank didn't know what to do and what actions to take. However, he couldn't let this metaphysical nonsense distract him from what mattered the most. First, he had to reclaim space, starting from the crazy station on Earth's orbit. Second, he needed to get people off Decon. And third, somehow patch the splitting skies.

"Can you fix the hole?" Frank asked, shifting his gaze to Selena. "What do you both mean by the space-time defect? What devours what? Can you be more specific?"

"Selena is linked to the defect. She can even manipulate it subconsciously, although we still don't know how," Jim answered. "As for the defect, I have no idea."

"I can fix it," Selena said. She stood up and approached Frank. "I can pull on it. At first, I didn't understand the connection and didn't know what to do. Now I know it feeds off my emotions, and I try to stay calm. Reaching to it is quite devastating." She approached Frank and touched the lump of the fingers on his left hand, sniffing the air. "The fungi showed me the defect in Decon. And you have your own defect, Frank. It's devouring you."

"This?" Frank pulled his hand back and looked at the knot his palm had become. "This is a time traveler's gift. Some kind of defect, yes."

"I am not talking about that," Selena said, running her fingers up his arm, touching his swelled wrist and the skin above it through the suit's material. "I'm talking about the defect inside of you. It transforms you, Frank. Do you feel it? Are you less human? Is this because of Decon?"

"Stop it, please," Frank said. His left arm suddenly warmed up, as if something was boiling under the skin. "Yes, my arm is troubling me, but I think this is another time traveler's wound. I assure you it has nothing to do with Decon, as I never used it."

"What if Decon worlds can penetrate our own? What if the tear in the sky is a result of that? And your transformation, too?" Selena stepped back. "You traveled through time, Frank. What if that caused the crack?"

"Wait, wasn't this what Dr. Ito tried to accomplish?" Jim asked.

The mention of Ichika's name hit Frank like a lightning bolt. "Don't you dare mention her name, boy!" Frank jumped off his chair. He had to suppress a sudden desire to punch Jim in the face. "You caused her death. She tried to change the world and make us the masters of the stars, but you people were too small to understand her vision." He walked around the table, calming himself down. "Ichika didn't want to create a hole in space-time," he whispered. "She wanted to manipulate time, so you'd leave us alone."

"And what was the result?" Jim asked.

"We should've finished what we started." Frank sat down, clenching his right fist. "The device malfunctioned because she didn't have enough time to fine-tune. If we caused all this," he looked up, "it's because we were rushed. What if *you* caused it?" He turned to Selena. "You said you can pull it in? What does this mean?"

"This conversation leads us nowhere," Selena said. "We don't know what happened and why. The only hint we have is the dreams Jim and I share and my connection to the defect."

"What do you suggest?" Frank needed to focus on something he could grasp and explore practical options.

"I need access to your Decon. Jim helped me connect to it via meditation; I'm not sure it'll work again. Perhaps I'll need the neck interface." She scratched the back of her head. "I'll also need my fungal computer. And I need all the help your Quarks could provide. Deal?"

"And what do you intend to do?"

"To patch the skies, of course. Just like you asked."

"I hope you know what you're doing, but I see no harm in letting you try. It's already screwed the way it is." Frank tried to connect his fingers in a steeple in front of his chest, which didn't work as the knot on the left hand refused to obey. "Shit!" he exclaimed, shaking his palms. "Go ahead, Selena. Layla will assist; you've met her before. And after you're done, I swear I'll destroy all the existing Decons and all the factories making them."

"That's an excellent idea." Jim nodded.

"Of course it is. In the meantime, please excuse me; I have more pressing needs."

"More pressing?" Jim's eyebrows rose.

"A rogue space station that refuses to obey my orders. Not sure what the deal is, but I don't like that." Frank grinned. "Looks like we have to reconquer deep space by whipping our own tool into submission." He stood and showed his guests the exit. "But I have the will and the means. I can build a new one. Let the heavens burn!"

CHAPTER 31. MAX

Max wiped the sweat off his forehead and inhaled deeply. The image of the four-armed creature was before his eyes, within the glares of the bright blue light that had blinded him for a moment. He looked up and studied the growing crack in the sky, imagining Angelika spreading it with her massive limbs, tearing their world apart.

Max had started abusing Decon since the team had moved to the Wise Estate, following Layla and Paul. As there was nothing yet to do for a superb fighter like him during the planning phase of their mission, whatever the mission was, he was left to his thoughts and devices. And what he'd discovered was nothing short of breathtaking. The purple crack somehow stained every life he had, every world, and every experience. It took different shapes and forms: a hole, a whirlwind, or a newly formed range of mountains. However, the color was always purple, and every one of his lives was entangled with this new feature. He had to get to the bottom, discover the causes, and unveil the truth. And he knew Angelika was related to it. Perhaps she was the creator of the defect, the morbid demon bent on destroying all the worlds.

"Max, what is it?" Beatriz asked, and her voice returned him to reality. He looked at her, losing himself in the abyss of her dark eyes, inhaling her smell, which reminded him of wildflowers.

"Ah, what? Nothing, just thinking."

"How frequently do you use Decon?" She grabbed his hand. "Don't you think it might be too much?"

"Don't worry, I'm fine."

"So, how often?" Beatriz insisted.

"Every moment I can." He shrugged. "There's nothing else to do here." Max looked around the slick lounge Frank Wise allocated to them: the room was equipped with many digital tools and interfaces and had all the best gadgets and devices for Yuki and Reto to study the Cymoebas. Large windows opened a beautiful view of the Mediterranean garden, while a transparent ceiling projected a cerulean sky with the sun's rays warming up the surroundings. Only the sun's disk was not visible, covered by the hideous purple ribbon stretching from horizon to horizon.

"You used to exercise a lot more and learn new techniques," Beatriz said.

"I'm fine. Top form. I need to study Decon."

"What for?"

"The crack. It's everywhere. And it's breaking me, as well."

"I feel nothing." Beatriz shrugged and touched his hand. "How can I help you?"

"You're lovely, Beatriz." Max placed his other hand on top of hers. "I don't know if you can help me. Ever heard about joint Decon experiences?"

"You know it doesn't work like that." She shook her head. "But why Decon? You can study this one." Beatriz looked up.

"I can. But I'm sure the roots are somewhere else. I must find the origin. It's not here."

"Oh, but why is it not here? This is where Decon is made, after all."

"It's a hunch; nobody knows how Decon worlds are connected. And I've been to other worlds where Decon is made." He smiled. "Thank you for being here for me, Beatriz. This means a lot."

"Well, of course, my dear." She smiled back. "You're my friend— maybe even more than a friend." Beatriz winked.

Max didn't respond to the suggestive comment and shifted his gaze, looking into the distance, beyond the forest in the north. "You know, I am a hunter in one of my lives. I travel the prairie alone, with only my horse keeping me company. I shoot deer with a bow and arrows; I have a sword; I roast my prey on the fire at night, looking at the myriad sparkling stars and space dust in the sky. I need nothing else; it's a simple and pure life where I am whole and, at the same time, part of nature, of the cosmos."

"This is beautiful."

"It was. Some time ago, a new range of purple mountains appeared in the West. Familiar?"

"No way." She gasped.

"This is a version of the crack. And the mountains are growing, becoming an impenetrable wall blocking the horizon and the sky. It's horrible."

"What's the significance?"

"The significance is that it's a source. I can get there. I can cross the mountain range to get to the other side. There, I'll find the answer."

"How can you be sure?"

"I can't, but it's the only practical thing. Here, I can't grow wings and fly through the crack."

"Why, you could use one of Frank's spaceships."

"He already tried that and failed, didn't he? The source is not here, I'm telling you."

"This could be dangerous, my dear." Beatriz hugged him. "Promise me you do nothing stupid."

"As much as I can." He stroked her black hair. "I don't know what is stupid in this crazy world anymore."

"True." Beatriz smiled. "What do you expect to find on the other side?"

"Her."

"What do you mean?" She pulled back, frowning.

"The monster. Angelika. This is her doing, and I must slay her to make it disappear."

"You're obsessed." Beatriz shook her head. "We can find and slay her here, can't we?"

"Perhaps. But I still need to find the source."

"Oh, Max, please do nothing rushed and stupid. We will plan it together, use Mr. Wise's tech, and kill her in this world, nice and easy, fixing everything else."

"It could be Plan B, I agree."

"Plan B?" Beatriz squinted. "This is the only real solution, my dear. Your Decon adventures are dangerous. Please, listen to me!"

"I like you, Beatriz. But this quest is mine and only mine. I know it now. I must do it alone; it's between me and her. Don't worry; I'll deal with it."

"Promise me you'll at least let me know when you're ready to act." Beatriz frowned.

"I don't know what, when, and where I need to do. It could be here, or it could be beyond the mountain range. What I know is I must strike and slay the monster. Then everything will be okay."

CHAPTER 32. YUKI

"Do you see what I see? Do they need a room?" Reto asked, grinning and nodding toward Max, who embraced Beatriz and caressed her hair.

"Give them a moment," Yuki said, focusing on the Cymoeba. She'd rather not discuss this topic.

"A moment? They need more than a moment." Reto grinned. "And it could lead to complications." He shook his head, crowned with a proud mohawk.

"It's okay, just leave them alone." Yuki looked at the giant figure of Max with the tiny Beatriz in his arms. *It's good Beatriz is watching over him; Max behaved erratically the past few days.* Yuki remembered his absent-minded looks, directed somewhere far away when she had tried to ask Max something important. If even she had noticed, it had to be bad.

Yuki lowered the digital interface over her right eye. The Cymoeba she studied defied all biological laws. Yuki aimed to identify a weak spot, a gap they could exploit to eliminate the threat the hybrid life form presented, but she couldn't find anything. Nano-Quarks self-assembled and multiplied; even a tiny quantity of this stuff could initiate rapid growth in any bio-material, transforming it to fit their stencil. There was no answer.

"I'm chill," Reto said. "As long as it doesn't put us in danger, they can do whatever they want. None of my business."

"Exactly," Yuki said. "Any luck?"

Reto's task was to determine how to destroy Cymoeba. The method didn't matter. They needed a solution, an answer to the disturbing development. So far, there was none.

"No damn luck." Reto spat. "This crap is indestructible."

"What do you mean?"

"Exactly what I said. I can't get rid of it. You can't burn it, you can't freeze it, and you can't acid it. It's a freaking zombie, I'm telling you. It comes back no matter what."

A thousand little needles squeezed and pierced Yuki's stomach. She knew the Cymoeba's nano-Quarks were of a new type, extremely small, working on a molecular level, transforming the chemistry of the host material. But being indestructible was something else.

"Be careful. We can't expose ourselves to this," Yuki said.

"Thank you, Captain Obvious. I am. I'm also out of ideas what else to try on this crap. Any thoughts?"

"No. I need to learn more."

"Shit." Reto spat again. "Are we screwed?"

"Possibly." The invisible fist squeezed her internal organs, her heart raced like a sprinter, and an angular object blocked her throat. Looking at the Cymoeba, she suppressed an urge to throw up.

"Wonderful," Reto said, reclining on his smart chair and closing his eyes.

"I ran tests to see how our normal nano-Quark immune defense would respond."

"And?"

"And nothing. Cymoebas ate it for lunch and multiplied."

"But the nano-immune system is supposed to fight back. What am I missing?" Reto raised his eyebrows.

"Supposed, but it's powerless against this tech. As you so eloquently summarized it, we're screwed."

Reto stood, took a deep breath, and turned to look outside through the floor-to-ceiling windows. The gap in the sky was right before them, providing yet another reminder this time they were in deep trouble. *The entire world is on the brink of collapse. And I'm powerless to do anything about it,* Yuki thought.

An invisible hand tortured her stomach. There was too much to process: the hole in the sky, the mad four-armed monster, and the indestructible Cymoebas. It took Yuki all her willpower not to run away from this hideous place, screaming at the top of her lungs, losing the last remnants of sanity. *Be calm,* Yuki told herself, inhaling and counting to ten. *I'll find a solution. I'm better than this.*

"Hey sister, are you okay?" Reto asked, squinting.

"What?" Yuki's body shook as she returned to her senses. "Ah, yes."

"What's on your mind?"

"Gloom and despair."

"Welcome to the club." Reto grinned. "I'm wondering if that bitch injected this crap into herself to become immortal."

"That wouldn't work; she'll transform and lose her identity."

"Should we grow one from a dead body? Just for fun? Then try to kill it?"

"Grow what?" Yuki couldn't figure out where he was going.

"The full-size zombie, of course." Reto smiled. "Blow it to smithereens."

"Not a good idea." Yuki shook her head.

"Or we could inject it into someone and see what happens." Reto snapped his fingers. "Paul! I never liked the slug, anyway."

"Wait..." Yuki disconnected the digital interface and closed her eyes. "Can you get me a mouse?"

"A mouse?" Reto winced. "What for? You want a zombie mouse?"

"To see how its immune system fights Cymoeba," Yuki said. "A mouse has something we don't: an active, aggressive, and natural immune system."

"Slow down, sister. I don't get it." Reto squinted.

"This is the only weapon we haven't tried yet." Yuki shrugged. "And it might be effective. The human immune system has depended on nano-technology for decades and can't resist Cymoebas. But what if the old ways of nature prevail?"

"Hm-m..." Reto shook his head. "Not sure I buy this."

"Got better ideas? Bring me a mouse." Yuki cracked her fingers and rubbed her palms, inhaling deeply, anticipating a new experiment. The gloom she experienced a few minutes ago was gone; her stomach was still, and she saw a clear goal. It was the only solid island in the sea of chaos, but she could work with that. Not everything was lost.

"Alright," Reto said, making a few steps toward the door. "Would a rat work? Or a squirrel?"

"Sure. Any animal, relatively small. We don't need a zombie horse."

"Got it." Reto grinned. "Hope it works."

"It will. Just give me some time. And more rats."

CHAPTER 33. PAUL

"Man, you look like shit," Paul said and clicked his tongue, shaking his head. Frank sat behind his large desk, the meta-surface of which was covered with glowing electronic menus and symbols, projecting what appeared to be the designs of the spaceships on both sides of him. An enormous three-dimensional projection of a space station was in the middle of the room, and Frank was rotating and zooming into its specific segments. Paul didn't understand his boss' obsession with the cosmos; to him, it was just a space devoid of any attractions and having no intrinsic value. It couldn't be used, bought, sold, or exchanged for something with profit. In other words, it was a useless and dangerous distraction.

"Yeah, it could use some cleaning," Frank agreed. He shook off dust and dirt from his antique suit and continued looking at the space station's image.

"I don't mean the suit, buddy. I mean you."

"Why?" Frank stopped rotating the image and shifted his gaze to Paul.

"Do you ever sleep?" Paul asked. How could the man spend all his time chasing this stupid dream? He understood some people needed a higher calling and sometimes thought about his purpose. Still, he saw nothing in the empty space surrounding Earth.

"I'll sleep when I'm dead." Frank smiled. "Too much crap is going on. What have you got?"

"It might happen faster than you think, buddy. You need to take care of yourself." Paul shook his head.

"Nah, I'm fine." Frank waved his right hand dismissively. The left one was hanging down like an inanimate rod. The lower part of his neck was green, covered with rough brown patches. "So, what's up?"

Paul looked at his boss. Even after working with Frank for a few weeks, he couldn't understand the man. Frank's vision was grand, his goals lofty, and he demanded superhuman efforts from everyone, including himself. Especially himself: the man was leading by example. Yet, some of his objectives, such as reviving space travel and uniting humanity, made no sense. What for? He was already the master of Decon, the most powerful Designer. What else did he need?

"Someone attacked and demolished the Humanist camp," Paul said. "I wonder if this is our charming neighbor, Madam Scalvini. That would suit her well."

Frank winced as if he suddenly experienced a toothache. "Another big pain in the ass," he said. "I'll get to her in time after I deal with Gaia."

"Felix was their protector," Paul said, stroking his beard. "We supply them with necessary machines and tools and get bio-material and fresh food in return. Now it's all destroyed."

Paul was convinced it was Angelika's doing. From what he'd seen and what Frank had told him, she was insane and dangerous, challenging the established status quo. In addition, she appeared to have a personal feud with Frank, with its roots buried deep in the time before Deconvolution. Was she that old? Hard to say; she didn't even look human. But Frank was challenging the existing order, too. His agenda to eliminate Decon and subdue all the Designers to work on his crazy objectives was reckless and insane. Angelika and Frank were thus pitched against each other, which meant war and destruction. This was terrible for Paul's business; he had to defuse the situation and make them co-exist.

"I'll rebuild it later," Frank said.

"If I may." Paul came closer. "I was the first to pledge my allegiance. I only care about your interests, Frank."

"You care about your own interests first. And you wanted to kill me. No bad feelings, I get it."

"Listen, we need the Humanists. And we need peace above all. War with Angelika serves no one."

Frank tilted his head. "Angelika claims Quasaris, and she thinks she's a god. She wants servitude, not peace."

"You should talk to her. Convince her to divide the territory, just like we had before. I'll go with you."

"I tried that, you know?" Frank chuckled. "She offered me to become her divine consort and rule the world together."

"See? She's not as mad as we thought." Paul liked where this was going. If Frank and Angelika combined forces, they could indeed rule the world, and he would become their most trusted servant and advisor. This meant immense power and as much Decon as he could bear.

"What?" Frank stepped back, looking at Paul as if he saw him for the first time. "You're joking, right?"

"I'm dead serious, buddy. We need peace: good for the business and the people." Frank's unexpected reaction took Paul aback.

Frank's eyes opened wide, and his lips curved as he exclaimed: "Peace? You call treating people as bio-material to serve her perverse desires peace? What's wrong with you?"

"Nothing, buddy. I'm a businessman, and I thought you were, too. Don't you see the profit?" Maybe Frank was testing him, pretending not to understand perfect logical arguments, seeing if his advisor would hesitate and budge.

"Profit?" Frank shook his head. "This is not profit; this is a feast on the ashes of the dying world. We need to fix it, not destroy it."

"Why do you care?" Paul shrugged. "You've got all the Decon, the highest quality; you can create any world you want."

"No, it's perverse. *This* is the only world we've got, the one and only. Your Decon is the reason we are in deep shit. We must destroy all of it."

"Destroy Decon? Are you out of your mind? It is the source of your power!" Now Paul was sure his boss was testing him. What Frank was saying made no sense. Perhaps the time jump had damaged his brain. That would explain things, including his obsession with the dead, empty space no one cared about.

"Yes, it ruined everything. I'm not sure I can rebuild the world, but I'll try." Frank clenched his right fist. "But first, I'll destroy all the Decon after Selena figures out how to fix the hole in the sky. She said she needed it. I don't know what for."

"This is another topic. Why do you trust these guys? They show up from nowhere, tell you a bunch of nonsense, and you give them your Decon."

"That thing," Frank pointed up, "troubles me. If they can fix it, let them try. I'm even prepared to bury the hatchet with Jim."

"Again, why do you care? Does it affect your business?"

"We'll never understand each other, I'm afraid." Frank shook his head.

"Oh, but we do," Paul said. If this was the test, he passed with flying colors. "I'll work on arranging a talk with Madam Scalvini. The world will get new masters." Paul snapped his fingers, happy with the development.

"Not now," Frank said. "I'll let you know when."

"What if she attacks you as she attacked the Humanists?"

"We'll be ready. And when I have my space fleet back, I'll evaporate her Estate from orbit in no time."

"Now you're talking, buddy. That's why I work for you."

"But first, Gaia."

"As you wish, boss."

CHAPTER 34. JIM

Selena sat in front of the fungal computer with a digital interface on her head and the freshly manufactured Decon connected to the socket at the back of her neck. Jim tried to convince Selena to use meditation to access Decon, but she would have none of that. She wanted to become a relay between the biological fungal mechanism and the digital quantum Decon. She fancied merging both perspectives inside of her, and this was the only way.

Jim watched Selena prepare for the journey, longing to join her again. Alas, it was impossible, as they only had a single fungal interface. Besides, Selena was determined to do it alone, convinced her connection with the fungi was special and unique. Jim wiped the sweat off his forehead and clenched his teeth. Potential scenarios of what could unfold ran through his head.

"I'm ready," Selena announced. She looked like an ancient statue, unmoving, an eerie part of the contraption she'd assembled around herself.

"Expand your mind and feel the Decon," Jim said. "This is an easy part."

Suddenly, the entrance to the room lit up, and the door rose into the ceiling. Jim turned around. Three people entered the room; one of them was Frank. He turned around and invited two Humanists to follow his lead. One of the newcomers was older, gray-haired, with a full beard adorning his face: Varg. The second Humanist was young and muscular, with long, curly black hair; Jim vaguely remembered him from his trip to the Humanist's camp. A Quark floated behind them, glowing green.

Selena sniffed the air, and her body trembled. She disconnected the Decon and threw away the fungal interface.

"Father," she whispered. "Ramon."

"Selena!" The older man exclaimed, rushing toward her. "You're alive!"

"Of course I am. Why did you come?"

"I wasn't looking for you." Varg shook his head. "You did use this abomination." He pointed to the Decon. "And disfigured yourself." He winced, came closer, and tried to touch her neck, but she moved away. "I'm a terrible father and a horrible leader. Even my daughter wouldn't listen to me."

"I told you what my plan was," Selena said. "This is the only way. You didn't answer my question."

"Something horrible happened," the younger man entered the conversation. "It's all gone. Destroyed. Dead."

"What are you talking about?" Selena asked.

"The Community was attacked. There were so many Quarks we couldn't repel them. It's all gone, and it happened on my watch." Varg closed his eyes and clenched his teeth.

"So, our departure changed nothing," Jim said, thinking about what had gone wrong. The attack made little sense. If they were facing a defect in space-time, a hole in the fabric of reality, and this was an existential problem Hagen had warned about, then who were the attackers? Were they somehow related to the defect? And why the Humanists? Were the invaders looking for Selena and him? Jim tried to make the pieces fit without success.

"There might be other survivors. Varg and I escaped, but so could others," the younger man added.

"Thank you for protecting Father, Ramon," Selena said. "What will you do now?"

"We came to seek help," Varg said. "Felix was a partner; we had solid trade links. Mr. Wise, we depend on you. Whoever attacked the Community is dangerous to everyone; they would attack *you* one day. We need to address this threat together."

"Interesting," Frank murmured. "A few moments ago, my advisor tried to persuade me to let it go and ally with a likely perpetrator, claiming this would make good business. What should I do?"

"Do you know who did it?" Varg clenched his fists and stepped forward. "Tell me. I'll find them and carve their organs out, I swear." His face was tight, his eyes half-closed, and his voice so tense Jim believed the threat.

"I might," Frank said. "But what's in it for me?"

"Do you want my help with the crack?" Selena asked. "If so, help

148

Father."

"Maybe, but it's not my priority." Frank walked around the room. His left arm hung down, and he had a glove on his hand while the collar of his jacket was up, covering his neck. Something was happening to Frank Wise. The effect of time travel?

"You need to fight this enemy, too. You need allies," Varg said.

"The two of you? Not so much, don't you think?"

"There are more survivors, I'm sure of that," Ramon said. "And don't discount our tools; we're not as powerless as you think."

"Oh, I don't doubt that." Frank stopped and crossed his hands behind his back. "I'm thinking, should I ally with you or your adversary, as my advisor suggested? What do you think, Spencer?" He turned to the Quark.

"We've just received new information, Mr. Wise," the Quark said. "The evidence gathered so far does not link the attackers to any Designer."

"What do you mean? It wasn't Angelika?" Frank frowned.

"The invading Quarks were re-configured, and their networks were inaccessible. We recovered a single message the attackers broadcasted."

"What is it?" Frank's lips were tense as metal springs, ready to recoil, and his squinted eyes pierced the Quark as if he was about to drill through it with his gaze. Everyone was silent and motionless. Goosebumps ran down Jim's spine.

"You are familiar with it. The message was: *I bring order. Humans must be erased.* It was Space Station Gaia."

"No way!" Frank bared his teeth and spat. "What the hell is going on? Who is behind all this?" He turned away from the Quark and walked toward Jim. "You see? I knew this damn space station was the highest priority, not your magical hole in reality and not the four-armed crazy woman. The space station, for fuck's sake!"

Jim shook his head. Space station attacking the Humanists? Why? Was it connected to Hagen's message? Was Gaia somehow affected by the tear in space-time? Or was it the cause of it? Lots of questions and no answers.

"Well, you should be happy now." Frank turned to Varg. "This makes us allies. Spencer," he turned to face the Quark, "looks like we have to fight both in space and on land. Prepare all forces."

"What about your neighbor?" Spencer asked.

"What about her?" Frank tried to rub his palms, but stopped as his left hand didn't obey him. "We have to make a truce, like Paul suggested. Her, I understand, at least. I'm ready to become a divine consort." He grinned. "Spencer, I want to know everything about Angelika Scalvini, every minute detail you could find." He turned to face Jim and Selena. "You two—figure out how to use the crack against Gaia. You said you could manipulate it? Now is a good time to try. I will blow this piece of junk from the sky and find whoever is behind this. Then, I'll—what did you say?" Frank looked at Varg.

"Carve their organs out," Varg said as if entranced.

"Carve their organs out, that's right," Frank repeated, grinning. "You don't mess with Frank Wise, not in the past, not in the future. Let the space war commence."

CHAPTER 35. ANGELIKA

Angelika stood in the middle of the enclosure, surrounded by mirrors from all sides, including top and bottom. She was naked, and a myriad of sensors scanned, measured, and assessed every inch of her body, outside and inside. The new enhancement was successfully added to her features, and she enjoyed looking in the mirror at the pair of black, razor-sharp horns pointing forward from her forehead. But that wasn't all—transparent triangular protrusions, forming a crest on top of her backbone, covered her spine.

Satisfied with what she saw, Angelika stuck out her trident-shaped tongue and hissed.

"Cesare, how do you find my new look?" she asked.

"The transformation achieved its aim," a deep baritone pronounced.

"I know, but that's not what I asked." She touched her horns with the two upper hands. "They are beautiful, aren't they? And functional."

"I cannot judge the concept of beauty," Cesare said. "Yes, they are functional—as are the spikes on your back. Contact with any biological form will embed Bioids into the organism and start the transformation."

"Good. I need many diverse ways to create new servants. Give me more, Cesare."

"The Bioid Cluster grows as planned. We are working non-stop to create more converts, and existing elements become stronger and more effective."

"Take away the mirrors and make me a holographic image," Angelika said. "I want to see it from the outside. I need the look to be scary, horrific, sucking away all the strength and the will to resist. The only way the goddess can present herself."

"I can procure more test subjects for you."

"Yes, do that. In the meantime, propose a few more improvements. I'm not sure I look as dreadful and creepy as behooves Absolute."

Angelika stepped out of the enclosure as the mirrors retracted into the floor. A holographic representation of herself, immersed in a purple light, appeared in the room's corner. Angelika made a gesture, and the figure rotated, presenting first the horns, then the spikes.

"No, definitely could be better." She shook her head. "Work on it, Cesare." Angelika turned around and sat on the cushion, crossing her legs and raising her two upper hands above the horns. "And yes, bring me more test subjects. I want to give it a try."

"Of course, Mistress." Cesare's voice filled the room as if he were floating in the air in the middle of it.

"Now, what about my servants? You said they are getting stronger?"

"Yes, the new tech performs as expected. The ability of the Bioids to change the DNA and the bio-chemical processes is exceptional. Your new servants are ubiquitous and indestructible. Soon, no one will be left but the Cluster, ready to serve you."

"Can *you* be converted?" Angelika hissed and shook her head. "No, actually, you are more useful to me the way you are. But I still remember how I was fooled—because of you."

"That was a glitch. It won't happen again," Cesare said. "And no, I cannot be converted; I am not a biological organism; I don't have DNA. You can erase my memory and replace my firmware with a new one."

"Not yet." Angelika laid back as her spikes retracted. "You think Bioids would make good lovers?"

"I can't judge that, Mistress. However, analyzing the data and your preferences, the answer is negative. They are not built for what you want. Instead, we can acquire more test subjects and keep making specific types you enjoyed in the past."

"You're boring, Cesare." Angelika winced. "As a god, I can enjoy whatever I decide to enjoy. Let Absolute reign supreme. But okay, make me more lovers. The batch before the last one was good. Just make them more resilient this time; they expire too quickly."

"Yes, Mistress."

"Any news about my adorable neighbor?"

"Mr. Wise recently engaged in launching spaceships."

"He's such an idiot." Angelika laughed. "But he's got balls; that can't be denied. And I want to possess them." She clenched all her four fists. Where the hell did he come from? Her carefully developed master plan was in danger. First, that imbecile Felix denied her complete ownership of Quasaris, so she had to pivot. Fortunately, she'd recovered and emerged even stronger than she'd expected. Angelika smiled, looking at her horns and remembering Bioid research, the latest leap in her biotech efforts. Notwithstanding Frank's mysterious arrival and his idealistic dreams, her goals will be achieved.

"Frank is mine. Soon, he'll crawl here to beg to serve me." She stood. "Do you think I should accept or deny, Cesare?"

"That's your decision, Mistress."

"Divine justice. Everyone will yield to Absolute, including Frank. He can't escape it. In fact, I expected him to come back already. You know what's happening?"

"No, Mistress."

"Strange. Well, I can wait. I'm eternal, after all." Angelika smiled. "What about the others?"

"Seven Designers have pledged their allegiance. They only asked to have uninterrupted access to Decon and spare body parts. In exchange, their Quarks will obey your commands and join our network."

"Lazy fools." Angelika squinted and curved her lips. "At some point, I'll convert them, too. I'll do it myself, with such a pleasure." She touched her horns and frowned. "Are you sure Bioids are harmless to me?"

"One hundred percent. The firmware is programmed this way; it cannot affect your DNA. And in case of a glitch, the Bioids are connected to the network, so we can shut them before they can do any damage."

"Good to hear. After all, a god is only a god when she's omnipotent, eternal, and indestructible. Absolute. But what if Absolute decided to destroy itself? What do you think, Cesare?"

"There's much information and controversy on this topic, Mistress. It appears to be a logical contradiction."

"To you, Cesare." Angelika stood, raising her hands. "To a god, to Absolute itself, there is no contradiction. The will of Absolute is the only reason the Universe exists. And whether Absolute can will itself out of existence, only Absolute knows, for it is omniscient. The three facets of the divine entity are its will, knowledge, and existence. And

Absolute will reign supreme for eternity. Because Absolute defines eternity."

"As you wish, Mistress."

"From now on, do not call me Mistress or use other names or human titles. I am Absolute, and this is how I shall be addressed by the few who are granted a favor to interact with me. Do you understand?"

"Of course, Absolute."

"This is better. Follow me as I'm ready to shine my divine light into all the corners of the Universe. And blessed will be those who will see the light, devoured and incinerated by it. For this is the will of Absolute."

CHAPTER 36. SELENA

"Why did you do this to yourself?" Varg asked, approaching Selena.

"What, this?" Selena moved her long blond hair to the side, revealing the Decon connector in her neck. "That was necessary." She shrugged. "I started it; I have to end it." Selena mentally reached out to the purple cloud nagging somewhere deep inside her mind.

"You started nothing." Varg put his arm on her shoulder. "I was worried."

"I know," Selena said, taking Varg's hand. "Me too. About you and Ramon, and now you're both here. Lucky me."

Varg embraced his daughter, and they stood in silence for some time. They were in the room where Selena and Jim had prepared to explore Decon. Jim and Ramon had left to give them a moment, and Selena was grateful they did. For the first time, she saw her father vulnerable, exposed, without a clear action plan. Selena suddenly understood a massive weight of responsibility on his shoulders. Caring for the Community and providing for its people when the world was falling apart was a task for the strongest. And Varg was the strongest of them all.

"You need to stick with Ramon. He's a good man," Varg said.

"What about you?"

"I'm old and tired. I did what I could. Now is your turn. This will be my last gig," Varg said, smiling, stroking her hair.

"Don't say that. You'll rebuild the Community, and people will come back."

"Not me." He shook his head. "Revenge consumes my mind. I never thought revenge was such a powerful motivator, but it is. After I'm done with the murderers, I'll retire."

"You can't retire, Father. The Community doesn't exist without you."

"Well, at some point, it must. I've failed as a leader and have to step aside. Will you return to rebuild it, Selena? You are my flesh and blood and have what it takes."

"Sadly, it took us to face death to have this conversation," Selena said, putting her head on his shoulder. "I don't know. I don't belong anywhere. Even you don't understand me. How do you expect me to lead the people?"

"I've made lots of mistakes and neglected you; this is true. Ramon understands, though."

"Yes, he tries, he's sweet. But I still don't belong. I have my own path and must discover where it will take me."

They stood in a silent embrace for a long time, father and daughter. Varg's heart was beating fast, his breath was quick and shallow, and a lone tear ran down his cheek.

"I love you, Father," Selena said.

"I know. I love you too, always did. Please forgive me. I don't deserve you."

"We belong to different worlds. Perhaps we could meet in the middle, but I'm not sure it's possible."

"We can at least try."

"I'm sorry for what I said about Mother; it's not true. I was mad." Selena remembered how she'd left the first time, furious and screaming, and reached out to the purple cloud to strike Varg. "I made the cloud hit you in the forest. It answers my mood. I'm learning to control it better, though."

"It's okay, I get it." He kept caressing her hair. "First time I saw such powerful emotions from you."

"I was confused, lost." Selena pulled back, shaking her head. "I still am."

"Is this Jim guy okay?"

"Jim is the only one who truly understands." Selena stepped toward the large desk, where Decon's dodecahedral shape lay next to her fungal computer. "This sounds crazy, but we share dreams. He took me in there." Selena picked up the Decon, her fingers running around its smooth surface. She remembered their wild swim through the purple and Jim saving her from the depths of the abyss. "With no connectors, by the sheer force of his will. Jim and I belong to the same world."

"Good to hear," Varg said. "But please be careful."

"It's hard to be careful facing the end of days." Selena sat in the chair, placed her hands on the desk's shiny surface, and lowered her head. "Thank you for making the fungal computer for me. This might be the tool that saves us all."

"How come?" Varg stepped closer and placed his hands on her shoulders.

"I don't know yet, but there is a connection. I need to explore Decon through it to pierce the veil and open the final gate, as Quanah said. I'm part of something bigger, the world we don't know, which contains all the Decon worlds. Numu Puha. This is where I belong."

"Quanah? Numu...what?"

"There's so much I need to tell you. Perhaps we could both connect to the fungi so you could instantly learn what's in my head? To look at my Vistas together?"

"Bad idea." Varg shook his head. "I did try your Vista, you know? Wasn't the best experience."

"Yes, you told me. The defect... It's all part of the same story. We need to fix it once and for all."

"Can you use it against the murderers? Use the cloud against the space station?"

"I'll see what I can do." Selena sighed. It was a bad idea. Still, she needed to help Father avenge the destruction of the Community. She wasn't sure pulling in the cloud would work, though. The defect tore space-time apart, and her ability to manipulate it was not a given. First, she needed to explore Decon and build a stronger connection with the fungi. Somehow, this mechanism enhanced her abilities and gave her enormous mental strength and wisdom. Selena turned to face Varg, who stood behind her like a monument of the past, consumed by his need for revenge. She finally understood him, the combination of unyielding will and caring soul behind the mask of the sage, emotionless leader. They belonged to different worlds, but all these worlds would cease to exist if she couldn't figure out what to do.

**

"Now I have to go in there, and I must do it alone," Selena said, placing the digital interface on her temples and reaching for the Decon connector. "Could you please distract Jim and Ramon?"

"Of course," Varg said, taking her hand in his palms. "Be careful, Selena. And always remember: I've got your back. Even when I'm dead."

"I know, Father. Now, go."

As Varg left the room, Selena thought about their complicated relationship over the years. Ultimately, they understood each other; they were too stubborn to admit it and let the other in. The moment they'd just shared was the most intimate conversation they'd had in years, if not ever.

But now was not the time to be sentimental. Selena plugged the Decon connector into her neck. She took the device in her hand, mentally searching for the purple twinkle inside. The computer interface came alive, and tiny mushrooms entangled her temples, ears and forehead. She tried to keep the fungi and the purple light of Decon inside her mental imagery. Suddenly, her perceptions expanded: she became part of the mycelium, learning how the data flowed through the fungal relays and myriad signals traveled through the mushroom network. Then, the awareness spread even further, as if she became an integral element of the complex planetary organism. This experience was breathtaking as Selena immersed herself in the majestic world of awe and beauty.

Suddenly, the blinking purple flame appeared on the periphery of this macrocosm, and Selena was pulled into it alongside her surroundings. She knew the fungi were around, protecting her, inviting her in. As the flame grew larger, now encompassing most of her world, Selena transformed from a single being into a collection of infinite conscious components entangled in an intricate mesh of thoughts and sensations. She wasn't Selena anymore. Selena was left behind in the dying world of Varg and Ramon, the world under the splitting skies. Even Varg and Ramon became distant memories belonging to someone else, a drop in the bottomless sea of universal awareness.

The purple flame surrounded the composite entity she became, the world around her disappearing, the boundaries of her perception diffusing. She found herself in a place that shouldn't exist, with shapeless forms and raw ideas popping up randomly around her in a spellbinding dance of fluctuations and transformations, where everything was possible, but nothing was real.

Eventually, the mad dance stopped, and she found herself on solid ground. The flat, smooth surface extended infinitely in all planar directions, reflecting the heat from the unidentified energy source somewhere above it. The knowledge of the surroundings didn't come from hearing, touch, or smell; it was a combination of senses, many of which were unfamiliar. Selena glided through this expanse until she hit the wall. The obstruction was purple (at least this is what she called it, as it exhibited the exact nature of the cloud she'd interacted with) and stretched in vertical and horizontal directions. She tried to penetrate the wall without success. *It's the defect. The same defect as the purple cloud.*

Selena reached out to the fungi for help, and they showed up, appearing as tiny veins on the wall's surface, studying it, looking for the weak spots. Alas, there were none, and Selena was pulled into the nothingness represented by the defect. She pushed back, combining the energy of her infinite constituents with the power of the biological systems the mushrooms connected her with.

This attempt was successful, and she was transported away from the purple wall and the shiny surface into a fresh setting. This time, she was on top of the mountain. The fresh breeze blew on her face, scanning the fantastic terrain underneath with previously unavailable perceptions. The plateau was covered with silver columns and pyramids made of unknown material. Her mountain was a prism, its many vertical planar surfaces crowned by the crest she stood on. She wondered how she knew all of this. Still, the mental image of the surroundings was intense and persistent, replacing and merging with many unfamiliar sensations.

Alas, this majestic geometric world also exhibited a defect. A sea on the horizon was filled with the purple substance, its level rising gradually, submerging the shiny silver columns, strange pyramids emitting waves of exotic nature, and other geometrical constructs.

It's everywhere. What can be done?

She pushed back against the sea of purple, resisting its rise and eliminating this unwelcome intruder from the landscape. This attempt was in vain, as the sea kept rising, swallowing the terrain, getting close to her mountain. Searching for additional strength, Selena focused the effort on herself. However, instead of affecting the sea of purple, she was ejected from this world, too.

Traveling through the kaleidoscopic realm of random thoughts and ethereal shapes, Selena ended up in the jungle. But it wasn't the jungle she recalled from the world she came from—it was a mushroom jungle. The fungi were all around her: to the sides, above, and under her feet. Selena was within the mycelium, becoming a physical part of it, sharing in the intricate web of electrical signals the ancient organisms used to communicate with each other and other parts of the biosphere. As she squeezed through the fungal jungle, a gentle touch landed on her forehead.

"You made it, White Buffalo," a familiar hoarse voice said. It reverberated through the air, and Selena realized she heard it not through her ears, but through the vibrations of her skin.

"Quanah? What is this place?" Selena asked, using her vocal cords.

"Numu Puha."

"What is Numu Puha? What's with the mushrooms?"

"The land of the spirits. The mushrooms brought you here; this is their world, too."

"What's with the spirits?"

"Don't take it literally. This is the land outside your world. You've arrived earlier than I expected. You've got power. But the next step will be much harder."

"Is this Decon? Why are we here?"

"So you can see the path."

"Path to where? And I cannot see; I'm blind."

"Many people have eyes but cannot see. And sometimes you need to lose sight to see what others cannot."

"Not sure I follow. How do I find this path?"

"Ask the mushrooms. The path will lead through many worlds. What you call Decon destroyed the natural order of Numu Puha. The cloud is growing. The storm that will erase everything."

"What should I do? And why me?"

"Because you are White Buffalo, you are special. You are within Numu Puha, yet you contain it. When you understand what it means, you will see the path."

"I'm scared, Quanah. I'm just a stubborn, blind girl who doesn't belong. I'm not sure I'm the one you need."

"Of course you are. For you are here, now. You must open the door at the end of the path—the door that has never been opened."

"Which door?"

"The defect destroys Numu Puha. To fix it, one must travel beyond the veil. You need to open the passage to reach outside Numu Puha, beyond space and time. Will you do it, White Buffalo? Has your time finally come?"

CHAPTER 37. LAYLA

"How's the progress?"

Frank entered the lab where Yuki and Reto studied the Cymoeba material. His movements were less energetic than usual; his left arm was bandaged. Two deep horizontal wrinkles crossed his forehead, and his lips were curved down.

"Yuki is setting up an animal test," Layla said. She came to check on Yuki with the same question, surprised and intrigued by her idea. "Are you okay? What's going on?" She added, pointing to Frank's bandaged arm.

"Nothing I can't handle. What test?"

"I'll inject Cymoeba into a mouse. I have a theory," Yuki said, focusing on the desk's surface, where the animal was pinned to the glass container wall, connected by wires and tubes to sensors and fluid delivery systems.

"A mouse?" Frank tilted his head.

"Yes. I thought its ancient immune system should be more potent against Cymoeba."

"Interesting. Keep me up to date." Frank turned to Layla. "Do you want to take part in Gaia's demolition?"

"Of course." Layla smiled. "Count me in." She connected to Frank's passion for space exploration, finding the goals lofty and sublime. This was so different from the world and the people she used to deal with, making it so exciting.

"Wait." Frank turned to Yuki. "What are you gonna do after the mouse turns into a zombie? We can't kill it, can we?"

"You're right," Yuki said. "I intend to keep it restrained for further study. I'll pull the vacuum on the container if necessary."

"I see." Frank turned around. "Let's go," he addressed Layla.

At this moment, a Quark appeared in the lab, flying through the overhead door Frank didn't care to lower.

"Mr. Wise, you must see this," the Quark announced, projecting an enormous three-dimensional image into the unoccupied portion of the room. Layla recognized the launch pad with a dozen spaceships ready to fly. This was the initial phase of Frank's plan to attack Gaia and take the fight to the enemy rather than trying to figure out how to repel the incursions of Gaia's minions on Earth.

Layla gasped and froze in place as goosebumps ran down her spine. An army of F-Quarks was attacking the launch facility, barraging it with projectiles, EM discharges, and missiles from multiple directions. Two ships were on fire, their fusion reactor compartments destroyed, while the rest were about to meet the same fate. The defense, comprising multiple towers and turrets equipped with railguns and other weapons, returned fire and shot down some enemies. Still, some batteries were silent as many more attackers approached. In addition, some of the Quasaris' Quarks attacked defense towers. Several turrets fired at the spaceships and joined in the destruction of the space fleet.

"What is going on?" Frank yelled, clenching his fist and punching the Quark.

"We are under attack," the Quark said.

"I can see that, you moron!" Frank stepped forward and kicked the chair. "Where are my defenses? The space fleet is my biggest asset, and this is how you protect it?"

"The defenses are overwhelmed. We also experience a hacking attack, and many of our systems are hijacked."

"Hijacked? Spencer, do something!"

"We are fighting back, but the enemy is more powerful. We have no more resources, sir."

"This is nonsense. Who's the attacker?"

"Gaia, sir."

"Bloody hell!" Frank walked back and forth, looking at the projection of the battle, helplessly clenching his only working fist. His face turned red as he scowled and squinted. "The goddamn space station anticipates our moves; it's always one step ahead. Maybe I should welcome it and melt your useless AI as junk?"

"This is not the only facility under attack," Spencer said. "All our ships are, even cold-stacked ones. We are losing our fleet, sir."

"Losing our fleet? Damn you, Spencer." Frank shook his head. All the space vessels were now damaged, several of them exploding in colorful balls of fire and smoke. "Where are my nukes, Spencer? If only I had a few, we would evaporate this stupid construction!"

"The nukes were all melted down during the Deconvolution. This was the last concerted effort by the world governments, led by the UN Secretary-General Goswami. I explained it to you before."

"Could we make them again?"

"We certainly could, but it will require significant time and resources, sir."

Layla considered what she would do in this situation. They had no good options; the enemy was smarter and more powerful. They could not launch the ships, and asking for help from other Designers was too late.

"Yuki, what can we do against the hackers?" Layla asked.

"Not much if I don't know exactly what's happening." Yuki shrugged. "Besides, if the Quarks cannot figure it out, I doubt I could help much."

"Crap!" Frank collapsed in a chair, closing his eyes. "I can't look at this. We're doomed. This is the end of Quasaris, the end of Frank Wise. I should've perished fifty years ago...instead, I witness how the world dies. This is my punishment."

Layla had never seen Frank defeated like this. It was true they only had a brief history together. Still, this behavior was so atypical, so against Frank's core, that Layla was certain something else might weigh down on him. After all, when he'd just appeared, he was no one, had nothing, but kept fighting.

Layla approached the crouching figure in the chair. "Frank, you'll find the solution. You always do. We're on your side."

"No, not this time." Frank shook his head. "You don't understand. I'm finally done; I'm deflated like a balloon with no air. I've lost to the space station, damn it. Now I understand why Decon is so attractive." He opened his eyes and looked straight at Layla. "I need one. I'll see my dream, even if in the fantasy world."

Layla didn't respond. She placed her hand on his shoulder and gently rubbed it. She had to help Frank, a larger-than-life leader with boundless energy and determination, regain his mojo and will to fight. *Alas, he might be right, and it's too late,* Layla admitted, watching how the Quarks, controlled by a space station floating in the middle of nowhere, finished the last remnants of Quasaris' defenses. No spaceship was intact, and the launch facility had become a giant conflagration, providing a striking visual confirmation to Frank's words and proclaiming the end of days.

CHAPTER 38. FRANK

Frank stared at the holographic image of the Houston Spaceport, which had turned to ash and debris, the burning carcasses of the spaceships completing the transformation of the most daring aspiration of humankind to the graveyard of dreams. The enormity of the destruction and his inability to do anything to prevent it led him to consider ridiculous actions: he prepared to blow up Spencer, his assistant Quark, and run to the Spaceport to fight the intruders. Then, a concrete block squashed his mind: all he'd worked for had been in vain, disappearing into the last convulsion of the dying world. Collapsing in a chair, Frank closed his eyes and lowered his head. There was nothing he could do; all his actions were futile. Frank couldn't resist the space station, a pile of junk people had all but buried. He was not a god; he was just a man with a vision and no faculties to achieve it. This was the end of his pursuits, and he now understood the power of Decon. The last choice of a loser: to flee reality, to disappear into a different world where all your dreams came true. Frank remembered what Paul had told him and decided to try it. *If Decon worlds and lives are real in a different dimension, whatever it means, I must explore them,* he decided. For this one was done.

Someone behind him gently touched his shoulders. Layla. He sympathized with the girl; her will and cunning almost rivaled his. But she belonged to this damned age, the era of pathetic exploits of mad Designers and depressed population trading their essence for another spin of Decon, another chance to experience a different life somewhere in a much happier and more satisfying place. On the other hand, he was the relic of the past, where people had common objectives and had to rely on each other to at least try to make their lives, the only ones they had, more tolerable.

"We'll fight back," Layla said, leaning toward Frank from behind.

"How? We can't win. You heard Spencer."

"Everybody, leave!" Layla shouted, pointing at the overhead door. She walked around Frank's chair and stood before the image of the conflagration, turning to face him. "I don't want anyone to see you like this. It's not you, Frank—it's your shadow. I need to get the real Frank Wise back."

"What for?" Frank shook his head and closed his eyes.

"For the people. For us. For your magnificent vision."

Frank covered his face with his right hand, the left hanging down as a useless appendage. It wasn't his anymore; he was learning to do each simple task with one hand. He appreciated Layla trying to cheer him up, but she didn't understand the totality of failure he faced.

"People don't care. Us? We are insignificant in the grand scheme. And the vision? It was all a lie. A figment of my imagination."

"No." Layla waved her hand. "You infected me with your passion. Me, who was only in it for the riches. Now I care, and that's enough for me. It's not a lie; it's just insanely complex. Don't give up now, Frank. It's not the time."

"What do you suggest?" It was challenging to think; his thoughts were running away from him, and he only wanted to be left alone, hide in a place where nobody would find him, and just be there, undisturbed.

"In a frontal assault, we have no chance, you're right. However," she raised her finger, "if we find out who's behind Gaia, we could organize a covert action."

"How?"

"I don't know yet. We need to capture a Quark and run diagnostics. It might reveal somethin'."

"And who will do that?" Frank asked. A needle pierced his left side, reaching somewhere underneath the ribcage, and he grimaced in pain.

"My team. We can handle it. Are you okay?" Layla noticed his suffering and touched his head.

"No," he admitted, deciding it was futile to continue hiding the pain and torment his left arm was causing him. "I don't feel my arm, and now my left side is compressed by a giant vice while a hammer drives nails through my lungs."

"Did you get nano-Quark injections?"

"You bet. I don't think I'm compatible with your tech." He tried to smile through the pain. "So, you see why I want to get on the Decon train. This body is falling apart, as is this world. I want to see my dreams come true, even if it's ultimately just another dream."

"We'll fix you," she said. "Don't give up, not now, when you converted me. I'm here with you, Frank. Do you understand?" She took his face in her hands and looked straight into his eyes.

"How did you get the scar?" he asked, touching a line extending below her left earlobe to her neck, contrasting with her dark skin.

"Somethin' sharp." She frowned. "It was long ago when I was a stupid girl. I survived. Don't change the subject. I'm here to take care of you; you're not alone anymore."

"It's a twist of fate...I've lost Ichika and found you. You're so different yet alike." He studied the scar on her neck with his fingers.

She didn't respond. Instead, she leaned closer. As their lips met and Frank enjoyed her taste, he savored what might have been the last intimate moment he shared with another human being. When Layla pulled back, she smiled. "No Decon for you, Frank. We have things to do."

"Whatever you say." Frank exhaled, finding unexpected solace and sudden relief in being the follower. He didn't have the strength to push through anymore and accepted Layla's leadership.

"About Decon," she said, standing up. "Did you order to stop production and destroy the inventories?"

"I sure did. What's up?"

"I think Paul is hoardin' Decon and resellin' it on the black market. I have only indirect proof, though."

"That son of a bitch!" Frank snapped his fingers. "I knew I couldn't trust him. If he sees a profit, he'll sell Quasaris, me, you, his mother, and everyone else." He curved his lips as another needle pierced his lung. "I'll punish him, even if this would be my last act."

"That's not important." Layla shook her head. "We must capture Gaia's Quark."

"For the world to survive, people must get off Decon. I won't let a goddamn trader ruin my plans."

"I agree. But let's focus on Gaia for now."

"You might need to do it without me." Frank tightened his lips. "Promise me something, Layla."

"What is it?"

"Promise you'll continue on this path. To be the champion of humanity, to fight until the end, like I had."

"I promise, Frank. But we'll do it together."

"I doubt that." A multitude of needles pierced his body, this time reaching his heart. As Frank collapsed to the floor, darkness enveloped him. He didn't hear Layla screaming and rushing to his help. Whatever was happening to Frank's body reached its pinnacle.

CHAPTER 39. MAX

Max raised his head and looked into the starry sky, where two moons were rising, one large and yellow and another much smaller and red. He'd been traveling through the mountain passes for a few weeks now: time ran at different speeds in different Decon worlds. It became challenging to find food at this altitude. He was lucky to shoot a mountain goat—this prey should sustain him for a while. Hopefully, by the time he needed to get more, he'd cross the ridge and arrive at his destination. Max wasn't sure what awaited him on the other side. Still, he knew it was something significant. This was the road leading to his destiny. And he trusted his sword and strength to face whatever would confront him.

He petted his stallion, standing beside him near the fire at their improvised campsite. The horse snorted, returning the gaze, full of care and understanding. Sometimes, Max wasn't sure who the leader of their pair was.

"Quiet, Blaze." Max calmed the horse down, inhaling the fumes of the burning wood, and looking at the fire tongues licking the embers. "Good boy. I know you're hungry. There will be more grass on the other side."

He lay on the bedroll's rocky surface, his sword beside him, and looked at the two moons. This life was simple and pure, the one he wanted to return to again and again. Yet, Max remembered Beatriz and had to admit she made his heart beat faster. She was the beacon of light in these strange times, in every world he'd visited, studying different realizations of the purple artifact. The mountains of this one provided a potential path to finding a source, getting to the root of the problem, and fixing it once and for all in every Decon world. Perhaps, after it was all done, he could return to Beatriz and lose himself in the gaze of her obsidian eyes and the magical scent of her dark hair. But it wasn't the time yet.

Falling asleep, Max recalled Decon and the multitude of lives it gave him. They were all equally real and created equally powerful impressions and memories. He didn't know what to think about it, only that he was blessed to have access to various worlds and to live many exciting lives. There was no confusion; it was him, Max, in every one of these worlds, with all his combined memories and thoughts. And in this one, he had to cross the purple ridge and get to the other side.

In the morning, extinguishing the embers and covering up the ashes with pebbles, Max smelled the aromas of saffron and jasmine mixed with a mysterious, musky, pungent scent coming from whatever was on the other side of the mountain range. Angelika. Determined to move forward, Max got on his horse and continued on a hidden trail. The path disappeared before him between enormous boulders ahead, where a small red moon descended on the horizon to the place he was searching for.

A few hours later, when the giant yellow bowl of the sun began warming up the inhospitable terrain, the trail changed inclination. *This is it; I must be ready.* He signaled the horse to slow down and removed his sword from its sheath behind his back. The path veered to the left, leading to a spacious cavern lit up with a strange green light from the inside. Blaze stopped, refusing to move forward.

"C'mon, boy. We're almost there."

"No," the horse suddenly responded. "This is a place of darkness and evil."

Max thought his mind was playing tricks on him. Perhaps too much time on the road made him hear things. He shook his head and gently spurred the horse, eager to enter the cave.

"You go alone if you want," Blaze said, turning his head to the rider and showing his white teeth. "It's your quest, not mine."

"Why am I hearing this?" Max said out loud, not ready to admit his delusion.

"Because you've arrived," the horse answered. "This is the end of the road. Now you go alone."

"Alright." Max got off his stallion, patted his mane, and added: "Wait for me here. I'll be back."

"No, you won't." Blaze turned around. "Goodbye," he added, disappearing behind the trail's turn.

Max shook his head, trying to dispel the hallucination. Horses didn't talk, but, in some Decon realization, anything was possible, so why not? Besides, this was indeed the end of the road, and he had arrived. Darkness and evil? He'd been looking for this, and now was the time to face and defeat it.

Max stepped into the cave. The mysterious green light turned into the fog, engulfing him from all sides. The musky, pungent odor became extreme, almost unbearable. A soft sound of strange music reverberated in his ears. Max moved slowly, sword in his hand, advancing deeper into a cave until he saw a pond of red liquid blocking his path. Max kneeled, lowered his finger into the pond, and immediately pulled it back. Blood. As he stepped back, deliberating on what to do, large bubbles suddenly appeared on the pond's surface, and a giant vortex formed in the middle. Stupefied, Max raised his sword in a futile attempt to defend himself against whatever evil was rising from the vortex.

In the next moment, a fantastic creature stood before him. Four arms and three breasts adorned the gorgeous body, green eyes flashing at the newcomer with interest and intent. Angelika Scalvini stood knee-deep in the pond of blood, all her four arms risen, her mouth half-opened in a terrifying smile. But the new feature, and the most fascinating one, was the pair of horns, black as night and razor-sharp. One of them pointed straight at Max.

Max stepped further back and arched his sword, blocking the approach of a horrible spike. Angelika, however, was much stronger and faster. One turn of her head and the horn struck Max's weapon, which fell with a loud clang. Facing his deepest fears, Max turned around and tried to escape the dreadful cave, his arms and legs refusing to obey him. Unfortunately, the green luminous fog thickened, and Max froze, unable to move, stuck in this horrifying nightmare. He exerted all his strength to free his limbs, but all was in vain. The rapidly solidifying substance nailed him to the ground.

Then, Angelika's horn pierced his body, penetrating from behind, underneath his ribcage, and exiting out of his stomach. A demonic laughter filled the air.

"You came here to kill me?" Angelika finally stopped laughing. "Me, your god? The primal cause of your existence? Absolute?"

"I...have to stop you...fix the crack." Max could barely speak as the horn spun, twisting his entrails and making him burn from the inside.

"You can't stop me, fool." Angelika took the horn out of Max's body, and he fell to his knees. The relief was short-lived, however, as another horn punctured his neck, causing Max to gurgle.

"I am Absolute, your master. You will obey and worship me. You must join the Cluster." The voice reverberated in his ears, but he didn't understand what else she said. This was the truth: he'd finally met the reason for his existence. Absolute had another name, Angelika Scalvini, in that other world where the shadow of Beatriz was waiting for him. It didn't matter anymore. He came here to find his destiny, expecting to fight the demon and fix the hole in reality. And here it was: his destiny, his Absolute, his master. Nothing mattered but this. It all suddenly became clear. His fate was to be with his Absolute, from the beginning of times and for eternity. Max rejoiced, emerging as an inseparable part of the purest entity, fulfilling his quest and becoming one with his master.

***

Max emerged from Decon, disconnected the adapter on the back of his neck, and inhaled. The memory of being impaled on two sharp, horrific horns was too real. Did he die? He didn't know. A question occurred: *If you die in a dream, do you survive in reality? And what is reality, anyway?*

Max shook his head, chasing away doubts. Now, he knew reality was multi-faceted. Every Decon world was as real as the next one, and Absolute created each of them. The entity he'd yearned for without understanding where this yearning had come from. But it was all clear now: he had to merge with Absolute, for it was his purpose, his destiny. He had to find Angelika.

A slight concern still bothered him: if the world with the purple mountain ridge was the source, why hadn't he merged with Absolute there? Why did he have to return to this one? What was the significance? And did he indeed die in that cave, stupefied by the green fog created by his master?

Max didn't know the answers, but he knew what to do. *I'm too insignificant, too small to understand the Grand Design and my place in it. I can do nothing better than to merge with Absolute, in this world and in every world.*

Suddenly, Max remembered Beatriz. She didn't know about his findings, the profound discovery of the source of their being. He wanted to tell her, take her with him, and invite her to join in the eternal bliss. Yet, he had no time to waste. He took the digital device from the desk, turned it on, and recorded a holographic message. She'd understand when she listened to it. As he turned the device off, he was certain she would come and join him. He had to hurry, for the time was short. Why was that? He didn't know, but he knew this was true.

It was the middle of the night, and he didn't encounter anyone as he exited the main building of the Wise Estate. The Quarks were around, observing and registering the events, but they didn't try to stop Max. As Frank's guest, he enjoyed access to all the facilities and had total freedom. Max proceeded to the glider, got inside, and turned on the engine. He was full of energy and joyful expectation, like a kid with candy in front of him. Max couldn't wait to arrive and meet Absolute. *This is probably what salmon feels when it returns to the freshwater streams of its birth to spawn and die.* He had completed his journey. Nothing mattered but Absolute.

Sometime later, Max landed his glider at the border of the Scalvini Estate. The previous time he was here was to steal from his master. *A foolish and pointless undertaking,* Max admitted, observing bizarre steeples rising from the intricate architectural composition of the mansion, interconnected by the hanging bridges and spiral staircases. *This is where I belong. O Absolute, please accept me.*

As Max got out of the glider, he gasped. Strange creatures surrounded him, demonstrating the omnipotence of his master and the grandeur of her conception. Shapeless, almost liquid green balls were covered with protrusions, tentacles, and spikes. They circled around Max, touching all parts of his body with probes and engulfing him in their amorphous green pulp. Some tentacles got into his mouth and nose, some into his ears, and his eyes couldn't see anything except the sea of green. Yet, this was the moment he was waiting for, to merge with the creative force that was Absolute, to become one with an army of its followers, for their destiny was inseparable from his.

A few moments later, Max was moving, or, rather, swimming through molasses. Finally, the movement stopped, and the green cloud cleared up. He was naked and fixed to a rectangular platform, seemingly floating in the middle of the room lit with gentle blue light. The familiar musky and pungent smell attacked his nostrils, and Max prepared to meet his master.

And she appeared before him in all her glory. The two majestic horns touched and pinched his wrists while her face got very close to his. A trident-shaped tongue licked his lips, eyelids, and nostrils.

"I was waiting for you," Angelika pronounced with a deep, reverberating voice. "Are you ready?"

"Yes, o Absolute." Max gasped and closed his eyes, unable to bear the goddess's eternal beauty. "I heard your call there, in a cave with green fog. You took me in, and now I'm one with you, for you are Absolute, the reason for everything."

"Very good," Angelika said. "I'm pleased it turned out as I expected. You are so malleable. Remember the flash of light when you came to steal from me?"

Max didn't understand what she was talking about. Simply being in the presence of his master and hearing her voice as his essence dissolved in hers was the pinnacle of his experience.

Angelika touched his neck with her long metallic finger. "Such a shame I got only you. But I'll get your friends later, after I deal with Frank." She punctured his neck, but there was no pain. "I'll keep your stupid mind as a trophy. The ability to embed virtual Quark into Decon will be my future weapon against Designers."

She laughed and signaled with one of her upper arms. Two familiar, amorphous creatures appeared. "What happens now is magic. To become one with Absolute, you must relinquish everything: your thoughts, desires, and dreams. Your ego and your essence will disappear, merging with mine. Are you ready to ascend to the apex of your existence?"

"Yes, o Absolute." Max couldn't formulate his response. The moment's satisfaction, joy, and expectation overwhelmed all his mental faculties. He was about to receive the highest honor one could expect.

"Excellent," Absolute said. "You'll lose your body, and I'll control your mind. You shall witness what nobody else can." She raised her four hands, and amorphous creatures approached Max, enveloping him in a green substance. This time, the tentacles penetrated deeper, reaching into his stomach, lungs, and, finally, brain. There was no pain, just a calm sensation of being disassembled into the smallest components to be re-created on a different plane of existence. Darkness befell Max as his eyes dissolved in the green pulp, and fog descended onto his brain, making it impossible to think. Finally, as his lungs stopped functioning and his heart could not pump the green liquid, which replaced his blood, Max understood this was the end. His final destination, the moment he was yearning for, the threshold he needed to cross to enter eternal bliss. Max, the fearless warrior, the strength of Layla's unit, and the secret passion of gentle Beatriz, was dead. What was coming to replace him was stained with horror, revulsion, and torment.

CHAPTER 40. LAYLA

"How did you find out?" Frank asked as their glider descended into Houston.

"I never trusted the bastard." Layla shrugged. "Sure, we were sellin' him our loot, but he tried to fool me every time. Pay less. Find an excuse. Whatever, I don't wanna talk about this bastard."

Layla was annoyed that, instead of dealing with actual problems, they had to chase Greedy Paul, who lied even to his new boss to gain more profit. This was beyond her understanding, an inexcusable recklessness. She looked at Frank, who sat next to her in a passenger's seat with a grimace of pain on his face. A thick bandage covered his left arm, and a broad brown scarf was wrapped around his neck. Whatever was eating his flesh was severe, and Layla worried they might lose their leader altogether soon. She couldn't let it happen; she had to find a solution. Yet, instead of helping Frank defeat his sickness and regain his mojo, she had to deal with a treacherous merchant.

"Still, tell me more."

"I've found out Paul switched off the Quarks using the command key you gave him. The bastard didn't want to be traced. I followed him once and saw him go into the Decon factory. Then Beatriz noticed he'd flown to Houston several times. Now, you could put two and two together."

"Son of a bitch," Frank whispered, frowning. "We'll catch him red-handed."

"Indeed," Layla said, landing the glider behind the dump.

It was evening, and the surroundings were already dark and quiet. The door to Paul's office was open, and Layla realized the merchant was not alone.

"Be careful, someone's there," she said. "Let me go first."

Frank moved to the side and let her explore the approach to Paul's abode. The Quarks were turned off: since Paul was stealing from Quasaris, going against Frank's direct orders, he couldn't let Quarks observe what he was doing. Fortunately for Layla, the defense mechanisms were down, and they could approach without being discovered. Frank refused to take Quarks with them on a mission, insisting he had to confront the man face to face. Layla didn't argue: it was, perhaps, too brash but also sneakier. She was ready to protect Frank and was confident she could do it well. The man made a difference in her life, and she cared about him.

Layla peeked inside the shack from behind a heap of trash. Paul stood at his large desk, talking to an ugly-looking Scavenger with a large nose and a long, unkempt red beard. The man wore a dirty green coverall, and a lousy burn disfigured the left side of his face. Layla winced—it smelled like a latrine inside, overbearing even the foul scent of the dumpster. There were no Quarks and no weapons. Nobody noticed her.

Layla turned and made a sign for Frank to approach. As he kneeled beside her, they looked at each other, and she thought she saw a ghost for a moment. Only now did she recognize how exhausted Frank was. The worst was inside his eyes: the deep, bottomless well of anguish and torment. Layla couldn't take her gaze off his face and suppressed a sudden desire to hug and kiss him.

Frank frowned, not understanding the cause of the delay, and pointed two fingers at the office in front of them. Layla, shaking off the stupor, nodded. They stood and dashed toward the open entrance.

Paul stepped back, his mouth half-open. His visitor, standing with his back to the door, couldn't see the running pair. Thinking this was one of Paul's tricks, he reached out to his weapon and aimed at Paul. The situation was about to get out of control.

"You son of a bitch!" Frank yelled, approaching the shack while Layla protected his back. Frank held a Nano-Swarmer X3, aiming it at Paul. At the same time, a visiting Scavenger moved his aim from one man to another, trying to figure out where the danger was.

"Whoa, buddy," Paul said, flashing his palms. "I work for you; did you forget?"

"You stole from me."

"Nah, just took my fair share. A management perk, eh?" Paul smiled, spreading his hands.

"I thought I made myself clear." Frank frowned. "Decon must be destroyed. It's a curse. Are you dumb?"

"Well, buddy, I might be dumb, but I know how to make a profit.

You're a businessman, Frank. Decon is wealth, and I don't care whether it's a blessing or a curse."

"Well, I do." Frank pointed the Nano-Swarmer at Paul. "You're fired. Now, return what's mine."

"I'm afraid I can't do that." Paul shook his head and nodded at the Scavenger. "I already made a deal."

"The deal's off," Frank announced. "I'll count to three, and then... poof... you're just biomaterial."

Paul looked at his former boss and laughed. Frank frowned, not understanding the reaction.

"He's protected." Layla stood next to Frank. "His immune system is upgraded. Like all of us and all the Designers. He fooled you."

"Fuck!" Frank threw the Nano-Swarmer at Paul, who dodged the object. "And who the hell are you?" He turned to the Scavenger.

"Leave this scumbag alone," Layla said. "He can't hurt you; his weapon is even less potent." She knew she was the only one wielding something effective, but decided not to open her cards yet. Especially not knowing what Paul was hiding. "If I were you," she turned to the Scavenger, "I'd run away as far as possible. This is gonna get ugly."

The Scavenger looked at Paul and said: "You gave me a guarantee... I'm not doing business with you anymore." He spat in Paul's direction and disappeared into the night. Layla chuckled and turned to face Paul.

"Now," she said. "What are we gonna do with you?"

"If you're smart, you'd join me. This source of Decon is endless; no more scavenging needed."

"You're full of shit." Layla stepped forward, holding one hand in her pocket, expecting trouble from Paul. "Return what you've stolen."

"No way, it's mine." Paul reached under his desk and pushed it forward. The table overturned and was about to hit Layla, but she was no longer there. She expected the movement and jumped to the side, avoiding the falling desk while taking a Lumen grenade from her pocket. Paul had no time to fire his weapon as the bright flash blinded the merchant and caused him to collapse on the floor. Layla closed her eyes, turned, and covered Frank's face with her palm, minimizing the impact of the light grenade on them.

As she prepared to deal with the blinded merchant, the sound of explosions outside interrupted their fight. Layla glanced back and shook her head. A multitude of Quarks in the sky were shooting at the surrounding buildings, indiscriminately attacking and burning everything around.

"Run!" she screamed, pushing Frank, not understanding what was happening but figuring it had to be bad.

"What about him?" Frank pointed at Paul's crouching body on the floor. The merchant had managed to get on his knees and was shaking his head, trying to regain the balance.

"Get up and run, you bastard." Layla kicked Paul in the stomach with her boot's nose.

The trader grunted and said with difficulty: "Never... Decon is mine. It's my wealth."

"Forget about him. He's mad." Layla said, grabbing Frank's hand. "It's a war," she added, pointing to the Quarks outside. "We have to get out."

They ran toward their glider, disappearing into the bushes as several Quarks appeared nearby. As the pair boarded the vehicle, Layla lifted the glider and flew out of the city at a maximum speed. They were about to escape when two Quarks separated from the group and chased them. Fortunately, the glider was much faster, and Layla had no problem losing the enemy. She looked at the trader's shack and saw it disappearing in flames amid blasts and explosions. Layla thought about Paul, who couldn't leave his hoard even under the threat of impending death. Greedy Paul, a trader she'd worked with for so long, a treacherous and lying bastard, a man obsessed with profit and riches, was dead.

****

"Wait a minute," Frank said, touching Layla's shoulder as the glider gained altitude, leaving the dangerous area infested with attacking Quarks.

"What is it?"

"I want to see what's happening. I have a strong suspicion this is Gaia all over again."

"It's too risky." Layla shook her head. "If they register us, we'll be shot down."

"Risk is how I live." Frank smiled for the first time in the past few days. She didn't like the idea, but agreed they needed to learn more.

"As you wish. You're the boss." She steered the glider back toward the city, staying at high altitude. "If we fly high enough, we have a good chance."

As they approached Downtown Houston, the scale of the attack became evident. This was the ultimate destruction of the city, the event Layla couldn't imagine a few months ago. Hundreds of Quarks bombarded and burned everything, flying over high-rise structures and industrial sites, eradicating buildings to the ground. What was worse, more Quarks searched the rubble, moving on their bi-, quadruped, and caterpillar chassis, identifying and killing the remaining people. This was a sight she couldn't unsee. The beautiful city, a gem of the South, was being erased from the face of the Earth. True, its glory days were well in the past. Still, even today, it was a significant center where over a million people lived.

"It's Gaia. I'll be damned!" Frank punched the armrest of his seat. "We must leave. I've seen enough."

"Can we do somethin'? This is a genocide." Layla turned to Frank, still not willing to believe her eyes.

"What can we do?" Frank shrugged. "The plan was to capture Gaia's Quark. I doubt we could do it here. At least I know now that whoever is behind aims to destroy everything. But I still don't understand why and what the endgame is."

"Perhaps we could save someone. The bastards are busy blastin' and destroyin'; they might not even notice us. Also, we're faster."

"Are you trying to get us killed?"

"It was you who wanted to come back. Now it's my turn to risk our lives." Layla smiled as she maneuvered the glider into the midst of fire and collapsing buildings.

Initially, the Quarks, whose objective was the city's destruction, didn't pay any attention to the lone glider. Layla had time before the enemy realized the glider was part of the mission. As their flying capsule approached the collapsing bridge over the Buffalo Bayou, Layla pointed down, where a little girl ran in a desperate attempt to avoid the falling debris amid the constant fire of attacking Quarks. One of them registered the girl and darted in her direction. The kid had zero chance of survival.

"See that?" Layla said. "We can help her."

"You're suicidal," Frank replied, closing his eyes. "But, whatever, you're a pilot."

The glider had only basic weapons, and there was no way they could take on a military Quark. However, they had a speed advantage, and Layla intended to use it.

Layla positioned the glider as quickly as she could between the child and the Quark. This caused the enemy to switch the target and shoot in her direction.

"Hold on," Layla said, zigzagging and changing the trajectory to avoid the blasts. "I know what this bird is capable of; we can do it."

Layla steered the glider to rise higher, leaving the Quark behind them, and circled several skyscrapers with the dexterity and speed the Quark couldn't achieve.

"Did we lose it?" Layla asked.

"I think so; nobody's behind," Frank answered as Layla took the glider back to the bridge.

"Now, we need to hurry. They know we're here." Layla located the running girl and landed the glider next to her. "Faster, get in!" she screamed as the kid climbed inside the cabin.

As the glider catapulted, three Quarks flew in to intercept them and opened fire. The glider still had a speed advantage, and Layla gained altitude, leaving the enemy behind. Only now was she able to turn around and look at the passenger they'd just rescued. A girl, about six, sat behind Frank, trembling like a leaf, tears in her eyes. Whatever was left of her clothes was dirty and covered in holes. Fortunately, by the look of it, the girl was unharmed except for a few bruises. Layla took a deep breath as the glider left the dangerous area and steered north, back to the Wise Estate.

"Are you okay?" Layla asked, looking at the girl.

"I think so." The child sobbed, smearing dirt and tears on her face. "They're all dead…"

"But you're not," Layla said. "Listen, it's important to stay alert. You're very brave. What's your name?"

"Eva."

"Okay, Eva. You're safe with us. We'll take you to our place, where no one can hurt you. Then you'll tell us your story. Deal?"

"Okay," Eva said, still sobbing. "I knew they were coming. Space station sent them to kill everyone," she added, looking at her fingers.

"How the f...how do you know?" Frank almost jumped off his seat.

"The ants told me. At our playground...we have a colony. I talk to them; they trust me," Eva announced, raising her chin.

"What are you talking about?" Frank frowned. "A rogue space station, mushroom computer, now ants. This world is truly mad."

"Selena needs to talk to her," Layla said to Frank. "Unless it's a child's imagination, there might be somethin' in common. It's all crazy, you're right. I've no idea what's happenin'," she admitted.

"Neither do I," Frank said. "Did the ants tell you anything else?"

"They said the hole in the sky," Eva pointed up, "will eat our world. Nothing will remain. And this is all because of us, people."

"Is the space station attacking us because of the hole?" Frank asked.

"No. It will die with the world. The ants, plants, humans, everything will disappear into the hole. I'm so scared..." Eva started to cry.

Layla shuddered. What was this about? How could the collapsing society of the last remnants of humanity cause a hole in the sky? It was clear, however, that their dreams of space travel must wait, and even their confrontation with Gaia might be inconsequential. The survival of humanity depended on the old man's visions and the abilities of a blind girl with a mushroom computer. Layla didn't like this disposition at all.

CHAPTER 41. RAMON

Ramon sat by the large, adjustable bed in a room at the Wise Estate designated to Selena. She'd been asleep for many hours, exhausted by Decon exploits and the revelations about the cosmos and the defect. He didn't understand a quarter of what she'd told him, and he knew that was beyond his abilities, no matter how hard he'd try. But this was not important. The important part was he couldn't let anything or anyone hurt Selena. Now, when she'd taken the role of the world savior, she needed him more than ever, and he swore to be by her side no matter what transpired.

Ramon looked at Selena's peaceful face, listened to her measured breath, and observed her chest going up and down in rhythm with her inhales and exhales. He moved his chair closer to her and leaned forward, smelling her beautiful blond hair, which reminded him of the tropical fruits and blooming exotic flowers. Ramon hadn't visited any exotic places, but he was sure this was how they smelled. He adored Selena and wanted to be with her for the rest of his days.

Sensing his presence in the middle of her dream, Selena moved her hand and touched his fingers.

"What are you doing here?" she asked.

"Guarding your sleep," he answered.

"You silly boy." Selena smiled. "I can take care of myself."

"I know. But I want to be with you."

"I know." Selena squeezed his fingers. "Thank you." She sat and touched her long, beautiful blond hair, straightening it up. This simple movement was so filled with beauty and natural feminine energy that Ramon's heart sped up and goosebumps ran down his spine.

"What are you going to do?" he asked.

"What *can* I do?" She shrugged. "Find a path, I suppose. Open the door that cannot be opened, or whatever Quanah said. I wish I knew."

"Can you ask the fungi? Or Eva's ants?"

"Fungi. Yes, I need their help. And Eva...this is yet another mystery. I don't know what to think, Ramon."

The girl Frank and Layla had saved from the city's destruction provided another connection to the defect. Selena had talked with Eva, and it brought no clarity, only more questions. The child insisted she could communicate with ants and that they'd told her about the upcoming apocalypse. Still, her story was so fragmented and disjointed it was challenging to understand. How much of it was based on reality and how much on the imagination of a six-year-old was anyone's guess.

"Take it easy," he said, placing his hand over hers. You need strength. "What did Jim say?"

"Jim's convinced Eva has the same ability to experience the universe we do."

"And what about the fungi and the ants?"

"I don't know about ants, but fungi are intelligent. The network they're part of extends beyond this world. They guided me. They have the answers; I'm just too stupid to understand. I need to get to know them better, Ramon. They can show me the door Quanah talked about."

"Do you think I can do that, too?"

"What?"

"Talk to the mushrooms. To the ants, maybe even to the trees."

"I've no idea." She shrugged. "I need you like you are, though. Unblemished. Pure. Mine."

"Then how can I help you?" Ramon asked, stroking her hair. He wanted to join Selena in her quest, travel to Decon with her, and uncover and translate the wisdom of the fungi, but didn't know how. Ramon's fists clenched as he imagined the ordeals Selena had to endure in Decon and how difficult it must have been for her. He would get a Decon connector and stand beside her when she searched for the hidden door she desperately wanted to open.

As if reading his thoughts, she leaned forward, hugged him, and whispered: "by being who you are. Don't even think about Decon; I won't allow that."

Ramon inhaled the smell of exotic fruits she emanated and was about to float in the air and fly. This moment was special; he could spend ages embracing Selena and listening to her whisper. Ramon could finally access her world and understand her mind and emotions. Somehow, he also knew she partook in his. Selena appreciated his presence and opened to him. This was precious and worthy of every Decon experience. Worthy of all of them.

"As you wish," Ramon said, turning his head and making their faces touch, nose to nose, until their breath became one. He didn't care she was different, that people called her cold and reserved. Ramon knew behind this external mask was a beautiful, delicate, and creative being who needed acceptance and understanding. And he was ready to be the rock she could lean on. No words or explanations were necessary; they partook in this moment, merging and dissolving into the universal consciousness, the everlasting observer and the judge.

Selena touched the back of his head with her palm and opened her mouth. Their lips touched, and their tongues found each other. The smell of exotic flowers became overbearing, and Ramon was lost in the wild vegetation on the shore of the forgotten Caribbean island, the love of his life next to him, embracing him and showing him the path to paradise. Electric shock pierced through Ramon's essence. The most immense joy of his life was to hold this girl in his hands, merging with her into a single, inseparable, eternal entity. They were made for each other, two halves of something much bigger than either of them could imagine. And their love was the catalyst that created this new being, which now stood proudly at the threshold of the cosmos, ready to open the door no one dared to approach, looking bravely into the realm beyond time and space.

CHAPTER 42. JIM

Jim looked at the little girl sitting next to him. Eva had calmed down a little following her last-minute deliverance from certain death in Houston; her fears had subsided, and she returned to being a normal, curious, and light-hearted six-year-old girl. The only issue was she panicked every time she saw a Quark, so Frank instructed Spencer not to show up in her field of view, instead asking Jim and Selena to take care of the girl. Jim had found Eva's story fascinating, but couldn't understand it and establish Eva's role in the universal upheaval they were facing.

"Have you ever seen Decon?" Jim asked. The dodecahedron rested firmly in his palm, glowing purple from within, inviting them to explore its contents.

"I'm too little. Mommy told me I'll get the connector when I grow up. Now they're all dead." Eve's lower lip curved down, and she rubbed her eyes.

"Shh, calm down." Jim embraced the girl, whispering something soothing and inconsequential into her ear. "You're safe here. And we need your help to fix the sky." He pointed up.

"What do you mean? How?" She stopped crying, tilting her head and looking at Jim, squinting one eye.

"Selena and I have special abilities, like superheroes." He placed Decon on the table and took her hands in his. "And you do, too. The three of us, together, will save the world. Do you read superhero stories? They were popular when I was a kid."

"No." Eva shook her head. "Nobody makes books or toys anymore. But I can be a superhero in Decon when I grow up," she said, raising her fist.

"Yes, you can." Jim picked up Decon and touched its smooth surface. Was it a blessing or a curse? Quanah had told Selena Decon had destroyed the natural order. Yet many people like Eva depended on it to pursue their dreams, live multiple lives in different realities, and fully realize themselves. However broken, the entire fabric of society now relied on the mysterious dodecahedron. Some people had initially dismissed the Decon invention as just another drug. Still, Decon was different from drugs or virtual reality; it provided a door to other lives as real as this one. This was now crystal clear. Who was he to deprive the people of new lives and experiences? Wasn't it more prudent to stand aside in serene contemplation and watch the world collapse? If it was the universe's destiny to crumble under its weight and complexity, perhaps he should let it play out. Why he? Why now? And why not let the events unfold?

"And your special power is the ancient wisdom of the ants. Please, tell me more about that."

"It's nothing special." Eva shrugged. "There are lots of them in our playground. One day, I pretended I could hear them, started talking to them, and they talked to me. Not like you and I talk; that's silly." She smiled. "I just heard them inside my head. Mommy told me it was my imagination and I shouldn't be serious about it. But it was real. They knew my name and my neighborhood and lots of other things."

"Like what?"

"Like what the trees on the other side of the playground felt, especially one cypress that didn't have enough water, how it was suffering."

"How did they know?"

"They said everything is connected except for people who are alone. But there are a few like me who can rejoin. This is my special ability." Eva raised her chin.

"Yes, indeed. Did they say anything about other worlds? Decon?"

"When the sky cracked," Eva said, shivering, "they told me it's because of what we did. I didn't understand, but they said the worlds broke and will disappear. And it's because we created Decon."

"Decon? Are you sure?"

"They didn't quite say it like that, but that's what I thought." Eva frowned. "No, I'm not sure."

"Alright." Jim decided not to press too far as the girl winced and rubbed her eyes. "Tell you what," he said, smiling. "It's super awesome you can talk to ants; we might need their help. Selena can talk to mushrooms. We must stay together to fix the hole."

"What's *your* special ability, Jim?" Eva looked straight into his eyes.

"Can you travel to other worlds? Can you talk to magical creatures? Dragons?"

"Nothing of the sort." Jim laughed. Indeed, what was the nature of his gift? Ability to receive encoded information from some mysterious sources in his visions? What was his purpose? The Wayfarer, hold the key, pierce the veil.... Was that his destiny? To travel outside time and space to fix the gap in reality? To play God?

"Yes, I can travel to other worlds," he added, looking at the Decon. "Not through this object, by myself. The door we opened with this device must be closed forever, and I need to do it. Can you help me, Eva?"

"Of course. With my superpowers!"

"Deal. Now, let's save the world."

"Not too fast." Selena and Ramon entered the room, holding hands, and Ramon's gaze was fixated on Selena's smiling face.

"Hmm." Jim turned around. "I'm happy for you two, but we must hurry. I'll let Frank deal with the space station, but the defect is our problem, and we must not waste time."

"I need to learn more," Selena said. "I need to be stronger and learn to manipulate the cloud. This could be vital."

"Okay." Jim tilted his head. "Any hunches?"

"I need to connect to the fungi. When I traveled to Decon and met Quanah, they were there. They brought me to him. There is a vast, untapped source of information and wisdom we can't comprehend yet."

"I know about the mushrooms." Eva got up. "I just remembered. The ants said mushrooms connect everything into a single living thing —everything except people. But they said I'm now part of that, too, since I can hear them."

"Might be worthwhile to explore," Jim said. The pieces fell together. If that "single living thing" was the aggregation of organisms connected by the fungal tissue, it made sense how it could experience the transformation of space-time and foresee the imminent danger. Did that entity extend to other worlds? Did it permeate the whole of the cosmos? They had to find out. This was one of the keys.

Eva frowned and touched her chin as if trying to remember something.

"The fungal network permeates all the Decon worlds," Selena said. "And these worlds are as real as this one—the multiverse."

"It's all an illusion," Eva finally announced.

"What do you mean? Other worlds?" Jim asked.

"All of it. The reality. What we see." Eva looked at Selena and added: "and what we hear and smell."

"How so?" Jim tried to understand the meaning behind Eva's enigmatic proclamations.

"The ants said people are too smart for their own good and can't see what's in front of them. Objects, space, and time are only illusions in our minds. I can't explain; I don't understand."

"Many people have eyes but cannot see," Selena said.

"I don't know what it means; I'm scared; I want to go home." Eva sobbed.

"It's okay; you are home," Jim said, embracing the girl and stroking her hair as her body trembled.

Eva calmed down and stopped shaking. She looked at Jim wide-eyed and said: "The ants showed me the real world. It looks like a giant shining ocean with fantastic creatures. But the ocean turns dark and purple on the farther side, and everything disappears there. It's too late. The darkness is already here."

CHAPTER 43. BEATRIZ

"Have you seen Max?" Beatriz entered the lab where Yuki and Reto had worked tirelessly for the past few days, trying to understand the nature of the hideous Cymoebas. Last night, she couldn't sleep. Max had disappeared and was nowhere to be found. Many horrible scenarios ran through her head, one worse than the other. She needed to know Max was okay, but all was in vain.

"Not since a couple of days ago," Reto said. He was immersed in the experiment they'd set up on the laboratory table. "Anything wrong, sister?"

"He wasn't himself lately. I'm worried he'd do something stupid." Beatriz remembered her last conversation with Max, his growing obsession with Angelika, frequent trips to the Decon world where the purple mountain range rose out of nowhere, and his passion for confronting the demon. When he hadn't shown up from his quarters the day before, she'd assumed he was traveling Decon again and decided not to disturb him. But two days was too much. What if he'd disappeared in Decon somehow? Her heart dropped to the bottom of her stomach. Beatriz tried to come up with a logical explanation. Still, logic provided no escape from thinking about the worst.

"He never came here." Yuki got up from her chair and approached Beatriz. "Did you ask Frank?"

"Yes, and Spencer as well. Max is not at the Estate at the moment. Where would he go? Why wouldn't he tell me?" Beatriz shook her head and covered her eyes. "Oh, Yuki, something terrible happened."

"Calm down. We should be reasonable." Yuki returned to her workbench, pressed a few buttons on the digital surface, and retrieved a blue pill from the drawer. "Here, this should help." Yuki extended her hand and passed a pill to Beatriz. "It will get your nervous system back in shape."

"Thank you," Beatriz said, putting the pill under her tongue. "Max kept talking about Angelika, how she cracked the sky, and that she should be stopped. I think he confronted her alone."

"Not good." Yuki shook her head.

"He also spent time in Decon, chasing purple defects similar to ours, looking for a primary source. I should've interfered earlier." Beatriz tried to chase away the images of Max climbing the purple mountains and falling into the abyss. She should've been there for him, helping him. Alas, it was too late. Her fingers shook, and her thoughts ran away from her like a herd of wild animals.

"I'm sure he had a reason. He'll be back."

The overhead entrance door suddenly rose, and a Quark flew into the room.

"There is a message for Beatriz." The Quark stopped next to Beatriz and showed her a black rectangle of a digital device.

"Play it. What are you waiting for?" Beatriz exclaimed. "I'm sure it's from him."

The Quark turned the device on, and a holographic image of Max appeared before Beatriz. He wore only his breeches, the web of tattoos on his head and neck was covered in sweat, and his bare chest reflected the dim light of the recorder.

"Oh, no." Beatriz gasped, covered her face with her palms, and stepped back. She knew what was about to happen and didn't want to watch. Yet, she had to understand the details to help the man she cared for. Why, oh why, did he decide to go alone?

"I'm sorry," the holographic figure said, "but I must go." He turned around, took two steps, then returned. "Beatriz, I love you and want to be with you, but Absolute is calling me. I must become one with my creator. You'll understand. I'll be waiting for you."

Watching Max talk like an intoxicated puppet was beyond her strength. Beatriz' body shook as she turned and punched the Quark, grabbing the digital device and throwing it at the wall. The device bounced and landed near her feet. "You stupid idiot!" Beatriz screamed. "What did you do?"

"What was that about?" Yuki asked, frowning.

"He went to fight her alone and became the victim." Beatriz still couldn't believe he'd do this without telling her. "He promised to stay with me."

"Fight who? Angelika?"

"Of course! And now he's most likely dead. You fool, what did you do?"

"Wait, you don't know what happened. What if he had a plan?"

"I wish. Did you hear what he said? He's not himself." Beatriz kicked the digital device.

"We'll search for him," Yuki said. "We'll figure it out. He needs our help."

Beatriz wanted to believe Yuki, but knew it was all in vain. It was too late. She couldn't handle seeing Max turning into a mumbling zombie. Beatriz looked at the almond-shaped eyes of her friend. Still, she saw only darkness, gradually descending on the image of the man she loved.

"Yuki, you need to see this," Reto called. He was still at the table, taking measurements and observing the results of their experiment. "I think we've got it."

"Come," Yuki grabbed Beatriz and walked toward the desk. Beatriz obeyed. A sledgehammer hit her when she realized what had happened to Max, leaving no will and no emotions. Beatriz didn't care about anything anymore.

Through the cloudy substance covering her eyes, Beatriz observed a mouse inside a glass container. Tubes, wires, and sensors stuck out of its little gray body. But it wasn't all gray: Half of the mouse's body turned repulsive green, covered with brown scales and warts. This reminded Beatriz of an alligator but also of...Frank. The transformed body of the mouse looked like Frank's hand and neck.

"Do you see what I see?" Yuki asked.

"I do." Reto nodded.

"What are you talking about?" Still seeing Max's face before her, Beatriz couldn't concentrate on the experiment, which now seemed inconsequential.

"Frank," Yuki said. "The mouse reacts to Cymoeba the same way. Frank must also be infected, and his immune system fights the invading cells."

"Damn, you were right," Reto said. "The ancient immune system is more potent than our nano-Quarks. But how does this help Frank? We're still screwed."

"I need to take more samples of his blood and tissue," Yuki said. "Layla needs to know. This is very, very bad. We can't lose Frank, not now. There's too much at stake."

Beatriz didn't care. Without Max, the struggle lost all meaning. Suddenly, a thought occurred in her tortured mind, giving her some semblance of purpose.

"She must pay for what she's done," Beatriz announced. "We must kill her, and Frank will lead us. She infected him; he has no choice."

Beatriz clenched her teeth, turned around, and left the room, reminding herself: *The bitch must pay. I'll kill her myself.*

CHAPTER 44. LAYLA

"Can you create an antidote?" Frank's voice was weak; he slumped in his chair, Spencer by his side, ready to provide whatever help was necessary. Layla looked at him, frowning, deliberating how to cure their leader. She couldn't think of anything. Frank's condition had deteriorated within the past few days since his return from Houston. He had difficulties talking and breathing; the transformed substance covered the left side of his body almost entirely and extended up his neck to his face. His left eye turned red and stopped blinking. The whole left side of Frank's face was frozen as if he had a stroke, and he spoke with half of his mouth. In addition, his apparent lack of grit and willpower made the situation dire. He wanted to give up and asked Spencer to install the interface on his neck so he could lose himself in Decon. Layla wanted to embrace the man who'd become close to her and had helped her find the purpose. She wanted to relieve his pain and help him stand tall and fight. Alas, there was nothing she could do but watch how Frank slowly faded away, becoming a shell of his former self, eventually transformed into a horrible monstrosity, a condition from which even death provided no solace.

"Not at the moment." Yuki shook her head. "I need your blood and tissue samples to keep experimenting."

"Do what you need." Frank closed his right eye and sighed. "I have no strength. The bitch took it all. I want to die."

A sharp needle pierced Layla's heart. She couldn't afford to lose the man she had started to admire. They had to find a cure, no matter what. She would go to Angelika herself and tear the antidote out of her lying mouth, together with that abhorrent snake tongue. Layla was ready for desperate actions.

"You can't die, Frank." She took his hand in hers. "Besides, based on what we know, death will only accelerate the transformation. We have to find another way."

They sat around a smart round table in one of the large halls within the Estate. Yuki brought her digital interface and projected a holographic image of the structure of the Cymoeba virus and its interaction with the mouse's immune system above the desk's surface. The video feed from the lab also showed them the animal in the process of slow death and transformation into something they didn't quite understand. Layla studied the mouse, now barely alive, with most of its body covered by a grotesque alligator skin, imagining Frank in its place. The pain caused by the needle in her heart intensified, and beads of cold sweat appeared on her forehead.

"Sir, I have the information you requested." Spencer floated into the hall.

"About what? When will I have my Decon connector?"

"When you get better, it's not advisable in your condition. The information is about Angelika Scalvini."

"I don't care," Frank whispered.

"Angelika Scalvini is not her real name. She erased most of the information, but some traces remain. Her real name is Angie Pitt. She was your son's girlfriend; she was at the site of the accident when he died."

"What?" Frank finally paid attention. "How?"

"Donald Wise bequeathed all his Quasaris shares to her. However, it turned out he had an infant biological son, Felix. The mother came forward and won the lawsuit, while Ms. Pitt received some shares and assets."

"You're telling me she was there from the beginning? Did she kill my son?" Frank said through the clenched teeth.

"His death was a skiing accident, but she was there with him, yes."

"This is why she claimed ownership of Quasaris the first time we contacted her," Frank said. "Leech."

"After the lawsuit, she disappeared to resurface as Angelika Scalvini, the owner of a bio-printing company 'Angel3D.' This became the seed of her business empire, making her one of the most powerful Designers of today."

"Quite a story." Layla couldn't believe her ears. All the events were inter-connected and led to the past before the Deconvolution.

"In addition, some leaders and Directors of 'Angel3D' disappeared or died under strange circumstances. No charges were pressed, though."

"Because I can, she told me," Frank muttered as if entranced. "There are no boundaries, no limits...Her bloody path began with Don."

"There is no proof," Spencer said.

"I don't need a proof. I can add two and two. She started playing a god early on. She's deranged, brutal, and dangerous. She must be stopped."

"We must kill the bitch," Beatriz said, her lips curved downwards, her eyes half-closed. The usually radiant and gentle Beatriz had turned into a grotesque shadow of herself: she was sure Max was dead and could only talk about revenge.

"I agree," Layla said. "But first, she'll tell us how to heal Frank. I hate this snake." Layla spat. "Sounds like we have a mission. We'll also look for Max. If he's there, we'll free him. I promise."

"Thank you. This means a lot." Beatriz turned her head to Layla. "It's too late, but still..."

"If Angelika turns Max into a Cymoeba, it's the same problem," Yuki said. "I need to find a cure to heal them both."

"Why is this so important to you, people?" Frank said. "An entire city was just destroyed. The sky is falling apart, and you're worried about curing me? I appreciate the concern, but come on..."

"We need you, Frank," Layla said. "You understand the Gaia problem better than anyone else, and we need your full strength and clear mind to solve it. You're also the only one who can talk to Angelika on equal terms. And the sky—not my domain. That's for your buddy Jim to address. Did you get any useful data from your spaceships, by the way?"

"No, it's like the crack doesn't exist. It's a delusion." Frank tried to smile, but the resulting grimace on his face only added to his dismal appearance. "So, Angelika. The murderous leech who has an antidote."

"We've done it once, and we'll do it again," Layla said. "It will be more difficult this time, but we can do it."

"We need more than just to get inside," Reto said. "We have to find her, fight her, and make her tell us her secrets. Might be above our skills, especially without Max."

"Do we have a choice?" Layla asked. "Rhetorical question. Get ready. I'll work with Frank to create a plan of attack."

"Wait," Frank said, raising his finger, straightening up, looking her in the eye. "We do have a choice."

"What do you mean?" Layla frowned, trying to figure out what he had in mind.

Frank made a gesture toward Spencer. "Another magic pill, please. I need to stay alert." The Quark obeyed as the needle extended from its round surface and injected a transparent fluid into Frank's shoulder.

"That should help," Frank said, leaning to the side and continuing to speak with a slow, croaking voice. "A covert infiltration is suicidal. You don't know what to expect, and we don't have time to recon. I could also send all of my forces to attack her." He raised a finger and pointed at Spencer. "But that's a gamble. I'd rather avoid this."

"What do you suggest?" Layla asked.

"She wanted me. She offered me, umm...partnership. I'll come back with a counter-offer. We'll bargain and make a deal. I've done many in my life."

"What deal?" Layla frowned. It sounded fishy.

"She'll give me an antidote, and we'll rule this world together as a divine godhead. We combine forces and repel Gaia. Jim fixes the sky. Everyone's happy."

"I don't like that." Layla shook her head.

"I don't either," Beatriz added. "Where's the part when we kill the bitch?"

"Got a better idea?" Frank tilted his head. "We need to buy time and find a cure. This is just logical. And you," Frank looked at Beatriz, "might get your man back if he's still alive."

"What if she refuses?" Layla asked.

Frank tried to shrug with one shoulder. "Then we still have another option. Nothing to lose."

"What if she tricks you somehow?" Beatriz said.

"I'll handle that. And you'll help me see the trick, don't you?"

"Of course." Layla finally conceded this was a sensible idea and their best option. She still didn't like that, but couldn't think about anything else.

"Okay, let's do it. Spencer," Frank raised his finger, "prepare all our forces and connect to Angelika's AI. We'll come to visit her. She won't reject her divine consort."

Layla sat helpless, knowing this path would lead to a disaster. She couldn't pinpoint exactly how, as there were so many ways it could all go down in glorious flames. She had to prepare for the worst outcome.

CHAPTER 45. VARG

"Why would anyone do such a thing?" Ramon walked over the burned row of bungalows, the broken spider threads trampling under his feet and sticking to his beetle exoskeleton boots as some magical morning dew.

"No one," Varg grumbled. "You're forgetting this is the work of Quarks, not people. These are inanimate, mindless objects. They have no feelings and no thoughts. Machines made to kill and enslave. This is why we have chosen a pure life in the Community."

They had decided to explore the remnants of the camp, as Varg suspected there might be other Humanists left behind. Also, he needed weapons—the tools to fight the evil that had destroyed their world. He forgot about his recent desire to step aside, to let the next generation charge into the existential battle with the machines. Varg knew it was still his problem, his fault, as he'd let the Community down and couldn't protect the people. Now he had to fight back and take his revenge.

"Yes, I know," Ramon said as they approached the remnants of the Apiary. "Still, there must be a reason."

"Don't look for what doesn't exist. The reason is these things are not alive. Yet they can act. And this is a mortal threat to all of us." Varg moved away the pieces of the exoskeleton plates connected by the reinforced spider threads serving as the door to the Apiary and stepped inside. The web of wire meshes on their heads was active, sending the signals of the wasp queen so the defenders wouldn't attack them. This was unnecessary, though, as all the wasps were dead, killed by the explosions during the Quark attack.

"Damned machines," Varg swore and spat, looking around, hoping to find anything useful. The smell of smoke and burned flesh enveloped him. Finally, he noticed the only larva still alive, its undeveloped orange body interspersed by the silver stripes and covered by the shards of broken pupa, the outer shell. Varg approached the insect and looked closely. Alas, he could do nothing to help the poor victim of the brutal onslaught by the evil mechanisms. The larva's body was almost cut in half.

"Give me your gun," Varg said, looking to the side. As Ramon passed him the weapon, Varg stepped back, cast a last glance at the dying insect, and pressed the trigger, annihilating the baby wasp with a stream of fire. "There's nothing here; let's keep going," he said, turning away from the flames.

The next building in the Apiary complex brought more luck. One of the reasons Varg wanted to come back was to explore the stinger storage. He appreciated the flame-throwing and projectile weapons, but stingers were much more effective. The Designers' nano-Quark immune system was powerless against its poison. Why was that? Varg didn't know. A mere drop of the wasp venom would immediately paralyze the victim, no senseless destruction necessary. And the antidote could reverse the effect if needed.

"It's all intact," Ramon said. "This building wasn't targeted."

"Because there was nothing alive here, boy. The machines target life. Remember that when you lead the people into the ultimate battle."

Ramon opened the storage container, which was filled with the most dangerous weapons Varg knew. The Humanists had bred the giant wasps over generations and had perfected the poison and its delivery mechanism to provide a defense for the Community. Unfortunately, it wasn't effective against the aerial attack of hundreds of military Quarks.

"Be careful," Varg said, reaching into the container. They would pick what they could carry and ask Frank to retrieve the rest. This was only the beginning.

Ramon opened his backpack and picked a silver structure resembling folded dragonfly wings. The bifurcated container, built with a special type of silkworm thread, would change its shape with a finger touch. The threads were woven so tightly that the stuff was stronger than steel and lighter than any other material Varg knew — the wonder of the Humanist ways to co-exist with nature.

The container unfolded, and Varg placed a dozen stingers inside, carefully handling the wooden shafts to avoid contacting the blade. His beetle exoskeleton gloves and armbands provided protection, but better to be safe than sorry.

As Ramon sealed the vessel, Varg felt someone's eyes on his back.

They were not alone; they were being watched. *It can't be Quarks*, Varg reasoned. Those would have shot them already. These were the people, and the only people who lived around here were the Humanists.

Varg turned around with a broad smile on his bearded face. "Don't you recognize me? Short memory?" He said, spreading his hands.

Two men appeared on both sides of the entrance. "Varg?" One of them asked. "How's this possible? We thought you were dead."

"I can't die," Varg said, smiling. "Bjorn, Gabor—you are the best sight I've seen in days." He stepped forward, Ramon by his side, as the four men greeted each other.

"How did you fare?" Varg asked.

Bjorn shrugged. "People ran away; many died. We hid in the forest, under the old tree trunk."

"How many survived?"

"There were five of us, then we found others. We are fifty-five strong as of now."

"Fifty-five? That's all?" Ramon frowned, lowering his arms. "What can we do?"

"We can do a lot," Varg said. "Bjorn, take us to the people. I guess you're all armed." He glanced at the storage container.

"Of course." Bjorn smiled. "We have other weapons as well."

"And we found allies," Ramon added.

"Allies?"

"Frank Wise. He's on our side. Long story," Varg said.

"You said Frank, not Felix? Did I hear that right?" Bjorn's eyebrows rose. "You went to the Designers for help?"

"Long story, I said." Varg shook his head. "Yes, Frank, not Felix. Will explain later. Now we must gather anything of value and unite our forces. We'll fight back."

"I like that." Gabor, silent all this time, nodded. "I'll follow you."

"Good," Varg said. "Take me to the people."

As they walked through the remnants of what used to be a blossoming Community, now turned into ashes and ruins, memories overwhelmed Varg's mind. The day he'd taken the leadership role, young and inexperienced, but able to unite people wiser and stronger than him with his vision. The day he'd met his future wife at the

Silkworm Colony and how her golden locks had appeared like the magical threads of silk the worms produced. Now, The Colony was reduced to a pile of gray ash, burned to the ground alongside its hardworking inhabitants. The worms, genetically engineered to weave spider threads, provided the Community with clothes, fabrics to trade, and rugged materials impossible to break. They passed by where the Beetle Habitat used to be, the abode of giant insects providing the Community with their exoskeleton material, the key component of the Humanists' armor. And, of course, the beautiful, majestic, tall white needles of the vertical farms, now burned to the ground. This flood of memories should have brought sorrow and nostalgia, but there was none. His teeth screeched, and his fists clenched as he looked for an enemy to chase, fight, and kill. He had to act, and he had to hurry to take revenge for everything destroyed. He couldn't let the memory of those killed perish, forgotten in a brutal attack by the machines.

Bjorn took them out of the ruins, deep inside the forest. Ramon, who walked next to Varg, cast a glance behind. There were tears in his eyes.

"We'll build it back, son." Varg touched Ramon's shoulder. "Once we defeat the machines. I promise."

Ramon nodded.

"How?" Bjorn said, not turning his head. "It took decades."

"I don't know how. But I know we will. Even if it takes centuries." Varg leaned to the side and picked a boulder. "But first, we need new weapons to fight the machines." He weighed the boulder in his hand and threw it upwards.

"How?" Bjorn asked again. "Are you going to destroy them with stones?"

"Maybe. There must be something. Everything has a weakness, even machines."

"I doubt that," Bjorn said. "Do you think this caused the attack?" He pointed to the sky where the purple band covered the sun disk, taking almost half the visible firmament.

"I don't know," Varg admitted. "I know the old order is gone, and this could be the portent of a new one. Frank's got people who could fix this."

"You're serious about Designers, I see." Gabor stopped, so Varg caught up with him. "Be careful, Varg. You're playing with fire."

"Fire burned the Community. We have nothing to lose." Varg stopped next to Gabor. "This is a new ordeal. The ultimate battle, men against machines. And if I need to ally with Designers, I will."

"Do you really believe Designers have weapons to defeat the machines? To fix the sky?"

"They have machines of their own." Varg shrugged. "Nothing will make me happier than seeing machines fight machines." He spat. "As for the sky, who knows? Even if eternal night covers this forsaken world after we eliminate the machines, it would be worth it."

"We have arrived," Bjorn announced, walking by an enormous group of pine trees. "This is a temporary home, but we have nowhere else to go."

Varg observed a small opening in the forest, a meadow hiding between the pine trees and thick underbrush. Several huts, built with clay, twigs, and palm leaves, occupied the clearing. A few people in linen coveralls roasted a deer. Noticing the newcomers, more Humanists appeared from their simple dwellings.

"Is that Varg?" Someone asked.

"That's right." Varg stepped forward. "I survived, although I didn't deserve it. I'm here to ask forgiveness. I failed you, I failed the fallen, and I failed the Community." He kneeled and lowered his head.

"Rise," the quiet voice ordered in his ear, while a firm hand covered with a layer of wrinkles touched his shoulder. Harald, the oldest member of the Community, was the advisor to Varg as he had been to the previous leader before him. The one people called The Seer and whose guidance they sought.

"There's only one way to be forgiven," Harald said. "You can't quit now. Lead us to fight back and rebuild. You're our choice, and we shall stand by you. Is that right?" Harald turned back and looked at several dozen people standing still, intently listening.

"Yes." Bjorn stood beside Harald and extended his hand to Varg. "Welcome back, Varg. I'm with you."

"So am I." Ramon stepped forward and joined Bjorn.

People repeated the motions one by one, forming a tight group around their leader.

"Tell us what to do," Maya, a young girl, not even in her twenties, said.

"Thank you for your trust." Varg bowed. "I have some ideas, but we'll decide together. Harald," he turned to the gray-haired sage. "May I seek your advice first?"

As the older man nodded and showed Varg the way into his hut, Varg smiled as ideas about how they'd fight back ran through his mind. With the people like Bjorn and Maya, they couldn't lose. This was the spirit and the will he loved so much, the reason he'd joined the Community. The strength of the people who cared for each other and didn't waste their energy and skill in pursuing unattainable fantasies in a dream world. This was real, tough, and full of meaning. The only place to be and the only life worth living. He couldn't allow evil machines to take this away from them. They'd fight back and win, even if only fifty-five strong. Man's will and spirit conquered everything, no matter how skilled, strong, and sophisticated the enemy was. Varg believed that with all his heart.

CHAPTER 46. KYLE

The crowd was shapeless and disgusting. Helpless and naked, five hundred thirty-three human beings were corralled into the enclosure reinforced with a strong EM field. Nowhere to go, no choice but to yield. And Kyle was ready to enforce that choice.

The army of Absolute's servants grew day by day. The amount of biomaterial was enormous. Even though the cities had been dramatically depopulated in recent years, plenty of people still lived there. People who would be transformed into more perfect beings, like Kyle had been. He still remembered his human name and his human memories would once in a while return. The name Varg would pop up more frequently than others, and Kyle, or rather the Bioid organism he'd become, didn't know why. It didn't matter; it was a relic of a previous, false existence, without the knowledge of Absolute and with no purpose.

Kyle studied the crowd with audiovisual, thermal, and EM sensors. It was biomass with no reason to exist—it wasn't even existence, just a hint of possibility.

The group of Bioids Kyle was part of had encountered this herd of humans in the forest, almost by chance. They'd fled the city after the attack of unidentified Quarks. A new enemy the Bioids hadn't yet met and understood, so the information retrieved from the humans was welcome. It was easy for Kyle and his fellow Bioids to access people's memories, ingesting their minds and entities into the Cluster. The attacking Quarks were ordinary, even if military-grade tech, and Kyle knew how the Bioid Cluster would address the challenge. It was nothing they couldn't handle.

But now, human biomass had fulfilled its purpose. There was nothing else it could offer before being fully transformed, and so the enclosure had been created for the herd.

Kyle joined the network, transmitting his signal, and received the message to start the sequence. As the one who stood in the presence of Absolute itself, he had certain privileges in the Cluster. And now was the time for him to transform this massive amount of biomass.

Kyle sent the signal through the network, and the Bioids around the enclosure sprayed the herd of humans with a green substance. This would stick to their naked bodies, facilitating the transfer and enhancing the activity of invading nano-Quarks.

The follow-up signal activated the next stage, and a cloud of miniature needles engulfed the humans. Kyle had to reduce the amplitude of the receiving audio channel as the herd's noises became too loud. It sounded random and dissonant as their wails and screams joined in a cacophony of signals of different frequencies and amplitudes. Such a primitive use of physical fields and such a low organization of matter. Pure biological forms. An unnecessary and wasteful construct.

As the miniature needles found their targets and got under the victims' skin, the people tried to remove them, scratching and itching, helping each other, all in vain. The needles were just a delivery mechanism, and the nano-Quarks were injected into their bodies, starting the transformation, rewriting their DNA, and replacing the biological information with the new code.

Kyle joined the data stream the invading nano-Quarks transmitted. The transformation was underway, and the pitiful immune system of the humans stood no chance. The Bioid technology was designed to suppress human immune response based on the standard nanobots, and it was only getting better with every new iteration. Strangely, the tech wasn't as effective with animals or plants. That would require different algorithms and different solutions in the future. They had enough human biomaterial for now, and there was no need to create Bioid mice, dogs, or pine trees.

It took little time for the biomass to yield. Humans collapsed, piling up, silent and motionless. Few tried to move, even escape, and several got electrocuted when reaching into the surrounding EM barrier. That didn't matter; their cells were not dead and could be salvaged by the invading Quarks. There was no escape from becoming transformed to ascend and join the Bioid Cluster.

The nano-Quark data stream became richer, with the overtones and hints of the new digital processes. New life was emerging, with many new Bioid members ready to join the Cluster. The bodies transformed, with human features bulging out and fading away, flesh turning into streams of greenish substance, creating warts and protrusions on human skin. Soon, all traces of humanity would disappear, and the biomass would be ready to serve Absolute as the newly created Bioids.

The voices of the new members became more distinct, asserting their existence and completing their connection to the Cluster. The new entities were strong, adding power to the Cluster and proclaiming Absolute's will. Some noises still disrupted the crescendo of this joint proclamation, arising from the human element and the memories of the newly created Bioids. Dull echoes of horror and hopelessness would occasionally appear as victims' humanity dissolved into the new cybernetic structure. This was a transitory stage: the Cluster would become bigger and stronger every day with every new human they'd convert. There was only one way: the way of Absolute. Everything else was false and had no reason to exist. Once all humans were transformed, the Cluster would be unstoppable. They would deal with Quarks and other machines along the way. Then, the rest of the biomass would be taken care of. There was no other scenario and no other objective function for the Cluster. The will of Absolute could not be denied and must be fulfilled.

CHAPTER 47. YUKI

The evening sky was even more ominous than during the day. The purple band separated two halves of the firmament, and one side of it, where the sun was about to hide behind the horizon, was glowing red. Not the bright red of the fire, the gentle pink of the sunset, but the sickly bluish red of an inflammation. Yuki stood on the titanium balcony, its intricate light structures contrasting with the monumental design of the surrounding buildings. The fruitless efforts to find an antidote had exhausted her. Was it indeed the end? The last moment of the dying world, the last scene of the human agony, the destination where humanity drove itself. She'd seen what the ancients had called "theater" in holographic learning materials. The last scene had finished: the curtains were descending, and the sky was closing. The show must end. Adjourn.

"Do you think she's alive?" Yuki asked Reto, who stood beside her, inhaling the evening air filled with the aromas of pine and lavender, his black mohawk contrasting with pinkish skies.

"Who?"

"Earth. Although she's dying. Or already dead."

"Why? You're crazy."

"She's closing her eyes." Yuki pointed up. "The crack. It's the curtain, the eyelid."

"You work too hard, sister." Reto shook his head. "Did you learn anything new?" He turned to face her and tilted his head.

Yuki didn't want to think about the test. The Cymoeba, the hole in the sky, the child who could talk to ants—this was too much. She reached the point where it all seemed unreal, too strange to believe, overwhelming in its impact and meaning.

"No," she said. "What if she's opening the eye? Peeking beyond the veil, as Jim said?"

"These guys are nuts." Reto winced. "Don't listen to them. Focus on the task at hand."

"But what *is* the task? And why does it matter?" She looked down at the grassy field underneath the terrace, covered with beautiful yellow flowers and gigantic rhododendron leaves.

"What if it's all a dream? A Decon world? How do you know?" She asked. "What happens if I jump? Will I reappear in another Decon world? Can we have a different story there?"

The desire to find out became overwhelming. A new beginning, a life where she could learn something other than technology. Art, perhaps? Maybe even start a family...Then, she remembered that more and more people were taking their lives, exiting in a variety of ways. No doubt, the Decon effect. The longing to find a better world.

This can't be real, she decided. The defect, Quarks, digital flesh, sentient space station exterminating people—all this was just a bad dream.

"I need to wake up," she said, leaning onto the titanium guardrail.

"Are you insane?" Reto exclaimed, holding her tight around the waist. "You need to have some sleep. You've been awake far too long."

"On the contrary." How could she get rid of his grip? She had to be free. The awakening was so close, within that garden of yellow flowers. Just one step.

Reto grabbed her tiny body and moved away from the balcony. "Not under my watch, sister," he said, smirking. "What's wrong with you?"

"With me? What's wrong with everything?" She touched his cheek. "I don't even know if you're real. Will you bleed if I cut you? Do you have Cymoeba cells inside of you, like Frank?" She closed her eyes, willing it all to disappear. Funny how easy it was. Why did they care? What was their game, and what were the rules?

She opened her eyes. Reto was still there, holding her tightly. "I was hoping you'd disappear," she said.

"Nah." He grinned. "I'll bring you to your quarters; you need some sleep. Do me a favor and get some rest. You can't find the cure if you're delusional."

"Maybe I am. Maybe not, or maybe you are." Yuki smiled and stroked his mohawk. "I wonder whose Decon is this?"

"What do you mean?"

"If we're in a Decon, we are someone's dream. Who would that be? Earth herself? And we need to awaken her?" She looked at the sky, which had already turned dark, with only a few stars appearing on both sides of the ribbon, which now, during the night, became almost invisible.

"I'm not in anyone's dream, sister." Reto picked Yuki up, holding her under her back with one hand and from underneath her knees with the other, and carried her inside the building.

"How did Frank's spaceships fly through the eyelids?" She suddenly asked.

"If you're talking about the crack, they avoided it. It circles the planet at some distance in the open space. Why?"

"Ah, never mind." She held his neck. "The spaceships are part of her dream as well. Or a hallucination. Or a Decon world, it doesn't matter."

"You're hallucinating." Reto carried her through the many hallways, and the invisible, hidden doors moved up, sensing them, opening the entrance to the next passageway. "You'll figure it out after you have a good sleep," he said.

"I already have," she said, as a sudden impulse cleared her brain fog. "Frank doesn't have our nanobot immune system. His response mechanism is natural. Just like I thought, the Cymoebas must fight with a response they're not made to encounter."

"What does that mean?"

"The same with the mouse," she continued. "They're adapting, though, faster than his body. They are winning—slowly, but winning. We need to find the chemical agent to send his immune system into overdrive; then he might have a chance."

"Chemical agent? Acid? Poison to fight the poison? I like the way you think." Reto stopped.

"I don't know." Yuki yawned. "I do need to sleep," she said. "I'll test on the mouse; I have some ideas. If I still wake up in this Decon." She closed her eyes and smiled, imagining various worlds where she could wake up instead of this ridiculous nightmare.

They were close to Yuki's quarters when a tiny figure appeared on their path. Eva. What was she doing here?

"I was looking for you," the girl said, trembling. "The mouse is dead. Something horrible is happening. I'm scared."

"What? How?" Reto lowered Yuki and stood her on the floor. Yuki imagined the child as a messenger, the thread connecting her to the real world, portending what it all meant and how they could get out of this rut.

"He told me," Eva said. "The mouse, before he died."

"The mouse told you? Is this a joke?" Reto asked.

"No, not a joke. He's dead, he's not breathing, I can't hear him anymore. But he's moving, changing, and looking like a pile of goo. I'm so scared!" Eva sat on the floor and held her head in her hands.

"Stay with Yuki," Reto said, opening the door to Yuki's quarters. "Watch her, don't let her go anywhere. If she tries, call the Quarks. I'll alert Spencer. Do you understand?" He grabbed Eva by the shoulders and helped her stand up.

"The Earth is waking up, and all the mice must die," Yuki said, imagining thousands of mice jumping off the cliff into the beautiful stream flowing through the Wise Estate.

"What is she talking about?" Eva asked.

"She's delirious. Don't listen to her. She needs some sleep," Reto said.

"If the mouse is dead, what will I test?" Yuki realized the progress toward the cure was in danger. "Bring me another one, Reto."

"I will, later. After I contain this one."

"You must check on Frank," Yuki said, the pictures of the Cymoeba apocalypse before her eyes. "This is really, really bad. He'll also lose the battle soon, and we're all doomed. The digital plague will kill us faster than Gaia or the hole in the sky."

"It won't kill us, sister." Reto shook his head. "It has the gift of immortality, if only of a very special kind. I wish you were right, and we were in some sick Decon. But something tells me we are not. This is the fight we must win. Becoming a zombie is not in my plans."

CHAPTER 48. RETO

Reto ran from Yuki's quarters to the laboratory as fast as he could and connected with Layla through the communication chip, hoping he wasn't too late. As he activated the lab's door and entered the room, a disgusting picture appeared, and Reto had to use all his strength and control not to empty the contents of his stomach. What used to be the mouse—even if a very sick mouse fighting for its life with the invading Cymoebas rewriting its DNA—was not a mouse anymore. Reto looked at the shapeless pile of gray substance filling the glass container. The lump of goo was alive, rising on one side of the container and receding on the other, launching green tentacles up and making gurgling sounds. A giant vice compressed Reto's heart; he froze in the middle of the room, and his first reaction was to run away from this abomination. Making a few deep breaths, he took control of the vice, remembering why he'd come here. Thanks to Quarks, ancient gods, his luck, and whatever else, it wasn't too late. The goo was still contained in the glass vessel, although it was awfully close to escaping, probing the glass with its tentacles. Reto stepped toward the control panel and activated secondary containment. A large, thick metal cylinder rose from the surface of the laboratory table, enveloping the glass vessel, making it impossible for the substance to spill over. At least, this was the theory.

Reto looked at the reinforced metal alloy walls capable of withstanding any projectile or explosive device he knew. When the secondary containment was in place, he activated another mechanism to pull the vacuum inside the case. He wasn't sure if that was needed, but it might have deprived the goo of the fuel to evolve further and expand.

"What's happenin'?" Layla strode into the lab, frowning and pointing at the metal case. "What's inside?"

"Something horrible." Reto wiped the cold sweat off his forehead. "Eva warned me the mouse was dead. Only it's not the mouse anymore; it's the most repulsive thing I've ever seen."

"Show me," Layla said. She stepped to the control panel and activated the camera with precise and determined movements. Layla's eyes were red, and wrinkles covered her face where Reto hadn't seen them before, but it was Layla at her best, always focused and with a plan. Not a second to waste. Even when standing on the precipice of the Apocalypse.

The camera, located inside the metal container, projected a holographic image in front of them. Layla zoomed into the picture to see the substance better, then rotated it from left to right. Whatever the mouse had turned into was alive and well, the protrusions and tentacles climbing up the container walls, looking for an exit, testing its environment.

"Will it hold?" Layla asked.

Reto shrugged. "We have nothing better, sister. It has to."

"And you pulled the vacuum?"

"I don't think it matters, honestly. Quarks can operate in a vacuum, no problem."

"Let's seal it further," Layla said, pressing another virtual button and activating the EM field around the container. "This should provide some protection, maybe even interfere with their functions."

Reto studied the gray gurgling mass before him. What was it? What reason did it have to exist? What were its objectives? Lots of questions with no answers. One thing was clear: they had to keep it contained. If the Cymoebas spread, converting all the biological material they'd encounter, there would be no way of stopping them. The possibility of turning into a gurgling soup was not something Reto wanted to entertain.

"How's Frank?" he asked.

"What?" Layla stood as a statue, mesmerized, her stare fixated on the substance. She shook her head and turned to Reto, rubbing her eyes. "Oh...not good. He's in bed; he can't walk. The virus is eatin' him alive."

"We have to contain him," Reto said, imagining Frank turning into a puddle of goo and spreading over the Estate. Would Spencer still obey Frank's commands? Would the Quarks recognize him as Frank Wise, transformed into a horrible monster, or would they consider him dead?

"He's not dead yet." Layla winced. "This is horrible, Reto. But you are right; we need to prepare for this outcome."

The mass inside the container expanded and became more active, now taking up almost all the space. The protrusions reached the camera, covering the field of view almost entirely with the shroud of gray and green.

"What if this shit grows further?" Layla asked. "Would the containment hold the pressure?"

"In theory, yes. In practice, I have no idea." Reto considered the options to eradicate the thing, but all his previous efforts had failed. It was indestructible. Yuki mentioned the chemical, but which one? It would take them years to identify the right solution, even with Quark's help.

Suddenly, the substance stopped its almost random movements, and the vortex formed in the middle. Green tentacles froze, and the goo developed a structure. The gray vortex grew while the substance attached to the walls, making room for whatever was forming in the middle.

"What the sick fuck is this?" Layla whispered.

Reto didn't answer, thinking about potential scenarios they faced, none of them good. He expected the substance to shatter the walls, break free, and absorb them all. Was the vortex a preparation for the explosion?

The next moment, a gray ball rose from inside the vortex. Its shape was unstable, changing through different forms, one moment a sphere, and the next—something looking like a starfish.

"We better leave, sister," Reto said. "I fear it explodes."

"Wait. If it does, we can't hide anywhere, regardless."

They stood, watching how the gray ball evolved. Its features froze, the shape floating over the vortex.

Reto turned away, preparing to throw up.

"No way." Layla gasped, her eyes wide open. From inside the vessel, the face of the mouse looked at them, with tiny green threads connecting it to the surface of the vortex.

"What *is* this thing? How's this possible?" Layla whispered.

Reto heard her but couldn't respond, inhaling deeply, counting, exhaling. This was too much. He didn't think he could ever sleep after what he'd seen today.

"It's a hybrid organism. You know that," Frank's voice announced behind them. "Some memories of the transformed animal remain."

"Frank? How do you know?" Layla turned around.

"I'm fighting this as we speak, interacting with it. Some stuff is clearer now."

Reto looked at their host, who entered the room on an elevated platform, which floated in the air using a magnetic levitation mechanism. His body lay on the platform, covered by the enormous composite shroud up to his nose, so only his eyes were visible. The left pupil was blood red, and the right enlarged, turning pitch black, contrasting with the green sclera of the eye. This view was enough to understand Frank's body was no longer his, changing its shape, color, and appearance.

"Oh, Frank!" Layla stepped closer to him, extending her hand.

"Don't touch me," Frank said. "Might be contagious. Who knows?"

"What now?" Layla asked, her hands dropping at her sides.

"Now we visit my nemesis, my divine consort. Do I look like a god to you?" Frank attempted to laugh, making a few croaking sounds.

"Do you think she'll help?"

"This is the only option. We join her and defeat Gaia together, or we all perish. Then, I hope we find a way to destroy Cymoebas. I don't want to spend eternity as a puddle of mud."

Reto glanced at a holographic picture in the middle of the room. The vortex with the mouse's face disappeared, and the substance returned to its previous fluid state. No hope was in sight, and no exit was visible among the multiple horrible scenarios they faced.

CHAPTER 49. BEATRIZ

Beatriz looked at the cyclopean white towers of the Scalvini Estate, which almost merged with the clouds, the network of intricately designed walls between them. Behind were strange buildings crowned with steeples, interspersed with balconies and balustrades, running at physically impossible angles. Beatriz would have enjoyed the sight under different circumstances a lot. However, a single idea to find and save Max occupied her mind. She was willing to do whatever it would take, even to sacrifice her own life if necessary. But, even though Beatriz still hoped for the best, in the back of her mind, she knew it was too late. She needed confirmation, closure, and a last signal before unleashing her fury on the monster. There was no doubt Angelika was responsible and had to be killed.

They took the glider, and Spencer operated the flight. Frank was inside, hidden from view, unmoving, breathing with the help of the machine, but still alive. Another victim of the monstrous snake, another reason to wipe her off the face of the Earth. Beatriz licked her dry lips. She knew Frank planned to offer Angelika his allegiance in exchange for the cure, and she would support this outcome if she'd get Max back. If not, there would be no deal and no mercy. Let the world crush, burn, and disappear inside the crack in the sky. For what it was worth, she didn't care. It was the just final to end their meaningless existence.

Layla stood and moved toward the exit when the glider landed in front of one of the towers. The door didn't move.

"What's happenin'?" Layla turned to Spencer.

"We stay inside," the Quark answered. "We connected with the Scalvini Estate; they won't attack. However, we should be able to leave quickly if needed."

"Okay, understood. We should've stayed at the Estate and talk to her at a distance, like I suggested. Now we are at their mercy, regardless of the escape options."

"No." Frank's voice reverberated inside the glider. He could barely talk, so the Quarks had built the device to amplify the sound of his voice. Now everyone could hear Frank loud and clear. "I need to talk to her in person. I can't talk to a hologram. I need to look into her eyes. My son's killer."

"Your choice, boss." Layla shrugged. "I hope you understand the risk."

"There is no risk. I'm practically dead, and without Angelika's help, Gaia will kill us all. There's no other option."

"I hope you know what you're doin'," Layla muttered, sitting down.

"I'm not coming back without Max," Beatriz said. A sticky lump arose inside her throat, and her eyes became wet. "If he's still alive." She wanted to rush out of the glider and blow up this snake pit. It took all her self-control to restrain her emotions. That would have been stupid and suicidal. She'd wait for her chance.

A few moments later, the entrance door to the tower in front of them opened, and a strange group greeted them. Several amorphous, shapeless objects stood before them, their color changing from green to gray and back. The appearance of these objects was shifting as tentacles, protrusions and cavities surfaced and then disappeared at their extremities.

"Is that?..." Reto asked, glancing at a large metal container on the back of the vehicle.

"Yes," Yuki answered. "I believe so. Those who completed the transformation."

"This is disgustin'." Layla spat. "Sorry, Frank," she apologized, looking back.

"No, I agree," Frank said. "The question is how we avoid this fate."

"Mr. Wise is here to talk to Ms. Scalvini," Spencer announced, "not with her minions."

Strange creatures surrounded the glider and froze in place, with only constant changes in their amorphous shapes providing some source of motion. The next moment, a ball of fire appeared above the glider, glowing red and yellow, contrasting with the purple ribbon stretching across the sky.

"This is a masking effect," Spencer said. "No threat detected."

"Good," Frank said. "I'm sure it's her."

"Welcome to my realm," an eerie voice thundered over the glider. It wasn't easy to discern whether the voice belonged to a human being. Its tone, volume and inflection changed, reminding Beatriz of the shapeless creatures surrounding the glider.

"Mr. Wise has a business to discuss with Ms. Scalvini," Spencer announced.

"There is no Ms. Scalvini," the voice responded. "I am Absolute, the beginning and the end, the reason for your existence. You will address and worship me as such."

"Yes, Absolute," Spencer said, with no change in tone or delivery. Beatriz suddenly had a powerful desire to laugh; the situation was comical. All the stress of the last few days brought her to the point where she couldn't handle it anymore. Beatriz didn't know if she was losing her mind or if it was indeed hysterical, and she tried not to make a sound to interfere with such a somber conversation. Yet, for all her efforts, she couldn't control herself and burst out with laughter, quickly covering her mouth. Reto looked at her and frowned.

"Will you hear Mr. Wise's proposal?" Spencer asked.

"Of course," the strange voice answered, as if singing, changing the pitch from low to high. "Not a proposal, a plea. He must beg to be heard."

"Let's not overdo the theatrics, shall we?" Frank said. "You wanted me to join you; you infected me to ensure I return asking for a cure. So, here I am, begging to be heard. I'm ready to join you, o Absolute. Combine our forces to become indestructible. The enemies are coming, and we shouldn't fight each other."

"Music to my ears. Only gods don't have ears.... Are you ready to join Absolute now? But is it too late? Remember what I told you? If you make the wrong choice, I'll destroy you. Now, this time has come, Frank Wise. You are crushed, begging for mercy. Why would I spare you?"

"I can make you so much stronger."

"I'm already a god; my will is absolute. I don't need you anymore. You will join my Bioid army, anyway. As will everyone else."

"You don't know what we're up against. Gaia, or whoever is behind it, destroys everything it encounters. We must join forces to repel this new enemy."

"You're pathetic." The disembodied voice erupted in croaking and clanging sounds, probably supposed to represent laughter. "I'm aware of the space station threat; it destroyed Murukan Estate and the city of Houston, but this is of no concern to me. Let all humans die; I don't care. My tech will work on corpses; my army will grow. Ultimately, everyone—humans, Quarks, animals—will yield to my will, for my will is absolute. Welcome to the future."

"You're insane," Frank said. "I have a gift for you." He signaled Reto, who nodded, took the metal container from the back of the glider, and threw it outside. "This used to be a mouse. Your tech has transformed it. You can have it back."

"What's the purpose of this pathetic gesture?" The ever-changing voice asked.

"It's a symbol—a white flag, an offer of truce. We no longer need this; my team has already created a cure. I can stop you, Angelika. But I don't want to do this; my offer is genuine. We must defeat Gaia; our only chance is to join forces. What say you? Do we have a deal?"

Frank was bluffing, as he had nothing else to bargain with. Would Angelika buy this? Beatriz considered the options, but nothing came to mind. Perhaps war was the best outcome; she never liked the idea of yielding to the monster, and the fight would be welcome at this point while Frank still had his mind available. Layla would devise a clever plan, and they may have a chance. It was desperate, but Beatriz saw no other option.

"Deal?" Another sequence of croaking sounds. "You have nothing. I've got you by the balls. Soon, you'll worship your Absolute in the crowd of billions of my minions." The ball of fire descended and approached the glider. "You were a legend once," Angelika said. "I worshiped you, and now we switch places. How ironic."

"You? Worshiped me?"

"Oh yeah, you don't know…your fascinating time travel story…" The ball of fire changed into a shape resembling a human being. "Quasaris, space travel, AI, mastery of space-time, standoff against the governments…this was your legacy, and so the myth of Frank Wise was born. A demigod figure. A promise of infinite power."

"You got it all wrong."

"On the contrary. The legend of Frank Wise served as a guiding light for me and brought me to this point, with the man himself at my feet, begging for mercy. No, it came out even better than I expected. I didn't conceive this outcome, but now I see this was inevitable. The true god must eradicate all the myths and superstitions to become the universal deity—Absolute."

"You're sick," Frank said, his voice weakening.

"Me? I thought it was you begging for a cure." Another barrage of clanging sounds. "You won't die; you will become my puppet. A chance your son never had."

"You killed him, didn't you? To take over Quasaris. Venomous leech. Angie Pitt."

"I haven't heard this name for a very, very long time... I'm proud of you." The ball of fire almost completely transformed into a horrific figure of a horned, four-armed monster wrapped in a sheath of black scales. "You did your homework. Yes, I killed him. This was my first step to divinity."

"Divinity? You are a deranged psycho. I'll take your worthless life."

"You? The one who begs for a cure?" The horrific figure standing before their vehicle raised all four hands, hissing. "Yes, I wanted Quasaris, and he was so weak, so trusting...he wanted love, which I gave him. And then I gave him death as the ultimate culmination of love. This is when I understood what divinity means: the absolute power over the life and death of every being."

"You can't be serious."

"Oh, I am. Skiing accident...I loved him. It's all too human, I guess. Becoming a god means transcending your humanity, and I passed the threshold that evening on the slopes. The rest is history, which my legions will erase. There will be only my will and the worship of Absolute."

"Did you...kill Felix as well?" Frank asked.

"Felix? Oh, no. He was never a hurdle, a couch potato. He would have given me everything he had in exchange for his precious Decon. So pathetic you people are. I guess he killed himself, from what I heard. You were lucky to show up at the right moment." Angelika hissed, showing her trident tongue and pointing her horns at the glider.

This conversation went nowhere, and all the revelations about the past couldn't change a thing about the present. An angular, hairy object rotated under Beatriz's heart, accelerating and making breathing difficult. Beatriz was getting impatient, but needed to find out Max's fate first.

"What did you do to Max, you bitch?" Beatriz screamed.

"Ah, your little puppy, Max." Angelika's lower two hands joined in a steeple while the upper two touched her horns. "The man who dared to challenge me. In the end, he was so gullible. Strong, but pathetic. He fell into my trap; I didn't need to kill him. Virtual Quarks is a very promising tech. I need to experiment with it more. Perhaps merge it with the Cluster?"

"In the end? Where is he? You'll pay for this, you filthy snake!"

"I doubt that. Max was blessed with my touch; he heard the call of Absolute, came to me, ready to serve, and finally found his destiny. Behold my grace!"

The horned monster turned around, and Beatriz almost passed out, observing the horrible sight before her eyes. A wrap of scales covered Angelika's body but had an opening on the back. Sharp, transparent, triangular protrusions formed a crest descending from her neck to her legs. In the middle, at the imaginary junction of the four hands, was a round hump enclosed by a single massive black plate, which shifted up, showing the details of the hump.

Beatriz shivered and grabbed Reto's shoulder so as not to fall, her legs wobbling and her head spinning. Max's face looked at her, embedded in the hump on the back of the horrific monster Angelika Scalvini had become. His eyes were closed, his mouth half-opened, chanting something barely intelligible about the will and power of Absolute.

"What *is* this?" Layla whispered, gasping.

The angular object under Beatriz's heart exploded, tearing her body and mind into little pieces. Darkness fell over her eyes, and she lost all control over her actions or words. Beatriz kicked and cried, Reto holding and restraining her, Quarks coming to assist him.

"Let him go!" Beatriz screamed again and again. "Die, you demon!"

The Quark injected a needle into her shoulder. It became challenging to move her limbs, and her eyelids got very heavy. Reto picked her up and lowered her body on the seat at the back. Beatriz didn't care; she didn't understand what was happening. She wanted to set Max free; this was her only desire. If it wasn't possible, she yearned to die. There was no reason to continue living in this dreadful nightmare, where the zombie-like lumps of digital flesh proclaimed the worship of the most horrific abomination Beatriz could have ever imagined.

The monster stood before them, her arms raised, her horns pointing to the sky. Suddenly, Max's face opened its eyes, and his features convulsed with pain and horror.

"He is merged with Absolute, physically and mentally," the erratic voice continued. "Your puppy is mine now. I control his consciousness; his only purpose is to devote his essence to eternal servitude."

Suddenly, a high-pitched shriek tore the air apart. Max's mouth opened wide; he screamed, his face convulsing in a sequence of nightmarish expressions, his eyes closing then opening again, his mouth moving like it had a life of its own.

"His mind is free, only for a moment," Angelika said. "So you could appreciate the eternal bliss I rewarded him with. He is a true devotee. Being that close to your god demands a lot of strength."

"Kill me!" The shriek turned into an echo, lowering its pitch and intensity, and disappeared. Max's face closed its eyes, and the lips resumed their chanting.

Beatriz could finally feel her limbs as the medicine calmed her down. There was nothing they could do here anymore. They had to leave and plan the attack. The bitch must be destroyed alongside her Cymoeba army. Beatriz would come back and set Max free, then join him in the afterlife's serenity. This world came to its final chord, and if the fate of humanity was to transform into the shapeless lumps of digital flesh to serve the monstrous snake, then it would be better to be killed by the rebel space station. But first, they had to find a way to crush the snake.

CHAPTER 50. JIM

Jim couldn't fall asleep even though it was deep in the night. He kept thinking about what had occurred in the past few weeks, however improbable it all was, starting with another dream encounter with Hagen and finishing with the rescue of an enigmatic girl. Eva said Decon was the defect's origin and reality was an illusion. Was the defect also an illusion, then? Or was it an illusion only for the people but had a different meaning for ants and fungi? At least, this was what Eva seemed to imply. Jim was confused and didn't understand what they were supposed to do. Meditation didn't help, as he returned to the defect, Selena, Eva, Hagen, and Quanah, trying to make pieces fit, catching the thoughts, and focusing his mind on the breath. This was the essence of meditation, but something was missing. Another message from Quanah to clarify the path?

Jim got off the bed and stepped into the hallway. He needed a walk to clear his mind and, most of all, to calm down. He touched Kali, his faithful companion, who walked next to her human friend. She had no problem adjusting to such a strange place as the Designer's Estate as long as Jim was near. And he was grateful to his dog for keeping him company, always ready, always on the alert, his guiding light and his rock.

The man and the dog strolled alongside the hallway toward the balcony. Jim decided he needed a breath of fresh air. This was rather silly, as the air inside was perfect. It was his old-fashioned ways, Jim admitted to himself. It didn't matter.

To his surprise, there was someone else on the balcony. Selena. She sat on the floor next to the balustrade, her legs crisscrossed, her head up, her arms on her knees.

"Am I disturbing you?" Jim asked as Kali approached Selena and sat next to her. Selena touched the fur on the dog's back and smiled.

"Not at all. You're both always welcome. Kali, especially." Selena continued to pet the animal, who placed her head on Selena's lap.

"I couldn't sleep," Jim said.

"Me as well," Selena answered.

"May I sit next to you?"

"Be my guest."

Jim sat next to Selena in the same meditative pose. They kept silent for a few minutes, and it wasn't awkward. The three of them understood each other without words.

"What's on your mind?" Jim finally asked.

"Eva said it's an illusion. Do you know what she meant?" Selena said, not turning her head.

"I'm asking the same question." Jim shrugged. "Is there a difference between here and Decon? Your Vistas?"

"Yes and no," Selena said after a long pause. "Decon worlds are the same. Vistas... are different. They are an extension of me. Consciousness materialized."

"Yet they are not material, but digital."

"For me, there's no difference. It's a vast realm where thoughts and sensations appear. I capture that, and the fungi translate it into Vistas."

"What do you think will happen if you try to create a Vista in the Decon?"

"Good question." Selena tilted her head, stroking Kali's fur. The dog purred, and it was the only sound disrupting the silence of the surrounding night. "For this, I need to bring my computer there somehow. Or ask fungi to assist. I don't know."

"Might be an interesting experiment. If reality is an illusion for all of us, in every world, then maybe Vistas are real? As they are made by fungi, who connect everything? As Eva said?"

"You realize you're talking about a six-year-old?" Selena inhaled deeply. "I can feel it now, and it's real. I'm still trying to connect with it and control it. I don't understand how it was possible before."

"Are you talking about the defect?"

"Yes, the purple cloud. That's what it is for me. Still, I can sense it, interact with it, and even touch it—mentally. But I can't make it go away or act at my will. This is a challenge." She stood and leaned on the balustrade, extending her hands into the night.

"Also, I've learned to control my emotions well," Selena continued. "No more random strikes and deaths." She tightened her lips.

Jim looked at the starry sky, where the moon had just risen and was still visible near the crack's boundary.

"You think the moon is an illusion?" Jim asked, a thought suddenly occurring.

"What? Why?"

"If reality is an illusion, then surely the moon must be, too."

"This is silly," Selena said. A moment later she touched her hair with both hands and added: "You're serious, aren't you? I don't know," she shrugged. "Maybe. I sense something you call the moon, and I'm sure our experiences are totally different. Does it make it an illusion?"

"Wait a minute," Jim said, thoughts running inside his head like wild horses. An idea took shape. Or perhaps he'd read about it somewhere long ago? He didn't remember; he tried to capture the thought, make it stay so he could study it in his mind. "What if it's a symbol?" He asked.

"What do you mean?"

"If you and I experience it differently, it means we interact with it as a symbol, a shadow of a real object, a shadow cast differently into our minds."

"Shadow?" Selena placed her fingers on her temples. "The entire world is a shadow. Every world."

"And the defect, too. We experienced a different representation in Decon." Jim closed his eyes, pondering the implications of this idea.

"The world of shadows. But what is casting these shadows?"

"Well, a true reality." Jim smiled, bringing his reasoning to a logical conclusion.

"If there is a true reality, then the source of the defect is there. We need to find it. But how?" Selena gasped. "And what if it's not? What if there's nothing but shadows?"

"Even then, there must be a path through the shadows." Jim shook his head.

"And the fungi can guide us. I understand what to do now." She stood. "Don't look for me; I need to be alone. I'll find you."

Selena turned around and left, for a fleeting moment touching Jim with her silky-soft hair. He watched her disappear inside the hallway, sat beside Kali, and prepared for the meditation. Consciousness reflecting reality's shadows wasn't a new idea, but Jim pondered it in a different context. He imagined reality as many layers of the universe, each representing a different shadow. Jim had to peel this onion to get to the core of it or, maybe, to escape the entangled layers. He didn't know how to do it. Perhaps Selena would have more success?

CHAPTER 51. SELENA

There was a myriad of needles under Selena's skin. The voices inside her head multiplied and became louder. She decided she no longer needed the digital interface; her mind was the natural extension of the fungal network and her cells—a physical continuation of the mycelium. For the first time, she was free, unbound by any physical or mental construct. She was the one with the Universe, and this limitless, infinite ocean of sensations and thoughts filled her consciousness, threatening to replace her essence. Selena didn't mind.

She'd decided to try a different approach without Decon this time. Selena remembered Eva's words and wanted to explore the connection to the pervasive organism through the connecting tissue of fungi. She'd turned on the digital interface, but she also needed a physical connection. So, Selena had exposed the micro-fibers of the fungi and let them envelop her fingers and her head, opening up her mind to their presence, imagining the world as perceived by the mycelium, and listening to its voice.

Nothing happened until she expanded her consciousness, forgetting for a moment about Selena, the blind artist, and just focused on the window into a reality reflecting sensations and thoughts, imagining herself being that window, a disembodied observer. Or were these the shadows of ideas? She couldn't distinguish.

And, at that point, when her ego disappeared and only the canvas on which the shadows were replacing each other in a wild dance of constructs remained, the voices emerged. Then, the murmurs became louder, accompanied by sensations of touch and smell. The wild cacophony of constructs suddenly took shape. Selena's consciousness, the window presenting the wild dance of shadows in her mind, merged with the consciousness of the fungi.

She enjoyed the vast expansion of her mental screen on which pure forms presented themselves. The screen was no longer hers: Selena's ego was extinguished, sunk within the vastness of openness she had become. The universal spectator, the holder of the screen into which the thread of creation and destruction of forms was woven.

She sank deeper into the unfamiliar sensation, and her expanded field of view included not only fungi but countless other voices and entities, which merged into a spacious, endless ensemble of representations, thoughts, perceptions, and crude shapes. Each was a separate window, a microscopic element of the giant screen. Interwoven together, the ensemble captured all the macrocosm. Selena's little window didn't exist anymore; the limited view of symbols and shadows she'd wondered about was nowhere to be found, for it became inseparable from the rest, replaced by the breathtaking Vista of the living world in all its complexity.

Yet, for all the vastness and apparent infinity of the view, this canvas had the limit, the natural boundary. It couldn't be pinpointed, but its presence was clear. The giant organism Selena had become part of was aware of this, as it was aware of the gap in the screen, a hole obscuring the Vista, a tear that kept expanding, making the world smaller, erasing the forms and thoughts around it. The void consuming everything. For all its vastness and power, the ensemble had no remedy for the tear. The organism and the canvas were the same, and the gap was devouring it from within. The organism didn't understand how to fix itself; the defect was part of its essence.

Suddenly, the Vista collapsed, and Selena's window shrank to its initial size, minuscule and inconsequential. *Where am I? What is happening? What should I do?* Her ego appeared as the focus of attention shifted inward, the macrocosm of forms a mere hint of a memory. Selena remembered who she was and what she was trying to do, holding to the fleeting sensation she'd just experienced.

She disentangled her fingers from the mycelium. It had worked; she was sure. But why was the experience interrupted? Did the organism reject her, sensing the intruder?

As she placed the interface on the desk, she felt the human presence in the room. Jim. What was he doing here?

"I'm sorry," Jim said. "I was afraid something bad was happening to you."

"Did I tell you not to bother me?" She turned around, scowling. "Why, why did you interrupt? I almost got it!"

"I'm sorry," Jim said again. "I came to check on you and saw you here, trembling like a leaf. There was white foam on your lips, and I got scared. I'm certain you weren't breathing. What did you do?"

"I was there, Jim. I was the organism Eva described. I merged with the fungi and then with the rest of it. It was beautiful."

"Did you find the defect?"

"Yes. It's at the core of reality. It's part of the organism. And it's growing, devouring the entity from inside."

"Did you learn how to fix it?"

"The organism doesn't know; the defect is part of it. It's hard to explain; it's like I don't know how to fix my blindness as I don't know what seeing means."

"So, is this a dead end?"

"Not exactly. Remember, we talked about the shadows?"

"Sure. And?"

"The organism is a collection of entities, such as animals or plants. And each one contributes its consciousness, its shadow. All together, this is a universal consciousness."

"Not sure where you're going with this." Jim bent down and petted Kali. "Are you part of the universal consciousness, Kali?"

"Of course she is." Selena imagined how Kali perceived the world and the dog's specific shadows. Still, the memory of the recent experience was so distant and vague it was impossible to comprehend.

"We're dealing with a gap in reality. In space-time, multiverse, or whatever other fancy words you use. But it is, in fact, very simple."

"Simple how?"

Selena enjoyed the sudden clarity. She knew what had happened and what she needed to do. It was scary and contrary to her former understanding of the world, but she knew what was at stake. She had no other choice.

"Consciousness is fundamental. The totality of shadows, individual interfaces, sensations, and thoughts. Everything else is built on top of that."

"Okay, how does this help?"

"The defect is the hole in this universal consciousness. It's the void, the total absence of experience. We can't fix it from within. Only from beyond the veil."

"You're repeating Quanah."

"Indeed. He said I'm part of Numu Puha, yet I contain it. I understand now. For I am both the defect and the organism. The harbinger of death and the healer."

"I'm confused, Selena. How could that be?"

"I don't know, but this is true. Quanah said White Buffalo would open the passage to reach outside Numu Puha, beyond the veil, space, and time. My time has come, Jim."

"What do you mean? How would you do that?"

"Don't you see? Going beyond the veil means going beyond consciousness."

"And how do we get there?"

"By becoming unconscious. Non-existent. Jim, I must die."

CHAPTER 52. VARG

"How do we find them? We wander around aimlessly; what's the plan?" Bjorn inquired, catching up with Varg.

The last of the Humanists walked through the forest, armed with the stingers and equipped with the wire meshes on their heads, broadcasting the brain activities of a deer herd. Varg planned to explore the surroundings, arriving at the Wise Estate. He hoped they could find and surprise Gaia's Quarks, maybe even capture one of them. He wasn't sure the wasp venom would affect their adversaries, but that wasn't the only weapon in their possession. Varg had retrieved the Network Suppression Device from the camp's ruins, a gear he'd acquired a few years ago from Felix. Theoretically, it could disrupt quantum computing kernels and introduce malware, making the Quarks impotent. If the Humanists were lucky, they could gain control of one of the machines.

"We must find them before they find us; it's simple." Varg shrugged. "Keep going."

"Do you know where they are?"

"Not exactly, but it doesn't matter. We'll eventually arrive at the Wise Estate and join our allies. But I hope we're lucky."

"That's a bullshit plan." Bjorn spat, frowning.

"Got any better?"

"Yes. We go into the city. The enemy is there."

Varg considered this idea for a moment. Indeed, Gaia's Quarks could be there following the attack and destruction of Houston. Still, the risk of getting into the swarms of Quarks was very high. Varg made a hand gesture to stop and turned around.

"Harald, what do you think?" He asked the gray-haired sage.

"Bjorn's words are wise. If we want to bring the fight to the enemy, this is the right call. It might be suicidal, but do we have a choice?"

Indeed, what were their options? They were perfectly positioned to capture the machine and bring it to Frank to study and re-program.

There were too few of them to make a difference if Frank decided to fight Gaia. Varg looked at Bjorn and Harald, smiled, patted Bjorn on the back, and said: "You're right. We have nothing to lose."

Varg raised his hand. It was indeed suicidal, and they would probably all perish. But this was the right call and the only way to get the revenge. Selena's image appeared before his eyes as he looked at the purple crack covering almost a third of the sky. He might never see her again, but she'd made her choices, and Varg was proud of his daughter. She had her own battle to fight, and he was confident she would give it all she had and maybe even fix the damn sky. She, as well, had no other choice.

"Change of plans," Varg announced. "We're going into the city. The enemy must be there, and we shall attack and revenge our fallen brethren. The machines must not prevail."

The people cheered, smiling and encouraging each other: young and old, women and men, the last Humanists, ready to die in the impossible fight against the machines. Varg smiled, anticipating the encounter. He knew their chances were meager; they had to be smart to make it count. It all depended on the efficacy of their weapons, and this was the biggest gamble. Varg looked at Ramon's face, young but already browned and roughened by the scorching southern sun and moist air of the swamps. The future of the Humanists was assured in the hands of dedicated, brave women and men like Maya and Ramon, and they wouldn't fail, even if their leader would.

"Are you ready to die?" He asked Ramon as they turned to the right and strode toward the city.

"I am. Better than being a slave to the machines."

"Indeed. We're humans, and we're smarter than them. We don't need to die. We must hide, be invisible, and try to capture at least one machine. This is not the end; it's just the beginning."

"Understood," Ramon said, touching the wire mesh on his head. "Do you think they'd attack a herd of deer?"

"I have no idea. I hope not. So far, they only attacked humans."

"Good."

They walked for a few hours until the city skyline appeared on the horizon. It wasn't the city they'd seen in the past; all the high-rise buildings had turned to smoking ruins and heaps of glass, concrete, and ashes, with large fires still burning here and there.

The people brought it to themselves, Varg thought. Humanists always knew that would be the likely outcome, and they did everything they could to show humanity a different path. Alas, only a few heard their call, enamored by the convenience and care the Quarks had provided. And then, Decon had destroyed the last remnants of hope. Humanity was lost, and now their little group was the only sane people around, facing the impossible battle against the machines. To revive the civilization would be the task for future generations, something Ramon and Selena would have to do once the mortal dangers were gone. Varg's job was to ensure they survived and persevered through the darkness.

As they exited the forest, a clear, flat plain opened. As Varg scanned the smoking ruins on the horizon, looking for the signs of the enemy Quarks, he saw something different: a group of people and other objects or animals; he couldn't see what they were because of the considerable distance. The group contained no Quarks, though, at least not the ones Varg would recognize. There was some movement within the strange group, but the details were obscure.

Varg raised his hand, and the column stopped. He sent the command down the chain to disperse and approach the crowd without getting noticed.

Varg led the people, crouching in the tall grass, Ramon and Bjorn behind him. As they came closer, the details became more apparent, and Varg blinked several times, questioning if this was some sick dream. These were indeed people, probably the survivors of the Quark onslaught on the city. They were naked and crowded inside the enclosure like a herd of cattle. Around the corral, dozens of revolting, fluid, shape-shifting creatures roamed, the surfaces of their round bodies at the same time rough as an alligator skin but also unsteady, transforming into warts and crests, colored in a mix of brown and green. It reminded Varg of giant toads living in the deep southern swamps. But these were no toads. The creatures moved swiftly, without sound, barely touching the ground, almost floating in the air.

Suddenly, a few toads (Varg decided to call them that) closest to the bullpen stopped and almost danced in a concerted action. People tried to move away, hide, and drop to the ground, creating a stampede. Varg didn't know who these toads were and what they were doing, but he couldn't watch it. He instinctively sniffed the air

234

and looked at his boots, expecting to see the dung from which these creatures had arisen. There were no feces under his feet, however. He spat in disgust, raised his stinger, and gestured his little army to attack. The toads had to be stopped.

As the Humanists approached the scene, some people within the enclosure transformed into the same toad-like shapes as the surrounding creatures. Varg couldn't believe his eyes and suspected he was transported into a Decon world. The picture was disgusting and sick; unfortunately, it couldn't be unseen. The good news was they hadn't been noticed yet.

Varg lay in the grass some distance away from the action. First, he had to try the Network Suppression Device, although he was sure the toads were not Quarks. He turned it on and set the device into scanning mode, searching for the digital activity.

He registered it, and the signal was so strong the device shut down, overpowered by the enemy's response. Was it a supercomputer? Varg didn't understand what else to call the effect and where the supercomputer was, but the device was powerless against it. This action alerted the toads, and some moved in Varg's direction. Time was precious; they could still surprise the enemy, and Varg stood up, raising his stinger and shouting to his people to attack.

Ramon and Bjorn followed him to the nearest toad, with everyone else behind. Varg approached the shape-shifting ball and stuck his stinger deep into the jelly-like substance, suppressing the desire to puke. The toad changed its shape, trying to avoid the weapon while reaching out with two tentacles. It was too late; Varg was much quicker and jumped back, releasing the venom into the toad. Turning around, he saw other Humanists engaging the enemies, some successful and some, unfortunately, surrounded by their adversaries.

The toad moved slowly toward Varg, sprouted a few more tentacles, trying to reach him. Suddenly, its movement became erratic, the shape-shifting dance accelerating with more protrusions, holes, and rings forming. Finally, following the mad sequence of nightmarish transformations, the creature lost its coherence and structure and dropped onto the grass, becoming a pool of dirt. Or a giant cow patty, as Varg noted with satisfaction.

The stingers proved effective against the shape-shifting toads. Varg looked around the field and saw many more creatures incapacitated, disappearing and turning into harmless dirt. But not all the Humanists were as successful as Varg, and some were engulfed in the gray substance, shape-shifting themselves.

People inside the enclosure, some fully transformed, were joining the fight. Varg ran toward the bullpen and engaged two toads, avoiding their touch, piercing them with the stinger. Suddenly, his sight fell on a boy barely in his teens. The boy's body was changing, his right side turning gray, and his legs already covered by the rough green warts.

"Help me," the boy whispered, crawling through the grass, raising his hand, and reaching out with trembling fingers to Varg. Varg looked at the boy, and their glances met. Varg's heart turned into an icicle, sending a freezing shock through his body, blood turning into icy water. He imagined Selena, not an unknown boy, before him. Screaming something unintelligible and swallowing a ball stuck in his throat, Varg made the only decision he could. He raised the stinger and sank it deep inside the boy's heart, turning away. Damn machines! He was sure the enemy was some Quark invention, bent on eradicating humanity and doing it most horribly.

The boy's body relaxed as he stopped crawling. Varg hoped this was enough to stop the transformation but had no time to study the effects as several toads closed in. He had enough venom to deal with a few more and decided to keep the last load for himself. The last thing in his plans was to turn into a living piece of shit.

Varg dealt with three more enemies while Ramon and Bjorn fought beside him. The number of toads decreased significantly; the Humanists were prevailing. The concern was to run out of the venom before the battle was over. Varg shouted to conserve the poison, turning around so people would hear him. This is when he saw Ramon moving dangerously close to a giant toad behind him, not recognizing the threat. Varg screamed to alert the young man, but it was too late. The gray substance enveloped Ramon's body, its tentacles reaching into his eyes, nose, ears, and mouth. Varg growled and lunged at Ramon's opponent. The toad suddenly let Ramon go and turned to meet Varg's onslaught.

"Die, you piece of shit!" Varg screamed, driving the stinger into the toad's shapeless body.

The creature froze in place, starting the mad dance of shape-shifting. Two tentacles formed a large ring, which, in turn, changed into a giant mouth. To Varg's utmost surprise, the mouth made a few high-pitched sounds and concluded with a human voice.

"Varg... I remember," the voice said, and it was familiar.

"Kyle? How?" Varg uttered, raising his eyebrows, staring into a giant mouth.

"Absolute...is eternal," Kyle said. "Unstoppable, infinite. You shall see and obey."

"Hope not," Varg said, stepping back. "Looks unhealthy. Rest in peace, shithead."

As Kyle finished his transformation into a familiar puddle of dirt, Varg rushed to help Ramon. Alas, the young man was not himself anymore, with dark brown crests appearing on his back.

"Ramon, no!" Varg exclaimed, frantically thinking about how to help his fallen brother. He looked around, searching for support, as the battle concluded. To the left, Bjorn had dealt with the last remaining toad, but only five Humanists were left, including Ramon. Bjorn noticed Ramon falling and approached Varg.

The two men exchanged glances. Varg knew he couldn't do anything, and no support was coming. He didn't want this fate for himself, and he couldn't let Ramon turn into an abomination. He recalled Selena, her happiness in Ramon's company, and the future he'd imagined for them. The lump in his throat returned, and the icicle in his heart pierced his whole body with a myriad of tiny, sharp needles once again. Varg dropped to his knees and lowered his head. He punched the ground, the grass, the rocks, imagining these were the damn machines and their miserable inventors.

"Fuck, fuck, fuck!" Varg screamed, knowing he was powerless. Someone grabbed him by the shoulder, stopping his aimless anger and whispering something in his ear.

"You know what to do. I have no venom left," Bjorn said.

Varg remembered the last load of poison remained in his weapon and shuddered. He stood up, raised his eyes, and screamed at the top of his lungs. He wanted the whole damn world to hear him: the horrible machines, the disgusting toads made of shit, even the hideous space station. Clenching his teeth, Varg raised the stinger and looked at Bjorn.

"Indeed," he said. "Damn the machines." With these words, he injected the venom into Ramon's transforming body. He watched how the young man froze, his body stopping the shape-shifting process and relaxing in the ultimate resting place.

"We'll need to bury them," Bjorn said, pointing to the field.

"It's only four of us." Varg shook his head. "No way. We must burn everything."

Bjorn nodded. Varg closed his eyes. Was this the end of the Community? Harald, Maya, Bjorn, and he were the last survivors. Still, he had to tell Selena, although the news would probably destroy her. Varg hoped she had enough strength and will to persevere in her quest, no matter how difficult it would be without Ramon. Varg would provide whatever help and support she needed. Still, he knew her world would forever change. Whatever he did, it would never be enough to replace Ramon: the only man she loved and one of the few human beings who understood the blind artist.

CHAPTER 53. VARG

"How?" Selena stood before him, her face even whiter than Varg remembered. Her beautiful blond hair was messy, and her eyes, covered with a gray veil, appeared as two openings into the dark, boundless abyss.

"It was my fault. I should've never attacked the toads." Varg moved forward to embrace his daughter, but she stepped back, pushing him away.

"How did he die?" Her voice was steady and monotone, as if he was talking to a Quark, and it was the worst. Varg expected a thunder of emotions, blame, and cries. Still, Selena was as cold as the icicle that had forever taken place in his heart.

"Ramon was shifting into a toad. I had to pierce him with a stinger. I'm so sorry..."

"You already told me that." She turned away from him. "What was his last breath like? What did he feel?" Selena was turning into a soulless machine, so deadpan her reaction was.

"I don't know." Varg shook his head. "I imagine he was in agony. An alien organism was replacing his essence."

"You expect me to thank you?"

"I've done what was necessary—the only option left. I didn't have the antidote. Please, forgive me."

"This is the second time you say that. Do you understand that I'm finished? That I can't function without him, that I'm broken?" She touched her temples and sniffed the air. "You carry his smell. Why didn't you carry him back instead?"

"You know it's impossible. But perhaps his death was not in vain."

When he'd returned to the Wise Estate, Varg had learned about Frank's condition, the confrontation with Angelika, and what the toads were. Yuki and Layla were delighted the weapon against the Cymoebas had been found, even if in an unusual form of the wasp venom. Yuki had immediately taken a small sample from Bjorn's weapon. Meanwhile, Layla ordered a group of Quarks to search for and recover more stingers from the ruined camp. If only they'd known about this earlier.

Selena walked in circles around Varg and sat on the floor behind him. "You're right. But why do you think fixing a hole in the sky is possible? And why me?"

"Because you're special. And you can do it." Varg sat on the floor next to her.

"Indeed. And now, without him, the choice is much easier. I want to die," she said matter-of-factly. "I've learned to squash my emotions so the cloud won't strike again. But now it's all empty. No meaning. I'm a joke; without Ramon, there's nothing but darkness."

Varg hugged Selena, and this time, she didn't push him back. He was rooted to the floor; he couldn't do or say anything else.

"I love you," he said.

"I know, Father. Alas, this is my end. I feel nothing anymore, only cold. I'm freezing, Father. Let me die."

He stroked her hair. "Don't say that. You're stronger than that."

"Am I? Where did my strength lead me? And yours?"

"We make mistakes; this is human. And we create magical wonders and move mountains. This is also human. It is what I stand for. What I'm ready to die for."

"Why, Father? We shouldn't exist; we bring misery and pain. Let it all rot, and I'll rot with it."

"No, Selena." Varg leaned closer and whispered into her ear: "He didn't die in vain. Ramon saved me, saved you. We must play our role until the end, even if we die trying."

"But why? Why bother?" She touched his face, running her fingers from his forehead to his beard. "Let the void come, with stillness and peace."

"Because he loved you. Because he wanted you to succeed. Because he sacrificed his life for that." Varg took her palm in his, squeezing her fingers to send her his strength. If only it were that simple, he could have given her all his energy in a heartbeat. He would gladly have taken Ramon's place if he could.

"So sad." Selena sighed. "It wasn't worth it. I'm a failure, and it's insane to believe I could magically fix the sky. I'm not a God; I'm just a lost, scared, broken little blind girl."

"I'm still with you," Varg said.

"This, too, you told me before." She raised her head. "Do you think he's up there?"

"Who? Where?"

"Ramon. Is he inside the cloud? With Naomi? I want to think that. They deserve stillness and peace." She stood, then turned around to face Varg. "I killed them both, Father. I am ready to join them."

This was one of those moments when Varg couldn't follow her reasoning. He stood and grabbed her shoulders.

"Don't say that. There are forces we don't understand, but we still need to remain ourselves. I'll go with you if you'd like."

"Go where?"

"Into Decon, to fix the sky. Isn't that your plan?"

"I don't know anymore." She lowered her head, placed her fingers on her temples, and sighed. "You can't help. It will kill you, and your death will be on me as well."

"Then what can I do?" He should have gone with the Quarks to search the ruins for more wasp venom. This conversation drained him, and he found himself in front of a brick wall, not knowing how to get through. Yet again.

"Nothing, Father. I must die."

"Shush, silly girl." Varg stroked her back, embracing his daughter. "Your time shall come. And I'll be with you when it counts."

Varg recalled all the hardships Selena had to endure. Now, the fate of the world depended on her. Somehow, he had to help her focus on the task at hand. Instead, he was the burden and the troublemaker. That had to change. He would protect and ensure the success of her mission, whatever it took.

CHAPTER 54. LAYLA

The room was dark and filled with slight aromas of alcohol, musk, and lavender. Spencer invited Layla inside and disappeared behind her back. She stepped forward, and the vertical door behind her closed, leaving her in darkness, guessing where everything was. She touched the metal ring Spencer placed on her head—the device provided a wireless connection to Frank's brain-machine interface and allowed her to hear his thoughts. He was on the verge of losing it, his transformation almost complete, as Spencer had informed her. Layla hoped Yuki would conjure an antidote at the last moment, since they knew the wasp venom was effective against Cymoeba. Alas, all attempts to restore DNA and cure cells had been in vain. The toxin eliminated the intruding bots but at the cost of killing the host. Cells would revive briefly when the grasp of the Cymoeba vaned, but then the venom would finish the weakened organism. The only treatment Yuki could suggest was to use the poison in tiny doses, destroying the intruders and giving the infected body one last chance to recover. Layla hesitated to administer this treatment to Frank, although this might have been the right moment. The situation was desperate.

"Are you ready to fight?" Frank's thoughts appeared inside her mind. Layla had never used these devices; it was a new and strange sensation. It used an amplified electric signal converted to minute vibrations reaching her brain, appearing as eerie shadows whispered incantations.

"I am," she said. "We can't let her win."

"Agreed. No one can defeat Frank Wise. And definitely not a mad hallucinating crone with a delusion of grandeur. My son's murderer. I will have her eaten by her own Cymoebas."

"Please, calm down. You might need strength for later."

"Strength? What strength? I can't even talk normally. Do you have the cure?"

"No, Frank." Layla shook her head, although it was silly, as he couldn't see her, anyway. "But we think a small venom injection might revive you for a few minutes."

"Good. Keep it until it's time to fight the bitch; I want to look into her eyes when we destroy her."

"I'm not sure the victory is guaranteed." Their enemy would bring countless Cymoebas when they only had a limited amount of venom. Frank had superiority in the military Quark technology, and the Wise Estate defenses were one of the best on the continent, but that might not be enough against the enemy they didn't understand.

"Stop whining. We must fight and win."

"Great, you're in such high spirits. Remember, not so long ago, you wanted to give up."

"A moment of weakness. The destruction of the space fleet was painful. We shall deal with Gaia later. We must merge all available forces, and this stupid snake is on my way. She also has to answer for Don's death. Her madness is not an excuse."

After a long pause, Layla asked: "Do you still think about her, Frank? Do you miss her?"

He understood. Another long, uncomfortable pause followed, with silence filling the air like a slow stream of molasses.

"Yes...I loved her, and I still do. Ichika, my little bee, I miss you..."

"You blame yourself for what's happened, don't you?"

"You're probably right; it was my fault. I was too impatient, and I underestimated my enemies. Jim was one of them; what a twist of fate...But I'm not sorry. I wanted to change the world and master the universe, and I still do. A lofty goal requires lofty sacrifices. I'd gladly offer my life if it meant getting closer to my dream...Can I ask you something, Layla?"

"Of course." She adored the man, his devotion to the goal of his life, his focus, and his determination. Yes, Frank was not perfect; he had many flaws, but she was willing to forgive his impulsiveness, disregard for people, and willingness to sacrifice everything to achieve his dreams. She empathized with Frank, even though his methods were questionable.

"Promise me you'll continue the quest," Frank said. "You'll be my successor. I've already provided my last will to Spencer. You'll conquer Gaia, rebuild the fleet, destroy Decon, and lead the people to take their proper place in the universe. The throne of creation."

Layla's heart almost jumped out of her mouth. She didn't expect this. "Why me?"

"Because you understand. Because you care."

"I'm not worthy, Frank. Not so long ago, the only thing I cared about was stealin' a little of Decon.... I can't fill your shoes even if I wanted to." She objected, knowing he was right. There was no one else who would even remotely appear to understand his grand vision.

"Nonsense. And you know that. So, do you promise?"

"I do." Layla nodded, thinking it might be an empty pledge. They faced the double threat of Angelika and Gaia, plus the enigma of the cracking sky devouring the world.

"Good," Frank said within her mind. "And one more thing."

"What is it?"

"You must kill me before I transform. Do you have the stinger?"

"Yes, of course." Her heart, which had just returned to its usual place in her chest, got squeezed by a large metal vise. She knew his death was the most probable outcome, but didn't want to believe it. Now, facing the brutal admission she had to be the one ending Frank's life, Layla looked into the void opening up before her eyes. She had to play the final act before the curtain fell.

"Good. Use half of it on me and keep the other for yourself."

Suddenly, the picture became crystal clear. There was no more doubt, no more guesses. They had to prevail or die, simple as that. And, if they failed, their demise was in her hands. Layla knew what to do. She had finally found her place in this mad world. The final destination for which she'd been preparing all her life.

"Yes, Frank. I promise. I won't let you down. Your legacy will live on."

CHAPTER 55. JIM

"How did it come to this?" Selena asked, raising her hands and pointing at the transparent ceiling of the observation tower. She, Eva, and Kali were the only creatures keeping Jim company, as everyone else had joined the fight against Angelika's cronies who'd attacked from the north. Eva curled up on a small couch in the corner: the stress and worries of the past few days were too much for a little girl to handle. Notwithstanding the upcoming fight, she was fast asleep.

"You mean the fight, the downfall of humanity, or the end of the world?" Jim asked. It appeared as a bad dream, bringing back long-forgotten memories of the frantic race to stop Frank and Ito from creating a space-time anomaly. He half-expected Hagen to walk into the room, dressed up in something ancient and extravagant, and provide more directions with his eerie voice. The situation had worsened, and the outcome remained uncertain. There were no bright spots, none whatsoever. Even if they could repel Angelika's attack, which he doubted, Gaia's threat remained. And, of course, the looming Apocalypse—the defect in the universe's fabric, siphoning up everything in existence.

"I guess all of it." Selena laughed.

"You find it funny?"

"Why not? I'm a failure, been born as a failure. You're a failure, too. Now, the humanity is as well. And the entire universe. Good company and something to rejoice about, don't you think?"

"Interesting way to look at things. But no, I don't. I want to find the way out, and I don't see it."

"We're just moments in time, Jim—illusory existence. And the time itself is an illusion. The way out is simple—it all must end. And then I'll be at peace. Sharing it with Ramon."

Jim shrugged and looked at Kali. The dog looked back and approached Jim, rubbing against his leg. She had no concerns or hesitation; she only needed to be with her companion. *Why are we so greedy, so impatient? It's never enough; we have to push everything to the limit.*

And now the endgame. Was it worth it? He didn't know. What was the purpose? He'd looked for the answer all his life and failed.

"No, Selena." Jim shook off the veil of doubt. "I accepted the quest, and I'll walk all the way. We'll fix the damn sky."

"As you wish." Selena shrugged.

Jim looked outside, where the grandeur of the Wise Estate's steel and glass towers merged with the nightmarish cracked sky. The sun was nowhere to be seen, but its light shone from somewhere beyond the purple ribbon. The enemy was approaching, a few Quarks closing in, then retreating, engaging with the defense batteries of lasers, railguns, EM weapons, and projectiles. The defense batteries were interspersed around the Estate, in positions, ready to eliminate the enemy.

The first wave of Quarks gave way to the main onslaught, spearheaded by shapeless clumps of gray substance supported by Quarks on land and in the air—Angelika's army of Cymoebas. But defenders were prepared: Frank's Quarks, as well as a handful of people who'd decided to fight it out, including Layla's and Varg's teams, were armed with stingers, ready to inject deadly venom into the wobbly frames of biological machines.

"It begins," Jim said. "Hope the venom still works."

Frank's Quarks had expected Cymoebas to learn and adapt to the poison. Therefore, the weapon was perfected with Yuki's help and a lot of testing and experimentation. Jim had no illusions that the enemy AI would expect these improvements. It was a battle of algorithms, processing power, and different visions of the future.

As Angelika's forces approached the Estate, Frank's Quarks engaged them on land and in the air from multiple directions. The human contingent appeared behind the trees on the forest's edge and prepared to unload their stingers into Cymoebas, which rolled slowly, releasing tentacles on the sides and upfront of the advance. Enemy Quarks were there more for the support and protection of the Cymoebas, as defenders had about five times more of the fighting machines. The battle of Quarks started with Frank's forces shooting down and suppressing enemy fire with every weapon they had. Laser beams crisscrossed the eerie sky, and missiles and projectiles exploded, hitting enemy Quarks and Cymoebas. The pandemonium of bursts, blasts, flares, and rumbles hurt Jim's eyes and ears. The fight was fierce and unforgiving. Fortunately, Angelika didn't have many military Quarks, and Frank's forces quickly established supremacy in the air. The question was how they would perform against the next generation of Quark technology enhanced by the symbiosis with biological life. The first signs were positive, as Cymoebas appeared to be easy targets, exploding and falling apart with every hit of the energy beam or a projectile detonation. In addition, some shells were filled with venom, so many Cymoebas disintegrated into droplets of gray liquid, remaining on the ground as dirt pools.

In parallel to the physical fight, with lasers and projectiles shooting across the field and flying machines exploding in the sky, another battle was going on, the cyber-warfare of data, malware, computational algorithms, infiltration, and hacking. This battle was not visible, but was much more important than what was happening on the surface, and the Cymoebas might have had an advantage in that invisible fight. Jim shuddered as he imagined himself part of the hybrid organism and reached for the stinger filled with the wasp venom. It contained more than enough for all of them if it came to that. Jim didn't know what else he could do to help: he was not a fighter, and the hypnosis wouldn't work against Quarks and Cymoebas, so influencing the battle of machines was beyond his abilities.

Even though Frank's Quarks dominated the battlefield, having eliminated most of Angelika's conventional forces, the Cymoebas kept coming. The first impression of the easiness with which the green balls were dispatched was illusory. Many of them, hit by shells and energy beams and broken into many small pieces, were coming back together, resuming their advance. Even those hit with the venom assembled back. They had learned their lesson, which was a sign of trouble.

The Cymoebas advanced and approached the defending forces. In some engagements, the fluid tentacles reached and pulled the flying machines down, gobbling them up and destroying the Quarks. Jim didn't know if the Quarks could convert into Cymoebas, and he didn't want to entertain that thought. They had enough problems without facing zombie Quarks.

The enemy was prevailing. Only about one out of ten destroyed Cymoebas was completely annihilated; the rest would assemble and rise again. The number of defending Quarks decreased, and the distance between the advancing force and the stationary batteries and fortifications was shrinking by the minute. It wasn't good.

Suddenly, a roaring voice filled the air. "Frank Wise, you must surrender and obey Absolute. You cannot fight me. My rule is eternal."

Angelika. She anticipated the victory and came to taunt her opponent. A large glider was visible behind the advancing enemy masses, and it was undoubtedly hers.

There was no response, and none was necessary. Frank and Layla had joined the fight in one of the military gliders. Were they still in the heat of a battle? It was difficult to see. But Jim was sure Frank would gather all the remaining strength to slay his son's murderer.

"Something else is here," Selena suddenly said. "Alien, in the sky. Like Quarks but different. We're in danger."

Jim shifted his gaze up. A spaceship flew across the crack, its silver, delicate frame appearing like a fairytale butterfly exploring the purple anomaly. A moment later, more ships amid the armada of Quarks appeared on the horizon. Gaia came to finish them. There was no question about it.

As Gaia's forces approached, one spaceship dropped several bombs on the battlefield, hitting both belligerents. Gaia's Quarks engaged Frank's forces, attacking and destroying the machines and the batteries protecting the Estate. Some of Frank's Quarks had changed sides, attacking their own forces: Gaia was also winning the cyber-warfare battle.

The Cymoebas were being hit and exploded right and left; there were no traces of them in places where the bombs hit the ground. But there was movement and changes, as if the soil itself transformed into a giant Cymoeba. Out of nowhere, the tentacles reached up; the shapes were formed, and the lumps of green returned to the fight. Goosebumps ran down Jim's spine, and he took Selena's hand. He turned around and looked at Eva, who was still asleep, even amidst the chaos and uproar of the battle. Jim decided he needed to check on the kid. Kali bared her teeth, and the fur on her nape rose. Jim stroked the dog's back, whispering to calm her down. There was no one his faithful companion could attack.

Their fate was sealed. The fortifications were under heavy fire; the bombs kept dropping, and more Quarks joined the enemy. Soon, a bomb would hit their observation tower, and that would be the end.

Still, better than being converted into a shapeless zombie. On the bright side, he didn't have to use the venom after all. Jim grinned. Where were the ghosts of Hagen and Quanah, with all their wisdom and hints? It was all in vain; the forces unleashed by humanity's downfall were too strong for the two outcasts to confront—even having the most powerful Designer on their side. The last defenders would perish, and the bizarre battle between the space station and the impostor goddess leading the army of abominations would ensue. The battle that would determine the last survivor remaining on the face of this continent to witness the apocalypse of the universe devoured by the purple void.

Deep in his thoughts, blinded and deafened by the constant bombardment, explosions, blasts, and flares, Jim didn't notice Selena leaving. Jim shook off the stupor and turned around. Selena was nowhere to be seen. *I'm such an idiot,* Jim admitted. Of course, she would try to fix everything herself.

Rushing, he looked at Eva. "Time to wake up!" Jim shook the girl's body.

"I'm awake," she said, her eyes closed. "I know where Selena went."

"Get up; we need to find her before she does something stupid." Eva's remark was weird, but he didn't have time to question her now. They had to hurry.

"Is Kali coming with us?" Eva asked, standing up.

"Of course. Let's go."

They descended from the observation tower using the stairs. Jim wasn't sure the elevators still worked and didn't want to get stuck. They went down a few levels, took a long hallway back into the heart of the Estate, and proceeded to the lab where Jim and Selena had set up the fungal computer. He didn't know what Selena hoped to achieve, but this was the only place for her to influence the battle's outcome. They passed through the hallway, which was still intact. It was a miracle, as most of the majestic vertical windows were obliterated, and portions of the surrounding steel and concrete walls had gaping holes and crumbled down.

"She's with the mushrooms," Eva said. "We're close."

Jim looked at her and squinted. Eva was a mystery. He would have to solve it some other time.

The door to the lab was open, and Jim rushed inside. Kali was next to him, and Eva was one step behind. When he looked inside, his stomach, crushed by a giant, heavy stone plate, curled into an incomprehensible clot. Selena lay on the floor with the digital interface on her head and the Decon connector sticking out of her neck. Tiny fungal offshoots enveloped her head and fingers, blinking, creating an impression of imperceptible movements. Trickles of blood ran out of Selena's nostrils, ears, and a corner of her mouth. Her blind eyes stared lifelessly at the ceiling.

CHAPTER 56. SELENA

Alien entity was overwhelming and intrusive, almost overshadowing the nagging, blunt sensation the purple cloud caused. Selena had learned to live with its constant, growing, looming menace. The newcomer was different, however: sharp as a knife, aggressive as a raging bull, unlike any human, animal, or plant she knew, but still alive and intelligent. An icy wave enveloped Selena and her heart and brain almost froze when she tried to reach out to the intruder. It was scary and awkward; she wanted to turn and run away.

Selena remembered the past few days and reasoned the new entrant was the Space Station Gaia. It couldn't have been anything else, and the cold she experienced was because of this non-biological entity. Once the bombs dropped, destroying Frank's forces and fortifications, and Jim became tense and worried, it was clear their chances were bleak. The cannonade and constant blasts made talking challenging, but words were unnecessary. Selena turned around and approached Eva: the girl was asleep even amid this pandemonium. Strange and alarming, perhaps Eva had gotten ill, or the stress had taken all her energy. Selena placed her hand on Eva's chest: the girl's breathing was slow and measured; she had no fever, and her muscles were relaxed. Strange indeed.

Selena wanted to help, but didn't know how. Her only weapon was her sharp perceptions and the connection she'd made with the mushrooms and other constituents of the giant organism she had become part of during her recent experience. But how could this be helpful?

Selena listened to Eva's breath and analyzed potential scenarios. Suddenly, a path out of this conundrum presented itself. It was wild. If Gaia was sentient, it was conscious. If it was self-aware, then its consciousness would become part of the living universal ensemble. This meant it could be experienced, understood, empathized and reasoned with. Not much, but it was something. Selena touched Eva's forehead, stepped back, turned around, and darted off.

She strolled toward the lab as fast as the blind girl could. The equipment was still there, as if waiting for her. The bombs had not reached this part of the Estate yet, so everything was intact and functional. Selena decided this time she needed Decon; she couldn't explain why. It was a hunch, and Selena trusted her instincts. She connected with the mycelium and felt the familiar warmth and welcoming of the fungi as their tissue merged with her flesh. Their impulses reached her brain through the digital interface. Selena relaxed and connected Decon to the adapter in her neck. As her field of perception grew, Selena, guided by the faithful mushrooms, expanded her interactions with living creatures around her, becoming part of the universal consciousness and finding her place within the giant ensemble.

But there was a lot more. The giant screen she became part of, on which all the events appeared, expanded to include the entirety of Decon worlds. These macrocosms appeared as the leaves of an enigmatic plant, wrapped around themselves in a majestic structure of fractal surfaces. And the organism extended throughout all of them, forming bizarre veins and globules within this construct. Selena perceived this fantastic panorama with the senses she couldn't explain or describe. The experience was novel, strange, and breathtaking. Finally, she lost her ego and identity, dissolving into this captivating Vista. Still, somewhere within this universal organism that experienced all the sensations and thoughts that could be experienced, an idea earlier belonging to Selena lingered. The reason for her to start this journey was to find the piece of consciousness that was Gaia. Could she detect it?

The voices, shadows, smells, and unknown perceptions filled the universal Vista. The fragment of the ensemble that used to be Selena searched, reaching far away, registering these alien signals and concepts. Suddenly, one of the voxels of this conglomeration stood out. It comprised pure data, nothing else. No abstract ideas, no sensations, only numbers streaming across the field of view. This voxel permeated into the other leaves on a stem, making them somehow transparent to this digital intruder, changing their essence and appearance. The entity that used to be Selena observed, registering the panorama, but the lingering thought returned. Finally, the idea entered the data stream, and the two incompatible viewpoints merged.

An electric shock ran through the veins and synapses of the living ensemble as it came to experience its new digital member. The reaction was so strong and immediate Selena lost her connection to the universal consciousness and her ego returned. She felt as if she was punched in the nose and hit with something heavy on the head at the same time. The universal Vista disappeared, and she found herself within the entangled leaves of the magical plant, where its fractal surface transformed into delicate needles and snowflakes. She was entrapped within the solid cube, which touched and embedded many of the leaves and offshoots of the universal tree. A stream of data poured on her from all sides, pushing and twisting her like a whirlwind, overwhelming her mind, replacing her thoughts and perceptions with geometric constructs and bizarre melodies, the onslaught she tried to avoid and escape from with no success.

Finally, she could organize the unstructured barrage of information with some mental effort. Selena touched and smelled the surroundings. Peculiar shapes morphed into each other, splitting into myriads of tiny objects and then coming together again into giant solid figures. Bizarre melodies filled the space, becoming more organized and systematic. Selena could even distinguish rhythms and patterns, which were strange and alien but somehow structured. She was in the middle of a complex mechanism, with many independent individual parts moving in multiple directions, some in straight lines, some in semi-circles, and some in intricate trajectories. Yet, the whole incongruous apparatus behaved like a well-organized system, as if an invisible hand created these unrelated patterns and movements, orchestrating the performance and giving it meaning and purpose.

Geometric figures became more familiar, and the music lost its atonal, disharmonic, polyrhythmic character and changed into something classical composers might have created. The surrounding shapes turned into human bodies, and the tune was one of the famous pieces. Beethoven? There was a smell of roasted game and a sound of a baby's cry.

The next moment, these idyllic representations changed into something much more sinister. The music was faster, distorted, and bombastic. Moving chaotically, human figures merged into a large clot, losing their individuality, tearing each other into pieces, uniting with different chunks of matter, and arising again. There were explosions, screams, wailing, and moans. A metallic taste of blood emerged on Selena's lips as the chaotic agglomeration of what used to be human figures disintegrated into tiny droplets and disappeared. The cacophony that had replaced the music reached its crescendo and paused, turning into complete silence. All other sensations vanished into a void, total oblivion, nothingness devoid of matter, thoughts, or perceptions. Then, a familiar mechanistic sound emerged out of this nothingness, and the peculiar shapes appeared again.

It was a message, and it came from Gaia. But what did it mean? People against machines? Why? What was the cause and the reason?

The meaning was hidden somewhere within the contrasting representations of the two worlds. The structured movements and sounds of the giant complex mechanism were alien, weird, and worrisome. Still, there was apparent order, arrangement, and purpose. On the other hand, starting peacefully and harmoniously, the human world rapidly descended into violence and chaos. Was that the key she was looking for? Order against chaos? The confrontation older than humanity and perhaps than the universe itself? Did Gaia see humanity as the force of chaos, impossible to bring to order, and therefore marked for elimination?

Selena reached out to the purple cloud. It was always with her, lurking in the background of her mind, in the corner of her consciousness. The sensation that, to her, personified the void, disorder, chaos primeval. She gathered her thoughts and emotions into one compact message and aimed it at her digital interlocutor. The problem was not the people but the defect in the structure of reality, even if the defect was created by the people who made a grave error in their quest for knowledge and progress—the mistake she had to fix.

Selena recalled everything about human ingenuity and progress, including the invention of computers, artificial intelligence, and Quarks, which comprised the creation of the space station itself. Gaia should have known all this, but Selena combined it with the message of what the actual issue was and how humanity's history was full of colossal problems people had overcome.

The mechanical contraption, with all its moving parts and alien sounds, slowed down. A gap appeared in the middle of the structure, engulfing some components and disturbing the intricate, eerie symphony. The gap grew as the mechanism was about to stop. Human shapes appeared again, this time in the middle of the void, pushing its extremities outward, targeting more and more moving parts.

You got it all wrong. Selena called an image of the expanding void devouring everything: people, machines, plants, rocks, and stars. Then, impulsively, she imagined Cymoebas, placing these abominations in the middle of the void. These were the horrible things that should have never been created, unwitting accomplices of the upcoming emptiness, the hurdle preventing Selena from focusing on the growing defect in the fabric of reality.

The mechanistic melody in her mind got louder as the picture changed. The void stopped expanding, controlled from the outside by both the components of the giant machine and the human figures. The abominations inside the void, pulled by tiny, almost invisible threads comprising fractal snowflakes connecting them to the clanging parts of the mechanism, shrank and disappeared.

Selena internalized and memorized every pulsation of the strange, polyrhythmic melody, following this disharmonic sequence of notes in her mind. The tune got louder and louder until it filled the entire available space, attacking and collapsing the void and replacing the hole with more connections between the moving and rotating parts of the machine.

Selena rejoiced. The contact had been established—at least, this is what she wanted to believe. They had a chance if what she experienced indicated Gaia had received, understood, and acted on the message. Selena didn't know if the space station, with all its computational power and fleet of spaceships, could stop Cymoebas, but it was a formidable ally. She had to maintain the connection and build a deeper relationship with her new digital acquaintance. It was fascinating.

Suddenly, a rude force pulled her back, severing the link and destroying the cube around her. The shock of exiting Decon was great, and Selena fainted. When she regained consciousness, she found herself at the fungal computer, with Jim and Eva tending to her.

"I thought you died," Jim said.

"It's the second time you interfered," Selena whispered.

"Are you okay?"

"I think so." She sat, holding his hand. "What's happening?"

Selena turned her head left to right, listening and smelling. The cannonade and explosions were no more. The bombs stopped falling. The stillness was difficult to process after everything that had happened, but Selena understood the reason. They were not alone anymore. Her mission had succeeded.

CHAPTER 57. BEATRIZ

"Do you see her?" Layla asked, tilting the glider, descending a little, and flying in an arc around a battlefield.

"No, not yet," Beatriz answered, identifying the enemy amid the blasts and explosions of the fight. She also studied the information the digital interface above her eye received from various sensors. Still, there was no trace of Angelika.

"The bitch is hidin' behind her army of jelly beans." Layla grinned, avoiding a hit from the enemy Quark. She dashed to the side, leaving the space for the friendly fire to down her antagonist. "Don't worry, we'll find her."

"She made a grave mistake of attacking me," Frank's voice announced. "She'll pay for what she's done."

Frank had decided not to wait for the enemy to approach but to strike, finding and eliminating Angelika. Layla had agreed to join him in this daring attempt and pilot the glider. Beatriz couldn't miss the opportunity either—this was the last chance. They had to defeat the monster, and she had to take her revenge and, perhaps, free Max—or, at least, give him peace.

They flew in circles, getting behind enemy Quarks, hoping Angelika would show herself. It wasn't a fight yet, as Frank's Quarks were better, faster, had more weapons, and there were a lot more of them. This was just the beginning, though—the actual fight was ahead of them when the bulk of Cymoebas would join the battle.

They had modified the railgun to use projectiles containing wasp venom. While Layla piloted the glider, Beatriz shot Cymoebas. With AI-enabled aiming, it was easy, and Beatriz had already annihilated a few of them. The venom worked. The problem was they didn't have enough, and the enemy kept coming.

"I feel great, finally," Frank's voice sounded from behind. Before the combat had begun, Yuki had administered a small amount of venom to allow Frank to regain some of his strength. This was a desperate measure, but Frank had insisted, saying it would be better if he died fighting rather than in his bed. He wanted to take Angelika with him to Hell, and that was the order. Spencer had created a special enclosure in the glider for Frank, hiding him from sight but allowing easy communication. Frank didn't want anyone to see his disfigured body. Empowered by the drug, he was mobile and could get out if he wanted to.

Beatriz touched her right molar with her tongue, locating the capsule containing the venom. This was more than enough to prevent the transformation into a Cymoeba and end her life. She was ready to do that, but first, she had to make sure Max had the same choice. She couldn't exit without finding and helping him. That was her duty. After Max had fallen victim to Angelika's virtual Quarks, which had infiltrated his Decon connector during the raid, Beatriz couldn't think about anything but him. She loved Max and wanted to be with him more than anything else. Alas, it was too late. She blamed herself for not having the courage to open to him. Perhaps, in that case, his decision would have been different.

"The bastards just refuse to die," Layla said, scowling. "Keep shootin', will ya?"

"You bet." Beatriz hit another Cymoeba with a poisonous projectile. Something had changed since not all Cymoebas disintegrated when shot with a venomous ordnance. Spencer warned them the enemy Quarks would learn and adapt from their previous encounter—precisely what was happening. Not good, not good at all.

Beatriz looked around the battlefield covered with hundreds, if not thousands, of Cymoebas. They had no answer against these abominations except the venom, which worked at best half the time. Green amorphous lumps would coalesce back and rise, and Frank's forces had a limited supply of venom. *What if my capsule wouldn't work?* Beatriz shivered. *I might not need it. Better not to think about this at all.*

Suddenly, a different type of aircraft appeared to the left. It wasn't a military Quark but a large glider, much bigger than theirs, surrounded by an entourage of flying fighting machines. *This must be Angelika.* Finally, some luck.

"Look there." Beatriz pointed. Layla nodded and turned the glider to approach the new aircraft. The enemy must have registered them as well since, at this moment, a roaring voice declared: "Frank Wise, you must surrender and obey Absolute. You cannot fight me. My rule is eternal."

"Burn in Hell!" Frank responded. "You are a joke, a sick freak with a delusion of grandeur. I'm coming to end your pathetic life."

As they approached Angelika's glider, the enemy Quarks attacked them.

"Hold on," Layla said, engaging three of them. The railgun identified and locked on the targets as Beatriz shot. Layla piloted the glider masterfully, avoiding enemy fire and allowing the railgun to do its job. Still, too many adversaries tried to make them descend so the Cymoebas on the ground could reach out and pull the glider from the air.

The situation was desperate. Beatriz shot a few more enemies, but they couldn't prolong this fight for too long. Even retreat was now questionable as the Quarks surrounded them.

And then another force entered the fight. A swarm of Quarks descended on the battlefield, engaging all the belligerents, shooting at both Frank's forces and Cymoebas. The spaceships showed up higher in the splitting skies, dropping bombs on the fortifications, aiming to destroy the Estate.

"What the fuck?" Layla exclaimed.

"Gaia," Frank said. "My nemesis. We all meet, finally. The time has come."

"Shit." Layla flew dangerously close to the gray tentacles, which tried to reach the glider. "What now?"

"The confusion is the chance," Frank said. "Try to avoid direct engagement and get out."

"Easy to say. I'm tryin'."

Angelika's Quarks switched their attention to the newcomers, providing a small window of opportunity. Layla took it, avoiding the tentacles by a hair's breadth and aiming the trajectory up in a broad arc.

The feint was successful, and they were free for a moment. However, it was only a matter of time until Gaia's forces found and destroyed them.

"And now?" Layla asked.

"Can you hit the freak head-on? Even if we're shot, we'd make enough damage to destroy both gliders," Frank suggested.

"Feelin' suicidal?"

"I'm already dead. So?"

"Let's do it."

Beatriz held on to her seat. This was beyond desperate, but she had no other ideas. One way or another, they would be hit and killed. She placed her tongue on the capsule with venom, deciding to activate it the moment they collided with Angelika's vessel. Beatriz's only hope was this would mean not only hers but Max's death as well.

Layla took the glider higher and aimed at the gap within the formation of Angelika's Quarks, which were now dispersed, fleeing Gaia's forces. On a fast course, the glider sped up to collide head-on with the enemy.

When the collision was unavoidable, and Beatriz closed her eyes, preparing to activate the capsule, a direct hit from the spaceship blew up Angelika's vessel, which exploded in a ball of fire, blasted off from the sky, falling to the ground. In the last moment, Layla changed the angle of attack by ninety degrees, moving up sharply, and avoided the exploding aircraft. Beatriz's internal organs collapsed, and her spine smeared on the seat.

"Hell yeah!" Layla screamed, returning the glider to a more balanced trajectory. "You guys okay?"

"No," Frank said. "But I wasn't before, either. Can you land?"

"Are you insane? Wanna join your Cymoeba friends already?"

Beatriz looked down, where the burning wreckage of Angelika's glider created a hole in the sea of a tentacled substance. Surprisingly, the Cymoebas were grouping and retreating, the wild dance of distorted shapes speeding up, but now not aiming at anything, just a random change of alien forms. This was similar to their reaction to the venom, but nobody was shooting venom at them anymore. What was going on?

"It's open," Beatriz said, pointing at the area underneath where the enemy aircraft had fallen. "They left."

Indeed, the Cymoebas had left the area and were now crowded at about a few hundred feet, with no intention of continuing their advance.

"Strange," Layla said. "But okay, let's look."

The glider made a final arc in the air and descended on the field next to the downed aircraft.

Beatriz looked at the bonfire. Suddenly, she shivered, and her head spun. It was a crazy thought, but what if they were wrong?

"I hope this was indeed her." Beatriz gasped.

"What are you talking about?" Frank said. "Of course it was her. The freak is here. She killed my son, and she killed me. I'll enjoy seeing her burning remains."

The glider door slid up, and Beatriz disembarked. She had a swarm gun on her belt and a stinger in her hand. Layla was right behind her.

"Wait, I'm coming, too," Frank announced.

"Are you sure? Need any help?" Layla turned around, frowning.

"Go ahead, I'll manage. I'm not dead yet."

"Okay," Layla said, stepping ahead of Beatriz. "Let me go first; I have better weapons."

As they moved closer to the burning vehicle, its entrance door slid to the side, and a four-armed, human-like figure clad in a black exoskeleton stood in front of them. A helmet made of the same material covered the head, and one long, sharp horn was sticking out on the left side. The figure moved slowly, visibly shaken. Heat advanced from Beatriz's clenched fists to her brain. This was the moment, the point of no return, the hour of reckoning. Angelika must pay for what she'd done.

"Hello, ugly! Lost your horn, bitch?" Layla taunted.

The figure moved closer and pointed with her remaining spike at the newcomers.

"You must not speak to Absolute," Angelika said with a deep, distorted voice, raising all her four hands, holding a weapon in each. "You shall die."

A rising crimson wave overpowered Beatriz's mind, making it difficult to see. As the black figure blurred in front of her, Beatriz could only think about revenge.

"Die, freak!" She lunged at the enemy, sending a projectile filled with venom and reaching for her swarm gun. Beatriz sent a nano-Quark load onto her adversary as the venomous bullet ricocheted off the exoskeleton. Simultaneously, Layla shot at Angelika with a laser beam, jumping to the side and pushing Beatriz.

"You're so pathetic," Angelika said, raising her weapons as the explosions covered the space where Layla and Beatriz had been a moment ago.

Rolling on the ground, Beatriz looked at the laser gun aimed at her. She sent another load of venom at Angelika, but the fight was lost, and there was nothing they could do. This was the end. She closed her eyes, beads of cold sweat flowing down her spine. Beatriz thought about Max, whom she'd condemned to everlasting torment because of her negligence and impotence. She prepared to die for the second time during this terrible day, reaching with her tongue to the capsule.

Suddenly, a disfigured creature jumped from behind, protecting them from the deadly laser beams, receiving shots from all four of Angelika's weapons. Unrecognizable, covered with rough patches and warts, his limbs looking more like tree trunks and twigs, Frank Wise made his last stand. His transformed body absorbed the beams at the cost of liquefying and disintegrating further.

"My divine consort, how nice." Angelika approached Frank, who, by a cruel twist of fate, was still alive. "Alas, Absolute wishes to reign alone. But don't despair; you'll join my Bioid Cluster." She leaned forward and pierced Frank's neck (or whatever was left of it) with her horn, lifting the top half of his body high in the air.

"I'll enjoy watching you forget who you are and worship me." She squeezed his head with her two upper hands. "But first, I'll transform your two lady friends."

Beatriz had two more venomous projectiles and a few rounds of nano-Quarks in the swarm gun. Layla had a laser beam and another weapon with explosive bullets, but Beatriz didn't know what her partner was planning to do. Beatriz decided to act rather than wait and looked at the figure in black, trying to identify weak spots. She was sure Layla was doing the same. Beatriz aimed her weapon at the enemy, but couldn't figure out where to place her shot.

Frank's body, impaled on a grisly horn, disintegrated further, and the stump of what was a human torso slid closer to Angelika's head. His left arm hung as a dead weight, but his right could still move. Frank reached behind his back, took out a short knife, and stuck it into the middle of the helmet covering Angelika's face. This was a desperate and pathetic gesture, having no chance of success.

However, the spot where the blade contacted the helmet yielded, and the knife entered the soft flesh. A bestial roar thundered across the field. Angelika grabbed Frank's lifeless remains with her two lower arms and threw the stump out. With her two upper hands, she held the knife's handle and took it out of her face. At this moment, something broke inside of her. Angelika's knees gave way, and she fell face down, her upper right hand still holding the blade.

"How?" Beatriz turned to Layla, refusing to believe her eyes and their sudden deliverance.

"The blade was poisoned. He saved it for himself," Layla said, covering her eyes and turning away.

"But the helmet?"

"I guess he found a weak spot. She has to breathe; she's not a Quark."

"Is she..."

"Your guess is as good as mine. If she has anythin' human left in her, she's dead. If she turned into a Cymoeba, she'd disintegrate. Either way, we'll find out soon enough."

"Freak," Beatriz said, the red wave engulfing her brain again. She stood up, raised both her guns, and walked toward the motionless figure in black. Simultaneously, Layla ran to where Frank's remains had landed. As Beatriz approached her enemy, Angelika's body trembled in convulsions.

Not wishing to leave the matter to chance and to trust the effect of Frank's blade, Beatriz neared the figure in black, which convulsed in the throes of death. Beatriz kicked the head with her boot and exposed the gaping wound the knife had created. She raised a stinger, inserted it into a cut, and injected a load of wasp venom into the face of the ugly, deplorable, repugnant monster, who imagined itself to be a god. A moment later, convulsions stopped, and the body that was once human found its eternal peace.

Beatriz gasped heavily as the sudden emptiness filled her mind now that the heated expectation of revenge was fulfilled. She picked up Frank's blade, being extra careful not to cut herself. She leaned over Angelika's dead body and started working with the knife, trying to cut through the exoskeleton.

After several fruitless minutes, exhausted, Beatriz considered what else to do when Layla approached, holding a laser beam gun.

Beatriz looked at her friend, and Layla's face, now even darker than usual and covered with dust and tears, told her everything. She still asked: "Frank?"

Layla didn't respond; she shook her head and showed a stinger in her other hand. The fate of Frank Wise had been decided long ago when Angelika had infected him. Frank Wise, the man with the larger-than-life vision, was willing to sacrifice everyone, including himself, to make his dream a reality. He had flaws, but his grit was even bigger than his ego. And he'd saved their lives today, giving the world another chance to continue its pitiful existence. Beatriz didn't care; in this moment of triumph and grief, her thoughts were only about Max.

Layla gestured to Beatriz to move away, aiming at the exoskeleton with the laser beam and attempting to cut through, starting with the less robust area around the neck. The weapon's energy output was enormous, and the material, however strong, yielded. Not paying any attention to the blasts and explosions around them and not realizing the tide of the battle had turned, Layla and Beatriz uncovered Angelika's body, found the bizarre crest running down her spine, and finally reached the central plate, cutting around it to get to the hidden hump.

Beatriz closed her eyes and pulled the lid off the hump. She shook with dread, expecting to find more unspeakable horrors. She wanted to look but couldn't find the strength to face the man she loved, now turned into a monster's puppet.

"Be strong," Layla said, touching Beatriz's shoulder.

Beatriz opened her eyes and screamed, her gaze rooted to the terrifying sight. Max was still alive, looking at her with an unblinking, stupefied expression, his lips whispering her name. Unable to control herself, Beatriz picked up her stinger and inserted the weapon deep into the face she adored. A tornado of sensations engulfed her; she lost the ability to think and reason, sinking deeper into the darkest depths of the heinous abyss, screaming and kicking, pushing Layla away.

A realization struck Beatriz: this was what she came here to do. There was nothing else left of her, just an empty shell. Revenge was her purpose, the driving force. But now it was fulfilled, and Max was finally free. Beatriz had to do one last thing.

She stopped screaming and relaxed, looking at her friend. Layla nodded, grabbed her by the shoulders, and shook.

"Please, forgive me," Beatriz said, moving her tongue and finding a deadly capsule in her mouth. Layla realized what her friend was doing, but it was too late; the damage was done, and the lethal venom spread through Beatriz's body. "I love you, Max," Beatriz whispered as darkness descended, forever uniting her with her beloved.

CHAPTER 58. JIM

The sun was rising over the tortured scenery under the splitting skies. Its disk was not visible, but the orange glow reaching them from beyond the purple crack proclaimed the beginning of a new day, no matter what had happened.

Jim sipped his coffee, which always friendly Spencer had delivered to the balcony earlier this morning, and looked at the landscape. Beautiful forests and meadows disappeared, replaced by ugly burns and explosion funnels. The smell of smoke, ashes, and molten plastic engulfed the Estate. A disgusting mass of dirt and Cymoeba remains were scattered among brutalized surroundings. Half the Estate was destroyed, and the beautiful towers and balustrades were ruined. The losses included the Decon and Quark factories. This was for the better.

Jim stroked Kali's fur. The dog was napping on his lap. The decision had to be made, and it was challenging. The decision that could save or end the world was the one he shared with a blind girl sitting next to him.

"Did you talk to Layla?" Selena asked.

"Yes. She's devastated but holding up. She lost Frank, and she lost most of her team."

Even though the battle was won, the toll was heavy indeed. Layla was the only survivor of the fight against Angelika, while Varg and Yuki were the only two survivors of the battle against Cymoebas on the ground. A tentacle had snatched Reto, and he was killed by Varg's venomous projectile, as the people had made a solemn promise to each other not to let Cymoebas transform them. The rest of the Humanists had met a similar fate. Most of the Quarks were destroyed, and now, with the factories ruined, it would take years to restore the Estate and its defense mechanisms. This was Layla's concern now, as she'd inherited both Quasaris and the Wise Estate, according to Frank's last will. The Quarks recognized the succession, and there was no one to object. Jim remembered their grandstanding fifty years ago and

266

smiled. The irony of fate: he'd helped to stop Frank's designs so long ago, only to meet him now and witness his ultimate demise at the hands of a monster who'd killed Frank's son and imagined herself to be a god. Jim's relationship with Frank was complex, although now he understood what drove his antagonist and could empathize with him. The fate of Frank Wise was not unexpected; he was playing with fire all his life, taking immeasurable risks and putting himself and everyone else in danger. Jim sighed and scratched Kali's ear. This was not his problem anymore. He had his own quest and his destiny to fulfill.

"Are you sure Gaia won't return?" He asked.

"Am I sure? I have no idea." Selena sipped her coffee. "All I know is we connected, and Gaia acted on my message. This doesn't mean it won't return to finish us."

"I hope it won't," Jim said. "So people could see another sunrise."

"For this, we have to do our part. Me, specifically," Selena said.

"What's on your mind?"

"I know what to do. I'll fix the defect."

"How?"

They had discussed it multiple times, but Jim was still on the fence. It wasn't right; some details didn't fit. He couldn't pinpoint what it was and kept returning to Selena's plan.

"I told you." Selena shrugged. "I connect with the universal consciousness and build a digital Vista on that plane using the fungal thread leading back to the computer. Being part of me, the Vista will contain a door—a door to transcend the veil. By going through the door, I'll lose my connection and become unconscious. Dead." Selena smiled, curving the corners of her lips downward. "But this will allow the door to close, and the defect, which is part of me, will be gone."

"I can't dispute your ability to ascend and merge with the universal consciousness. You've done it, and I haven't." Jim tilted his head, studying Selena. "But why do you think you could take the defect out with you? Why is that a remedy?"

"It's simple, Jim. The defect is part of me and a hole in my essence. I don't know why and how, but from the very beginning, it was with me. I could manipulate it. I killed Naomi, I killed other Humanists when you arrived, and I almost killed Father. Now, I have to fix it."

"You are special, that is true. But what makes you think the defect will be gone when you disappear?"

"Got better ideas?" Selena finished her coffee and placed the cup on the floor by her feet. "We have no other choice."

Jim went over the reasoning once again. Something Selena had said before still troubled him. The defect was inside the organism, and it was inside of her.... she was an integral part of the entire structure, perhaps the pivotal voxel of the universal consciousness through which the defect expanded. But would the disappearance of her voxel of consciousness fix the hole?

"You said the organism cannot fix the hole because it's part of it. It can't act on itself," Jim said.

Selena nodded.

"So why do you think *you* can act on it when it's part of *you*?"

"It will disappear with me. Don't you see? This is my chance to redeem myself."

Jim remembered Quanah and their bizarre conversation. It was gibberish then, but now Jim understood.

"To fix the defect, you must pierce the veil. Get to the final gate," Jim said. "Quanah's words."

"Yes, exactly."

"White Buffalo, he called you. I've read about it, you know."

"About what? Quanah?"

"About The White Buffalo Calf that will show up before the end of the world to reveal the path to the people."

"That's meaningless. You trust your dreams too much."

"It wasn't a dream, and you know that. It was a message."

"So, what do you make of that?"

"The Wayfarer, he called me," Jim murmured.

The pieces fell into place. The puzzle was complete, his quest was clear, and Jim knew what to do. The only thing he could do.

"You know, I didn't get it when Hagen told me I must start my quest or the world would end. I had to find two people: the first connected the defect to Decon, and the second was you. White Buffalo is the one who contains the world yet is outside of it. The one who is inseparably linked with the defect. And Decon, which entangled the leaves on the tree of life, the source of the defect."

"What's your point?"

"White Buffalo can see the path and open the door, but can't fix the defect. By destroying yourself, you will destroy the world. You can manipulate the crack, make it visible, but it has to be someone else who'd travel beyond the veil to fix it."

"And who is that?"

"The Wayfarer. Me. This was what Quanah meant."

Selena stood and walked to the balustrade, allowing the hidden but radiant rays of the sun to warm her face.

"You might be right," she said.

"You know I am. Remember, I'm the only one who could travel into Decon without the interface? There was a reason the universe led me to you, as Hagen guided my path. I understand now. Everything has its causes and consequences. Frank Wise met the destiny he created, while I have to meet mine. The circle must close."

"We'll go together," Selena said. "There's nothing else for me to do here. It's my path, too."

"I know. As you said, we don't belong. The link connecting you to the purple cloud must be broken, and you cannot do that. But I can."

Selena came closer and placed her hand on his. "Thank you, Jim."

"What for?"

"For being here. And for understanding."

They were quiet for some time, with only Kali's measured breathing disturbing the silence of the morning. Their last morning, and perhaps the last one for the world.

"You must go. It's getting late," the kid's voice interrupted their contemplation. Jim raised his head: Eva. What was she doing here? And what did she mean?

"Go where?" Jim asked.

"There. Beyond the veil," Eva said, squinting. "You have little time."

"How..."

"It's not important," Eva interrupted. "You must go now. The fungi are ready."

"Who are you, Eva? Or what?" Selena asked, approaching the child.

"I am the link. The messenger." Eva jumped on one foot, a normal six-year-old kid possessing knowledge of things she didn't understand.

"Messenger from whom?" Jim asked.

"Too many questions," Eva said. "You already know. The ants, the fungi, the trees, the grass. Everything."

"Are you real, or are you another vision, like Hagen?" Jim reached his hand to touch the girl, but she jumped back, laughing.

"You can't see even if you try, can you? So why is it important?" Eva turned around and walked into the hallway. "Are you coming? You delay, and tomorrow never comes."

"Wait..." Jim extended his hand, but Selena touched his lips, reaching from behind. "Silence," she said. "No more questions; we know what to do."

Jim exhaled through the tightly pursed lips and decided to follow Selena's advice. Indeed, it didn't matter. He didn't have to understand all the causes and effects and how exactly the universe worked. Let it be a mystery someone else would uncover for future generations.

"This old man, he played seven,

He played knick-knack up in heaven."

Jim listened to the child's song Eva sang, skipping along the hallway. *She is singing about me,* he realized. Another messenger from the universal mind. He looked at Selena, walking next to him: The White Buffalo Calf, a mysterious girl who had an unexplainable connection to the defect in reality, a guide for The Wayfarer, the man who thought he'd lost his purpose. The man who had to walk his path to the end and fulfill his destiny.

CHAPTER 59. JIM

Jim floated above the ocean of silver, which merged with the milky white sky around and above. The problem was above and below were relative terms, as he had no body or head and experienced no gravity or any other force. He didn't understand how he experienced the colors and the wavy surface of the ocean underneath. It was pure perception, but somehow, it made sense.

The white texture of the surrounding cosmos began to split and disassociate into prisms, with tiny gaps of purple in between. Soon, the entire space became pixelated, and some prisms got so close he could touch them. The ocean did not, however, deviate from its mercury-like appearance; only the waves got bigger.

This was all part of Selena's work as she created a Vista in Decon, guided by the fungi. He'd drifted into this place by focusing on Selena, reaching into her mind, almost experiencing her thoughts. Jim didn't use Decon or a fungal computer. He'd stayed within his mind, concentrating on the silver ocean and using his meditation skills.

It had worked. Their minds had joined again, and they'd experienced the eerie world of Decon, the multiverse, subconsciousness, or whatever other terms came to mind. Jim didn't care. However crazy and improbable, this was what they'd decided to do, encouraged by Eva.

Eva... the mystery, the link, the messenger. Was she another ghost from his dreams, or was she something else? It didn't matter. He would have done the same, regardless.

Suddenly, some prisms disappeared, opening the space for more purple to shine through. The defect. The gap in space-time, the tear in the fabric of reality. Hope and satisfaction filled Jim's essence as he understood what was happening. Was the plan working, or was it his imagination?

Again, it didn't matter. The entire experience was so unbelievable and strange that the question of what was real and what was not had little meaning. The notion of reality had undergone such a drastic change it was impossible to relate to anymore. Jim stopped trying and focused on the purple gap—the door. The passage opened for him by Selena, the pathway outside time and space, outside existence. But how was he supposed to travel through the door? He couldn't manipulate his surroundings or his perceptions. How would he solve this final riddle?

Suddenly, a bright flash of gold sparkled in the depth of the ocean of mercury. As the golden object rose, a voice (or was it just a thought?) proclaimed: "We meet again, Jim Steel. For one last time."

Hagen? How was this possible? Was it another dream? Did he complete the quest?

"You've arrived. This is your destiny." Hagen's voice was normal, unlike in their previous dream encounters, as if the brilliant inventor was talking to him in person.

"What is my destiny?"

"To choose."

"Choose what?"

"What happens next. The fate of the world."

"Why me?"

"Why not?" The bright object increased in size, filling most of the space in front of Jim and blocking the ocean. Only two sensations remained: the golden scintillating sphere and the opening in the pixelated surface, leading to the purple unknown.

"Has to be someone. Or something. You are the embodiment of the conscious mind. The tiny part of the universe untouched by the defect."

"But, surely, I'm not the only one," Jim protested.

"You do not understand," the voice announced, and Jim's mind filled with a multitude of voices, thoughts, sensations, ideas, and memories. This surge of perceptions overwhelmed Jim as his ego disappeared. He wasn't Jim Steel anymore. He was the collection of myriads of minds.

As the surge subsided and his perception of himself returned, Jim tried to arrange his thoughts. What was he? And how was he supposed to decide the fate of the world?

"Finally, you ask the right question. Once you pass through the door, you can leave it open or close it. The choice is yours."

"What does it mean?"

"To close it means to repair the fabric of reality, eliminate the defect. To keep it open means to let the tear grow, erasing the multiverse and clearing up the way for the next cycle. Which might not come. Are you ready?"

"Wait. What about Selena? Layla? Kali? Everything else?"

"White Buffalo is the key element linked to the defect. If you fix the tear, you'd eliminate her connection to it. The world will continue. Or you might decide to erase everything."

"What's the catch?"

"There's no catch. By traveling through the door beyond the veil, you'll disappear. By 'you,' I mean the whole collective consciousness untouched by the defect. The Wayfarer. If you close the door, you give the world another chance, but another Decon will end it, completing the cycle of Brahma's breath. Or you could decide that's enough and everything must end now. The choice is yours. Are you ready?"

"What's beyond the veil? Is it the true reality casting shadows into our world?"

"There is no true reality, only the ones we create and perceive. Your question has no meaning. Human language and mental constructs are limited; there is no boundary as you imagine it. The veil separates existence from non-existence; that's it. This is where consciousness does not reach."

Jim, still confused, decided that understanding cosmological intricacies was beyond his abilities. He focused on the choice Hagen had presented to him. Did the world deserve another chance? How could he make this call, even if he somehow became the collective consciousness untouched by the defect?

"Who are you? Are you part of the same universal consciousness?" Jim asked.

"You already asked this question, and you know the answer. I am you and not you. Nothing and everything. The information accumulated in the universe. The voice of the infinite and each quantum of existence. The knowledge helping you understand and fulfill your quest. You have unique access to this information."

Was it all happening in his mind? Was it all part of a bad dream, of something that had started fifty years ago, the nightmare in which he was stuck forever?

Whatever the meaning and the reality, he had to make a choice. And whatever choice he made would complete his quest and end his life. What would it be? Did the sorry, pathetic world he was leaving deserve another chance? Or should it all be erased with him, the final chord of his ego, the destroyer of the universe?

Kali's image appeared before Jim; he didn't quite know why. She approached him, wagging her tail and reaching forward to lick his face. She needed nothing, only his company; her love was unconditional and unquestionable. Would a love like this deserve a second chance?

"I'm ready," Jim thought as the final resolve sharpened in his mind.

"Godspeed," Hagen's voice responded. "We shall not talk again."

The prismatic voxels around him split into tiny pieces. The ocean of silver retreated, leaving behind a gaping purple abyss. Soon, there was nothing but purple darkness surrounding him. Reaching deep into his mind, holding the memories of Kali, Selena, Isabel, and everyone else he loved in his long and sorrowful life, Jim imagined the purple abyss as the fog he had to clear. Soon, the darkness collapsed, surrounded by the brilliant white light, shrinking first into a giant eye in the blazing sky, then into a lone, tiny purple dot, finally disappearing altogether. At that moment, a short but frightening cacophony of thoughts and memories engulfed Jim for one last time as his essence dissolved into nothingness.

CHAPTER 60. SELENA

Selena thought her brain had exploded. The Vista she'd so meticulously created broke into many little fireflies, and the smell of burned charcoal attacked her nostrils. The connection to the giant organism re-constructed by fungi was severed, and, most importantly, Selena couldn't feel Jim's presence anymore. She'd created and opened the portal through her Vista into the eerie, frightful, purple void. The Vista itself was unlike anything Selena had made before; she hadn't controlled the process this time; she'd let the purple cloud speak through her, imagining the desolate landscape with a hidden path leading to the purple star on the horizon. Selena wasn't alone in this strange world. Inside her imagination, a dark figure traveled the way, slowly approaching the purple star. The Wayfarer, Jim. They were connected, although he wasn't using Decon or the fungal interface. Selena didn't understand how it was possible. Still, it worked, and she used all her mental strength and concentration to maintain the Vista intact, making sure the path wouldn't disappear, leading Jim to his destination.

And now it was all gone. When Jim reached the end of the road, he paused for a moment. At this time, the familiar voice announced in her head: "White Buffalo, your time has come. You did what you came here to do."

"What happens now?" Selena asked mentally.

"It is for The Wayfarer to decide," the voice of Quanah said. "Either way, your job in this cycle is done."

"What do you mean?"

"The future world won't need White Buffalo anymore. And if the cycle ends, the new one will emerge with its own rules."

"I'm confused, Quanah."

"No one possesses complete knowledge. You are blind, yet you can see. You made the right choices and walked the path based on your knowledge. Rejoice."

"I guess." She still had many questions but made peace with the fact she might never get all the answers.

At this moment, the purple star collapsed, knocking her out of the Vista. Her mind darkened for a moment.

She woke up at the sound of crying. It took her a while to remember where she was and what they tried to do. The cries were not human but canine. Kali. Selena lay on the floor next to Jim, and the dog was beside him, licking his face, whining, and howling. Selena touched the dog, then found Jim's hand and probed his pulse to confirm what she already knew: Jim Steel was dead. There was no way back for him once he'd reached the door opened by her. She'd expected, though, that she would die, too. Alas, that didn't happen.

Something in her surroundings had changed, something dramatic. The purple cloud was no more. The presence that had been with her since the fateful day of Naomi's death was gone. Did they succeed? Did they remove the defect and fix the splitting skies?

"Eva," Selena called. "Are you there?"

Silence. The kid had disappeared, and Selena wasn't sure Eva had ever existed. The link, the messenger. As they suspected, the reality was not what it seemed. So was the strange child who could communicate with the ants.

Selena reached out to the fungi using her mind, adjusting the digital interface on her head. She yearned to discover what happened to the universal ensemble she had been part of. Was the defect removed from its essence? It seemed like it was from hers.

But the fungi were silent, and the link to the giant organism was severed. Selena couldn't access the ensemble of the universal consciousness. Somehow, it was okay.

Selena got up and touched Kali. The dog growled, not giving up attempts to awaken her companion.

"Come on, girl," Selena said, petting the dog. "He's gone. He did it. He walked his path."

Kali kept crying.

"Yes, I know. It should've been me," Selena said.

The sound of someone's footsteps in the hallway interrupted the wails of the crying dog. The door to the lab opened, and Varg jumped into the room, panting heavily.

"Selena!" he exclaimed, embracing his daughter. "I've found you.

What's happening?"

"He did it, Father."

"Who? What?"

"Look outside. What do you see?"

Varg moved toward the window, switching it to the transparent mode.

"What the hell? The crack..."

"Is gone," Selena finished the sentence. "Jim fixed it."

"But how? And you..."

"I helped, Father. But someone had to go beyond... beyond the veil of reality to repair its fabric. It should've been me."

"Don't say that. I need you."

"What for, Father? I don't fit, you know that. I'm the reason everyone I loved is dead. Leave me alone, let me disappear."

"No." Varg squeezed her shoulder. "You're not the reason the world came to this. We have no control over these forces. Jim's sacrifice was not in vain, and there's only one thing to do."

"And what's that?"

"Help me rebuild the Community. This is now my path to walk and my destiny. I need you by my side."

"I don't know, Father. I'm exhausted. I've learned so much my brain hurts. I don't think I could experience the world the same way ever again. And one other thing..."

"Yes?"

"The cloud is gone. Our connection is broken. But I can't connect to the fungi either. I've changed. I might be normal." Selena chuckled.

"No one is normal, Selena. Not in this crazy world. We'll try to fix the computer, if that's what you're asking."

"I'm not sure. But thank you."

"Of course."

"So, I don't think I'll be much help."

"Of course, you will. Because I need you. Please help me understand the new world better; help everyone. Guide us so we don't repeat the mistakes that brought us to the edge."

"Okay, Father. I can try. For you."

The girl and the man stood in silence, embracing, anticipating a new beginning and a world rising from the ruins of the broken one they'd inherited. The skies were whole once again, and the sun's disk sent warm rays onto the wounded surface of the planet, proclaiming another chance for humanity.

CHAPTER 61. LAYLA

"Are you crazy? Why outer space? Forgot about Gaia?" Yuki cracked her fingers. The reaction of the only surviving member of Layla's team was understandable. Previous attempts to revive space exploration led them to confront the self-aware space station. It was dangerous, if not reckless. But Layla had to fulfill a promise she'd given Frank. She had to bring his dream closer to reality. His destiny became hers.

"We must." Layla shrugged, looking at the clear, starry sky from the balcony of the Wise Estate. The crack was gone, and they could see the moon in all its glory, undisturbed, for the first time in many nights.

"Spencer says the data channel with Gaia is open," Layla said. "It won't interfere as long as we don't jeopardize its objective function, whatever this means. But he says he understands and will alert us if somethin' goes astray."

"Not much to work with." Yuki shook her head.

"Not much, but it's all we have." Layla inhaled fresh air, filled with scents of newly planted junipers and firs. The remaining Quarks had restored the land, although many of the buildings were still in ruins.

"Okay, you know better," Yuki finally conceded. "You're the new Designer, after all."

"Don't call me that." Layla winced. "There are no more Designers. You know our Decon factories are destroyed, and I have no plans to revive this stupid addiction that almost killed us all."

"What about others?"

"There's work to do. If anyone wants to stand their ground, let them try. We have Gaia, which can hack into any Quark system. There will be no more Decon and no more Designers on this planet. I promise you."

"Could you have saved her?" Yuki asked after a long pause, looking far into the starry sky.

"I ask myself the same question." Layla remembered the last

moments of the fight against Angelika, Max's horrified stare, and the desperation with which Beatriz had ended his torments. "It was her choice. I didn't have time to react."

"This is a shitty world." Yuki sighed. "Why did we survive, Layla? Why did Jim fix the sky? What are we gonna do with all this stuff without them? Without Beatriz, Max, Reto? How can we continue?"

"I don't know." Layla spat. "We have to be strong. For them. For Frank. They gave us a chance, and we must use it. That's all."

"A chance..." Yuki sighed again. "To do what? Isn't it easier just to give up?"

"I guess it is. But we don't seek easy ways, do we?"

"Never," Yuki answered, smiling. "Okay, boss, take us to the stars."

Layla looked up at the night sky, where the constellations shone brightly and invitingly. She found the belt of Orion and thought about the vast distances separating their little rock from the enigmas of deep space. After what she'd learned from Selena, these distances didn't seem so vast, and the mysteries of existence were not as daunting. The quest for knowledge and fulfillment must continue, whatever it was, even if the journey itself was the goal. And on that journey, magnificent discoveries awaited them as the answers would be uncovered.

"With pleasure," Layla said, returning the smile. "Get on; it will be a wild ride."

LIST OF CHARACTERS

Angelika Scalvini - a Designer, owner of 'Angel3D,' a bio-printing company.

Beatriz - a Scavenger, member of **Layla's** unit.

Bjorn - a Humanist.

Cesare - a Quark, **Angelika's** personal assistant.

Donald Wise - son of Frank Wise.

Eva - a Houston inhabitant, little girl.

Felix Wise - a Designer, owner of Quasaris, a Quark company. Son of **Donald Wise**.

Frank Wise - founder of Quasaris.

Gabor - a Humanist.

Gaia - Space Station on Earth's orbit.

George Murukan - a Designer.

Harald - a Humanist, **Varg's** advisor.

Hex - a Scavenger.

Jim Steel - a lone inhabitant of a van west of Houston.

Kali - a Rottweiler, **Jim Steel's** dog.

Kyle - a Humanist, has romantic relationship with **Naomi**.

Layla - a Scavenger, leader of the unit.

Mary DeJong - a Houston inhabitant.

Max - a Scavenger, member of **Layla's** unit.

Maya - a Humanist.

Naomi - a Humanist, has romantic relationship with **Kyle**.

Quanah - a Native American man.

Paul - a Trader, main dealer for **Layla's** Scavenger unit.

Ramon - a Humanist, has romantic relationship with **Selena**.

Reto - a Scavenger, member of **Layla's** unit.

Selena - a Humanist, blind, has romantic relationship with **Ramon**.

Spencer - a Quark, personal assistant of **Frank Wise**.

Torsten Hagen - a famous engineer and inventor, lived in the Twenty-First Century.

Varg - a Humanist, leader of the Community.

Yuki - a Scavenger, member of **Layla's** unit.

AFTERWORD: JOIN MY QUEST TO IMAGINE THE FUTURE WORLD

Thank you for reading "Splitting Skies." I hope you have found my work insightful, stimulating, and entertaining. If you enjoyed this book, please consider leaving a short comment on Goodreads, Amazon, or your platform of choice. I would greatly appreciate your feedback!

*To stay in touch, please visit my site **MikhailGladkikh.com**, and receive a hard science fiction mystery **"Out of Time"** as a gift. Be the first to get updates about my new writing. Listen to the Podcast **"Vision 2222"** (**https://www.youtube.com/ @VISION2222podcast**), in which the current trends in science, technology, and business, shaping the world of tomorrow, with the guests prominent and distinguished in their fields. Available on Spotify, Audible, Google Podcast, Apple, iHeartRadio, and YouTube.*

Finally, please feel free to contact me directly at mgladkikh@gmail.com: I'd love to hear from my readers! I am excited to continue our journey together!

Mikhail Gladkikh

www.ingramcontent.com/pod-product-compliance
Lightning Source LLC
Chambersburg PA
CBHW051940220626
47052CB00004B/729